PRAISE FOR

THE INVISIBLE L

#2 on the *Independent*'s (U) Novels of 2015 List

"Flavored with truly unique mythology and a dash of the eldritch. Such clever, creepy, elaborate world building and snarky, sexy-smart characters! Also, remote-controlled alligators. You just can't go wrong with that."   —N. K. Jemisin, author of *The Fifth Season*

"A breath of fresh air. . . . With a companionable heroine in Irene and a satisfyingly complex plot, *The Invisible Library*—the first of a series—is a book in which to wallow."   —*The Guardian* (UK)

"Written in a similar vein to Deborah Harkness's All Souls trilogy . . . contemporary meets fairy tale in this novel."   —Big Issue

"Thoroughly entertaining."   —*Starburst*

"Fantasy doesn't get much better. . . . If you're looking for a swift, clever, and witty read, look no further."   —Fantasy Faction

"Highly entertaining. . . . It reminded me a lot of Jasper Fforde's Thursday Next series."   —The Book Plank

continued . . .

BY GENEVIEVE COGMAN

The Invisible Library
The Masked City
The Burning Page

THE
BURNING
PAGE

AN INVISIBLE LIBRARY NOVEL

GENEVIEVE
COGMAN

New York

ROC
Published by Berkley
An imprint of Penguin Random House LLC
375 Hudson Street, New York, New York 10014

Library of Congress Cataloging-in-Publication Data:

Names: Cogman, Genevieve, author.
Title: The burning page: an invisible library novel / Genevieve Cogman.
Description: New York: ROC [2017]
Identifiers: LCCN 2016044535 (print) | LCCN 2016051595 (ebook) |
ISBN 9781101988688 (paperback) | ISBN 9781101988695 (ebook)
Subjects: LCSH: Librarians—Fiction. | Secret societies—Fiction. |
BISAC: FICTION / Fantasy / Historical. | FICTION / Fantasy / Paranormal. |
GSAFD: Fantasy fiction. | Alternative histories (Fiction)
Classification: LCC PR6103.O39 B87 2017 (print) | LCC PR6103.O39 (ebook) |
DDC 823/.92—dc23
LC record available at https://lccn.loc.gov/2016044535

Pan trade paperback edition / December 2016
Roc trade paperback edition / January 2017

Printed in the United States of America
1   3   5   7   9   10   8   6   4   2

Cover spot illustration by Adam Auerbach
Book design by Laura Corless

ACKNOWLEDGEMENTS

I can't believe that I've got this far. Thank you to everyone who's helped with this book, and with the ones before it.

Thank you to my agent, Lucienne Diver, who took a chance on me and has always been there to support and advise me. Thank you to my UK editor, Bella Pagan, and to my US editors, Diana Gill and Rebecca Brewer, who made this book a great deal better. You are all very much appreciated.

Thanks to my beta readers and friends—Beth, Jeanne, Anne, Unni, Phyllis, April, Nora, and everyone else. Thanks to the classification team and all my other friends at work, who give me support, friendship, and coffee. Thanks to all my readers and friends online who've enjoyed the previous books—I hope that you enjoy this one too.

Thank you to my family—my mother and father, my brother and sister, my aunt and uncle, and all my other relations. It's your support, and the books on your shelves, that have helped make this book what it is.

And thanks to all good libraries and librarians everywhere. You are needed and appreciated, and you always will be.

THE
BURNING
PAGE

OFFICIAL LIBRARY TRAVEL ADVICE

World A-215: Status—At War

This alternate world is currently in a state of global thermonuclear war and has had several live exchanges of nuclear weapons already. In the interests of personal safety, we recommend that no Librarians enter this world for at least the next two years. Anyone requiring further information should contact Vasilisa on the Library email system.

World A-594: Status—Chaos Infestation

The chaos level on this world has risen to a high infestation level and is at assumptive status, verging on conglomerative. For those of you who cannot remember your basic training, this means that the entire world is in danger of being completely absorbed into chaos. This is a real and present danger to any Librarians trying to visit. Attempting to go through the Traverse to this world risks exposing the Library itself to contamination. Don't make any doomed attempts to rescue books from this world. You will not be allowed to re-enter the Library afterwards. (N.B.: the statement about written permission from a senior Librarian does *not* apply to this world, as no permission will be granted.)

World B-12: Status—Power Struggle

This alternate world is currently the subject of a power struggle between the dragons and the Fae. The facts are uncertain, but agents from both sides have been attempting to gain control of the Ottoman Empire, which rules most of this world. In the interests of preserving our neutrality, we are currently staying out of the conflict and out of the world. Will anyone who has visited previously and has information on the political situation (however out of date it may be) please contact Chandidas on the Library email system.

World B-474: Status—Personal Vendetta

We congratulate Alastor on having retrieved a copy of Mary Shelley's handwritten and unpublished sequel to *Frankenstein*. This was discovered in the private library of the Fae known as the Lord Judge. Unfortunately this has caused the Lord Judge to issue a proclamation: that he will kill any Librarian who crosses his path for the next five years. Since B-474 is where the theft took place, all Librarians are strongly urged to avoid this world until further notice. Alastor is going to be staying in the Library for the next five years. He is therefore currently available to any novices or journeymen requiring lectures on Sensible Targets and Rational Threat Assessment.

World G-133: Status—Police Interest

The Traverse to this world is out-of-bounds for at least the next month. This is because the Franco-Prussian Empire's police force is taking far too close an interest in the site of the gate. We also wish to make it absolutely clear that Librarians should not attempt to use the Library to transport dinosaur eggs. And if they do disregard this rule, under no circumstances should they draw official in-world attention while doing so. In fact, we wish to remind all Librarians that they are here to collect books, not dinosaurs. Those Librarians who have problems distinguishing between the two should take a refresher course in Library basics.

World G-522: Status—Gate Malfunction

This Traverse has been demonstrating strange behaviour, and malfunctioned when Ekake was about to use it. The situation is currently being investigated, and travel to this alternate world is not recommended until further notice. Ekake is currently under Library medical care, and more information on this situation will be released once he is conscious and able to provide it.

PROLOGUE

FROM: Peregrine Vale, 221b Baker Street
TO: Inspector Singh, Scotland Yard

Singh,

For the love of God, can't you give me anything challenging? London is a stagnant pool, and its criminals are petty, unimaginative, and uninteresting. These last few weeks have driven me nearly mad with boredom. Nothing seems worth my time or attention. Even my research seems a waste of effort. I must have a decent case to occupy me, or else I believe the machine that is my brain will spin out of control.

In answer to your queries about Rotherham's murder and the apparent hauntings at the Thames pumping works, I would have thought it clear that the two are connected.

It should be obvious that the victim was decoyed down to

the new ultrafiltration membranes in the Thames pumping works and murdered there. His body was passed through the system to suffuse his lungs with fresh water in order to give credence to the claim that he was drowned in the Serpentine in Hyde Park, where his body was found. Check the financial holdings of Rotherham's niece, and her private library—I believe you'll find evidence of her scientific studies there. The alibi that the niece's husband gave her is also very dubious, and he will probably break under pressure.

Winters and Strongrock are out of London at the moment, on a mission to one of their parallel worlds. From what Strongrock has confided to me, Winters is suffering official displeasure for leaving her post in order to rescue him. Typical bureaucratic nonsense. Her superiors might not have condoned her methods, but she achieved the results they wanted anyhow But I dare say it could have been worse.

Give me a case, Singh. It will keep me busy, and God knows I need to be busy. Logical thought and reason are the best medicine for my current inertia, and will keep me from worse alternatives.

Vale

CHAPTER 1

The morning light glittered on the glass windows and on the blades of the guillotines in the central square. Pigeons squabbled noisily in the gutters, audible solely due to the general deadly silence. Only the creaking of cart-wheels and the soft padding of footsteps disturbed the stillness.

Irene could feel an even greater zone of terrified hush surrounding herself and Kai. Passers-by avoided their gaze, desperate not to attract their attention. It was because of their "borrowed" uniforms, of course: everyone was afraid that someday the National Guard might come for *them*, to drag them away for counter-revolutionary activities. And then would come prisons, and trials, and then the guillotine . . .

It made their outfits the perfect disguise for getting around unnoticed. Nobody was going to look twice at the National Guard. In case the National Guard looked back at them.

With a neat pivot, the two of them turned at the corner of the street and marched down it together, their steps in unison, out of view of the guillotines. Irene felt an illogical sense of relief in response. Even if they weren't out of danger yet, she was spared from having to look at the thing that might chop her head off.

"How much farther?" Kai murmured out of the side of his mouth. Even in the charmless National Guard uniform—heavy black wool coat and trousers, and tricolour sash—her assistant managed to look almost unrealistically handsome. The sun gleamed on his black hair and touched his face with a glow of pure health and physicality. When walking, he paced like an aristocrat, or a predator, rather than trudging like an ordinary man doing a nine-to-five job. There was very little they could do to disguise that, though. Smears of mud would have been out of place on a Guardsman, and disguising him as an ordinary citizen being taken for questioning would have been too risky.

"Next street," Irene muttered back. Next to Kai she was comparatively plain, to her occasional regret, and so she was much better at going unnoticed. Her own plain brown hair and regular features took actual work to make them look interesting, or really any more attractive than "neat and tidy." But since most of the time she *wanted* to go unnoticed, that was a benefit in her line of work.

Fortunately women served in the National Guard, and she hadn't needed to bind her breasts, or anything like that, to blend in. The European Republic that had spread from the French Revolution in this alternate world was oppressive, vicious, hard-line, and highly dangerous, but it did at least let women get themselves killed in the armed forces. Probably because they needed the manpower, as it were, due to the ongoing wars, but that was another problem.

They turned the next corner, and Irene flicked a glance towards the raddled old building that was their target. It was barely in one piece: decaying brick was seamed with ivy and cracks, the shutters were locked shut in place and covered with graffiti, and the roof was missing tiles. They marched up to the front door as though they had a perfect right to be there. Kai banged on it, waited for a response, then kicked it open. The two of them stomped inside.

Kai peered into the darkness. Shafts of light filtered round the edges of the shutters, enough to let them see the utter ruin of the building's interior. The staircase that led up to the first and second floors looked just barely passable, but all the furniture was gone, and the walls were covered with revolutionary dogma. It might once have been a library, but now it was a decrepit barn of a building that would probably have been turned down by passing cows as too uncomfortable.

"I don't understand how there still can be a link to the Library from this place," Kai said.

"Nor do we. But if it takes us back to base, that's good enough for me." Irene kicked the door shut behind them. Without the light coming in through the doorway, the place was even darker. "Sometimes it can take years for a world's entrance to the Library to shift. Sometimes it can take centuries. But with all the local libraries and bookshops shut down or under armed guard, this is our best bet."

"Would it be out of order for me to say that I don't like this alternate?" Kai asked. He unbuttoned his coat and reached inside, pulling out the book they'd been sent to fetch, and offered it to Irene.

She took it, conscious of its warmth from the heat of his body. "Not at all. I don't like it either."

"So how long before you stop getting..."

He was looking for a non-aggressive way of putting it, but Irene was irritated enough about the situation herself, so she felt no need to sugar-coat it. "Before I stop getting all the crap jobs, yes? God only knows. I'm on probation, after all. There isn't a fixed time on that."

And then she felt guilty at the way Kai's eyes flicked away from her, and at the flush on his cheeks. After all, her probation was his fault, in a roundabout way. She'd abandoned her duties as Librarian-in-Residence in another world at short notice, because she'd gone running off to save him from kidnapping and slavery—she'd also averted a war in the process. Clearly she was lucky to retain her post at all, but these types of missions were the price. It wasn't fair to remind him about it. And it didn't help to brood over it herself: the brooding tended to devolve into corrosive anger, or *they'll-all-realize-they-were-wrong-and-apologize* fantasizing, neither of which helped.

"Let's get moving," she said. "If the guards check their records, they'll realize that we were impostors and they could track us here."

Kai peered into the shadows. "I'm not sure there are any undamaged doors on this floor. Do we need an intact door and frame to get through to the Library?"

Irene nodded. And he was right—the place had been trashed very thoroughly. She wished she'd seen it while it was still a functioning collection of books, before the Revolution had gutted it. "We do. This could be awkward. We'd better try upstairs."

"I'll go first," Kai said, reaching the stairs before she could object. "I'm heavier than you are, so you should be safe to tread on a stair if it'll bear my weight."

This was not the time or place to get into another *will-you-stop-being-so-protective* argument. Irene let him go first and followed him gingerly up the creaking stairs, treading only where he trod and hanging on to the chipped balustrade in case of sudden falls.

Upstairs, the first floor was almost as ruined as the ground floor, but there was one door off the large central landing that was still hanging loosely on its hinges. Irene breathed a sigh of relief as she saw it. "That should do. Give me a moment."

She focused on her nature as a sworn Librarian, drawing herself upright and taking a deep breath, then stepped forward to lay her hand against the door, pushing it shut. **"Open to the Library,"** she said in the Language. Its power to reshape reality was a Librarian's greatest asset. So in a moment they'd be out of this place, back in the interdimensional collection of books they both worked for, ready to deliver one more volume to its huge archives.

What happened next *should definitely not have happened.* The door and its frame went up in a burst of fire. Irene stood there in stunned disbelief, barely snatching her hand away from the heat, a concussion of power resounding in her head like a car crash. Kai had to grab her shoulders and drag her back, pulling her away from the flames. They burned hot and white, catching on the wood faster than was natural and spreading across the wall.

"Fire, go out!" Irene ordered, but it didn't work. Usually the Language would interact with the world around her like cogs fitting together and moving in unison, but this time the metaphorical teeth on the cog-wheel didn't catch and the Language failed to grip reality. The flames rose even higher, and she flinched back from them.

"What happened?" Kai shouted, raising his voice to be heard above the crackle of the fire. "Was it booby-trapped?"

Irene gave herself a mental shake and pulled herself together, drawing back from the spreading fire. She'd been expecting to feel the usual drain of power, but what she'd touched had felt more like a live wire—an antithetical surge of power, which had exploded when she'd tried to touch it with her own. Fortunately it didn't seem to have affected *her*, just the door that could have been their route back to the Library. "I have no idea," she shouted back. "Quick, we need to find another entrance! And before this whole place goes up!" She clutched the book to her chest in a death grip: if she dropped it here and it went up in flames, god only knew how long it would take them to find another copy.

They stumbled to the stairs, smoke already coiling towards them and starting to drift through the shutters and outside. Irene led the way up this time, spurred by the rising crackling of the fire. She heard a crunch behind her as one of the stairs gave way under Kai, but he grunted at her to keep on going up, and a moment later his footsteps were behind her again.

Irene staggered out onto the second floor and looked around. It was as much of a wreck as the ground floor. There were no doors, only empty doorways and broken walls. There was more light, but only because of the large holes in the roof, and the floor was stained where the rain had been coming through.

Perhaps you should have used the Language more efficiently and succeeded in putting out the fire on the first floor. Rather than just screaming "Fire!" and panicking and running away, the cold voice of self-judgement at the back of her mind pointed out. *Might it have worked if you'd just tried a little harder? And don't step on those stained bits of floor,* the voice remarked waspishly, *they're probably rotting and unsafe.*

Kai strode across to one shuttered window, peering down at the street below through the cracks between shutter and wall. He went still, and even in the dim light Irene could see the tension in his shoulders. "Irene, I have some bad news."

Panic would be wasting vital time and energy, however tempting it might be. And the fire made it extremely tempting. "Let me guess," Irene said. "The National Guard has tracked us here."

"Yes," Kai said. "I can see a dozen of them. They're pointing at the smoke."

"I suppose it would have been too much to hope they wouldn't notice it." Irene tried to think of alternatives. "If I can stop the fire—"

"Possible—unless it's something to do with the Library or chaos," Kai pointed out. "That's stopped you using the Language before. Do you know what caused it?"

"No." Irene joined him at the shutter. There was a squad of twenty men and women out there, and the fact that the house was on fire was probably the only thing that had stopped them from coming in for the moment. She forced herself to speak with deliberate calmness, ignoring the clenching fear in her belly. "Dear me, we must have annoyed them back there. But I'm surprised they followed us so fast."

"I think I recognize that one." Kai pointed at one of the soldiers. "Wasn't she the one whom you convinced with the Language that we were officials from Paris?"

Irene squinted, then nodded. "I think you're right. It must have worn off faster than usual. Oh well."

Inwardly, she felt far more disturbed than she was allowing herself to show. It wasn't the squad of twenty soldiers outside. She could handle that. Well, she and Kai together could. It was the fact that the attempted gate to the Library had been shut down, and in a way that she didn't recognize or understand. Her current probation status meant that she was getting dirty work and dangerous jobs, such as this little waltz through a totalitarian republic and into their private vaults, to get a unique copy of *The Daughter of Porthos* by Dumas. But she should have been *warned* if there was a problem with reaching the Library from this world. It was a simple matter of common safety. If someone had deliberately sent her out here without telling her . . .

There would be time to settle that later. For the moment, they were in a burning house with angry soldiers outside. Par for the course. "Out the back door, then, before the first floor's impassable," she said.

There was a crash behind them.

"That was the stairs," Kai said, deadpan.

CHAPTER 2

"Right." It was amazing how being cut off by advancing flames focused the mind. And not just in the way that the first cup of coffee in the morning helped one concentrate, but more in the way that a magnifying glass directed all the minor fears into a single laser beam of pure terror. Irene had never particularly liked fire. More than that, the idea of fire getting loose among her books was a particular nightmare. Being caught in a conflagration was near the top of her Top Ten Ways I Don't Want to Die. "We break the shutters on this floor, go out, surrender, and escape later."

"Just like that?"

Irene raised an eyebrow. "Unless you have a better idea?"

"Actually, I *do*." Kai sounded half-proud, half-defiant, but overall determined. "We don't need to come back here, so it doesn't matter *what* they know. I'll change form and carry us both out of this world."

This threw Irene off balance. It wasn't something she had remotely expected. Kai hadn't bothered keeping his heritage as a dragon secret from her—at least, not after she'd found out about it—but he very rarely offered to do anything that would involve using it. And she'd never seen him in full dragon form before. "They've got rifles," she pointed out practically.

Kai snorted. Or perhaps that was the smoke. Which was admittedly getting thicker. Thank heavens there were no books in here to be burned now. She was a Librarian, after all: destruction of any books was loathsome. "Rifles are no threat to me, in my proper form."

Irene nearly said, *But what about me?* although she managed to shut her mouth before the words could get out. It was their only hope right now, after all. "Right," she said after a moment. "Do we have enough space in here?"

"Outside would be easier," Kai said. More smoke was drifting up between the floor-boards, and the crackling of flames was getting louder. "But there's just enough room in here. Please stay back against the wall."

Irene thrust the book inside her coat and stayed beside the window, her back pressed against the wall, as Kai walked out towards the centre of the floor. She did wonder if changing to a dragon was going to involve a loss of clothing, then mentally scolded herself for getting distracted at a moment of crisis. But she didn't look away.

Kai stopped and raised his arms, his back arching as he went up on his toes. But the movement didn't end there. The air seemed to thicken in the room, growing denser and more *real* in a way that outweighed the smoke. The light spilling through the holes in the roof grew heavier, glowing around him as his form shifted. Dazzle stung Irene's eyes, and she had to blink for a moment, however hard she tried to keep watching.

When she could see clearly again, Kai wasn't human any more.

Of all the pictures of dragons that Irene had ever seen, he looked the closest to the images in some of the older Chinese works. He lay in a serpentine knot of dark blue coils, his wings folded against the sides of his body. Where the light struck him, his scales were the clear dark sapphire of the deep ocean in daylight, and the traceries of scales along his body were like the ripples on the surface of a river. She thought he might be thirty feet or more long, fully outstretched, but it was hard to judge with him coiled up inside the room and in the smoke. His eyes were red as rubies now, with a light that didn't need the sun to burn, and as he opened his mouth she saw a great many sharp white carnivorous teeth.

"Irene?" he said. His voice was deep and organ toned, though still recognizably Kai's, and it hummed in her bones. The floor seemed to shudder in response.

She gathered herself. "Yes," she said. "Are you . . . all right?" It was a stupid question, she knew, but it was difficult to know what one should say. *Etiquette on dealing with apprentices after they have turned into dragons—another missing item from* The Big Book of Library Procedures.

"Absolutely," he rumbled. "This place is quite congenial to me. Stay back while I bring down the roof."

Well, the world was on the more lawful side of things, rather than on the chaotic end of the universe. The ruling despotic regime was an unfortunate side effect of that. As were the guards and guillotines. It would explain why Kai had no problems with being a full dragon here. In a more chaotic alternate world, which they'd unwillingly visited before, he'd been barely conscious in human form, and it would have been much worse if he'd been in dragon shape.

Kai reared up, his wings spreading till they bent against the walls, and set his back against the ceiling. The floor creaked ominously beneath him, but it was drowned out by the groaning of the ceiling as he shoved against it. Tiles came loose, falling to shatter against the floor, and through the dust and the increasing smoke Irene could see the remaining plaster cracking and falling away and the central rafters bending.

"Is anyone up there?" came a yell in French from downstairs.

The natural human response was to shout, No! Which said something about humanity. But Irene was too busy watching Kai, in any case, and trying to stay back, as more and more of the ceiling and roof came tumbling down.

With a heavier crash, the floor began to give way. Kai flexed his body, shifting to brace himself against the walls of the building, and lowered his great head. "Irene, get on me, between my shoulders—now!"

It would be bad manners to argue with the designated driver. Irene unslung her rifle and dropped it, then scrambled on top of the nearest bit of Kai's back, crawling up between his shoulders. It felt horribly lèse-majesté and improper to be crawling on all fours along the back of a dragon like this. His skin was like warm, flexible steel, rippling beneath her hands as his body flexed to hold him in position, and now that she was on top of him, Irene could smell the sea, stronger than the stench of dust and mould and fire.

Another piece of floor went tumbling. Fire came streaming up from below, leaping in the sudden burst of air, and Irene flung herself flat on Kai's back, her hands digging in as best they could. He was too broad for her to straddle, so she plastered herself against him and prayed. "Go, go, go!" she shouted. "Just go!"

Kai flung himself upwards in a twisting curve, scraping through the gaping hole in the roof, his tail lashing behind him as he rose into the air. Irene clung to his back, her face pressed against his hide, and felt his body flex underneath her in the sort of S-bend that should have been impossible—that *would* have been impossible—for a natural creature flying naturally.

But Kai was a dragon. He rose through the air as if he was simply moving from point A to point B like a painting on a scroll, and though his wings spread out in great blue arches as if to catch the wind, he flew against it. Irene could hear the screams and shouts from below, and the sharp cracks of rifle shots, but Kai's pace didn't falter as he drifted farther and farther up, till the city lay spread out beneath them like a photograph and the burning house was a distant blotch of orange.

"Irene?" He didn't turn his head to look at her. His flight path changed to a curving hover, tracing a wide circle in the air. "If I hold steady now, can you get a little closer to my shoulders? It'll be safer there for you, when we pass between worlds."

"Give me a moment," Irene said through gritted teeth. It helped if she kept her eyes on Kai's back, rather than looking down at the ground beneath. She wasn't fond of heights at the best of times, and sitting on a dragon's back hundreds of yards in the air made it hard to ignore exactly how high up she was. However, one consolation was that she wasn't being as wind-blown as she'd expected. Something was blunting the effect of the speed and the air currents on her—and on Kai, too, presumably. It must be to do with the whole dragon magical-flight thing. She added it to her list of questions for later, as she pulled herself slowly along Kai's back to between his wings.

"Now sit upright." She could hear the amusement in his voice.

"Like hell," Irene said. It was a very long way down.

"You'll be safe. We've carried people before, Irene. Sages, visitors, human favourites . . . Trust me. I won't drop you."

It's not a question of me not trusting you. It's a question of whether or not I can make myself physically let go of my death grip on you. Finger by finger, Irene released her hold on Kai's hide and pushed herself to a sitting position. Kai was too wide for her to sit astride, so she curled her legs underneath herself. Tendrils of mane flowed back from around his head, and she tentatively held on to a couple of them. It wasn't logical, but she felt much better for holding on to *something*. "What now?" she asked.

"Now I travel back to Vale's world." Kai's wings flexed, spreading to their full extent. The light glittered on them like the water on the surface of waves. "I know its place among the flow of the worlds, and I could fly to Vale himself, if I so desired. But he probably wouldn't like that," he said, abruptly losing his formality. "Where should we go?"

"The British Library," Irene said firmly. "You can land on the roof and I'll handle any guards while you change back. And then we can use the gate to the Library from there."

"That seems reasonable." Kai hesitated, the gesture more normal for a human than a dragon. "Irene, what happened back there?"

"I don't know." It was easy to admit ignorance, but more worrisome when it came to speculating about it. "If there's a problem with that world's access, I wasn't warned about it. And if it's a recent problem, then I need to warn other people. Urgently. I haven't heard of anything like this happening before, and other Librarians could be at risk." Her grip tightened. "Take us home, Kai. Before the people here invent a rocket ship to come up after us."

Kai rumbled a laugh, and she could feel the shiver in his body underneath her. *Well, I'm glad one of us is enjoying this.*

Then he dipped, losing altitude, his body curving through the air but not disturbing her, leaving her as well-balanced as though she were sitting on a chair in her own study. The wind was only moderate, ruffling her hair around her face, but they were moving faster now— fast enough that the air was shrieking as they sliced through it.

The air gaped open ahead of them, luminous and shimmering, a rip in reality. The roaring wind sounded like chanting voices, the words indecipherable, but the tone ominous and warning. Irene's stomach twisted in suppressed panic. She'd always been the one in control of travel between worlds. Of course she trusted Kai, of course she was sure he could handle it if he said so, and of course she wasn't going to *admit* to being afraid, but the terror of the unknown was a cold shadow on her heart. Yet curiosity kept her eyes open. This was, after all, something she'd never done before . . .

Kai flew straight ahead, into the rift.

CHAPTER 3

They plunged into an atmosphere that was as thick and dense as syrup. Irene could still breathe, after the first moment's panic, but the air flowed around them like water, and tendrils of her hair drifted round her face as though she were submerged. There was no sun, no moon or stars or any obvious source of light, but she could see herself and Kai with a vague dawn-like clarity.

They were gliding through an ocean of air in a thousand shades of blue and green. There was no obvious end or beginning to it, and no clear solid objects or real things except for the two of them. The only differentiation Irene could see was in the shadings and temperatures of the currents that constantly moved and shifted through the air, like vast streams of smoke or rivers entering the sea. And perhaps Kai could perceive even more than she could.

"Where are we?" she asked.

"Behind," Kai said. He didn't change his steady pace, gliding through the flux of watery air. "Outside. Travelling."

"Is it that you can't explain—or shouldn't explain?" Irene asked. Either would make sense.

"More the first than the second." He winged a long, casual turn. "I'm seeking the river that leads to Vale's world. I can't explain it any better than you can explain the Language to someone who doesn't have the Library brand."

"Fair enough." She patted his back reassuringly, then hoped that dragons didn't object to that sort of thing from passengers. "You won't get into any sort of trouble for this from your relatives, will you?"

"For protecting you? Hardly. They're still considering how best to reward you for your meritorious actions."

Kai sounded smug, but Irene didn't have quite so rosy a view of matters. Yes, she had helped rescue Kai, but tracking his kidnappers had meant leaving her post as Librarian-in-Residence and going AWOL and provoking a large number of Fae. This might have raised her stock with the dragons—or at least with Kai's family, who were, after all, kings among the dragons—but it had left her on probation in the Library. She was lucky she hadn't been exiled. Whether that was fair or unfair was something that wasn't worth arguing, and would only mark her as a troublemaker if she tried. Irene wasn't sure that she wanted to raise her stock with the dragons at the Library's expense. She was a Librarian, sworn to the Library, and that had to come first.

"That reminds me," Kai went on, a little too casually. "Have you considered Li Ming's suggestion?"

"Kai." Irene took a deep breath before she could snap at him. This was the third time he'd brought it up in the last three days. "I appreciate that you didn't ask for your uncle to send Li Ming to Vale's world. And I appreciate that Li Ming is only being courteous in offering to provide accommodation for you and your household. But I can't—not won't, *can't*—move in and live under his protection."

"You won't be under his protection," Kai protested. "You'd be under mine!" He seemed to realize that he'd said the wrong thing. "Besides, it wouldn't be protection as such. It's just that he'd be paying for it. And you'd still be keeping up your duties as Librarian-in-Residence."

"No," Irene said. She looked out at the endless flows and patterns of colour. It was enough to make anyone feel insignificant. Dragons must be immune, however, which probably said a lot about dragons and their in-built feelings of extreme significance. "I can't compromise the Library's interests by living in accommodation that's being paid for by a servant of your uncle."

That was the diplomatic way of putting it. The Library was neutral and stayed out of the way of both dragons and Fae, unless their interests came into direct conflict—usually over the ownership of a book, or an immediate life-or-death situation. They certainly weren't going to formally ally themselves with either side. It would be highly inappropriate for a Librarian to be living as a paid dependant of one of the dragon kings.

Irene's immediate reaction was a bit more visceral. She didn't object to Li Ming in person. He was always courteous and diplomatic, and while he was here to watch over Kai, he did so very discreetly and didn't stop Kai from going on jobs like the current one. But Irene was absolutely certain that in the long run Li Ming wanted Kai away from the Library and going back to his previous role as dragon princeling, with Irene either installed as a favoured servant or out of the picture. Which was fair enough. But in the end, it was going to be Kai's choice.

Kai was silent for ten minutes, probably reviewing his strategy. "What if I was paying for it?" he suggested.

"With money you got from Li Ming? Sorry, that won't wash."

"You're treating this as a major issue." Kai curved downwards: there was enough gravity to make it perceptible as "down" rather than "up," and Irene was grateful for that, since she was having enough trouble as it was in reconciling her perceptions with reality. "I just want to protect you. So does Li Ming. So does my uncle. He views you as a suitable friend for me. Why can't you understand that?"

"As your friend, I'm grateful for that." It would have been too blatant a kick in the teeth to say *I don't need your protection* or *Last time I was the one protecting you.* Plus there was the fact that Kai was the one who'd just rescued her, less than an hour ago. "But as a Librarian, I can't accept it. Not in that way."

Kai growled, and Irene felt the vibration underneath her, down the length of his body. "You aren't making this easy!"

"I'm sure I'm not," Irene said. "Have you asked Vale about any of this?"

The dead silence in response was indicative. Vale was a number of things: he was London's greatest detective in the alternate world where they were living, and he was a good friend of Kai's and—Irene thought—not entirely unattached to Irene herself. He was also very similar to a certain fictional Great Detective, but Irene didn't like to bring that up in conversation.

"Is that a 'Yes and he said no'?" Irene enquired. "Or just a plain 'No'?"

"Since when did you become so involved in my relationships?" Kai rumbled, with a deepening undertone of anger.

"He's my friend too," Irene said.

For a moment Kai was silent. Irene was congratulating herself on having found a conversation-stopper when he suggested, "I don't *mind* you having a relationship with Vale, you know."

"How very open-minded of you," Irene muttered.

"It wouldn't hinder our friendship, of course," Kai went on

blithely. "Nor would it matter if you were bedding me as well. I know you say that you feel that would be inappropriate, as mentor to student, but among my kind it would be considered quite natural. And if you'd like some suggestions about how to approach Vale . . ."

"Kai," Irene said through gritted teeth. "Drop the subject. Please."

"We're almost home in any case." The air around them was a deepening blue-green and was thicker in Irene's lungs, almost difficult to breathe. "Brace yourself."

Irene took a firmer hold of the tendrils of mane. "Where will we come out?" she asked.

"Why, where I choose." Kai sounded almost surprised that she needed to ask. "But I'll make it high enough that we don't have to worry about zeppelins."

"Good thinking," Irene said faintly. She hadn't even envisaged the possibility, until he'd mentioned it. She wasn't used to thinking in terms of air traffic. What she was thinking about was the ongoing struggle between the Fae and the dragons. This ability to choose exactly where they emerged in an alternate world would mean that the dragons could appear in any place they liked—if it weren't for the fact that high-chaos worlds were antithetical to them. Kai had been semi-conscious most of the time they'd been in a very high-chaos Venice, and he'd implied that he'd have been in an even worse condition if he'd been in his draconic form. Probably something similar applied to powerful Fae who had ambitions of invading high-order worlds. It explained why most of the fighting took place in the middle areas, in worlds that were somewhere between the two opposites.

Kai folded his wings close to his body, jerking his head and shoulders as if he were fighting against an oncoming tide. But before Irene could get more than mildly panicked, he roared, the sound reverberating through the empty space around them as if they were in an echo chamber. As the noise shuddered through the air, a rift split open in front of them, shattering light in all directions, and Kai dived through it.

They came out above the clouds. It was a very long way down, and bitterly cold. For some reason, Irene's fear of falling from a height like this was much greater than it had been of falling off in the space between worlds, where the fall could presumably have gone on for infinity. She pressed herself tightly against Kai's back. *Perhaps it's because I knew that he'd catch me if I'd fallen there, while here . . . I might just hit the ground.*

Kai drifted downwards: as before, the velocity and wind didn't reach Irene or do more than ruffle her hair, and she could enjoy the view of oncoming clouds and smog. Typical weather for this world, or at least for this London. "Can you go to any world?" she asked, curious.

"To any world I know, or to any person I know." Kai sounded smug again, which wasn't surprising: Irene's travel through the Library was rather more specific and limited. "I could find you wherever you were."

"Even in the Library?"

There was a pause. "Well, no. I can't reach the Library. None of my kindred can. It's barred to us by our usual way of travel. The only way I can get to it is by being taken there by a Librarian. Like you."

Well, that explains why the dragons haven't taken us over for our own good. Irene made some soothing noises of agreement, and wondered exactly why dragons couldn't reach the Library, and if she had a hope in hell of finding out while acting as mentor to a dragon apprentice. Her superiors could be very paranoid, and it might earn her some much-needed favour.

Kai snaked through the air. "Ready to go down?" he said.

It would have been nice to sit up here above the clouds for a while longer, discussing metaphysics and dragons and other interesting topics, but there was simply too much on her schedule. "Let's do it," Irene said.

They came down with a rush, slicing through the clouds and leaving streamers of mist behind them, with a speed that would have left Irene prostrated if it had been natural flight—well, as far as any flight on the back of a giant supernatural pseudo-reptile could be termed natural. She realized, with the technical part of her mind that wasn't occupied with *Oh my god please slow down*, that Kai must be going as fast as possible to make it less likely that people would see him. Even in London, a dragon might attract attention and would be hard to mistake for an airship.

She could see the British Library below, and the glass pyramid on top of it. There was a small zeppelin tethered to the roof, floating there ready for action, and Kai had to adjust his flight path to avoid it. Two guards had seen him incoming and came running to intercept him, hands on truncheons.

Plus several points for duty, minus a lot more points for intelligence, for running towards an approaching dragon rather than running away from an approaching dragon. Irene waited till Kai had settled to the ground, then slid off his back. Ideally she would have walked towards the guards, but for some reason her legs didn't want to work, and she leaned against Kai instead. "Good afternoon," she said, trying to sound charming.

The guards looked her up and down. Admittedly her National Guard costume, her harshly braided hair, and the fact that she'd been gently smoked (or lightly kippered) didn't make her look like the most trustworthy person. Time for the other option.

She pushed away from Kai, standing upright, and took a deep breath. Light flared behind her. That must be Kai turning back into a human. Good, it'd make the phrasing easier. **"You perceive that I and the person behind me are normal but unimportant people, who have a right to be here on the roof, but are not worth your time and interest."**

The use of the Language to affect someone's perceptions always took energy. She swayed as she felt the drain on her reserves. But it worked. The guards developed the vaguely puzzled look of men trying to remember exactly what had been so important. One of them waved her and Kai towards the door into the main building, with a mumbled, "Please enjoy your visit to the British Library."

Of course the problem with using the Language that way was that it might wear off at any moment. It was only useful up to a point. Kai knew that just as well as Irene, so the moment they were inside the building, he led the way in a rapid trot down the book-lined storage corridor, and they didn't stop till they were a few turnings away.

"Are you going to open a direct portal to the Library from one of these rooms, or do you want to go down to the fixed entrance?" he asked.

Irene ran her hands over her hair and grimaced at the amount of ash that came away. "I think we'll use the fixed entrance," she said. "I know we'll probably run into people on the way down there, but at least we know where we'll come out in the Library, that way. Besides, after last time, I stashed a couple of overcoats in the room next to it. It'll do to cover up these outfits till we can get back to our lodgings."

"We could just change clothing in the Library," Kai said hopefully. He had much better taste in clothing than Irene did, and frequently exercised it.

"Time," Irene said. "I'd rather get back here as soon as we can. We can collect any mail in the Library, but other than that . . ." She shrugged. "We've been away from here for nearly a fortnight. As

Librarian-in-Residence, it's my duty to make sure nothing's happened in our absence."

"Li Ming and Vale will both be glad to know we have returned, too," Kai agreed. "As you say, then."

Irene led the way down the stairs and passageways at a fast walk, ignoring the looks of surprise, shock, and sheer horror. Ladies in this world did not wear trousers. Zeppelin pilots and engineers did, but they weren't generally ladies, and they wouldn't go wandering around the British Library in them.

The room containing the permanent entrance to the Library was cordoned off with ropes and signs, declaring hopefully, REPAIRS IN PROGRESS. Irene had to admit to a certain responsibility there, involving a small fire and a pack of werewolves, but on the positive side, it did make it easy for the two of them to march in while looking like workmen.

Once inside the room and with the door safely shut, Irene looked around guiltily. This had once been a well-kept office, with glass cases full of interesting things, or at least antique ones, and cupboards and shelves properly full of books. Now—after the silverfish infestation, her duel with Alberich, and the fire—it was a wreck. The few remaining display-cases were empty and shabby, and the scorched floor and singed walls stood bare and unattractive.

It wasn't her fault. Not directly, anyway. But she still felt guilty.

With a shake of her head, she stepped forward to put her hand against the far door. In practical terms, it was a simple storage cupboard. But in metaphysical terms, it was a permanent link to the Library, like the one that had gone up in flames, and only needed a Librarian's use of the Language to activate it. **"Open to the Library,"** she said. A queasy worm of nervousness twisted in her stomach at the unwanted but inescapable image of the same thing happening here.

As if to quiet her worries, the door swung open at once, without the slightest hindrance. She took a deep breath, not wanting to sigh in relief *too* audibly, and ushered Kai through before stepping through herself and shutting the door behind her.

The room in the Library was familiar to them by now—one of the conveniences of using a fixed transfer point from an alternate world to the Library, rather than forcing a passage through and possibly ending up anywhere at all in the Library. The walls were thick with books, so much so that the black-letter posters warning, MODERATE CHAOS LEVEL, ENTER WITH CARE had to hang in front of them, for lack of clear wall space. As did the promised overcoats. Someone had installed a computer on the central table.

"That's new," Kai said, pointing at it.

"Convenient, though," Irene said. She sat down in front of it as she turned it on, and removed the book from her coat. "Could you just check down the corridor? There's a delivery point there, and you can drop this in and get it off our hands while I'm sending an urgent notification about the gate. Coppelia or one of the other elders might want to speak to us personally."

Kai nodded, taking the book. "Of course. Irene—"

"Yes?"

"What *do* you think that reaction was?"

"I don't know," Irene had to admit. "It wasn't some sort of linked-chaos trap. At least, I don't see how it can have been. There wasn't anything linked to it that I could see—did you see anything?"

Kai shook his head. He paced thoughtfully, in a way that Irene suspected he'd subconsciously copied from Vale. "I saw nothing, and I felt nothing out of the ordinary. If I had done, I would have warned you. It didn't even feel like a normal intrusion of chaos into that world—forgive my vocabulary, please; it's the best way I have to describe it. If I were to guess—"

"Which is an appalling habit, and destructive to the logical faculty—yes, I know," Irene couldn't stop herself from saying.

The corner of Kai's mouth twitched. On him, the streaks of ash looked merely like artistic dishevelment, the sort of thing a model would wear in a particularly outré fashion show. And on him, the National Guard uniform could have started a fashion. "If I were to *hypothesize*, then, I'd say that the problem was somewhere at the Library end, or between the two points. But I don't know if that's actually possible."

Irene nodded, logging on and starting to draft an email report to her mentor, Coppelia. "We didn't come *in* through that gate, because it would have meant dropping into the middle of hostile territory and an unknown situation. That was why Baudolino brought us in via Sicily, and we had to go overland from there." Baudolino was that world's Librarian-in-Residence, a frail man in his seventies and definitely not up to dodging revolutionary informers and handling a police state. Irene personally thought it was past time for him to retire to the Library, but it would have been tactless to say so. "And Baudolino himself can't have checked up on it recently, or he would have fallen into the same trap—if we can call it that. So . . . I don't know. I'll just have to report it and see how that goes. And about delivering the book itself . . ."

"Going, going, gone," Kai said, and the door closed behind him.

It took some editing for Irene to transform her first reaction. Which went something along the lines of *We nearly got roasted, so I am raising the alarm, and if someone else knew about it, then why the hell weren't we warned? This was a life-threatening malfunction!* She eventually managed a more tactful *I must report that when we attempted to activate the gate, we were the victims of high-energy side-effects, and I'm not sure that the gate is still in existence.* But she did end with . . . *The lack of information on the gate's status could easily have caused a total failure of the mission. If Kai and I weren't fully briefed due to some issues in communication, then I must raise this as a serious problem for future efficiency and safety. Librarians are a finite resource. And if this is a new problem, then other Librarians need to be warned as soon as possible.*

It was more management-speak than she liked, but it should get her meaning across. Irene sighed, putting her chin in her hands. Paranoia suggested that she had already been put on probation, and there was a direct line between that and being sent on dangerous missions with incomplete information. Common sense argued that she shouldn't attribute to malice what could perfectly well be explained by stupidity, or at least by organizational mistakes. But there wasn't anything in her waiting emails or in the *Current Events* bulletin about other gates going up in flames. So what could have happened?

Could it be sabotage? Could someone be attacking the Library? That was a dangerous line of questioning, and not one that she liked to consider.

Paranoia was self-fulfilling, she reminded herself. Mistakes, or even coincidental accidents, were more plausible here. But paranoia wouldn't be banished quite so easily.

The door creaked open. "All done?" Kai asked.

Irene nodded. "And nothing urgent otherwise. Book safely posted?"

"On its way." Kai inspected the spare overcoats, pursing his lips. "Buying the cheapest second-hand goods is a false economy," he finally said.

"I'm not thinking about that now," Irene said firmly, pulling on her overcoat. "I'm thinking of getting back to our lodgings and having a hot bath."

"You have a point." Kai swung his coat over his shoulders. "At your will, madam."

Their exit back into Vale's world, and out of the British Library, went unnoticed. It was verging on evening by now, and those people still in the British Library were more concerned with work or study than with watching passers-by. Irene was beginning to nurture hopes of a quiet evening without any further problems. Hot water first, of course, then a clean dress. Then perhaps dinner, or calling on Vale and seeing if he was available for dinner, and then—

Kai grabbed her arm, dragging her back to reality. "Who's that?" he hissed.

They had just left the British Library. A woman was standing on the far side of the road, watching the main doors. Everything about her was vastly inappropriate for the time and location. Her dark curls were twisted up into a knot and fell to brush her bare right shoulder. She wore a drape of thick black fur that stretched from one wrist to the other, hanging in thick folds behind her. Beneath it a dress of black silk clung to her body and legs, so tight that it looked as if it had been sewn in place. The smoggy sunset light turned her skin an even darker gold than usual, and her eyes were as vivid as cut obsidian. She held a leash in her right hand, which restrained a black greyhound. As Irene and Kai paused, it lifted its head from sniffing at the ground and gave a little bark, as much as to say, *Here you are—I found them.*

"Zayanna," Irene said. If her voice was numb with surprise, she hoped that it passed for a controlled assessment of the situation. The other woman wasn't actually an enemy. Well, probably not. She'd even been an ally of sorts, the last time they met. And she was Fae, but that was a different sort of problem.

The woman spread her arms in a delighted gesture. The greyhound yelped as the leash tugged at his neck, and she quickly lowered her right hand. She hurried across the road towards them, delicate on her high heels. "Irene! Darling! Have you any idea how difficult it's been to find you?"

"I didn't realize you were looking for me," Irene said, her social circuits cutting in automatically. Ignoring Kai's hiss of "Is that a Fae?" she held out her hand in welcome. "If I'd known—"

"Oh, there's no way you could have known, darling," Zayanna said. Ignoring Irene's hand, she embraced her, wrapping her arms around Irene and nestling her head against her shoulder. "I have to appeal to you for asylum, darling. You don't mind, do you?"

CHAPTER 4

Irene was conscious that she had gone board-like and unresponsive in Zayanna's embrace. One arm came up automatically and patted the other woman on the shoulder. "There, there," she said. She was aware that it lacked a certain something. "Perhaps we should discuss this off the main street?"

"Perhaps not," Kai said dangerously. "Woman, get off Irene and stop trying to seduce her."

Zayanna raised her head to look at Kai, and the dog growled, apparently echoing its mistress's feelings. "This isn't seduction. This is just—"

"Throwing yourself on me in the middle of the street," Irene said, conscious of the number of people who were obviously watching, and the even larger number who were pretending not to watch, but were watching anyhow.

"She's so good with words," Zayanna confided to Kai. "And she's so *popular*. You should keep her locked up, sweetheart. Actually, no, that's not a good idea, because she can't have daring adventures if you keep her locked up. But you know, it's the thought that counts."

"The thought has crossed my mind on occasion," Kai muttered. "Irene, who is this woman, and is there anything that you would like me to do?" The subtext of *such as getting her off you* came across very clearly.

We need to talk in private. But I'm not bringing her into my home. Even if I do owe her something for her non-interference in Venice. She'd needed all the help she could get when Kai was kidnapped. "Tea," Irene said quickly. "Restaurant. That is, we will go to a nearby restaurant and have tea, and Zayanna can tell us what the problem is."

"You've gone so terribly native," Zayanna said with a sigh, mercifully removing herself from around Irene's neck. "I don't suppose anywhere round here serves mescal?"

"I don't know," Irene said. Vale would, but then Vale knew London forwards, backwards, and upside down. And he could recite the London gangs from memory or identify a splash of mud with a single glance. "Why don't we go and find out?"

Kai's expression over Zayanna's shoulder suggested a whole variety of reasons why they shouldn't, but Irene didn't feel like arguing.

Fifteen minutes later they were sitting around a table in a tea-shop of dubious quality, whose back wall was lined with cobwebbed tin boxes of exotic teas, and whose lights were burning worryingly low. The fog had closed in outside. Zayanna's dog was lying beside her chair, snuffling thoughtfully and watching all three of them with red-lit eyes.

"You said that you wanted asylum," Irene said, coming to the point. Her tea smelled musty, with an undertone of metal. She would have preferred a better-quality tea-shop, but with the way the three of them were dressed, they would have been turned away at the door. "Could you give me a little more detail, please?"

Zayanna puffed at the surface of her cup of tea, blowing up a little cloud of steam. "Darling," she began. "You remember that I didn't try to stop you from rescuing your friends on the train back from Venice?"

"Vividly," Irene said. Something that had been nagging at the back of her mind clarified itself. "How did you know my name was Irene?" As far as she could remember, she'd been using an alias all the time that she'd been with Zayanna. It was a little worrying to think how the other woman might have found out.

"It was Sterrington," Zayanna said. "After you left the train, Atrox Ferox and I managed to have a word with her. She'd been told your real name by Lord and Lady Guantes. They were your arch-nemeses during that whole jaunt, after all. They'd also said you were a Librarian—working here, and everything. Darling, I was stunned! A real secret agent with me all that time, and I'd had no idea!"

"I'm not a secret agent," Irene said, knowing that it wasn't going to work. "I just collect books."

"Of course." Zayanna nodded solemnly. "Your secret is safe with me, darling."

"And with the whole of this tea-shop," Kai said. There was a stiffness to his posture that worried Irene. While she had managed to rescue him from what Zayanna so casually called a "jaunt," for Kai it had been kidnapping, and imprisonment, and the threat of being sold to his kind's worst enemies. He wasn't sleeping well at night, he was too ready to throw himself into danger, and he thoroughly disliked talking about any of it. This sort of conversation would be rubbing salt into his wounds.

"Oh, *them*." Zayanna shrugged. "They're just people."

Irene was lost for a moment, trying to work out whether that statement stemmed from sublime unconcern, a genuine lack of interest in ordinary humans, or a deliberate ploy to make her underestimate Zayanna. No, on the whole she thought it was simply Zayanna being Zayanna, and being Fae. To a Fae, the whole of humanity were fellow actors at best. They were the supporting cast or backstage scene-shifters the rest of the time. All Fae were convinced they were the heroes of their own stories. The dangerous thing was that in the more chaotic alternate worlds, the universe conspired to agree with them.

"But are *you* a secret agent?" Irene asked.

"Not exactly, darling." Zayanna sipped at her tea. "Things went wrong, you see. After Venice, I had to report back to my patron. He said that even if Lord and Lady Guantes *had* totally messed up the dragon's kidnapping, I shouldn't have let all three of you get away like I did. He was really cutting about that." She shivered artistically.

It's not as if you had that much chance of stopping us. Irene ignored Kai's atmosphere of polar frost next to her and reached across to pat Zayanna's hand. "I'm sorry you got into trouble," she said.

Zayanna looked down modestly, if the word "modest" could ever be used in connection with her cleavage. "I knew you'd understand," she murmured. "So naturally, when I had to break ties with my patron, I thought of you."

"I don't know what to say," Irene lied. She could think of quite a few things to say, but none of them would actually advance the conversation, even if they might make her feel better. "Zayanna, you do realize that I don't actually"—what was it that Zayanna had said she used to do for her previous boss?—"have any snakes that need looking after."

"We can get snakes, darling," Zayanna said reassuringly. "Do you prefer cobras or vipers? Or mambas?"

"Can you collect books?" Irene countered.

"I've never tried," Zayanna said. "But there's a first time for everything, isn't there?"

Irene was fairly sure there weren't any Library regulations about Outsourcing Jobs to Fae, probably because the area was mostly covered by Don't Associate with Fae in the First Place. But, she reassured her conscience, it would do for the moment, while she tried to find a better long-term solution. "Does Silver know you're here?" she asked.

Lord Silver was probably the most powerful Fae in London. He was the Liechtenstein ambassador (Liechtenstein was a hotbed of Fae, in this particular alternate world) and a noted libertine and reprobate, regularly making the front pages of the more scandalous newspapers. He had also technically been an ally during the whole business of Kai's kidnapping, helping Irene to reach the world where Kai was being held so that she could rescue him. Though that had only happened because Silver felt threatened by Kai's kidnappers. He was another person whom Irene would like the earth to swallow up. But if he could take Zayanna off her hands, then she'd even send *him* flowers.

Zayanna pouted. "I've been trying to avoid Lord Silver, darling. I don't really want to be indebted to him. I did think of asking him where you lived. But then I had a better idea, and I got this gorgeous little dog to help find you! I took him to your address and I've been tracking you since then. I think I'm going to call him Pettitoes." She drained her cup and put it down with a clink. "But I need to be serious too, darling. Someone out there wants to kill you."

It was rather sad that Irene's first reaction was not so much shock as resignation. Then she wondered whether there was a queue, and if someone was selling tickets. After all, in less than a year she'd managed to seriously annoy a number of people—the local werewolves, several local secret societies, one of the two masterminds who'd plotted to kidnap Kai (she'd actually killed the other), the notorious traitor Librarian Alberich, and probably all sorts of other people she didn't even know about. And Silver didn't like her very much, either. "Who?" she asked.

"I don't know." Zayanna leaned forward across the table, trying to capture Irene's hand in hers. When Kai interposed his hand, she grabbed that instead. "Darling—darlings—" Kai looked as if he were biting into raw garlic. "You must believe that I want to keep you safe. What would I do without you?"

That was another frequent problem with the Fae. They wanted fellow starring actors in their private melodramas, both friends and enemies. Irene had to figure out a way to disentangle herself from Zayanna—and fast—or she'd get swept into some improbable new narrative. "I believe you," she said. *Mostly.* "But if you can't tell us who it is, or when they're going to try . . ."

Zayanna sighed, and Kai took the opportunity to pull his hand away. "It's just a whisper of a rumour, darling. I'll try to find out more. But it's getting late. You'll be wanting to go out on highly sensitive missions and dance the tango, won't you? Can I come?"

"No," Irene said firmly. "I'm sorry. It's top secret. Where can we get in touch with you tomorrow?"

Zayanna took the dismissal surprisingly well. "The Carlton hotel, darling. I'll be waiting. But I'll stay here for the moment. This place has such a charming ambiance." She gestured around at the gloomy shelves and at the rafters with their hanging bare ether bulbs, then down to her dog. "Don't worry about me. Pettitoes will keep me safe."

Kai waited till they were out on the street and a couple of hundred yards away before saying, "Should we kill her?"

"Zayanna *helped me rescue you*," Irene muttered. It didn't make it any easier that she was considering that option as well. But simple inconvenience was not a good enough motive for murder. Even if it looked like being a really, really large inconvenience.

"Yes, but the woman is Fae," Kai answered. There was a brittle coldness in his eyes, and his gait had shifted from a casual stride to a much more dangerous and purposeful stalk.

Irene tried to think of some intelligent, logical, helpful statement that would convince him to stay calm. Nothing came to mind. What *could* she say to a dragon who'd been kidnapped by the Fae in order to start a war? Already-existing personal bias was being inflamed by post-traumatic shock, and he certainly wasn't going to have any sudden epiphanies in the middle of the street. "But *I* say you won't just remove her," she hissed, resorting to the fact that she was his superior, and knowing how temporary and stop-gap an answer that was. "*Understood?*"

Kai blinked, and the inhuman light—had it been there for longer than a moment?—receded from his eyes. "Understood," he said, his voice dark and low in his throat.

I'm going to have to talk this through with him later. And if I can't get him to see sense . . . Irene had a duty to her work in this world. She also had a duty of responsibility to Kai. Something twisted in her stomach at the thought that perhaps the best thing she could do for him would be to see him assigned to another Librarian. Or he could even be returned to his father's court, to safety among the other dragons . . .

"I'm not sure I trust her, either," she said. "We have no proof that she's telling the truth. But I think it's better to keep her under close watch for the moment, till we can establish what's going on. Keep your friends close and your enemies closer, and all that sort of thing. Besides, if Zayanna is telling the truth, then we might be able to get useful information from her."

"It might just be simpler to wait and see who's trying to kill us," Kai said.

Irene looked ahead down the street. In the foggy twilight, newspaper boards loomed on the street corners where vendors touted the evening papers, with barely visible capitalized headlines glaring at her like secret messages. BETRAYAL. MURDER. WAR. "True," she agreed. "But they might get lucky."

"Disguise someone as us, and then watch them from a distance?" Kai suggested.

"Mm. No, not really." A fuzzy memory of management training nagged at Irene. "It's not that I'm trying to shoot down all your ideas," she added. "It's more that I don't see how we could manage it, without the preparation being noticed. It may also be a question of how long they've been planning to kill us. We've been out of London for a couple of weeks now. Though in that case . . ."

"Yes?" Kai prompted when she trailed off.

"Well, unless the person who wants to kill us is getting information from the Library, or from Vale—both of which are very unlikely—then they couldn't have *known* we'd be out of London for the last two weeks. They may have been sitting around chewing their fingernails and wondering where we've got to."

They conversed quietly as they walked down the foggy street— just another pair of Londoners in heavy overcoats, with scarves wound round their faces against the evening mist and pollution. It would have been difficult to be more anonymous. Irene could glance down the street and see other pairs and groups of people strolling together, their heads close as they murmured to each other. Conspirators? Families? Friends? Apocalyptic plotters? How could anyone know?

"We should check in with Vale," Kai said.

Irene nodded. "After we've checked our lodgings. Carefully, of course. And I don't know if you've considered it, but Zayanna might be useful for information about another thing, too."

"What other thing?"

"If there's someone in the Library, or among the dragons, who's selling information about us, then we need to find out who it is." Apparently dragons were a monolithic block who would absolutely never betray each other to the Fae. Or so the dragons said. This could simply mean that they were very thorough about getting rid of traitors. "If Zayanna still has links to the Fae gossip networks, or however it is they share the news and conspiracies, maybe she could find out something."

"Or maybe she could sell me out herself," Kai said coldly. "Or you. I'm sure there are Fae out there who'd like a Librarian slave."

"I'm sure there are," Irene agreed mildly. She still had nightmares about a few aspects of her trip to that Venice. "But the fact remains that when push came to shove, she did help me. So for the moment let's stop going round in circles and playing *who-do-we-suspect*. Lodgings, bath, clothing, then Vale, and wait for the next mission."

When they reached their lodgings, the surrounding buildings had their lights on, but their own set of rooms showed ominous dark windows. Of course, that was how they'd left them, but it was hard not to imagine potential murderers waiting behind the drawn curtains.

"Let me check the door," Kai said, stepping in front of Irene. She knew that he had a minor criminal past, from his time in a more technological alternate world, so she let him get on with it. He would know how to check for tripwires, hidden switches, or scratches on the lock much better than she would. She glanced up and down the road. No obvious followers, no lurking minions, no shadows visible on the rooftops.

After a few minutes of inspecting the door, lock, step, door-mat, and surrounding area, Kai rose from his knees. "It looks clean," he said. "No wires. Nothing connected to it. No chaotic residue."

"Good," Irene said. "Though I wouldn't have thought it would be a bomb, anyhow. You know the Fae. A bomb would lack that personal touch. And it'd be over far too soon."

Kai stood back from the door so that she could unlock it. "You did say that Lady Guantes was the *efficient* type, though. And you did kill her husband."

"Yes, well," Irene muttered. "Let's hope that she hates me enough to want to take lots of time over it, and do it in person."

The key turned smoothly. Nothing bad happened immediately. She waited a moment, in case there was anything hiding to jump out at her, then thrust the door open.

Through the doorway, in the light from the street ether lamps, she and Kai could see a perfectly normal corridor. A scattering of post lay on the carpet, where it had been shoved through the letter-box, but none of it looked large enough to be dangerous.

All right, perhaps I am being paranoid.

Kai gave her a nod. They both stepped inside, and Irene raised her hand to the light-switch.

Something hairy touched her fingers.

CHAPTER 5

Irene froze. It wasn't a deliberate choice of action made from a careful assessment of the situation. It was an instinctive reaction to the soft touch of something thin and hairy against her fingers, something moving, and childhood memories of being told *Don't jerk your hand away, you'll just startle it*. It was very definitely something alive.

"Kai," she said, and swallowed to clear her throat. "There's something else in here with us."

"Do you think it's light-sensitive?" Kai demanded.

How on earth was she supposed to know? "Let's hope so," she replied. She still didn't want to move her fingers. She could dimly see the thing now, a large blotch of a creature about a monstrous six inches across, its body sprawled over the light-switch. But there was more than one way to deal with that. **"Corridor-ceiling lights, turn on!"** she commanded in the Language.

The ceiling lamps flared into sudden brightness as Kai slammed the door shut, and Irene had enough time to see the creature before it scuttled back towards the coat stand, leaving her fingers free and her heart hammering.

It was a spider. Irene had nothing particularly against spiders, and when she was at school she had more than once been the person who had to take them out of the room and release them into the wild. But she had a very definite reaction to spiders that were over eight inches across and covered with hair. She wiped her hand on her skirt, illogically and vigorously.

"That's a spider," Kai observed unnecessarily.

"It looked like one." Irene found herself backing towards him. The two of them stood together in the middle of the corridor, as far as they could get from coat stands, pictures, bookcases, or any other objects that might have spiders hiding behind them.

"Do you think it's venomous?"

Irene snorted. "Do you think there's even the remotest chance it isn't?"

"Right. Stupid question. Do you think we can fumigate the whole house?"

"I'm not going to sleep if there's the slightest chance of any of them still being in here," Irene said firmly. "Which means we need to clear the place. Especially if it's even remotely possible that they could breed, or get out into other houses."

"How do we clear the place?" Kai asked, putting his finger on the problem.

Irene frowned, thinking. "What's the largest reasonably airtight container we have?"

"Probably one of our suitcases," Kai suggested. "It's not totally airtight, but there aren't any cracks in it big enough for the spiders to get out, if they're inside."

"Right. And the suitcases are in the attic, aren't they?"

Kai took a deep breath. "Stay right here," he said and was running for the stairs before she could tell him to stop.

Technically she was rather relieved not to be running through the place, with spiders lurking in corners and ready to jump out at her—or should that be drop down on her?—at the slightest provocation. But she still felt a little guilty that he'd gone off to take the risk. Perhaps she was being overprotective.

She heard his footsteps upstairs, and the thump of the attic trapdoor swinging down from the ceiling, followed by the banging of cases and trunks being shifted round. It was far too easy to imagine huge, heaving cobwebbed nests of giant spiders in the attic. She forced herself to focus on her immediate surroundings—and look, the spider that had been crawling around by the light-switch was emerging again and picking its way down the wall. There were other little twitches and barely visible movements coming from the darkest corners of the hall. The light had been so bright and welcome a moment ago. But now it merely threw possible hiding places for spiders into stark relief. And there were far too many of them. Irene was abruptly very grateful that she was in boots and trousers.

"I'd almost prefer to be back in a burning building with the troops outside," she muttered to herself.

"Sorry?" Kai came thundering down the stairs, banging the suitcase he was carrying against the balustrade posts in his haste. Irene winced as she saw another twitching clot of shadow drop from under the stair-rail and scuttle for cover. "Any problems?"

"Not now," she said with relief. She took the case from him and opened it, placing it on the floor in front of them. "Get ready to brace me."

Kai simply nodded.

Irene took a deep breath, filling her lungs, then shouted in the Language, her voice loud enough to be heard throughout their lodgings, **"Spiders, come here and get into the suitcase on the floor!"**

The loose command structure of the sentence, and the fact that she was attempting to exert her will on living beings—if not humans—made her sway at the sudden drain of energy. Kai, with the expertise of both warning and experience, caught her with an arm around her shoulders and held her upright against him as the shadowy corners of their lodgings came to life.

Spiders as big as the first one came scuttling from the folds of coats hanging on the hat-stands, dropping from the upper corners of the ceiling, and levering themselves out from behind the shabby pictures that hung in the hallway. A couple of dozen of them came in a wave down the stairs, heaving and jerking along in a mincing eight-legged gait that was too fast for peace of mind. Irene watched as they clambered into her suitcase, forming a hairy, seething mat across the interior, climbing over each other and waving their legs in the air. A few normal spiders had joined the rush and ran round inside rather pathetically, tiny in comparison to their bigger cousins.

She gave it ten seconds after the last spider had climbed in, then kicked the lid closed and sat firmly on it, snapping the catches shut.

"We could throw it on a bonfire," Kai suggested. "No, wait, they might get out when the case burns. Perhaps if we throw it in the Thames?"

"Kai," Irene said firmly. "I'm surprised at you. This is a valid route for investigation. We don't simply want to destroy them—first we want to find out everything we can about them. But before that, I am going through this place with another suitcase. I'll use the Language to hatch any hidden eggs and make absolutely sure we've found them all."

Kai evidently hadn't thought about the possibility of eggs. He shuddered and glared down at the suitcase. "Disgusting creatures. How do you suppose they got into the house?"

"We won't know till we've checked," Irene said, brushing herself off. "Could be a broken window or a hole in the roof. It could be . . ." She looked at the front door. "Well, it would be incredibly blatant, but you could just about push them through the letterbox, if they cooperated."

"At least it'll interest Vale," Kai said with resignation as they went to find another suitcase.

The all-night pet shop down the road was an upper-class one, gleaming with up-to-date chrome and high-power lamps, and little steam-powered climate systems hissed along the rows of tanks and cages. It was complete with pedigree puppies, Persian kittens, glass tanks full of brightly coloured and probably incompatible fish, and a proprietor who didn't want to serve them. She was stick-insect thin, with straw-pale hair the same shade as the blonde ferret ripping toys apart in a cage behind her, and was dressed in spotless dark blue with heavy leather bracers on her forearms.

"It's not that I don't want to be helpful," she protested icily, "but I'm afraid I really don't understand what you could possibly want with a humble establishment like my own, which only serves the most refined of clients."

"We have two suitcases full of giant spiders," Irene said pleasantly. She'd taken ten minutes to change into proper clothing for this alternate world and get rid of most of the ash, so she knew that she looked like a respectable woman, if not a stinking rich one. "We need an expert's opinion."

The proprietor raised her near-invisible eyebrows. "Madam, I realize that a lot of spiders may seem large to you—"

"Eight inches to a foot across." Kai stepped forward, giving the woman his most serious and winning look. Irene wasn't normally a supporter of the *go persuade people through your good looks* school of thought, mostly because she didn't have the sort of looks that one needed to make it work, but she could appreciate it when it was being done to help her.

The proprietor hesitated. It might have been because Kai was handsome, well-dressed, and charming. Or it might have been because however much he tried to play it down, he inevitably came across as someone from an aristocratic background, with more money than he knew what to do with. "Well, I suppose I could take a look at them. Perhaps a consultation fee . . ."

"Of course," Kai said, with casual disdain for precise amounts. "Do you have a glass tank or something similar, which we can release them into?"

The proprietor signalled an assistant to fetch a large glass tank. Kai took the smaller suitcase and laid it inside the tank. It held the few stragglers that they'd found, plus some tiny specimens that Irene had forced to hatch early, and which she still eyed with suspicion, small as they were. Kai snapped open the catches but left the suitcase lid down. "When I open it," he said, "please stand ready to close the tank lid, and make sure that nothing has a chance to get out."

To Irene's relief, the proprietor nodded professionally. "Let's have a look," she said.

Kai flipped the suitcase lid back, pulling his hand and arm out of the tank in the same motion. Spiders came spilling out of the suitcase in a drift of waving legs and heaving balloon-like bodies the size of tennis balls. With an astonished curse, hastily cut short, the assistant brought the tank lid down firmly and slid the bolt shut.

The proprietor pursed her lips. "Why, I do believe— Can it be?" She leaned closer to the tank, nearly squashing her thin nose against the glass.

The spiders swarmed inside the tank, dashing up and down on the sandy bottom and running up the interior glass walls. Irene felt something squishy bump against her leg, and she nearly jumped away in automatic reaction before she realized it was a bystander moving closer to peer in fascination.

"How splendid," the proprietor exclaimed. "*Pelinobius muticus!* A king baboon spider! Dozens of them—an entire breeding colony!" Irene didn't need to be a mind-reader to see the little signals tipping over in the woman's head and pointing to EXCLUSIVE SUPPLIER and HUGE PROFIT. "Are you intending to bring them onto the market yourself, sir?"

Kai glanced at Irene. Irene stepped forward. "Not exactly, madam—"

"Miss Chester," the woman said, with a narrow-lipped smile that tried to look friendly and failed.

"Miss Chester," Irene said, "we recently had a crate of bananas delivered, a gift from a friend in Brazil." Did they grow bananas in Brazil? She'd forgotten her basic school geography and national products, let alone whatever they were in this alternate world. "We honestly didn't expect to find these, um . . ."

"*Pelinobius muticus,*" Miss Chester said, pronouncing it very clearly to make sure that Irene got it right.

Irene liked being underestimated. It made people less likely to suspect that she was lying. "We just didn't have the resources to take care of them ourselves," she said. She tried to look like a woman who might actually like spiders, rather than one who preferred the drown-them-in-a-vat-of-acid option. "If you feel that you can give them a good home, then perhaps . . ."

"I'm sure that we can come to an arrangement," Miss Chester said, her smile growing toothier.

"I t would have looked suspicious if we hadn't bargained," Irene said later. They were in a cab and were finally on their way to Vale's rooms.

"You don't think it looked suspicious anyhow?" Kai queried drily. "Two people showing up with suitcases full of giant killer spiders—"

"*Pelinobius muticus,*" Irene said. "I wrote down the details. We can ask Vale about them."

Kai brooded, leaning back and folding his arms. "Irene . . ."

"Yes?"

"I'm concerned."

"Well, that's quite understandable. Someone did probably just try to kill us." Not to mention the gate going up in flames. But were the two connected?

"And while we did survive . . ."

Dragons yet again proved themselves masters of the obvious. Irene nodded, waiting for him to continue.

Kai seemed to be looking for the right words to finish his sentence. Finally he said, "Should we reconsider our mission here?"

"In what way?"

"Well, we could move to a more protected environment."

Oh. Another attempt to bring her under the draconic wing. However, he had a point about people trying to kill them. After two near-death events in one day, it wasn't paranoia; it was simple caution. "I admit that the evidence shows that they—whoever they are—know where we live," Irene said. "And I also admit that doesn't make me particularly comfortable. However, I wouldn't call them very efficient murderers."

"You *want* an efficient murderer?"

"Heavens, no," Irene said. "Give me an inefficient murderer any day. I'd far rather have someone trying to kill me by shoving spiders through my letterbox than by hiring a sniper with a laser-sighted rifle or setting fire to our lodgings." Actually verbalizing the thought cheered her up. But she was by no means as insouciant as her words suggested. Dead was still dead, whether the killer was exotic, professional, or amateur. Getting killed was incredibly easy. Anyone could do it. Staying safe and alive was much harder.

Kai's mouth twitched and he began to smile, finally relaxing. "You have a point there. I hadn't thought of it that way."

"Not that I *want* to have someone trying to kill me," Irene hastily added. "But, you know, given the choice . . ."

The cab rolled to a stop and the driver called down from his perch, "We're here, madam, sir. Will you be wanting me to wait?"

"No, thank you," Kai said. He paid off the driver while Irene clambered out of the cab, already regretting her return to long skirts. One really didn't appreciate trousers until one wasn't wearing them any more.

The two of them looked up at Vale's windows as the cab rattled off into the fog, its ether lamps glaring eyes that vanished into the darkness. A dim light showed round the edges of Vale's curtains.

"At least he's in," Irene said. From time to time she regretted this world's lack of convenient mass communication. "It'd be annoying if he'd been out on a case."

Nobody answered Kai's knock, but Irene didn't have to use the Language to coax the door open. Kai already had a key. He led the way up the stairs. Irene followed. She reassured her slight flickerings of nervousness—why didn't anyone answer? was anything wrong?—by reminding herself that it was coming on to eight o'clock at night.

Vale's housekeeper might well be out. Vale himself would recognize their footsteps, and he might in any case be several miles deep in experiments or research.

"Vale—" Kai began, opening the door at the head of the stairs. Then he stopped in his tracks.

"What?" Irene demanded, ducking under Kai's arm to see what was going on.

Vale's rooms were in as much of a state of controlled clutter as usual. His scrap-books and files were organized neatly, scrupulously tidy and alphabetical, but other than that, the place was full of *stuff*. Laboratory equipment was strewn over the main table, with several crumb-dusted plates perched beside the test-tubes. Boxes filled the corners of the room, piled on top of each other in a desperate attempt to use all the limited space available. Various relics from past or current cases lay along the mantelpiece or fought for space on the bookshelves. The ether lamps were turned to half strength, leaving the room in dimly flickering light, and the fire had burned down to embers. Newspapers littered the chairs and floor, as if they had been frantically rifled through and discarded page by page.

Vale himself lay on the sofa. He was a tall man—but, sprawled as he was, he'd lost all his usual grace and was a lanky tangle of limbs. One arm was half-thrown across his face. He was only semi-dressed, in a dressing-gown over shirt and trousers, and clearly had not been planning to go out.

He didn't react to their words. He didn't even move.

It was astonishing how pure nightmare could quite literally put ice in one's veins. *An attack on us, now an attack on Vale, too . . .* She and Kai were both moving across the room in the same moment, without even having to say anything. The only reason Kai reached Vale first was that he'd entered the room first.

Kai grabbed for Vale's wrist, fingers clasping it tightly, then sighed in relief. "There's a pulse," he reported. "But it's slow."

The wave of relief that hit Irene was so strong she could taste it. "Thank god," she said. "But why . . ."

An answer came to mind. It wasn't a pretty one. She took Vale's wrist from Kai and peeled back his sleeve, checking his forearm. She wasn't entirely surprised by what she found. It did, after all, go with the territory of being London's greatest detective, in a world where stories could come true and life too often followed narrative. "Look," she said, pointing to the needle marks.

Kai bit back an oath. "But he said—" he began, then stopped short.

"What did he say?" Irene asked softly. She checked Vale's pulse herself. It was slow but steady.

Kai turned and walked across to turn up the lights. "He said that he didn't use it any more." He didn't look at Irene.

"When did he say that?"

"A few months ago. It wasn't long after we met, the three of us. I, you see . . ." Kai was nearly stuttering in his attempts to find an explanation. She hadn't heard that speech pattern in him before. "I found the syringe and the drug—"

"Which drug?"

"Morphine." Kai turned back to her. "Irene, I swear, he said he'd only used it occasionally, and not at all now that his practice had become more interesting. I don't know why he'd be taking it *now*." His face showed something of the panic of a child who'd found out that a fundamental pillar of his world was no longer solid. "Could someone else have forced it on him?"

It was certainly possible. It just wasn't very likely. "I suppose we won't know until we can ask him." Irene laid Vale's arm back across his body and brushed his dark hair back from his face. His skin was hot under her fingers. So human. So fragile. And if someone was trying to kill her, then was he a target, too?

She had to find a way to protect them—all of them. And she had to talk to her superiors, *urgently*. The time for professional detachment was over.

It would have been a perfect trap, the cold unpleasant voice at the back of her mind pointed out. Incapacitate Vale, arrange a bomb or something similar, and expect Irene and Kai to run into the danger-zone the moment they saw him lying there. It was a very good thing that the attempted murderer or murderers, whoever they were, didn't have Irene's own imagination.

She had to say something to Kai. "We're staying here tonight, of course."

"Would it be safer to take him to our lodgings?" Kai asked. "Or to somewhere else defensible?"

She gave him a few mental points for not actually saying *such as Li Ming's establishment* out loud. "I can set up defences here," she said. "Library wards. And we can sit up and watch for spiders together." She also needed to discover what had driven Vale back to his drugs. Under the circumstances, information was the best weapon she could have.

Kai eyed the room dubiously, obviously imagining how many places a spider could hide itself. "I suppose it might be better," he said unenthusiastically. "I'll put him in his bed. It'll be better than leaving him on the sofa. He might catch a cold."

Which is of course a profoundly serious issue, when compared to shooting up with morphine. But Irene nodded. "Check the bed first. We should be careful."

"We can't go on like this!" Kai burst out.

"No." Irene fought down the whirl of fury in her stomach. *Once is happenstance, twice is coincidence; three times is enemy action...* "No, we can't. We are not required to act like sitting ducks, just waiting to be shot at. We aren't being laid-back about this, Kai—we're putting up defences and finding out what the hell is going on. We also need more information..." She wasn't sure whom or what she was angriest with: the mysterious murderer, Vale for the drugs, or the whole day for being such a rollercoaster of near failure. "And we don't know that this, here"—she gestured at the unconscious Vale—"is specifically due to us."

"It's very coincidental if it isn't," Kai said. But his temper had cooled a little. He bent down and swung Vale up in his arms, carrying the man easily. Vale didn't stir, as loose-jointed as a strung doll, his eyes closed in fathoms-deep slumber.

I wish I knew more about the effects of morphine, Irene thought. Oh well, it was probably in one of Vale's own reference books. She could look it up while she was waiting.

The room was cold, now that she wasn't being distracted by Vale. Kai had been right. She went down on her knees next to the hearth to build up the fire. In her distraction, she almost missed the balled-up sheet of notepaper. It had been caught in the grate and had fallen a few inches short of the embers.

It was probably a private letter. It would be prying into Vale's personal life to look at it. He was a friend of hers, and he deserved better than this sort of morbid curiosity.

On the other hand, they'd come in to find him drugged out of his mind on morphine.

She picked it up and unfolded it, smoothing it into legibility.

It was expensive notepaper: she could tell that much, even if she didn't have Vale's expert knowledge of paper, manufacturers, and watermarks. And it was Vale's handwriting, carelessly untidy, scribbled with the sublime lack of concern of someone who thinks it's the other person's job to understand the message:

Singh,

> Stop wasting my time with these pitifully simple cases. I am not interested in these petty problems. I would have no qualms in giving these to even the slowest-witted among your colleagues at the Yard.
> I thought that you understood. My mind is a machine that is being stressed to breaking point, without any problems to exercise it. And if you can't help me, then—

The writing broke off there in a spattered trail of ink.

Irene hesitated for a moment, then crumpled the letter and thrust it into the embers. Her hands went through the motions of building up the fire, but her mind was elsewhere. The murder attempts. Zayanna. Now Vale. There was too much to do and too much to monitor. And what was she going to do if the Library ordered her off on another mission tomorrow?

She carefully diverted herself away from that thought. Because if that did happen, then one way or another, she was going to end up betraying *someone*.

CHAPTER 6

Kai had fallen asleep by now too, curled up on the sofa where Vale had been sleeping earlier. They'd agreed to keep watch in turn. After the day's events, neither of them had felt safe, even with Irene warding the place. Vale had enough books for her to draw the rooms into a temporary sympathy with the Library, which should keep out any immediate Fae attacks.

Sitting with a book in her lap next to the fire, with the lights turned down so that Kai could doze better, Irene half wished that they *had* an immediate attack on their hands. It might give them a bit more information. At the moment they knew very little: they were reacting rather than being proactive, running to catch up.

There was a faint mutter from Vale's bedroom. She put down the book on narcotics and went to investigate.

Vale lay on his bed, his bedspread half-thrown back, eyes closed but mumbling to himself. It was a step up from the drugged slumber of earlier, but it still wasn't wakefulness. The light from the open door fell in a slice across his bedroom, throwing his face into painful definition: his eyes were sunken in their sockets, and his cheek bones stood out viciously. Surely, Irene thought, surely he hadn't looked that worn, that desperate, when they'd last seen him a fortnight ago. Surely she would have *noticed* . . . wouldn't she?

She closed the bedroom door quietly behind her, so that the noise wouldn't wake Kai, turned the light on, then walked across to Vale's bed. She sat next to him and touched his shoulder, shaking him gently. "Vale?" she murmured.

His eyes came open. He was the sort of man who snapped into consciousness all in one moment, rather than Irene's own more gradual (and pitiful) slow clamber from sleep to wakefulness. He assessed his surroundings in one quick glance, then focused on her. "Winters."

"I'm not impressed." She'd run through dozens of versions of the conversation in her head. None of them really had a happy ending. At least he was addressing her by the relatively familiar *Winters*, rather than retreating to the more proper *Miss Winters*.

Vale looked away from her. "Not all of us have your strength."

"I don't understand."

He sighed. "One single night's indulgence, and for that I have you and Strongrock occupying my rooms and preaching abstinence. It seems rather unfair."

Leaving aside the moral aspects, there was a major logical fallacy in that statement. "One single night's indulgence does not result in a week's worth of injection marks," Irene pointed out. She'd inspected his arm while he was unconscious.

Vale snorted. "And now you'll attempt to play the detective at me, Winters? That isn't a game that you can win."

"It's not a game at all," Irene said. "I'm just . . . surprised."

"You aren't," Vale said. He rolled over to look at her, propping himself up with one elbow. "You're unhappy, but you're not surprised. I wonder why?"

Unwelcome as the question was, Irene would have liked to take it as a sign of improvement. But he spoke languidly, rather than with his usual keen interrogative tone, and she could see that his pupils were still too wide and unfocused.

"Are you being forced into it?" she asked.

Vale stared at her. "Do you honestly think so?"

"No," she admitted. "But Kai thought it was possible."

"Strongrock is a good man and refuses to accept some things as probable. He wouldn't understand why a man might need drugs to sleep."

"Which would be?"

Vale flopped back onto the pillow. "Oh come now, Winters. If I choose to take morphine, that is my business and not yours. And you're clenching your jaw now, in that annoying manner that suggests you're going to make a personal issue of the matter."

Damn right I am. "You know perfectly well that morphine is an addictive drug."

"Of course," Vale said. "That is, naturally I am aware of this fact. Your point being?"

"Merely that I am quite sure the criminal classes of London will be overjoyed to learn—no, to see the *results*—of you sliding into addiction and self-destruction in this manner." She kept her voice low but didn't try to take the edge off it. "Quite besides the feelings of your friends on the subject."

"You have an advantage over me, Winters." Vale sounded genuinely tired, rather than simply muzzy with the after-effects of the drug.

"What would that be?"

"An ability to admit your own failings." He stared at the ceiling.

"Of course, women are more prone to discussing their emotions than men. But even so, you have always been willing to acknowledge when you have made a mistake, or when your competency lies in areas other than the current situation. Almost too ready. Your opinion of your own abilities is frequently lower than it should be. Did you have the virtues of humility drummed into you at that boarding school you remember so fondly?"

Irene bristled, trying to work out if that whole little speech amounted to an insult, or if it was honest truth. "If you're trying to annoy me so that I'll walk out of this room, then I must tell you it's not going to work."

Vale sighed. "What a pity. But my point remains. You seem to find it quite simple to confess to error."

"Not really," Irene admitted. "I don't like being wrong any more than anyone else. It's more that I can't allow my pride to get in the way of my function as a Librarian. I have a job to do, Vale. If that means letting someone else take over who can do things better, well . . ."

A cab rattled past outside in the darkness, wheels grating on the road. "If you truly believed that," Vale said, "then you would have permitted your colleague Bradamant to take charge of your earlier mission—to find the Grimm book. From what Strongrock told me, you were quite firm in refusing her help."

Irene flushed. She still wasn't comfortable discussing the other Librarian. While they had agreed to a degree of truce at their last meeting—at least Irene had proposed one, and Bradamant hadn't actually said no—they hadn't seen each other since. And they had years of bad feelings to overcome. Then she realized the purpose behind Vale's words. "You're trying to distract me. The sooner you're honest with me, the sooner I can let you get back to sleep."

"Ah, and there lies the problem. Since that little trip of ours to Venice, I have had trouble sleeping."

If Vale was admitting that he had any sort of problem, then the problem in question was probably already too big to handle. "And therefore the morphine?" Irene asked.

"And therefore, as you say, the morphine. Though . . . I must admit that I have increased the level of the dose in the last few days." Vale looked up at the ceiling. "Are you now going to tell me that you have used that Language of yours to remove the drug from my body?"

"Frankly, I wouldn't dare," Irene said. "I could try telling it to come out of your body, but heaven only knows how it would come out or what damage it might do to your bodily tissues. It's the sort of thing I would reserve for emergencies. Please never give me cause to try."

"I wish I could give you that promise, Winters," Vale said slowly. "But if I am to be functional, then I need to sleep. And if I am to sleep, then I must have morphine."

"Why can't you sleep?" Irene asked bluntly.

Vale was silent for a long moment. Finally he said, "I dream."

The logical next question would have been: *What do you dream about?* Irene had never trained as a psychologist. Or a psychiatrist. She wasn't actually sure what the difference was, or which sort had more letters after their name. The closest she'd come to it was on-the-job training in persuading people to talk to her. Usually to get them to tell her where books were. She wasn't any sort of therapist. If Vale had been traumatized by his visit to that other, dark Venice, like Kai with his understandable post-kidnapping PTSD, then where did she start?

Silence seemed to be the right course of action. Vale finally spoke again. "I dream of moving amid a world of masks, where we are all actors, Winters, and where we are all on the strings of greater pup-peteers. I dream of a thousand, thousand worlds, all of them spinning at odds to each other, all of them gradually being lost to a random ocean of utter illogic and randomness, like flotsam in a whirlpool. I dream that nothing makes *sense*."

"Dreams can be chaotic—" Irene started.

"Of course they can," Vale said with exhausted patience. "But these are not just dreams where things from my daily life are jumbled together randomly. I dare say such dreams are common enough. These are dreams that exalt disorder and illogic, Winters. Nothing makes sense. The only thing that eases them is to throw myself into work, and even that is scarce—there are no problems large enough to challenge me, no mysteries complex enough to intrigue me." He was sitting upright now, grasping her wrist hard enough to hurt. "You must understand me, Winters. I cannot *endure* these dreams."

Irene looked down at her wrist meaningfully. Vale followed her gaze and let go of her, carefully unfolding his fingers. "Forgive me," he said. "I should not have done that."

"I asked the question," Irene said. And the answer made far too much sense. They'd visited a high-chaos world. Vale had been *warned* not to go to that version of Venice—Lord Silver had been quite clear about risks, even if he hadn't made it clear what those risks were. And now there was this threat—not to Vale's body, which would have been comparatively minor, in Vale's own estimation, but to his mind . . .

"It hardly takes a great logician to connect this to recent events," Vale said, echoing her thoughts. "But I will be damned if I go to Lord Silver for help. If I can endure these dreams until the influence of that world weakens, then I can reduce the morphine afterwards."

There were so many possible logical holes in that statement that

Irene could have used it as a tea-strainer. But she could see from Vale's face that he himself was aware of them, and it would have been no more than cruelty to have pointed them out, without something better to offer. Finally she said, "I could take you to the Library."

Vale blinked. Just once. His eyelids flickered, but his gaze was set on her face. "You have never shown any interest in taking me there in the past."

"You've always avoided actually suggesting it." *Probably because you knew I'd say no. It's not a tourist hang-out.*

"Do you honestly think it will help?" He left out the question *What would your superiors say?*, which was a relief, as Irene was trying not to think about that.

"I don't know," she admitted. "But we do know that Fae can't enter the Library. If I escort you in there, it might purge your system—I take it we're going with the explanation that you have been affected by overexposure to high levels of chaos?"

Vale gave her one of his best *neither you nor I are idiots, so do not descend to idiocy* looks. "It would seem the most obvious explanation. Though when you were infected with chaos in the past, you weren't even able to enter the Library, as I recall. Do you think I will be able to?"

Irene pursed her lips. "Well, if we try and find that you can't, then at least we'll be one step closer to identifying the problem."

"And locating a solution?"

"Let's take this one step at a time," she said firmly.

"Could you use your Language to force this infestation out of me?" Vale suggested. "You did it to yourself, as I recall, when you fell victim to chaos exposure."

"Um. There could be consequences." Irene could think of a number of undefined but vaguely unpleasant ways that such a thing could go wrong. It could be worse—both to soul and to body—than sweating morphine, and that was just the *first* thing she could imagine. Heaven only knew how many other ways something like that could go wrong. "The official line was that chaos infection would eventually be purged from our bodies naturally. And it's known that as a world shifts from chaos to order or back again, so do the people of that world. So if we can keep you steady long enough for it to equalize to your natural balance . . ." She was conscious that this wasn't being very specific, or even remotely reassuring. It might not even be accurate. She certainly wouldn't have wanted to hear it herself. "We can save it as a last resort," she said.

"Tell me, Winters, do you think . . ." Vale trailed off for a moment. "Do you think I am particularly vulnerable to this contagion?"

Irene hesitated. She hoped it would be taken for careful consideration. *Chaos likes to turn people into walking archetypes, main characters in search of a part. You're a great detective. And you already fulfil all the criteria for a certain* fictional *Great Detective.* She could easily see Vale being dragged deeper into stereotype and falling victim to chaos. But would it actually help to say that? He thoroughly detested the Fae, both as individuals and as a race. Comparing him to them would not help his mood or make him sleep any better.

Vale apparently took her silence for agreement. "Yes," he said quietly. "I don't talk about it, Winters, but you and I both know that my family is . . . unreliable. I broke with them because of their more dubious practices. Black magic. Poisoning. But there's worse. Winters, there is . . ." He swallowed. "There is hereditary insanity in my family. I thought I had escaped it. But now . . ."

"Rubbish!" Irene was surprised by the firmness of her tone. "This would probably have happened to any unprotected human who went there. You saw how the locals reacted." *They were puppets on strings, toys to be jerked around at the whims of Venice's Fae masters, backstage props and chorus to the ongoing drama.* "Kai and I were lucky enough to be protected. It's that simple."

"Ah yes. Your protection." Vale didn't look wholly comforted, but he did look slightly less despairing than he had a moment ago. "How did you obtain it?"

"I took vows to the Library," Irene said briefly. "A mark was set on me."

"Details, Winters," Vale prompted. "Details."

"We don't talk about it." She hunched her shoulders defensively. Now it was her turn to look away from him. She remembered bits and pieces of the night she took her vows to the Library. The questioning by a panel of older Librarians. The nerve-racking, stomach-clenching panic that she wouldn't be found worthy. And then a dark room, somewhere in the bowels of the Library, somewhere she had never found again. She had been alone in the silence there, and a sudden crashing flare of light had brought her to her knees and carved a pattern across her shoulder-blades . . .

"It would distract me . . . ," Vale said. Outside, another cab creaked past.

"I can show you the brand, if you want." It was harder to say the words than she had expected. She wasn't particularly body-shy, but the Library mark was something she automatically kept hidden and private. But it would still be easier to show it than to talk about that night.

Out of the corner of her eye, she caught the flare of interest in Vale's face. "If it wouldn't be too inconvenient," he said in an encouraging tone.

Irene turned away from him and reached behind her back to unbutton her dress. Her thoughts were complicated. Part of her mind was screaming that she was alone in a bedroom with Vale and was about to bare her back to him, and was this really a good idea? What would it do to their carefully managed friendship? Another part of her mind thought it was an excellent idea and was sotto voce suggesting directions that the two of them could take from there. And the rest of her mind was trying to convince her it was really just to distract Vale from his nightmares, and that if she ignored all the other thoughts and emotions, then they would simply evaporate.

She undid the buttons at the back of her neck, grateful that she was wearing a dress that buttoned down the back rather than the front. And this wouldn't require her to strip to the waist to show Vale her shoulders. That might be taking things a bit too fast.

But she was still utterly conscious of his presence, lying on the bed behind her in the quiet, dimly lit room, and of his eyes on her. When she'd been younger, she'd idolized great detectives and dreamed her own dreams. It had been part of the reason that she'd chosen her name. She knew—she accepted—that the man behind her was his own person and not some sort of fake-Holmes. But that didn't stop her from caring for him, for who he was. If she had to take him to the Library, then she would. She was already in enough trouble. What was one more breach of regulations?

And if it did all go wrong and she was ordered away from this world, then what?

She slipped the dress down from her shoulders, holding it modestly against her breasts, exposing her shoulders and back. She was aware that the straps of her brassiere partly obscured the markings across her back, but most of it should be visible. "Can you see it?" she asked.

"Yes." Vale sat up behind her. Irene didn't look round, but she could hear the creaking of the bed and the rustle of the pushed-aside bedspread. "It does look like a relatively normal tattoo, composed of scrollwork or Chinese characters . . . Why can't I understand it? I thought Strongrock said that everything in the Language would look like a man's native language if he tried to read it."

"Library marks are an exception to the rule," Irene said. She tried to relax and keep her breathing even, and not think about how close behind her he must be, how easy it would be to turn round and kiss him.

"Is it hazardous to the touch?"

"I don't think so. Nobody's ever died of it." She realized that might cast a dubious light on her behaviour and quickly added, "That I know of."

"If I may . . . ?"

Her throat tightened. "Of course," she said.

She felt the faint brush of his fingers against her skin, gliding along the lines of her tattoo. His fingers were feverishly hot—or was that just her?—and as he leaned in closer, she could hear his breathing come faster.

"It feels like normal skin and scarring," he said. It was the blandest of possible remarks. It didn't match the way his fingers trailed across her back. Maybe Kai had actually had a point when he suggested she should approach Vale. She'd always thought that any attraction on her side had been one-sided. She might have been wrong about that. Which meant . . .

Irene took a deep breath. Now or never. She swivelled round, her left hand holding her dress up in place. Vale was only a few inches behind her, his hand still raised. His cheeks were flushed, and no, she wasn't imagining it—there was the heat of desire in his eyes, in the way his lips were parted to speak.

She didn't give him the chance to ask her to turn back round. She slid her free arm around his neck, pulling him to her, and flung herself into a kiss. Part of her tried to compare this to Zayanna's earlier tactics, but she shot that thought down before it could get in the way. She was semi-undressed in Vale's bedroom. In this place and time, it was not an innocent situation, and both of them knew it.

And Vale responded. His lips parted against hers, and his arms came round to hold her as firmly as she was holding him. He made a small sound deep in his throat, sliding deeper into the kiss with the assurance of a man who has had his share of experience, as hungry for her as she was for him, as tired, as desperate . . .

Slowly the kiss eased. His hands shifted to cup her face. "Winters," he said. "Irene, I—"

"Don't *say* anything," Irene urged. "Please. I want this, too."

"You can't know what you're saying." Was it just the reaction of a man who would always think that women were less competent, less able to know their own desires? Irene had thought better of him. "I shouldn't have . . ."

"*I* kissed *you*." She tried to put genuine feeling into her voice, rather than retreating to her usual calm surface of sarcasm and distance. "Vale— Should I call you Peregrine?"

"Dear God, no!" he said. "Irene, I can't let you make this decision like this. Your pity for me shouldn't sway you into degrading yourself—"

"I would not be degrading myself," Irene said through gritted teeth. The heat of that kiss was wearing off under this sudden bath of cold indecision and self-loathing. "I have respected and admired you for months. I find you a very handsome man. If I choose to pursue you, then by all means tell me no, but please don't imply that I am somehow donating myself to you out of charity. It is *nothing* like that."

"You are far too attractive and deserving a woman to throw herself away on a man like myself." Vale was starting to sound terse. Perhaps it signalled a growing annoyance that she wouldn't simply withdraw and leave him to his self-indulgent bitterness.

"I'm an unprincipled adventuress working as a book thief," Irene snapped back.

"You're barely twenty-five."

"I'm in my late thirties."

Vale dropped his hands to her shoulders, seizing her as if he would like to shake her. "Have you no *sense*, Irene? I'm going insane. I'm no fit bed-mate for any woman."

"And I have just said I do not intend to let that happen!" Irene hissed, keeping her voice down, so as not to bring Kai in on them both. Though it would have been a pleasure to shout. "If you consider my judgement to be worth so little, then by all means throw me out of your bedroom, but allow me to point out that I would very much have liked to stay! What do I have to do to convince you that I'm an adult and I know my own mind?"

Vale took a deep, shuddering breath and then pushed her away from him, releasing her shoulders. "Get out of here, Winters. I don't blame you. I couldn't possibly blame you. This is my own fault for playing the fool, for leading you on . . ."

Irene didn't quite trust herself to speak at once. She pulled away and turned her back to him, doing her dress up again in quick, angry movements. "I am certainly not going to try to force you," she said. "We are both mature adults, after all. And if you want to wallow in your self-pity, far be it from me to stop you."

Vale didn't answer. The bed creaked as he lay back down on it.

Irene rose to her feet. "Get some sleep," she said coldly. She still wanted him. Even losing her temper didn't stop that. And for that moment, she knew that Vale had wanted her, too. Her eyes pricked with furious tears. The stupid, irritating, self-pitying, overly noble *idiot* . . . "We can talk later. When you aren't so tired."

"My decision won't change, Winters," Vale said coldly. He rolled over, turning away from her and dragging the bedspread up over his curled body.

Irene closed the door behind her, leaving him alone in his bedroom, and was quite pleased with herself that she didn't slam it.

CHAPTER 7

The fog had gone the next morning, and the day was as clear as it ever became in this London and this alternate world. Passing zeppelins above drew thin trails across the morning sky, which faded into feathery patterns of cloud, and newspaper sellers shouted their wares on the street corners. They formed small islands of temporary stillness in the hurrying crowds. Even in this pleasant weather, all of London had somewhere to go and some place to be, and nobody had the time to dawdle.

Irene herself was hurrying. She needed to find out if there was any reply to her report on the malfunctioning Traverse. She also wanted to add supplementary material, possibly in capital letters, on the subject of spiders and further murder attempts. If she and Kai needed to shelter in the Library, she wanted to do it sooner rather than later. She refused to risk both their lives.

She'd left Kai behind with Vale, with the excuse that this trip to the Library didn't need both of them, and that someone should stay with Vale in case he was targeted by whoever had sent the spiders. The more honest truth was that she'd wanted some time on her own. What little sleep she'd managed hadn't been good, and she hadn't felt very charitable to either of the men—even if Kai had done nothing to deserve it. And they could keep each other safe.

She was heading for the British Library again, despite her misgivings that it might be too obvious a move to any unfriendly eyes. It was a trade-off: she could force a passage to the Library itself from some other large collection of books. But then she couldn't control where in the Library she would emerge, and she'd only be able to hold the link open for a short time. There were too many urgent things going on for her to risk ending up in a distant corner of the Library. It was best to use the fixed entrance and run the risk of others knowing where it was. Hopefully nobody was planning to kill her this early in the morning.

"Read all about it!" the closest newspaper vendor shouted. Irene glanced at his display board. GUERNSEY ZEPPELIN BASE WITCH-CRAFT SCANDAL, it read. No, probably not related to her current problems. Not everything was about her.

Then the shock wave hit. It was a surge of force that felt like the Library at first, but wasn't—oh god, how very much it wasn't. It seemed reassuringly familiar, but it had an aftertaste of chaos that roiled her guts and made her choke. *Sweet to the mouth but bitter to the stomach,* half-remembered scripture quoted itself in her mind as she struggled for balance. It was hunting for Irene, or for any Librarian, like a bat screaming sonar waves into the darkness and waiting for a response. The Library brand across Irene's back blazed up so that she could feel each separate line of it, and the force of its weight made her stagger.

Nobody around her was reacting to it. Why should they? They weren't Librarians. A couple of people glanced at her as she missed her step, but nobody stopped, or did more than adjust their own trajectory so as not to step on her if she fell over.

Then, like an ocean wave, the blow hammered down around her and left its imprint on the malleable sands of reality, then drained away, withdrawing to wherever it had come from. She'd felt something like this before, when the Library (or, more accurately, a senior Librarian) had been sending her urgent messages, only it hadn't involved this feeling of chaos. The Library's message had been classic scattershot technique, targeting any Librarian in the vicinity, then printing the message on the nearest written material. She automatically looked at the newspaper display board again.

"Dreadful scandal—" The vendor broke off as he looked at his papers and saw that the print on them had changed. Irene knew it would be the same as the message that currently showed on the display board and on any other printed matter within a few yards of her. It was written in the Language, and anyone who read it would see it in their own native tongue, even if the words made no sense to them.

THE LIBRARY WILL BE DESTROYED, it read. **AND YOU WILL BE DESTROYED WITH IT. ALBERICH IS COMING.**

Irene throttled the panicked inner voice that wanted to retreat into a corner and start whimpering. There was no time for that. Her feet carried her on automatically, away from the black-and-white message on all the newspapers. What she had just seen made it all the more urgent that she reach the Library and report this.

It had been in the Language. There was only one person outside the Library who was tainted with chaos and who could have used the Language. It was Alberich who had left that message, and he had left it for *her* to see.

He knew she was in this world. He remembered her. And he was coming.

Irene breathed a sigh of relief when she reached the British Library without being accosted by Zayanna again. She did want to know what was going on with the other woman. It might be relevant. But the Library and its own interests had to take priority, and she needed to report Alberich's threat. It wasn't only a threat to her, after all. It was a threat to the Library as a whole. And if it had anything to do with what had happened yesterday to the Library gate . . .

She slipped through the British Library unobtrusively, adopting the preoccupied air of a student, and reached the door to the Library itself. As she closed the door behind her, she felt herself relaxing. Here she was safe. Safe from the physical dangers of spiders and guns, the emotional wrinkles of caring about the people around her, and, most of all, safe from the threats of the Library's greatest-ever traitor. Of all places, this was the one location where Alberich could never reach her.

But today, even this sanctuary seemed shadowed. The lights seemed dimmer, and the corners seemed darker. The very air seemed to whisper in the distance—like a ghost breathing, or the faint echo of a clock's tick.

The computer terminal was already booted up. Someone must have been using it recently and left it on. Irene thrust aside her nervousness, sat down, and called up her email, already starting to phrase her report on Alberich's warning.

The blinking message at the top of the screen caught her attention: READ THIS NOW.

It couldn't be spam. Nobody could spam the Library network. She clicked on it.

> An emergency meeting has been called. All Librarians will attend. Transfer shifts have been established at all junctions within the Library to permit attendance. The command word is "Necessity." Your presence is required immediately.

"Well, this is new," Irene said out loud. Her voice echoed in the quiet room. She was already logging off and pushing her chair back, not bothering to check the rest of her email. Whatever this was, it was urgent, and she cursed the fact that she'd been distracted and delayed by Vale, the newspaper, and the whole mess.

She couldn't remember ever having been summoned to an emergency meeting like this before. She couldn't recall ever *hearing* about an emergency meeting like this before.

In Library terminology, *junction* meant an intersection of passages where there was also a delivery chute to the central distributing area. They were plentiful throughout the Library, making it easy to drop off new books and get back to your assigned world. Transfer shifts were rarer. They were temporary creations arranged by a senior Librarian, which near-instantaneously transported a target from one point in the Library to another. They were also rather uncomfortable. If transfer shifts had been established throughout the Library to a central point, then this suggested a huge expenditure of energy.

The nearest junction was a few corridors away. An ominous light leaked in through the diamond-paned windows, and the sky outside crawled with clouds above an empty sea of high-peaked roofs. The floor in this section of the Library was black marble, smooth underfoot, with shadowy reflections of the crammed bookshelves, the high windows, and Irene herself as she hurried along.

A transfer-shift cupboard stood waiting at the junction. It looked like a battered normal cupboard, approximately six feet high and just large enough to hold two people—or, more usually, one person and a stack of books. The front had been engraved with a pattern of ravens and writing desks, and when Irene touched the wood, it hummed with restrained energy.

She stepped inside and closed the cupboard door. **"Necessity,"** she said in the darkness.

The cupboard jolted sideways, and Irene was flung against the wall before she could brace herself. She'd travelled by transfer shifts a few times before, but this was rougher than usual. The pressure held her pinned against the wall like an aeroplane passenger during a particularly vertical take-off. Unseen winds dragged at her hair, and the air was scented with ozone and dust.

With a thump it stopped.

Irene took a moment to recover her balance, then opened the cupboard door and stepped out.

The room she was standing in was all polished plastic and metal railings. It didn't look genuinely high-tech, but more like some fictional image of the future based on inadequate information, and it contained too many ramps and balconies. The ceiling was several storeys above her head, roofed with concentric panes of glass that looked out at the same ominous sky as before. Other wooden cabinets resembling the one she'd emerged from stood along the walls, incongruous in the pseudo-futuristic ambience.

A knot of people had gathered in front of the large metal door in the far wall. The door was closed. The people were arguing. Clearly they were Librarians. (Not that anyone else could have been here, but the arguing made it certain.)

Irene approached the group. Their assortment of clothing was as varied as their ages, races, and genders. The only real constant was something you'd only see if assessing a wide variety of Librarians for comparison. It was a certain quality of age and experience to the eyes, which went beyond the merely physical, and which was why Irene never looked too closely into her own eyes in a mirror.

"Is this the emergency meeting?" she asked the nearest person, a middle-aged woman in a high-waisted gauze dress, with gloves sheathing her arms from finger to armpit. "Or are we just waiting for it?"

"Just waiting," the woman said. Her accent was vaguely German. "Apparently they're doing it in half-hourly sessions. Next one is in five minutes."

"Do *you* know what's going on?"

The woman shook her head. "No, nor does anyone out here, though Gwydion over there"—she gestured at a sallow man with greying hair and black robes—"he said there was a problem with the permanent Library gate in one world that he visited."

Irene felt something congeal in her stomach. "Yes," she said, keeping her voice casual. "I had a problem myself with a Traverse yesterday."

Other Librarians were turning to look at her. "Share," said a young-looking woman with short pink hair, in fluorescent leathers that emphasized her figure. "You got something on this?"

"I was trying to pass through a gate back to the Library," Irene said. "When I opened it, in the usual way, there was some sort of chaos interference and it went up in flames. I couldn't put it out with the Language, and I had to leave by another route."

Gwydion had wandered over and was nodding. "Much as yours is my own tale, save that I came to find the portal aflame, without knowledge of whence came the fire or how it fixed upon it. Darkly the taint of chaos lay upon it, fierce the abhorrence that it held to the Library's nature. If aught can be said to make this matter clear, then may our elders do so."

"Well, my gate was just fine," said the pink-haired woman. "Though it was from an order-slanted world. You two—were those worlds chaos ones? You think this could be some new kind of infestation?"

Gwydion was nodding slowly, but Irene had to shake her head. "No, the one I came from was more order-aspected. The gate where I'm usually stationed was working properly, though. And that place is indeed more chaos-aspected."

"No proof, then," the pink-haired woman said.

"Hardly enough evidence to judge by," another man said. He smoothed the sleeves of his long blue silk robes nervously. "If our superiors have more—"

"Excuse me," a woman said quietly as he spoke, addressing Irene. "You wouldn't be called Irene, would you? Librarian-in-Residence to B-395? I think I've heard about you."

"Nothing too bad, I hope," Irene answered. She didn't recognize the woman, or the man who stood beside her. "I don't think we've met?"

"I'm Penemue," the woman introduced herself. She was comfortably middle-aged at first glance, with greying straw-coloured hair worn loose and an embroidered blue shirt and slacks worn even looser. She nodded to the man next to her, who was fiddling with his glasses while looking around the room. "This is my friend Kallimachos. I hear that you fought off an attack on your world from Alberich some time back?"

"That's drastically overstated," Irene said. "There was a book that Alberich was after, but it was more a case of me managing to avoid him than actually fighting off an attack. And it was only a few months ago. Might I ask who told you about it?"

Penemue shrugged. "Word gets around. I've been wanting to get in contact with you for a while now. Could we have coffee after our mysterious meeting?"

This all sounded perfectly innocent and reasonable, except for the metaphorical elephant in the room. Irene knew that she'd only managed to block Alberich from Vale's world because Kai had helped, using his natural abilities as a dragon. But hardly anyone in the Library knew that Kai was a dragon—or, at least, was *supposed* to know that he was a dragon. Native caution made Irene pick her words carefully. "Of course. Though I can't stay long, I'm expected back shortly and I wouldn't want to panic my assistant."

Penemue nodded. "Don't worry, I just want to set up some channels of communication. I've been doing some organizing among the people who work in the field, like us, and I wanted to get you in on it. I've heard so much about you, as one of the best operatives in the field." She offered Irene her hand to shake. "I'm sure that we'll be able to work together."

This was sounding suspiciously like a definite commitment, and Irene didn't like to commit herself until she knew what was going on. "We're both Librarians," she said, forcing a smile and shaking Penemue's hand. She wished she had some idea who the other woman actually was, and what her record was like. It was at moments like this that she regretted not keeping up on Library gossip.

"They're letting us in!" someone called from over by the large door. The conversation broke off as everyone hurried to go through.

The meeting room was what university lecture amphitheatres

dream of growing up to become. Deep banks of seats ran from floor to ceiling, enough to handle hundreds of people rather than the several dozen who'd been waiting to enter. The desks were of heavy iron, inlaid with green enamel vines and leaves, and the glass ceiling high above was fitted with spotlights that focused on the table at the centre. People's feet rang loudly on the metal floor as they made their way down the ramps to jostle for seats in the front row.

At the far end of the front row sat Bradamant. She hadn't been with the group that had just entered, but had already been in the room. It had been months since she and Irene had last met, but she still wore her hair in a sleek razor-cut, and her elegantly draped gown was a deep jade-green silk. She had a computer laptop open and was tapping quick notes, glancing up from time to time at the new arrivals. Her gaze met Irene's for a moment and then she carefully looked away, not quite quickly enough for insult, but precisely enough that it was clear she wasn't interested in interaction. Irene wondered why Bradamant hadn't left with the others in the previous briefing.

"Over here," Penemue said, beckoning Irene to sit alongside her and Kallimachos. "Let's hope they get through this fast. And while I've got you here, what really happened with you and Alberich?"

"It was really more of a controlled escape than actually stopping him," Irene said, looking around.

At the epicentre of the hall, a group of clearly senior Librarians sat behind a long oak table, which looked painfully out of place against all the glass and metal. Irene saw her own mentor, Coppelia, among them, tapping the clockwork fingers of her left hand against the table as she waited for the Librarians to settle themselves. Of the others, she only recognized one: another senior Librarian, Kostchei. She'd never had any personal dealings with him, but she'd been introduced once at a seminar, and he had a reputation—or possibly a notoriety—for cold competence. He was sitting at the centre of the table, with a pen and paper in front of him. His head was bald and his eyebrows barely there, but his beard was a thick braided mass that reached down to brush the table. And his face had ingrained lines of exasperation and temper around the mouth. The other Librarians were strangers to her but were all visibly old—apart from one exception, a middle-aged woman at one end of the table in a large wheelchair. The wheelchair would explain her early retirement to the Library, rather than being out in the field.

"If I can have your attention." The room fell silent as Kostchei spoke. He leaned forward, folding his hands in front of him. Irene couldn't help noticing that his knuckles were swollen with arthritis. "There will be a brief presentation on the current crisis, during which you will all keep silent. You may then ask questions."

He waited for a moment, but nobody was stupid enough to speak, and he finally nodded.

"Yesterday morning, by world-local time, we received a message from the traitor Alberich. He demanded that the Library surrender to him, accept him as its leader, and allow him to enter it. If we refused, he threatened to destroy us. Naturally, we refused."

He paused.

"Since then, we've received reports that a number of permanent gates to the Library have been destroyed. We've also received reports of assaults on Librarians who were stationed in those worlds, or in others. There have been several deaths. Confirmed deaths, that is. We have not yet checked on all Librarians who haven't been in contact with the Library for a while."

One Librarian started to raise her hand to ask a question. Kostchei stared at her silently until she lowered it again.

In the silence, the whole situation rearranged itself in Irene's mind. This wasn't just something directed at her and Kai: it was a threat to the whole Library. She felt as Kai had done when confronted with Vale's drugs—faced with something that couldn't be happening, that was a challenge to the very way she viewed the universe. She hadn't thought it was possible that the Library could be threatened. She'd always thought she might not survive, that Librarians might die, but the Library would surely continue . . .

But Coppelia was somehow down there, with other senior Librarians, confirming that all of this was true.

Irene wasn't sure now if the spiders were linked to Alberich. Would it be better or worse if they weren't? If they *were* his doing, that meant he had some way of reaching inside Vale's world, perhaps via an agent. And if they *weren't* his doing, then yet another person was out to kill her. Or Kai. Or both of them together.

She remembered a conversation with Kai's uncle Ao Shun, when Kai had been kidnapped. Ao Shun had said in tones of iron, "This is not to be tolerated. This *will* not be tolerated."

Anger crystallized in Irene's stomach. Indeed. She refused to tolerate this.

Kostchei waited another five seconds before continuing. "We haven't yet established whether the gate malfunctions are triggered by attempts to use the gates, or whether the gates are already destroyed and we only find out when we attempt to use them. Library Security has nothing to report, and we don't believe it to be an internal matter." In other words, there weren't any traitors inside the Library's walls. So the problem lay outside. "We have made enquiries from various sources, and the dragons don't appear to be involved in this. We're not sure about the Fae. Under no circumstances will we accept Alberich's terms. You may now ask questions."

Hands shot up. The pink-haired woman received the first nod

from Kostchei and fired off her question. "How many gates have been hit by this so far? And are they to law-slanted worlds or chaos ones?"

"The table recognizes Ananke. So far, twenty-five gates are known to be affected. The proportions of chaos and order worlds are roughly equal, and there is no clear evidence of more breakdowns on either side of the theoretical balance."

The man in blue silk was next. "Have there been any previous occurrences like this in the past? Could it be somehow cyclical?"

"Wishful thinking," Penemue muttered, but Kallimachos raised a finger to his lips to hush her.

"The table recognizes Sotunde." Kostchei tugged on his beard. It looked solid enough to be used as a weapon. "While it is a matter of Library record that gates may shift their positions inside a world, we have no previous reports of any going up in flames. We realize that this in itself doesn't prove that they can't go up in flames every few thousand years. Your comment is taken under advisement. Next!"

"Did Alberich give any means to locate him?" This was from a middle-aged woman in a neat grey linen kimono and geta sandals, her face painted to bland immobility. Circuit-embossed metal bracers encircled her wrists and forearms.

"The table recognizes Murasaki." Irene blinked. That was the name of the woman who'd recruited Kai as a trainee Librarian, but hadn't noticed the fact that he was a dragon. It would be interesting to speak with her later, if there was a chance. "Alberich said if we were to surrender, we were to publicly announce it on the media in several specific alternates and then have some of the elders leave the Library and wait for him to contact them. While we have agents checking those worlds, as yet they have nothing to report."

Interesting how little detail he's giving on where, how, or when Alberich made his announcement, Irene thought. *Could it be that Kostchei wants*

*to make sure nobody actually follows those instructions? Are they afraid
that some people would try to surrender if they knew how?*

"Brief was the mention of sources of enquiry." Gwydion had
wedged his way into a pause in the dialogue, without waiting for
Kostchei to signal him, and was frowning. "While none of us would
dally untowardly with our enemies, should our ears not remain open
in the service of the Library? If aught can be learnt, then surely we
should ask for information wherever we can find it."

Kostchei started to speak, then paused when the woman in the
wheelchair raised her hand. "The table recognizes Gwydion. I yield
to Melusine."

Melusine had dirty blonde hair, trimmed close to her head, and
she was in a plain checked shirt and jeans, rather than the more dramatic robes or dresses that some of the other elder Librarians wore.
Her voice was light and cool: Irene couldn't identify any traces of a
national accent. "To cut aside the circumlocutions: yes, we have
some contacts among the dragons and among the Fae. Yes, we have
spoken with them. No, the ones we've spoken to don't know anything
about this. However, the information we have access to is far from
exhaustive. If you have an inappropriate friend out there, don't be
shy. Get them to talk. Just be careful. There have been rumours that
Alberich has Fae contacts . . ."

Not rumour, fact. Irene had met a Fae or two who'd boasted of
his acquaintance.

". . . so be careful you're not being led up the garden-path."

Gwydion nodded, lowering his hand and looking relieved.
Nobody else actually made any signs of agreeing with Melusine's
comment, but a number of the other Librarians present were looking
blandly thoughtful in a way that suggested they were mentally
reviewing lists of their acquaintances.

"I've had some Fae interference in my work over the last week," a man in velvet coat and breeches said diffidently. His blonde curls had been carefully styled into position, and he held his feathered hat in his lap. "Nothing life-threatening, but meddling with a current assignment of mine. Could there be a link?"

"The table recognizes Gervase. We can't rule anything out at this stage. Please leave your information with my assistant, Bradamant, who will be showing you out." Ah, that would explain Bradamant's presence, Irene noted. "We'll correlate it and see if any pattern emerges."

Penemue had her hand up. "Has there been any actual consultation with Librarians in the field about this, or has senior management simply taken the initiative here?"

"That is senior management's job," Coppelia said, her voice as dry as sifting sand.

"I feel that we need a more complete picture of what's going on before we make any definite moves here," Penemue said. "I'm sure that I speak for everyone here when I say that we need more information if we're to give a properly directed response. And surely that includes full details on these threats?"

"My pleasure," Kostchei growled. "I will expand my statement about his threats. Alberich said that he would destroy the Library *utterly*. He failed to provide us with any helpful information about how. Any more questions?"

"Yes," Kallimachos said, picking up from Penemue as neatly as if they'd rehearsed it. Perhaps they had. "I think we may be overreacting here. Alberich has apparently existed for centuries. He is used as a threat to frighten new Librarians. But we know he's not invincible or invulnerable. We even have someone here who's dealt with him before." He pointed to Irene. "Are we seriously suggesting he's that dangerous? Shouldn't we consider a more measured response?"

Irene desperately wished that she could vanish into thin air, or at least hide under the desk. Everyone was looking at her. Worse, they were now assuming that she was allied with these two. Irene didn't object to the theory that junior Librarians should have a bit more say in how things were run, but she objected very strongly to an attempt to grab the metaphorical wheel in the middle of a meta-phorical multi-lane car crash. Even more so when they tried to involve her in the power play.

"It's obvious that the man's mad," Kostchei said. "He's also a meg-alomaniac."

"Doesn't that count as mad in any case?" someone muttered in the seats behind Irene, then fell silent as Kostchei stared in his direction.

"He believes the Library should take a more active role in influ-encing and controlling other worlds," Kostchei went on. "You all know that is not our role. We aren't here to make moral judgements about the Fae, the dragons, or anywhere in between. We're here to keep the balance and let the worlds in between stay free. What Alberich wants is completely against our principles." His voice lowered to a growl, and he pulled at his beard as if it were a hangman's rope. "We stand for preservation. We are not rulers. We are Librarians."

"Yes, but surely we can handle this in a more balanced way," Pen-emue said firmly. Her words came out with the smoothness of a pre-pared speech. "This is just one more case of a lack of communication, which has become far too common lately. The Library isn't served by having the people who are supposed to be running it ignoring the input of a large number of the people who actually do the work. There have been plenty of previous cases of this. I know I'm not the only person here who—"

Irene wished, again, that she was sitting on the other side of the room. She didn't want to seem associated with this faction. Which was no doubt why Penemue had arranged for them to sit together. Irene *hated* internal politics. Low-voiced conversations were breaking out among the listeners. Kostchei was lowering his head like a bull about to charge. The whole situation was about to degenerate into a list of complaints—and an argument between the elder Librarians and anyone who thought Penemue had a point. There wasn't time for that. This was an emergency.

Irene desperately thrust her hand in the air.

"The table recognizes Irene," Coppelia said.

CHAPTER 8

"I have some new information, which I haven't had a chance to tell anyone else yet," Irene said. "This morning I received an urgent in-world message in the usual Library manner, but it was tainted with chaos. It said—in the Language—that the Library would be destroyed and that I would be destroyed with it. That Alberich was coming. I'm guessing it was a message from Alberich himself."

The gasps and muffled exclamations would no doubt have pleased Zayanna greatly. Irene gritted her teeth and focused on looking professional. "I was coming to report it, when I saw the message to attend this meeting."

Kostchei tugged on his beard again. "The table recognizes Irene, Librarian-in-Residence on probation to alternate B-395. You are sure that this message was delivered in the Language?"

"Yes," Irene said. "Though it had a chaos aftertaste to it." She was conscious that the words *on probation* had affected the rest of the room. She was now officially *unreliable*.

"Did it name you personally?"

Irene shook her head. "It just said 'you.'"

"Then it could have been addressed to any Librarian in the area?"

"It could," Irene agreed. She tried to guess what Kostchei was suggesting here. Did he want to imply that any Librarian was in danger from Alberich? She let her eyes slide sideways to Coppelia and saw that the other woman had her lips pressed firmly together and was frowning. *I'll take that as a hint.* "I do have reason to believe that Alberich has contacts with the Fae, too," she added. "It's in an earlier report of mine, concerning a claim by one of the Fae. A few months back."

Kostchei nodded. His face was impenetrable, a stone mask with beard and ridged brow. "This appears to be another example of Alberich's threats. If there are any further such direct messages to other Librarians, they'll be examined for a possible triangulation on his location. Kindly speak to your supervisor after this meeting." He glanced across to Coppelia, who nodded.

"And someone tried to kill me just last night," Irene added, aware that it sounded a bit weak, tagged on at the end like that. "Though that could have been a coincidence."

Kostchei looked at her, his eyes liquid ice, and Irene found herself stuttering to a halt and closing her mouth. He had more presence in that glare than some Fae lords she'd faced down. It wasn't psychic powers, as some people would have described them. It was simply alpha teacher, channelled with a side order of extra ice and public humiliation, and it worked far too well.

Nobody else raised any questions. Penemue's drive appeared to have fizzled out with that interruption, and she was now pointedly not looking at Irene. *I'm guessing that the post-meeting coffee has been cancelled, now that I'm not quite so useful.*

Kostchei swept his gaze across the group of Librarians. "For the moment, the policy is to strengthen the Library's ties to the alternate worlds. As usual, this will be accomplished by gathering books important to those worlds and bringing them here. This means that you will all be getting urgent assignments, now or in the near future. Do the job, get the book, bring it back as fast as possible."

"What of our more prolonged missions?" Gwydion asked. "Several books have I now sought for years, and I would not set those tasks aside and waste my effort."

Irene resisted the urge to cover her eyes and sigh. Had she ever been that stupid? Possibly, but she liked to think that even when she was younger, she would have known better than to ask a question like that.

Kostchei glared at Gwydion. "Get your priorities right, boy," he growled. "This is not some sort of casual diversion. This is an emergency. The Library is in danger. Forget the damn long-term projects. What we are doing, right this minute, is shoring up our defences and making certain that our gates and links stay solid."

Irene glanced at the other Librarians out of the corner of her eye. Nobody was actually raising their hand to ask the ten-million-dollar question, namely: *Isn't this a very short-term approach? Aren't we just treating the symptoms, rather than the underlying problem? Shouldn't we be thinking about a long-term strategy, or attack, not simply defence? What if this doesn't work?*

Kostchei took a deep breath, visibly composing himself. "Any further developments or information should be reported immediately. Take all due precautions. Bear in mind that you are valuable resources and that the Library prefers you to stay alive. Get out there and do your job." He rapped on the table with his knuckles. "You are dismissed."

Irene had to push past a few other Librarians on her way down towards Coppelia. A couple of them gave her semi-friendly nods or sympathetic glances, and both Gwydion and Ananke muttered something about staying in contact. Irene made a mental note that she should probably make the effort. Assuming they all survived this. Penemue and Kallimachos both looked right through her, the sort of deliberate ignorance of her presence that would have been called *the cut direct* in certain times and places. *Well, fine,* she thought. *Thanks for making it so very clear why you were interested in me, and why you aren't now. It saves time.* A background murmur of debate rose behind her, far more tense than the earlier chat before the meeting.

She let Coppelia lead her into a small side office. Coppelia was in her usual dark blue, with a white lacy shawl round her shoulders, and her wooden hand was newly polished till it almost glowed. But she looked tired. There was a hollowness around her eyes and a sense of strain to the way she moved. Irene was reminded that senior Librarians became like this because they'd worked out in the field until they were old, and then finally retired to the Library—where nobody aged and no bodily time passed—to become positively ancient. At this precise moment, Coppelia *looked* ancient too, and weary.

The office was sparsely furnished. Coppelia settled into one of the flimsy-looking glass chairs with a sigh, and gestured Irene into the other. "Briefly, who's trying to kill you, and why?"

Irene gave a rundown of the last couple of days' events, trying not to imagine her chair collapsing beneath her. "I don't know *who* is responsible," she finished. "But Lady Guantes has an obvious motive. So does Alberich, but I don't think he can reach me in my current posting. Not after he was banished from there previously." The mere thought that he might be able to left a sour taste in her mouth. "And even if he did, he wouldn't just leave poisonous spiders in my bedroom."

"Venomous," Coppelia corrected her absently. "A spider is venomous: it creates the poison and delivers it by biting. Minus a point for incorrect terminology."

"Is this really the time to—" Irene started angrily.

"Yes," Coppelia snapped. "Yes, it is and it always *will* be. You use the Language, child. You have to be absolutely precise or you will get *hurt*. I have not invested all this time and effort into you to lose you now."

Irene took a deep breath. "How nice that I matter to you."

"Don't be silly, Irene. I haven't time for you to be juvenile. Can you behave like an adult, or should I have you wait outside while we take the next briefing?"

This was the second time inside half an hour that she'd been scolded as if she were still a teenager. It hit nerves already frayed from assassination attempts and threats from Alberich. "People are trying to kill me," she said, controlling herself with an effort. "The Library's been threatened by Alberich. Gates are being destroyed. Alberich sent me a personal message. I haven't time for you to treat me like a child. Is this really the moment for power games?"

Coppelia tapped a wooden finger on the table. "Just because you've stayed out of Library power games in the past doesn't mean that you'll always be able to do so. Do you have any relevant questions?"

"Yes. What should I do if Alberich tries to contact me again?"

Coppelia hesitated. "I would like to tell you not to bother answering him. But we desperately need further information. If you think you can get anything out of him, try it."

"Answer him?" Irene hadn't thought it was possible to respond to that sort of message. It was yet one more thing that junior Librarians didn't "need to know." The thought rankled, another brick on top of a growing construction of annoyance. Just think, if she'd been able to respond before, after receiving other emergency messages . . .

"How?"

Coppelia pursed her lips as if she was considering reproving Irene for her tone, but her answer was mild. "You need to overwrite the written material with your own message, using the Language. The person who sent the first message should still be focused on the link to your general area and will perceive it. The link doesn't last long, so you'll only have a chance to exchange a few lines."

"How safe is this?" Irene asked.

"Nothing's totally safe. What sort of guarantee are you looking for?"

Irene spread her hands. "Well, are we talking about me-being-led-into-sedition-by-his-hypnotic-messages unsafe, or Alberich-using-this-theoretical-link-to-drop-a-rain-of-fire-on-my-head unsafe?"

"Well, the Library couldn't drop a rain of fire on your head through that sort of link," Coppelia said. "So Alberich probably can't. It interests me that he can make the connection at all."

"It surprises me that he'd bother, given our previous British Library confrontation," Irene said. She wasn't entirely reassured by the use of *probably*. "Other Librarians must have managed to dodge him before. I can't be the first one."

Coppelia reached across the table and tapped Irene's forehead with her finger—one of the flesh ones, thankfully. "Use your brain, child. You read that book he was hunting for. He knows you'll have read it—and it was only a few months ago, so he won't have forgotten."

Irene frowned. "But it only told me that his sister had a child who was raised in the Library. It didn't . . . Oh." It came to her what Coppelia was saying. "But maybe he doesn't know that. Or at least he doesn't know how much I know, or what the book said."

"I'm tempted to order you to stay here," Coppelia mused out loud. "It might be safest for you."

Irene blinked. "You are joking, aren't you?"

"I'm quite serious. As Kostchei said, we don't want to waste you." She sighed. "That man has never liked chairing meetings. You can watch his level of patience go down like a thermometer being hit by a blizzard."

"Well, I'm being serious, too. I'm not sitting in here when there's work to be done." She leaned forward, trying to impress Coppelia with her determination and focus, then stiffened as she heard the chair creak under her. It spoilt the effect. "And why are we having meetings, anyhow? Why aren't you just broadcasting the news to all the Librarians as fast as possible?"

"It takes energy." Coppelia shrugged. "The Library's resources are not infinite. We're informing people who come in first, and we'll be broadcasting warnings to anyone who hasn't shown up or been in contact within twenty-four hours. And as for work to be done, I have a job for you. It's in a different world from your Residency post—but since Alberich won't know to look for you there, you should be as safe as if you were here. Safe from Alberich, at least," she corrected herself.

"What sort of job?" The very concept of a simple book retrieval brought a welcome normality into the discussion, and Irene relaxed.

"The usual," Coppelia said. "But under the current circumstances, we need the book as fast as possible. You won't have your usual time for preparations. We do know where you can find a copy of it, but it may be a little difficult to extract."

Which meant that it was probably going to be hideously difficult and dangerous. Still, at least Irene would be doing *something* to help.

Coppelia reached down painfully and flipped open the leather briefcase beside her chair. She slid out a thin folder of papers, offering them to Irene. "The book we want is *The Manuscript Found in Saragossa*, by Jan Potocki. He was Polish, but the manuscript was written in French. In a lot of alternates it was published without any problems, but something was different about it in this world, B-1165. The book was mostly destroyed. A few copies showed up in private collections. We have a lead on one of them, and since we're short on time, you'd better try for that one. Don't think you're being given an easy job to keep you occupied. This one's going to be difficult to acquire. We would have liked to get hold of it sometime back, but it was judged to be too difficult a mission. But under the current circumstances . . ."

Irene took the papers. "If it's a beta world, then it's magic-dominant?"

Coppelia nodded. "The major power is Tsarist Russia. The book's in the restricted collection in the Hermitage at St. Petersburg. There isn't a Librarian-in-Residence on that world, so you'll have to operate without backup."

Irene's feeling of relaxation was ebbing rapidly. "What do I do about Kai?" she asked. "I'm nervous enough about leaving him alone in Vale's world while I come in to report. Should I leave him here in the Library while I'm collecting this Potocki manuscript?"

Coppelia apparently considered, but she had a particular set to her lips. Irene recognized it as meaning that the older Librarian had already made up her mind. "You'd better bring him with you. The world's disputed ground, not high-chaos or high-order—but it is more order than chaos, so it shouldn't be too risky for him. And you might find his help useful."

Irene nodded. "All right. It'll certainly make him happier. But level with me on this one, Coppelia, please. I didn't ask this outside, in the meeting, but what are we going to do if this stabilization approach *doesn't* work?"

"Think of another one," Coppelia said. She cracked her wooden knuckles. "Melusine is correlating reports from Librarians across all the alternates as they come in. Once we get a lead on where Alberich's hiding out, we can move in a strike force."

"It's amazing how Alberich threatening to destroy the Library suddenly gets everyone interested in locating him and hunting him down," Irene said. She couldn't stop a certain amount of sarcasm seeping into her voice. "Rather more serious than just killing individual Librarians."

"Individual bias is fine in private," Coppelia said gently. "But be careful what you say in public."

"Oh, don't worry. I'll do my job." Irene realized she was echoing Kostchei, and was reminded of another question. "Did Kostchei deliberately play down my report?"

"He gave it what he considered the appropriate level of significance." Coppelia shrugged her thin shoulders. "He may follow it up later, but at the moment we're rating the destruction of Library portals and the deaths of Librarians as more significant than one threat to your life."

Irene hadn't wanted to ask, but she couldn't force the thought away any longer. "Has this affected anyone I know? My parents—"

"Not your parents." Coppelia met Irene's gaze. "Nobody you know. Some Librarians just haven't been in contact yet. We're trying to reach them. At least a couple are known to have died. So far they were on worlds where the gates have been destroyed. We think at least one was caught in a gate going up in flames."

Irene thought of how nearly the same thing had happened to her. "I understand you don't want to start a panic," she said. "But I'm wondering if this news perhaps *justifies* a bit of panic."

"Panic is the last thing we can afford," Coppelia said. "Panic will have everyone rushing off in different directions to try to 'save the Library.' Panic is the antithesis to good organization. Panic is messy. I am against panic on a point of principle." She checked her watch. "Do you have any other questions? The next briefing's in a few minutes, and it's my turn to chair it."

Irene had been carefully putting her other problem to one side, balancing it against her professional responsibilities and her duty to the Library. But that didn't make it go away. And Coppelia, an elder of the Library, might have an answer. "How would you recommend cleansing chaos contamination from a human's system?" she demanded.

"Dear me." Coppelia frowned thoughtfully. "Vale, I take it? Yes, I did wonder how he'd coped with that version of Venice . . . Don't look at me like that, Irene; chaos contamination wasn't a certainty, and in any case he isn't a Librarian. For a start, you won't be able to bring him in here."

Irene mentally cursed. "Why not?" she asked.

"The obvious reason—if he's reached too high a level of intrinsic chaos, the gate won't let him through, just as it wouldn't have let you through while you were contaminated yourself. But you know that. Why bother to ask me?"

"I was hoping I was wrong," Irene admitted. "What about moving him to a high-order world?"

"By other methods of transportation, I assume." Coppelia made a wiggly gesture in the air that might have been meant to mimic dragon flight. "Yes, that should work in the long term, assuming he survives it. If it's too deep in his system, he might simply calcify, the way that the high Fae do in such worlds. You'd need somewhere mid-order, and you'd be looking at a long-term convalescence. Or you could take him to another high-chaos world."

"How would that help?"

"It'd set his nature." Coppelia shrugged. "Again, if he survived. He'd acclimatize to being the same chaos level as other denizens of that world. Of course there would probably be some personality changes, and he'd be more vulnerable to Fae influence, but he'd live. You might do best just to take care of him as he is, and hope that he can ride it out. Eventually his body will resettle to a more normal level for his world."

Her Library branding had shielded Irene, of course. But that wasn't an option for Vale. He'd gone to that high-chaos Venice of his own will, in spite of all the warnings, to save Kai. Even though he'd known he would be risking his life. Even though he might have suspected he'd be risking his sanity. Irene found herself turning cold at the thought that she might lose him. Vale wasn't simply a civilian casualty. He was someone she cared about, someone who had a place in her life.

There *had* to be a way to save him. She would not accept otherwise.

Irene rose to her feet with a nod. "Thank you for the information," she said. "I'll be back with the book as soon as possible."

"Irene . . ." Coppelia looked for words, then spread her hands again. "Be careful, girl."

"You too," Irene said. "After all, if nowhere's safe"—she gestured at the walls, at the wider Library around them—"then this isn't safe, either."

Coppelia's mouth quirked into a smile. She nodded, and Irene left, making her way through a new group of Librarians waiting to be briefed.

She fretted all the way through the transfer shift and back to the portal to Vale's world, trying to think how best to handle matters. Assuming that this gate remained stable—and should she set up some sort of warning system, in case it caught fire?—she needed to ask those Fae she knew about Alberich. Zayanna. Silver. Anyone else she could find. Perhaps Vale could suggest a few names, if only from his local list of Dangerous Fae Malefactors. And she needed to watch out for any further messages from Alberich. She also needed to talk with Kai about Vale, and discuss where to take him, and if he'd agree to go. Oh, and she needed to find out who left those spiders. Though when compared with everything else, someone trying to murder her so inefficiently was a minor concern.

And she needed to go and steal a book.

She left the British Library in the middle of a jostling group of young students, mentally preparing an argument for Silver. He had to believe that it was in his interests to cooperate. But the sudden pain of a needle stabbing her hand broke her concentration. She looked up in shock to see one man sliding the hypodermic back in his coat, as another slipped an arm round her waist, gathering her to him as she began to sag. She opened her mouth, trying to speak, but she couldn't focus and her sight was darkening. She choked on the smell of sweat and hair and dogs.

Oh yes. And I was going to be more careful about travelling through a portal known to my enemies, wasn't I?

Whoops.

She sagged forward into sleep.

CHAPTER 9

When Irene woke, she was in darkness.

She lay unmoving with her eyes closed, waiting for any reaction, trying to get a sense of where she was. She was lying on a hard floor, brick or stone. But it was warm and dry, rather than cold and leaching the heat out of her. She wasn't bound or restrained in any way, but the folder she'd been given by Coppelia had been taken.

There were no sounds of anyone else breathing. She cautiously let one eye flutter open.

Near-total darkness, but faint lights in the distance. Irene sat up, her head spinning. Her hand ached from the needle, but not enough to stop her from using it. She was in an arched cavity set into the wall of a long brick tunnel. The lights burning in the distance in both directions were lamps. The corridor was thick with dust, too: she didn't have to see it, she could feel it where her fingers touched the floor, and she had to work not to cough.

What the hell was going on? If someone was going to kidnap her, why just leave her like a sack of potatoes, without even tying her up or taking away the knife in her boot?

Paranoia whispered reminders about Alberich and the other missing Librarians, but a more immediate and practical concern was Kai. Irene herself might just have been knocked out and dumped down here in order to get her out of the way while something worse happened to him.

She pushed herself to her feet and shook some of the dust off her skirt. Now that her eyes were getting used to the semi-darkness, she could see there was a faint trail down the centre of the passage, where the dust was less thick than at the edges. There were occasional footprints—some looked like heavy boots, but others were bare feet. Vale would no doubt have been able to identify the shoe; or, in the case of the bare feet, comment on the originator's height, weight, and posture. All Irene could deduce was that this was a frequent route for whoever came down here.

And the next big question was: who was that?

The tunnel shook. A deep, shuddering, grinding roar vibrated through the walls, making Irene jump and steady herself. For a moment she just wanted to run for it, in any direction whatsoever as long as it was *away*.

She controlled herself. Panic wouldn't help. The rumbling was dying away now, in a long clatter of motion that seemed somehow familiar. She began to head to her right, choosing the direction at random, keeping her pace as quiet as possible as she listened for pursuers.

The silence was complete again and the dust had begun to settle, when a wolf's howl came echoing down the passage. It would have been frightening enough on the moors by moonlight. In this confined space, in the near dark, given her total lack of knowledge about where she was, it made Irene's spine curdle and her legs twitch as she restrained herself from running. It wasn't even a normal wolf's howl, if one could use such a term. It had the full-bodied weight and impact that came from a larger-than-normal set of lungs.

There was a werewolf down here with her. No, make that *at least one* werewolf. She might as well assume the worst. And her kidnappers might be lurking as well. Or possibly her kidnappers were werewolves. It was like one of those Venn diagrams where all the possible Bad Things intersected to provide a Worst Possible Thing at the centre. But what she'd smelled when they kidnapped her was suggestive.

Irene picked up her pace to a jog as she headed for the light. While it wasn't quite a terrified run, it was faster than her earlier prowl.

The light was a dimming ether bulb mounted out of her reach on the wall. As she approached it, it gave enough light for her to see what was written on the wall beneath it.

LONDON UNDERGROUND SAFETY TUNNEL N-112

A trembling roar came through the walls again, but this time Irene knew what it was. It was a Tube train, passing by out of her sight and out of her reach, while she was locked in these tunnels with the werewolves who laired in them.

She'd heard about this part of London. Vale had warned her and Kai not to wander down there, if they had any other options. The tabloids regularly published INNOCENT STREET URCHINS MAULED BY BLOODTHIRSTY BEASTS headlines—no, wait, that had been the incident with the imported giant rats, not the werewolves.

She realized that her brain was doing its usual thing in a panic situation, which was thinking about anything else, in the hope it would distract from the immediate danger. She needed to be practical. She needed to find a weapon. A weapon larger and more efficient than the knife in her boot.

Irene had no idea where she might be in relation to London above her. Going onwards would presumably take her to a door, or a ladder, or some other way of getting out of these tunnels. There had to be some sort of maintenance exit, didn't there? Common sense dictated that there must be a way out. There had to be a way *in*, for her to be here in the first place.

It was tempting to use the Language to bring down a chunk of ceiling or wall and block the tunnel, or even squash some werewolves. But that might be bad for whatever part of London was above them. Also, once a ceiling collapse had been started, it could be very difficult—even impossible—to stop it. She knew that from personal experience.

Staying here wouldn't help. She set off down the corridor again, the light throwing her shadow in front of her. Ahead was darkness, but she thought she could see another flicker in the distance: presumably another ether lamp.

Another howl shuddered through the air behind her: it was closer, and imagination added a gloating edge to it. *Look at the poor little fleeing prey*, it seemed to say, *picking up her skirts and scuttling for cover. But there's nowhere to run in these corridors, little rabbit, little mouse— there's no way to escape . . .*

Irene found herself smiling unpleasantly. She was not amused. She hoped that very shortly she would be able to explain to these werewolves just how unamused she was.

The passage, fully dark now, came to a crossroads, and Irene halted. She could see dim pinpricks of light in each of the possible directions, so that wasn't any help.

Sniffing the air, she caught a very faint stink of sewage from the right-hand opening. The London Underground shouldn't have any open links to sewers, even in the maintenance tunnels. Which meant either some sort of rebuilding in progress or damaged walls. Which meant . . . a possibility.

She headed to the right at an increased pace, her nose wrinkling as the whiffs of sewage became stronger. The next light was still a good distance away, an unfulfilled twinkle in the shadows. Presumably maintenance workers—if any actually *came* down here—brought their own lanterns.

The tunnel shuddered above her, and dust fell from the ceiling, crusting on the shoulders of her ruined coat. That must be another Tube train, at a right angle to the previous one. She tried to imagine a mental map of the London Tube layout in order to make a guess at her current position, but there were too many possibilities.

Two more howls, one answering another, and both of them close behind her. The penetrating waft of sewage was a stink that went through her nose and drilled all the way to her lungs, but that didn't seem to be slowing down the werewolves.

In the near darkness Irene didn't see the pile of bricks against the wall. She tripped over an outlier, stubbing her toe and measuring her full length on the floor. Irene swore with her nose in the dust. Rolling over, she squinted at the pile. Several dozen loose bricks and a few half-bricks too, intended for the now-obvious hole in the wall, which reached up towards the ceiling. Perfect.

Instead of getting up, she clasped her ankle melodramatically. It'd be much easier if they came within range. "No!" she whimpered, trying to put some genuine pain into it. "My ankle!"

Another howl guttered away into a deep, throaty laugh. Movement whispered in the dark junction that Irene had just left. She strained her eyes but couldn't see any shapes clearly.

Lesson One of Practical Interrogation: people will gloat and tell you things if they think you're helpless. "Who's there?" Irene begged. "Why are you doing this to me?"

Shadowy forms differentiated themselves from the greater darkness behind, and eyes glinted red in the ether light. There were four of them: two were fully wolves, moving with the smoothness of natural animals as they prowled towards Irene, while the other two were half-man, half-wolf. They were hunched and clawed, with huge paws that scraped on the brick floor, and jaws that hung open and panted.

None of them answered.

They were less than twenty yards away now. And werewolves could move very fast.

Lesson Two of Practical Interrogation: know when to cut your losses.

"**Loose bricks**," Irene ordered in the Language, "**hit those werewolves.**"

The bricks hummed through the air like fast-bowled cricket balls, slamming into the oncoming creatures with audible cracks and crunches. Irene found herself wincing at the screams and whines, in spite of her awareness that the werewolves *had* probably been about to kill her. At least this probably wouldn't kill them. It took silver, fire, decapitation, or practically chopping one to bits to kill a werewolf.

But it would hurt them.

She scrambled to her feet, picking up a loose half-brick on the way, and walked towards the four downed werewolves. They were lying on the ground now, in puddles of their own blood. One of the lupine-form werewolves was clearly unconscious. The other was curled up, licking frantically at a shattered paw, and cringed away as Irene approached. The two more human-formed ones were both conscious—one of them lay sprawled on the ground with visible hollows in his ribcage, while the other was nursing a shattered right arm and shoulder.

"Talk to me," Irene said, keeping her voice calm and practical. "Tell me what's going on and why you kidnapped me."

The werewolf with the broken arm tried to snarl. Brick shards had ploughed across one side of his face, but the gashes were already closing up, leaving his fur and teeth matted with blood. "You'd better start running, woman, while you've still got a chance—"

"Ten out of ten for bravado," Irene said, then realized how much she sounded like Coppelia. The thought made her frown. "Look, do you *want* me to kill you? We both know that if I throw enough bricks at you—"

The half-turned werewolf lunged at her. Irene had been ready for that and stepped back, avoiding a slash from his clawed left hand. "Fine," she said. "**Werewolves, assume human form.**"

Using the Language on living beings was always awkward. They tended to resist it, you needed incredibly precise terminology, it had to be something physically possible, and you needed to be careful not to accidentally include yourself in any imperatives. Junior Librarians were encouraged to avoid it unless they really knew what they were doing—or, of course, for the classic reason that *I'll die otherwise.* Here, Irene could be reasonably sure that as she wasn't a werewolf, she wouldn't be affected. Which made life simpler. For her, at least.

The werewolf who had attacked her jerked away, claws melting back into his hand as it shortened to a normal human one. His toothed muzzle resolved into an unshaven face, his naked skin pale in the darkness. Fresh blood ran from the wounds on his shoulder and arm. The others were seized by the Language as well, their bodies painfully contorting as Irene's words forced them back into human form. The three conscious ones screamed: the unconscious one simply lay there, his body flopping and jerking on the floor as it shifted into that of a young man.

Even in the near darkness, they had one obvious thing in common. They were *young* men, no more than student age, and while they were mostly muscular and well built, none of them had the sheer muscle and lithe power that she'd seen before, in other adult werewolves. Irene recognized their faces now, and remembered that she'd thought they were students when they'd met her at the British Library.

Perhaps this was the time to access her inner Coppelia, or even her inner Kostchei. "What on *earth* do you think you're playing at?" she demanded, stepping forward.

The werewolf cringed back, his eyes still catching the light more than a normal human's eyes would, but wide and disconcerted. "What did you just do?" he demanded, his voice rising in panic. "What did you *do* to us?"

"Don't worry," Irene said briskly. "It's not permanent. But I want you to think, for one little moment, about exactly how much it would hurt to have more bricks hit you while you're like this. Use that mind of yours, such as it is, to imagine what it would feel like to have a brick go smashing through your skull and turning your brain into grey goo." She took another step forward. "Now, are you going to behave? Or do I need to make my point again?"

He cowered back in front of her, turning his head to one side and baring his neck. "I submit!"

Irene was tempted to toss the half-brick up and down in her hand, but common sense pointed out that it was heavy and she'd either hurt her hand or drop the brick, which would spoil the intimidating effect. "Some answers, then. Who hired you? What can you tell me about them? And where's the folder I was carrying?"

Her victim shuffled back to join the other conscious werewolves, who were huddling together, their hands running over their fellows' bodies as though they could restore their normal hairy forms by pure force of will. *And I don't know how much longer the Language will keep them that way, so let's not give them time to think* . . .

"It was a woman," the first werewolf stammered.

"Yes?" Irene said encouragingly. "And?"

"Well, she was a woman," he said, giving a perfect description of approximately fifty per cent of the world's population. "Nicely dressed."

"I am not in the market for half-answers," Irene snapped. "What did she sound like? Upper-class or regional accent? What *sort* of nice clothes was she wearing?" An idea about what werewolves might notice flickered through her mind. "And what did she smell like?"

"She was wearing far too many veils for good taste," one of the other werewolves said wearily. He cradled a broken hand against his chest. Freed of the snout and fur of his wolf form, he was well shaven and skinny, and his accent was middle-class London. "Nice scent. Spicy. Obvious she didn't want to be recognized. Veils on her face and hair, expensive coat, gloves . . ."

"Gloves?" Irene said. A chill seemed to whisper in the air.

Recently, during the business of Kai's kidnapping, she'd killed one Fae, and his wife had made a definite promise of vengeance. Both of them had used a gloves motif. Of course, this could be pure coincidence—any woman in London might wear gloves.

But it might not.

"Did she give you any concrete instructions about what to do with me?" Irene asked.

All of them shook their heads. "She just said, catch her when she's coming out of the British Library, here's a description of her, prick her with this needle and it'll knock her out. Then take her down to the tunnels and chase her a while, before you, um . . ." The first one paused mid-narrative. "Frighten her and let her go," he suggested hopefully.

Irene sighed. "Please don't treat me like an idiot. It's been a long day and it's going to get longer, and I am not in a good mood. Where's the poisoned needle?" Vale could probably analyse it.

"Davey's got it," werewolf number three piped up.

"And Davey is . . .?" Irene enquired.

"Not here," werewolf number three said, clearly wishing he wasn't there, either. As Irene's glare intensified, he added hastily, "Davey went to the throne room. And he took your folder, too."

Irene considered her options. The fact that she'd been left down here unconscious, to be chased and mauled to death, argued strongly *against* Lady Guantes. The woman was not a powerful Fae, but she was practical. (The two facts were connected.) She was the sort of enemy who'd hire a sniper with a powerful rifle to wait outside your workplace, and you'd never even know there was a bullet coming. Even if she had wanted Irene to be kidnapped and killed by were-wolves, she'd have given them some sort of warning about not letting Irene say anything. So if this was Lady Guantes, then it wasn't intended to be a *murder*.

But what if it was meant as a distraction? To keep her down here while something happened to Kai or Vale? The thought lay in Irene's mind like a curdled piece of shadow, suggesting a hundred worse possibilities. She had to get out of here and check that they were safe.

But she also had to get that folder back.

"All right," she said, lowering her voice to a tone of gentle calm. For some reason, the werewolves cowered even more. "We are all going to the throne room. You'll lead me there."

"We can't do that—" the first one started. The words caught in his throat as Irene raised her half-brick. "Tom here's unconscious! We can't just leave him."

"You can carry him," Irene said patiently. "There are three of you and one of him. It won't kill you." *But I might.* The words went unsaid.

"We're not supposed to bring outsiders there," the second one tried, unconvincingly.

"Then you'll just have to apologize when we get there," Irene said. Perhaps it was time for the carrot rather than the stick. "Look, gentlemen. You were clearly drastically misinformed about me. I'm not *particularly* angry with you. I'm angry with the person who hired you." Mostly true. She was *more* angry with the person who'd hired them. Getting angry with the hired thugs themselves was a waste of time and energy. "Take me to your throne room, let me get my folder and that needle, and you won't have to worry about me ever again. Isn't that the best possible outcome for all of us?" A train rumbled by in the background, providing echoing thunder to back up her words.

She was trying to be patient and project an aura of unhurried superiority, but her impatience nagged at her. Was it safe to be running farther into the depths of werewolf territory like this, while anything could be happening to Vale and Kai? Granted, Kai was a bit more careful these days, even if he didn't have Irene's own level of sensible paranoia. In addition, Vale was with him, and the two of them *should* be safer together . . . But anything could go wrong.

She locked gazes with her first victim, and again he backed down. "Right. Miss. Ma'am. We'll show you the way and then you'll be out of here, right?"

"I'm looking forward to it," Irene said grimly.

Half an hour later, Irene was struggling not to think, *What if something's happened to Kai or Vale?* with every second step. She'd considered sending one of her little pseudo-pack to warn them to lock the doors and be careful, but she wasn't sure that she trusted the werewolves out of her sight. They hadn't tried to run away from her, though, which said something about how badly she'd frightened them.

She found it difficult to feel really terrified about her current situation. Possibly she was becoming jaded after the last few months. In comparison with everything else, and especially in comparison with Alberich, a werewolf pack seemed like a pleasant walk in the park. Part of her knew this was not an intelligent attitude: just because a danger was less than world-threatening didn't mean it couldn't kill her. The other part of her was just plain irritated—with these idiot thugs; with whoever had hired them; with the heat and the darkness and the dryness and the dust; with this waste of time; with *everything*.

For a moment she thought she was imagining it and rubbed her eyes, but then she realized that it was actually getting lighter ahead of them. "Are we there yet?" she asked the nearest werewolf.

In the growing light, she could see the uncertainty on his face. "I'm not sure about this . . . ," he mumbled. "Maybe you should let us go in and find that folder thing for you?"

"No," Irene said firmly. "I don't think so. Try again."

"Maybe I should go and tell them you're coming—ask for an audience?" he hazarded.

"That's more like it," Irene approved. "Don't worry. I won't take long."

He swallowed and loped on ahead. His gait had been becoming visibly more animalistic over the last few minutes. Either the Language's hold was wearing off, or it had worn off some time back and he'd only just realized it.

"You could simply walk away, ma'am," one of the remaining werewolves said. He and his friend were still carrying their unconscious compatriot between them. "If you were to head straight out from here, there's a ladder to the north—"

Irene adjusted her hat. It was battered, dust-smeared, and probably ruined, much like her coat, and any professional cleaner would have them both burned on sight. "Gentlemen, you seem to think that I'm a lady of fashion," she said. "I'm not. I'm a professional, and I am the sort of professional who has just thrashed all four of you together. And then I let you live, because you're not a threat to me and I don't have any quarrel with you."

She'd spent most of her life playing the invisible underling in the background, creeping around in the shadows to avoid attention. Over the last few months she'd come to realize that taking the initiative and acting like someone who *deserved* respect might also be a valid strategy. She was not someone who was going to walk in there and apologize for the intrusion. She was a professional, a Librarian, and thoroughly dangerous. She was going to demand an apology for kidnap and theft. And if that failed, she'd damn well drop the ceiling on them.

They *would* listen to her. Or else.

The light ahead of them grew. It was a dim shade of reddish orange, but compared to the tunnels it was practically midday. Well, midday on an overcast October day with a fair amount of cloud, but still an improvement. It was accompanied by a growing animal wet-dog smell, which made Irene breathe carefully so as not to wrinkle up her nose.

The archway they came to was flanked by two piles of clothing, each with a large wolf nesting on top of it. They looked up and dropped their jaws in a growl, but didn't try to stop Irene as she walked forward.

The room beyond was an amphitheatre of sorts: it was large and circular with a sloping base. The floor was covered with tangles of werewolves. Some of them were in human form, naked or clothed, while others were in animal or part-animal form. Huge wolves were draped over their pack members like puppies in a litter. The place resounded with their breathing and panting. It caught in Irene's throat and made her pulse stutter. A battered chandelier hung from a hook that had been screwed into the ceiling, decorated with burning oil lanterns that flared red and orange. The place was full of an animal heat and danger, which even Irene—the most human person in the room—could feel.

At the centre of the room, in the middle of the amphitheatre, sprawled a well-dressed man in a city gentleman's clothes, right down to the bowler hat and striped waistcoat. He reclined on a throne made from battered Tube signs, patched together with wire and scrap and draped with fragile-looking velvets and lawns. Several other werewolves clustered around his feet or lounged beside him. The ones nearest him were either in wolf form or in fully clothed human form— a mixture of men and women in comparatively normal clothing.

One of them rose to his feet, a bruiser in half-animal form, with a human stance but a wolf's muzzle and paws. His pale fur was a bloody orange in the lantern-light. He cleared his throat in a parody of a formal butler's manners.

"You may approach Mr. Dawkins," he announced.

A growl rippled around the room like surf on the beach, and animal and human eyes caught the lantern-light as the inhabitants turned to look at Irene. These were not tame werewolves, or even romantic werewolves. Imminent violence hung in the air as thickly as the animal smell that filled the room.

Irene stamped down on the immediate urge to back out of the room and make a break for freedom. Running from a group of predators was the very thing guaranteed to get her killed. *And I am not prey. I am a Librarian.*

She stepped into the room.

CHAPTER 10

I rene strolled forward, keeping her pace nonchalant and casual. She had to pick her way across the piles of sleeping or watching bodies to reach the centre, and her skirt trailed across werewolves who couldn't be bothered to move. Her unwilling escorts hung back by the entrance, but didn't try to run for it.

Mr. Dawkins sprawled in his chair, watching as she approached. As she came closer, Irene could see that his face was scored with claw-marks—he might be able to pass for a city gentleman, but it would have to be a very battered one, possibly with a prior career as a lion-tamer. Unlike most of the werewolves she'd met so far in this world, he wasn't sprouting random tufts of hair.

Irene stopped about six feet from him: farther away would have been rude, but closer would have put her at too convenient a distance for a casual attack. She wondered what the proper etiquette was for visiting werewolves. She'd done vampires, Fae, dragons, and even university students, but never werewolves.

"So." Dawkins's voice was a deep, rolling bass. Probably the hint of a growl behind it was only natural. "Is Mr. Vale sending his spies into our tunnels now?"

"No," Irene said. "I'm here to reclaim property that was stolen from me. One of your people said it could be found in the throne room." She jerked her head to indicate the battered quartet near the door. "I hope this isn't an inconvenience."

"Remind me of her name again," Dawkins said to one of the women behind him.

The woman flicked a glance at Irene that was as sharp as cut glass. Her dark skin was ruddy in the lamplight, and her braided hair curved around her head like a nautilus shell. She was dressed in prim clothing that might have belonged to a shop assistant or a teacher. "She's called Irene Winters, Mr. Dawkins. Been here a few months now. Canadian."

"Now, you see," Dawkins said, leaning forward, "this is where it gets interesting. I keep on hearing your name linked to Mr. Vale, and connected to trouble with my people. Significant company, for a woman who's only been here for a few months. That has me curious about you. Not necessarily opposed, you understand. That would be unreasonable." His voice, if possible, deepened. "But if you're meaning to make me your enemy, then you've put yourself in harm's way."

Irene shrugged. "Your people do seem to do a great deal of work for the Fae," she said. "Lord Silver. Lady Guantes. I regret it if your wolves have been caught in the middle."

"Mm." Dawkins considered that, his hands on the arms of his throne. "And Mr. Vale?"

"My friend," Irene said. Just this once, she didn't care about the consequences of answering truthfully. "But that's not why I'm here."

There was a rising growl from the room around her. Messy images of the *I-am-about-to-be-torn-to-pieces* sort flickered through Irene's mind, and it took all her self-control not to turn around.

Dawkins raised his right hand. The room fell silent. "It's true that we can't always pick our friends, any more than we can pick our family," he said. "Let's not condemn her for that. But you'd better have a *fucking* good explanation for being down in our tunnels."

His sudden vulgarity ripped through the hot air as his voice rose with it. The pack was growling again, all of them rising and snarling, like surf on the shore in a hurricane, or like rain slashing the leaves of a forest.

He's reasonable, Irene thought. The surge of anger around her was reassuring, in its way: Dawkins had directed it, and Dawkins was in control. If she could deal with Dawkins, then the situation was manageable.

"Blame your own people," she said. "I was coming out of the British Library when I was jumped, drugged, brought down here, and had my property stolen." She pointed back in the direction of her victims without breaking his gaze. "I'm not here to make myself your enemy or to count their actions against *you*. But I want my property back."

"And someone here's got it?" Dawkins demanded.

"Davey. Or so I've been told. I'd like the needle with the poison they used on me, too. If you don't mind."

Dawkins leaned back in his chair, looking thoughtful. The scars on his face shifted into a new set of disfigurations. "And you aren't calling any sort of debt on my boys for snatching you?"

"Why should I?" Irene let herself smile. "They've already paid."

The tension dropped a few notches. Dawkins nodded. "Right. Now I've a question I want answering. If you can do that, I may be able to help you. Celia!" The woman with the braided hair tilted her head. "Go find me Davey."

Celia nodded, stepping back and into the crowd.

"So what's the question?" Irene asked.

"A while back, some of my boys took a job for that Fae woman you mentioned. Lady Guantes, in from Liechtenstein. She was the one doing the hiring. They left on a train with her, and I haven't seen them since." Dawkins's voice was a low, throbbing growl, almost as deep as the rumble of the passing trains. "What I want to know is: what happened to them?"

Oh, this was going to be a difficult one to answer. "Why do you think I know?" Irene parried.

"She was working against you," Dawkins said. "I'm thinking that you or Lord Silver are the two people I'm most likely to get an answer out of, and I don't want to pay Silver's prices."

Irene contemplated honesty. *They were left behind in a dark, paranoid Venice in a high-chaos world, and you'll probably never see them again.* Perhaps *tactful* honesty would work better. "That train went to a Fae world," she said. "I'm sorry, but if Lord Silver or Lady Guantes didn't bring them back, then I don't think they'll be coming back."

"You can't fetch them, then?"

"I wouldn't go there if I could—but I can't access that world," Irene admitted, "and I'd probably get killed if I tried. So no, I'm not going to be able to help you there." And she hoped that wasn't a bad omen for the future. Saying she wasn't going to do things under any circumstances was like using words such as *unsinkable* around big ships and icebergs. It was just asking for trouble.

There had been a stir of interest among the assembled werewolves at Dawkins's question, which subsided again at Irene's answer. It was interesting that Dawkins hadn't seemed surprised at Irene's suggestion of an alternate world. Perhaps working for the Fae left them more used to such concepts.

"All right." Dawkins shifted position in his chair slightly. The movement was echoed by the group of werewolves around him, but on a larger scale, like an orchestra's musicians following a conductor. "That's a fair answer. I'll not stand in the way of your talking to Davey."

It wasn't quite as helpful as *I'll make sure Davey turns over your stolen property*, but it would do for a start. Irene nodded in thanks.

Then the wave of chaos-tinged power hit her again, slamming down on the room in a silent burst that made her shake. She locked her knees and bit her lip, conscious that she was swaying but aware that if she showed weakness, her grip on the situation would be broken. It didn't touch the werewolves—they couldn't even feel it—but it ran across Irene's nerves in a burst of foul scent and heat, then leapt for the nearest printed material like an arcing current.

"What the hell is this?" Dawkins rose from his throne, inspecting it in confusion. Irene went up on her toes to get a better look at it, over the heads of the werewolves who were crowding around, and her heart sank even lower. All the carefully attached Tube signs were covered in graffiti or had changed their wording entirely, and the new writing was all in the Language.

I know you're there, it said.

Write something back on it, she'd been told. It was harder than she'd thought to pull herself together in the aftermath of that strike. It was probably also a bad idea to associate herself with the event in the eyes of the werewolves. But she needed answers. "Excuse me," she said, then raised her voice above the confused babble. "Excuse me! Does anyone have pen and ink?"

"I do," said one of the werewolves who'd been near the throne. He was an elderly man, with grizzled hair that ran down his face in long sideburns, paired with a draggly beard, and he was fully dressed. He fished in his breast-pocket. "That is, would a pencil do?"

"Perfect," Irene said, plucking it from his hand before he could object. "Mr. Dawkins, please give me a moment and I'll try to find out who sent this."

"Do you know what's going on?" he demanded.

"Possibly," Irene said. She squeezed between two werewolves to get at the throne, stepping on a set of bare toes to make some space for herself, and hastily scrawled in the Language on the nearest sign: **Alberich?**

This time she was more prepared for the shock of the response. It didn't make it any *easier*, but it did mean that she could brace herself against it. The writing on the throne changed, like sand being dragged into new patterns by an invisible tide. **My little ray of sunshine. Have you changed your mind about your future?**

Irene gritted her teeth. At least that *proved* it was Alberich. Only a very few people knew that her original name had been Ray, and he, unfortunately, was one of them. **From what, to what?** she wrote.

Dawkins leaned over her shoulder, with enough rolling power to his movement that it nearly burst the seams of his city gentleman's suit. "Perhaps you'd like to explain," he said. There was a non-optional tone to the suggestion.

"It's on my newspaper!" one of the nearby werewolves complained, holding up a sheaf of newsprint, which Irene recognized, from her acquaintance with Vale, as the agony page from the *Times*. "All the same stuff that's on there!"

Irene spared a moment to hope that Davey—and her folder— were well out of the effect's range. "It's from a man named Alberich," she said. "He's tried to kill me in the past."

"Why?" The tone of Dawkins's question acknowledged that people no doubt had perfectly good reasons to kill each other. It seemed he was asking merely to satisfy his own curiosity about their motivations, rather than from any moral imperative to prevent a killing.

Irene shrugged. "I stole a book, he stole it back, he betrayed us, these things happen—" She broke off at a new surge of power, and the writing on the throne changed again. **Join me, tell me what the book said, and be safe. Or perish with the Library.**

"Oh, you don't need to make excuses to us," Dawkins said. There was a thin round of applause and snarling from the mob. "So, you going to tell him what he wants to know?"

"No," Irene said. A sudden headache was rising to a blinding intensity. **I'm interested,** she scribbled. **I want to live. Tell me more.** All of which were true in themselves. One couldn't lie in the Language. She just hoped that together they'd give a totally false impression of surrender.

There was a pause, and then the words re-formed. **You're probably lying. But we'll talk later. If you live.**

The humming weight of power grew, swelling around Irene. She couldn't shake the feeling of being in the cross-hairs of some impossibly large gun. The metal Tube signs were beginning to shudder on the throne's framework, rattling against their fastenings in a rising screech of metal.

Her next conclusion wasn't born from logic. It was a leap of imagination, combined with a very vivid mental image of what would happen when the energy levels down there rose too high. "Everyone get back and get down!" Irene shouted, following her own advice.

The throne exploded. Shattered Tube signs scythed in every direction, humming through the air and slicing into everything in their way. Irene hugged the ground, her arms over her head, hearing screams and crashes but not daring to raise her head till the noise had stopped.

At least the bursts of power had ended too. Her headache was draining away, and she could think clearly. And her first thought was, *Dawkins is not going to like this.*

She looked up. Dawkins was standing above her. His coat was split down the sleeves, and his arms rippled with muscle. A healing gash dribbled blood from his forehead to his jaw, and while his face was still human, there were too many teeth in his mouth, and his eyes were pure red.

Saying *sorry* would have implied that this was her fault. "I'm glad you're not seriously hurt," Irene said as she stood up.

"I don't like people bringing their fights into my territory." Dawkins was echoed by a rising growl from the surrounding pack. Pieces of shattered metal were embedded in the floor, walls, and werewolves, and the throne couldn't have supported a poodle now. The chandelier was still in one piece, but that was only because none of the flying metal had spun directly upwards.

Irene met his glare. "And I don't like having to come down here to get my property, after *your pack* attacked me."

The place stank of blood now, as well as dust, werewolf, and heat. If she showed weakness, they'd take her down. So she couldn't afford to show any weakness. She wasn't just one human in the middle of a mob of werewolves. She was a *Librarian.*

Dawkins thought about that, and a little of the fire in his eyes ebbed away. "Fair point. So what's the Library, and who's Alberich?"

Irene weighed *things I should and should not tell outsiders* against *possibly unfortunate reaction of lead werewolf if I refuse him in his own den, especially after that explosion.* "The Library is the organization I belong to," she said. "Alberich is an enemy of the Library. Mr. Dawkins,

I ask you: am I really worth your time, when so many people are queuing up to kill me anyhow?"

Dawkins snorted. "I have to say that's not the sort of argument people usually give me."

"What do they usually give you?" Irene asked.

"Oh, their throats or their bellies, and whimpering about how they don't want to die. And that's the oddest thing about you, even for a friend of Mr. Vale." The brief amusement drained out of his eyes like sunlight from behind stained glass. "You're not scared. You're in the middle of the home turf of the biggest pack in London, and you're not stupid, but you're not scared, either. I'm starting to think that you may be right. Maybe I should let you go."

"Mr. Dawkins—" one of his closer followers began, a man in a butcher's rough clothing and blue apron.

Mr. Dawkins lashed out, catching the man by the back of his neck in one suddenly larger and clawed hand. He shook him from side to side, jerking him off his feet until the man's teeth rattled. "Did I ask for opinions? Did I ask for any fucking opinions?"

Nobody moved.

Dawkins released the man, dropping him to the ground. The man rolled over onto his back, panting for breath, and tilted his head back to bare his neck. "Right," Mr. Dawkins said. His voice echoed from wall to wall. "I've led this pack for five years now. And one reason why we're the biggest pack in London is that I know when not to get into a fight. Is anyone challenging me on this?"

Dead silence flowed through the room like a living thing. Irene could hear her own breathing. Then, one by one, the werewolves began to flatten themselves on the floor among the fragments of shattered Tube signs, heedless of their clothing or injuries, their heads lowered and obedient.

Dawkins nodded. "Good," he said. "That's right."

The woman who'd been sent to find Davey rose and stepped forward, dragging another man by his hair. Her victim stumbled forward, clutching an overcoat and a bagful of items to his chest. "This is Davey," she said. "He'd like to be . . . helpful."

"Hand them over," Dawkins snarled.

Davey dug into his bag and pulled out the folder. Irene almost snatched it off him, she was so glad to have it back again. She flicked it open and was relieved to see that the papers inside all looked as they ought to, and that the contents listing matched the number of pages.

"Anything else?" the woman enquired.

"The poison he used on me, if you don't mind," Irene said.

Davey reluctantly dug out a small pouch from his bag. "Bottle and needle's in here, miss," he said. "But we didn't take none of your money."

"Why did you take the folder?" Irene asked curiously. They'd left her purse on her, so why bother with her papers?

"Because the woman as hired us, she said not to let you keep any writing material nor papers," Davey explained. He glanced nervously at Dawkins.

Dawkins sighed. He reached out and cracked Davey across the face with a backhand slap that knocked the smaller man to his knees. "Didn't I tell you? Any jobs that involve magic, they go through me first." He spun to growl at his listening hangers-on. "You all hear that? Look what happens when some idiots try to be clever!" His gesture took in the shattered throne, the numerous injuries, and Irene herself.

After a pause that dragged out to almost unbearable lengths, he turned to Irene. "You're going to be walking out of here," he said.

"You're right, woman. We've better things to do with our time than get involved with your business."

Irene gave him a nod. "And I don't want to further complicate yours," she said.

Dawkins snorted. "You tell Mr. Vale that, and we'll see if he listens. Celia, show her to the exit."

Celia stepped away from Davey, who was still kneeling on the floor with the air of someone who hoped nobody would notice he was there, and gestured to Irene. "This way, please," she said. Other werewolves moved out of their way in a shaggy wave of fur and muttering.

The back of her neck prickled as Celia led her down a passageway, but the other woman didn't bother conversing with her. She simply pointed at a ladder at the end of the passage. "Up there," she said. "You'll come out in the basement of a workshop. Make your excuses and leave. Don't try coming back."

"I wouldn't dream of bothering you," Irene said politely, and tucked the folder under her arm before climbing up the ladder.

O nce back on the streets of London, somewhere south of Waterloo, Irene's next problem was hailing a cab while in her current state of dress. Fortunately an upper-class accent combined with a promise of a large fee did the job. She finally had a chance to open her folder and flip through it, as the cab headed for Vale's lodgings.

The report was nearly ten years out of date. And there was a note that the Librarian who'd done the research had been given the Potocki manuscript as an optional target, but had decided it would be too dangerous to make a try for it there and then. The target world's political structure was fairly stable, with the main powers being Russia on one side and the United Republics of Africa on the other.

Smaller confederations of states were scattered in between. Magic existed and was commonplace, mostly musically based and sung, or involving the control of natural spirits. However, it was generally under state control in the Russian Empire, the focus of this report. The technological level was a bit behind the current position in Vale's world, too—as often happened, having magical ways to get things done meant there was less impetus to create technological solutions.

But at least she probably wouldn't be chased by giant automata this time.

Research done, Irene reflected on the woman behind her kidnapping. She had apparently told the werewolves to deprive Irene of anything written, or anything that could be used to write. This argued that the woman knew Irene was a Librarian. So, maybe it really was Lady Guantes? But in that case, why so lax and incompetent an attempt at killing her? And if it was someone else . . . who was it?

At least Alberich couldn't get into this world directly to hire kidnappers, even if he could send her threatening messages and blow stuff up. His antics last time had meant permanent banishment from this world. That was one little ray of sunlight, to quote Alberich himself, in the general mess. More to the point, Irene herself would shortly be leaving this world for a while, so Alberich would have no idea where to find her. Even better.

She riffled through the papers absently as she considered what she'd need. Kai, for a start. Information on the layout of the Hermitage, which was part of the Winter Palace. Could she get anywhere by going through as a tourist? Did they even allow tourists in? There wasn't time for her normal approach of getting an unobtrusive job to check the layout and plan the theft. Maybe she and Kai could fake being foreign dignitaries? Kai was very good at impersonating foreign dignitaries: he had the perfect air of affable condescension that had people believing it was a pleasure to roll over and grovel for him. And they'd need clothing, money, a place to stay . . .

The cab drew up outside Vale's lodgings. With a sigh, Irene handed over the fee, plus a sizeable tip. There weren't any signs of drastic kidnappings, murders, or anyone trying to crash a zeppelin into the building, and she relaxed a little. Now she just had to explain everything—well, most things—to the men, and then be off.

The housekeeper met her at the door, answering the bell with a surprising turn of speed that suggested she'd been expecting someone. "Oh, Miss Winters!" She looked at Irene with an expression of shock. "What *happened* to you?"

"I'm very sorry," Irene apologized. "It's been one of those days. Are Mr. Vale and Mr. Strongrock in?"

"Oh yes," the housekeeper said. "They're just upstairs, and . . ."

For a moment Irene let herself relax in a great upswelling of relief. They were here; they weren't dead or kidnapped. And if the housekeeper was running around answering the door, then there hadn't even been anything dramatic like a zombie assault on the house or an attack by killer bees.

Are my expectations possibly getting a little lurid? she wondered. *Not really. After all, there is someone out to get me.*

". . . so is everyone else," the housekeeper finished her sentence.

Irene's sense of well-being and security popped like a balloon and sank without a trace. "Everyone else?"

"Well, the visitors." The housekeeper pursed her lips. "I must say, they were arguing quite a lot. Perhaps you might ask them to keep their voices down, miss? Mr. Vale's an excellent lodger, but really, there are limits . . ."

"I'll have a word with them," Irene promised, and took the stairs at a run.

CHAPTER 11

Irene could hear the shouting through the door even before she reached the head of the stairs. She recognized Kai's voice and Vale's clipped tones, but the woman's voice was unfamiliar . . . Wait, was that Zayanna?

She groaned to herself. Zayanna's involvement would be so much easier to explain if Zayanna herself weren't actually *there*.

" . . . and I don't care what you say, I'm not risking her safety any longer!" That was Kai. "I'm going to go and find her right now—"

Another voice, unclear through the door, interrupted, and Irene took advantage of the momentary pause to push open the door.

All of the people in the room turned to look at her. Vale. Kai. Zayanna. And Li Ming. Wonderful—just the person to make an already volatile mix even more explosive. A Fae and two dragons in the same room was asking for trouble under the best of circumstances, and Irene herself was probably about to set light to the fuse.

"Irene!" Kai made it across the room in three steps to grab her, his hands biting into her shoulders. "Where have you been?"

Vale rose from the chair that he was sprawled in to frown at her. He looked almost worse than he had last night, and his sleep had clearly done him no good: his eyes were still sunken, and his face was paler than usual, with a high flush on his cheek bones. He took in Irene's dishevelment and the dust on her coat with a single glance. "Apparently Winters here would rather gallivant around the London Underground with werewolves than trouble herself by coming back here directly. Instead she sends you all to fill my rooms, in the hope of distracting me."

So much for last night's softer mood. Irene reminded herself that Vale was prone to vicious sarcasm when worried. He wasn't the sort to express genuine concern, like Kai—in fact, she'd better reassure Kai fast, before his protectiveness tipped over into something irrational. "I'm all right," she said, holding up one hand. "I went to the Library. I just ran into some trouble afterwards. Zayanna, what are you doing here?"

Zayanna was curled up on the sofa, her shoes kicked off and her feet tucked underneath her legs. She'd discarded her coat somewhere, and her dress flowed in cascades of highly fashionable cream lace, which showed a lot of cleavage. She was nursing a glass of brandy and a clearly unpleasant mood. "You did say that you wanted to stay in contact, darling! And you weren't at home, so I thought I'd try your friend instead."

"I see," Irene said, suppressing an urge to demand some of that brandy. "I hope you haven't all been too worried about me. I apologize for my delay in getting back here. It wasn't my fault."

"Perhaps you'd care to explain to us whose fault it was," Vale said, relapsing back into his chair. "And what it has to do with the current situation. Please distract me, Winters. I am bored nearly to death with these infantile arguments. Did you get those papers from your Library?" His gaze was on the folder under her arm, and he was ignoring the irritated looks that everyone else in the room was giving him.

Irene nodded. "But when I left the Library, I was kidnapped."

She was aware that Li Ming was listening, but she couldn't think of any way to get him out of earshot that wouldn't be highly rude. It would probably insult both him and Kai too. As usual, the dragon in human form was impeccably dressed in silvery grey and could probably compete with Zayanna for the title of Most Fashionable Person in the Room. Kai would win the Most Handsome award, but he was looking attractively scruffy at present, not elegantly stylish. Vale would carry off the Most Brooding. And Irene herself would have to settle for the booby-prize in all categories.

Physically, Li Ming resembled a human female, with the same inhuman perfection that characterized Kai and the few other dragons that Irene had met. But among other dragons, Li Ming was considered male, and he acted that way in human form as well. Irene had given up trying to deduce the exact details and had asked Kai about it—as tactfully as she could. Kai had explained, in tones of kindly condescension at human convention, that social gender among dragons was what the dragon in question said it was. And since Li Ming said he was male, then he was male. Irene had thanked him for the information, and had broken off the conversation before Kai could get into any further commentary on human limitations, et cetera. Kai might be very non-judgemental when it came to personal gender roles, but he was extremely superior when explaining how non-judgemental he was.

"I was drugged by werewolves, carried off, and chased through the Underground tunnels," Irene reported succinctly before everyone else could get more questions in. "Then I extricated myself and came here. Apparently they were hired by a woman who gave them the poison with which they drugged me."

Vale looked interested. "Which poison?" he asked.

"Which woman?" Zayanna asked. "Was it someone local, or an old friend?"

One hand still on her shoulder, as if he wasn't prepared to risk letting go, Kai tugged Irene over to the armchair he'd been occupying. "Are you all right?" he asked. "I knew we shouldn't have split up—"

"Your Highness, you demean the lady," Li Ming put in. "Clearly, if she's here and safe, she was quite competent to handle herself. Though it is a shame that she caused you concern."

Irene sat down in the chair. It was easier than arguing with Kai about whether or not she needed to sit down. "In any case," she said, "I'm here and safe, and I'm glad to see that all of you are all right." Zayanna had risen and was splashing brandy into a second glass. "Oh, yes, *please*," Irene added.

"Some small payback, darling," Zayanna said, putting it into her hand. "Do you have any idea who the woman is?"

Irene had reviewed the possibilities several times in the cab. Lady Guantes was the standout candidate, but it could honestly be anyone. It didn't even have to be a Fae. It could be a dragon who objected to her current working relationship with Kai. It could even, if Alberich had a traitor working for him, be another Librarian . . . "Short of getting the werewolves to sniff all the possible candidates, no," she said. "Lady Guantes is the obvious candidate, but it was inefficient; and if she was hiring assassins, she might be more likely to use a proxy to contact them. I don't know." She sipped the brandy.

Kai's expression had darkened to a scowl at the mention of Lady Guantes. Of course, given that she'd been an equal partner in Kai's kidnapping, he viewed her as unfinished business. Irene also suspected that Kai didn't want to admit that he'd experienced any such emotions as post-traumatic stress, worry, or even outright fear. "We need to establish a safe base," he said firmly, glancing to Li Ming, who nodded. "Then we can track the kidnapper down and eliminate this threat."

It would have been nice to have had a private conversation with Kai, in which she could have broken the news about the current situation to him slowly and in detail, Irene reflected. Emphasis on the *would have been*. "I'm afraid that's not going to be possible." She took another swig of the brandy. "I have an immediate job from the Library. You and I will be leaving later today, Kai."

"Leaving this country?" Vale put in with a frown.

"Leaving this world," Irene said.

"I'm afraid I'm intruding," Li Ming observed. He rose from the chair he was occupying, his long silver braid slipping to hang straight down his back. "Your Highness, perhaps we can converse later?"

"No, stay," Kai said before Irene could stop him. "I need—that is, I'd be grateful for your help in that other matter. Irene, surely Li Ming isn't a threat here? You know that my family and our kin aren't enemies of the Library."

Li Ming waited politely, with the air of someone who would *of course* be glad to leave, rather than eavesdrop on a matter that didn't concern him. But his silver eyes, as bright and metallic as his hair or his fingernails, showed a confidence that he would be allowed to stay.

"I can give my word not to tell anyone else about it, darling," Zayanna said. "You know my word binds me. And I'd hate to just walk out if I could actually *help* you."

Vale leaned forward in his chair. "Has this something to do with the murder attempt on you and Kai, Winters?"

And here it all came down to the wire. Who did Irene trust? Kai, of course, but did she trust everyone that *he* trusted? Li Ming worked for Kai's uncle: it would be his duty to pass on anything he heard. And even if the dragons weren't *enemies* of the Library, they weren't the sort of neighbour who'd turn down a territorial advantage or ignore a weakness. Zayanna was Fae, and Alberich had worked with other Fae in the past. And just because Zayanna said she was Irene's friend, that didn't mean that she was a friend to the Library. Vale himself was currently suffering the effects of having helped Irene previously. Was it fair to put him in even *more* danger?

Common sense popped that last bubble of guilt and made it vanish. Vale would walk barefoot over broken glass to investigate a case. His behaviour wasn't Irene's responsibility.

"I don't know," Irene said. She looked around the room, considering. "Zayanna, if you want to stay in here and hear what I have to say, I'm going to ask you for that promise."

Zayanna bowed her head and put her hand on her heart. "I swear, on my name and nature, that I won't reveal anything you tell me to any other Fae, or anyone who may use it against you. And I won't use it against you myself." Her voice throbbed with conviction.

It was melodramatic, but it seemed sincere. And, to the best of Irene's knowledge, the Fae couldn't break their given word. They could be incredibly picky about how they interpreted promises, but they couldn't break them. Zayanna was safe, to a limited degree.

"Alberich has threatened the Library," Irene said. Neither Zayanna nor Li Ming showed any surprise at the name. *Well, that answers that question: they both know about him.* "I've been assigned an immediate retrieval mission, to fetch a book that should prove useful." She tapped the folder. "This has the details. And I'm sorry, Kai—everyone—but I need to leave as soon as possible."

"If I can be of any help in finding your book—" Vale began.

"It's not that I don't *want* to take you," Irene said quickly, then cursed herself for the sudden coldness in his eyes at her rejection. "But I *can't* take you. Kai and I need to travel through the Library. I'm sorry, Vale, but you're currently contaminated with chaos. I wouldn't be able to bring you inside."

Vale's expression closed in on itself. "I quite understand," he said curtly.

Kai frowned. "Wait, Irene, are you telling me we can't take Vale into the Library? I'd thought that if we could detoxify his system there, that might help."

"Chaos can't enter the Library," Irene said with controlled patience. "That was why we were stuck outside it last time when *I* was contaminated. Remember?" They'd got round that by forcing the chaos out of her. But she wasn't sure if she could do that to Vale. She didn't know if a human who wasn't a Librarian could survive it, and Coppelia hadn't given her any hope it might work.

Li Ming spread his hands. "I have to admit this is beyond my competence, Miss Winters. No doubt if Mr. Vale here were to spend time in a more orderly world, it would be good for his health. But I lack the strength to carry him there on my own."

"Just who precisely can travel between worlds, and who can't?" Vale asked. He tried to make it sound casual, but there was an edge to his voice. He was probably making a mental list of possible intruders and relevant counter-measures.

"I'm not of the royal blood and don't have the royal strength," Li Ming said. He indicated Kai. "The prince here, however, can carry more than one person, and my lord the king could carry hundreds in his train, if he wished."

"Well, don't look at me," Zayanna said. "Would any of you like some more brandy? No, *please* don't look at me like that, Irene—it's not my fault, I just *can't*. It's exactly like the charming dragon here was saying . . ." Her gaze went pointedly towards Li Ming, rather than to Kai. "I don't have the strength. It took all my power simply to find my way here, and I certainly couldn't carry anything more than my luggage. Or perhaps one other person, instead of my luggage. But who'd travel without luggage?"

Li Ming gave Zayanna a sidelong glance. Irene wondered whether the dragon had taken exception to the "charming" comment or intended to cast doubt on Zayanna's assertions. Probably the first.

"And I have to go through a library, or another large collection of books," Irene said. "Which limits what I can do. Now *please* can we get back to the subject under discussion?" She realized she was starting to get as emphatic as Zayanna, and she moderated her tone. "Zayanna, Li Ming, you both clearly know who Alberich is. Do you know anything about his current activities? Or anything else odd—anything at all—that's going on at the moment?"

Zayanna frowned. "Well, there was one rumour I heard, but I was rather hoping it wasn't true. I had been trying to keep track of Lady Guantes—casually, through the gossip networks—and I heard she'd been talking to Alberich. Then she'd dropped out of general circulation."

Irene's throat went dry with something unpleasantly close to fear. "You might have mentioned that before," she said.

Zayanna shrugged. "It's a rumour, darling. I don't panic over rumours. If I did, then I'd already be hiding in some backwater little London in a great detective's sitting room—oh, so sorry." She didn't look remotely apologetic. "But you asked. And I can't verify it. That is what you say, isn't it? When you're talking about being a good spy and trying to confirm facts?"

Irene touched Kai's hand reassuringly. She didn't look up at his face, but she could feel the tension in him. She couldn't blame him: if she was honest, that touch had been as much to comfort herself as it had been him. She turned to Li Ming, hoping he'd have something encouraging to contribute.

Li Ming was already shaking his head. "Nothing unusual," he said. "The only oddity at the moment is that some of the regular conflicts have quietened down. One might guess that forces have been withdrawn from known trouble spots, to be deployed elsewhere."

Vale opened his mouth, possibly to disapprove of guessing on general principles, then shut it thoughtfully. He finally said, "How recent is this? Would the timing fit?"

"The attacks on the Library have only taken place in the last couple of days," Irene said. "But perhaps Alberich was drawing in his forces beforehand, if he's using other agents . . . I don't know." She marshalled her thoughts. "All right," she said. "We'll leave it there for the moment. Thank you both for your comments. Immediate plans—Kai, I'll need your help. Vale, if you would—"

The door swung open, and everyone turned towards it. Irene couldn't help noticing that both Vale and Zayanna slid a hand beneath their clothing, clearly demonstrating who was carrying weapons. *Are we all feeling nervous? I think we're all feeling very nervous.*

Inspector Singh stood in the doorway, looking a little bewildered to find everyone's attention focused on him. He was in uniform, but the cuffs of his trousers were thick with yellow dust, and a few grains of it marred the whiteness of his turban. "I apologize if this is a consultation in progress, Vale," he started.

Vale relaxed, eyeing Singh's cuffs, his hand sliding back into view. "What have you been doing in Houndsditch, Singh?"

"A matter of some corpses being stolen during a plague-pit

excavation," Singh said. "I don't like to take you away from anything urgent, but you did say to call by if something intriguing came up. And there was a message from your sister that it might be connected to the Tapanuli fever investigations. Though those haven't been made public yet—"

His glance towards Irene and Kai wasn't particularly friendly. Irene could sympathize to some extent. Her own guilt kept on reminding her how much Vale's current situation was their fault.

"Tell me about it," Vale said, rising to his feet. He took Singh by the arm, hustling him towards his bedroom. "We don't need to bother the others with this," Irene caught him saying before the door closed behind them.

"I didn't know Vale had a sister," Kai said in tones of mild shock. It wasn't clear whether he was surprised that Vale had never told him about his sister or by the fact that the sister existed at all.

"You know he doesn't talk about his family," Irene said. She was desperately curious herself, but her growing sense of urgency insisted that she leave the gossip till later. Besides, it would be bad manners. "Zayanna, we may be away for a few days. Will you be safe?"

Zayanna put down her now-empty glass. "I think so, darling. I'll be careful. Are you sure I can't come with you and help? To your B-1165 world? And why is that folder of yours written in my own language, anyway?" She saw the incomprehension on Irene's face. "Nahuatl, you'd probably say. The Library isn't secretly based under my home or something, is it?"

Irene glanced down at the folder. Coppelia had helpfully labelled it with the world's designation, and since it was in the Language, anyone who wasn't a Librarian would read it as their own native tongue. "Ah. Trade secret," she said. "It's the Language. You're just seeing it as Nahuatl."

"That would explain why I've been seeing it as Chinese," Li Ming noted.

Irene resisted the urge to run her fingers through her hair and scream at the way everyone kept on wandering off-topic. "I can't take you through the Library, Zayanna," she said. "And I don't have any other way of getting there. But you can do one thing for me."

"Anything, darling," Zayanna promised, her eyes huge and dark with emphasis.

"Tell me how to help a human being who's been exposed to a world with too much chaos," Irene said.

Zayanna frowned. "That's not something people actually need *helping* with, darling." She looked around at Irene, then at Kai and Li Ming, neither of whom looked amused by the way she'd put it. "Oh, well, I suppose if someone like me had a favourite whose nature had been really unbalanced and was getting much too pliable, they could take them to the more rigid spheres. But you'd already suggested that. And if you didn't want your friend Vale to have this problem, then you shouldn't have taken him along with you to Venice in the first place."

"Pardon me," Kai said to Irene. He stepped across to where Zayanna was lounging and backhanded her across the face, slamming her into the sofa.

"Kai!" Irene snapped. "Control yourself!" God knows she'd wanted to hit Zayanna for that little bit of spite, but this couldn't possibly help.

"My friend has helped you, and for that you return an undeserved insult," he said, standing above Zayanna. Faint scale-patterns showed like frost marks on the surface of his skin, on his hands and face. "You will not do so again, or I will throw you out on the street, and your patron may have you back—living or dead—to serve his whim."

Zayanna pushed herself up on her elbow, her hair falling around her face in dark tangles. The imprint of Kai's hand showed scarlet on her cheek. She took a hissing breath, and for a moment Irene saw fangs rather than teeth in her mouth. The expression on Zayanna's face wasn't one of Fae pleasure at having found a new enemy to plot against: it was one of outright dislike, and a wish to see Kai dead— or worse. "Oh, so now you're being judgemental because *you* couldn't take care of your pets? Everyone knows how far beneath them the dragons think humans are! At least we get *involved* with them."

Irene caught Kai's wrist before he could hit Zayanna again. She had to strain to hold him back. "I told you, stop!"

"You creatures are users and destroyers of human souls," Kai snarled at Zayanna. "When you interact with them, it's never to their benefit. You get your perverse amusement out of playing your games with them—"

"We *love* them!" Zayanna shrieked. "You're the ones who are soulless: you don't understand them, you just keep them as pets, you're only spending time with Irene because you want her as a concubine. I *care* about her—"

Irene stepped between them, putting her free hand on Zayanna's shoulder to hold her back. "Shut up," she said, her voice as cold and hard as if she had been using the Language. "Shut up, both of you, or I'll *make* you."

For a moment she felt Kai's wrist tense in her grasp. Then he broke free with a twist of his arm and stepped back, folding his arms. His eyes had shifted to true draconic red in anger, and burned in a face that looked cut from marble.

Zayanna panted where she lay on the sofa, her shoulder soft and warm under Irene's hand. "He hit me," she murmured.

"Don't push me," Irene said. "I nearly hit you myself."

She glanced across to Li Ming, but he was still in place, still very much unconcerned, and he shrugged in response. "Is this any of my business?"

Well, scratch the idea of leaving Zayanna with Li Ming while we're out of London, Irene decided. *She'd probably accidentally fall down a well or step in front of an oncoming train the moment I was out of sight.*

She deliberately ignored certain words that Zayanna had said: *because you want her as a concubine . . .* There was more to her friendship with Kai than that. Just because Zayanna might be jealous, that didn't make her right. "I'm in a hurry," she said. "If you can't help me, Zayanna, then fair enough. But I don't have any time to waste."

Zayanna looked up at Irene through lowered eyelashes. "Can't I help?"

"Right now, I don't see how," Irene said curtly. "Kai?"

"Yes?" He was looking more normal and human again now, but his face was set in lines of resentment. And the way that he was eyeing Zayanna suggested that he was visualizing dropping her—from several thousand feet up.

"If you must argue, do it in your own time, please. We haven't the luxury for that now."

The door opened. Vale stood there, frowning. "I thought I heard shouting."

"You did," Irene said. "I think everybody's about to leave. No, wait: I have a favour to ask you, if you would. Two favours."

"Within reason," Vale said, but he looked intrigued. Which was much better than weary and self-destructive.

She offered him the small pouch holding the needle that had been used on her. "Please analyse this. It's the poison that was used to drug me. If you can trace it, I might be able to find out who hired the werewolves who kidnapped me."

"Excellent," Vale said, sounding genuinely pleased this time. "And beyond that?"

"Silver owes us after the Venice business, since we took down Lord Guantes. After all, Guantes was his arch-rival. I need to know if Silver's heard anything lately about Alberich or the attempt on our lives, and I don't have time to ask. Gates to the Library are being destroyed. I need to go and do my job. So, Vale, please, if you would, meet up with Silver and ask him if he knows anything."

"And how am I to tell you what I find out, assuming that Lord Silver is actually aware of anything beyond his immediate surroundings?" Vale demanded.

Irene was about to snap back, but then she heard the same tone in his voice that had been there earlier, when he'd been complaining about her absence. Expressing worry about anyone else was outside his emotional lexicon. "My mission is urgent, so naturally I won't be wasting any time," she said. "I hope to be back in a few days. I'll leave a message with Bradamant in the Library if I expect to be longer than that, so she can drop by to see you, if necessary. She knows you, and where to find you."

"Adequate," Vale said begrudgingly.

"Have you any instructions for me, Miss Winters?" Li Ming enquired. "My lord Ao Shun takes an interest in your welfare, after your actions in guarding the prince here." It wasn't quite clear whether he was being serious, or simply ironic. Then Irene caught the side-glance he threw Kai. He was being serious.

"No, thank you," she answered politely. "Though if you do hear of anything strange going on outside this world, I'd be grateful if you could pass it on to Vale here."

"I shall do that," Li Ming agreed.

Kai had moved into place next to Irene and was buttoning up his coat, the folder safely under one arm. "We should be on our way," he said quietly. Then he glanced at Zayanna and there was a glint of fire in his eyes again. "Before there are any more hindrances."

"Good luck, Miss Winters," Singh said, standing at Vale's shoulder. "Though I must say that if you are going to be *borrowing* books again, I'm glad to hear you'll be doing it outside my jurisdiction."

"I'd rather avoid complications like that," Irene agreed, and escaped from Vale's rooms onto the street, with Kai one step behind her.

CHAPTER 12

W hen they stepped into the Library, it was dark. The receiving room was full of shadows, with a wan emergency light bulb as the only source of illumination, and the titles of the books on the walls were illegible in the dimness.

Irene tensed in shock, and her hand tightened on Kai's arm as the door to Vale's world thudded shut behind them. "This is . . . unusual," she said carefully.

"Where are we?" Kai's eyes dilated and glinted in the remnants of light as he scanned the room. "Is this an outlying area?"

"I don't know," Irene admitted. They'd come in through the first library she could reach on Vale's world, rather than by the regular Traverse. As a result, they might be anywhere at all in the Library. "That's the problem with opening a random entrance. But we were in a hurry." The room unnerved her. She'd never before been in a part of the Library that felt so deserted and abandoned. "Come on, we need to find a room with a computer."

The corridor outside was lit only by a thin strip of emergency lighting that ran along the ceiling. The floor creaked under their feet, as if another pair of steps were echoing theirs. There were windows to their left, but they faced out onto a barren courtyard under a lowering sky, so full of clouds that there was no light to spare.

Five doors later, they found a room with a computer in it. Irene threw herself down and turned it on, and felt a surge of relief as the screen lit up. Kai leaned over her shoulder, resting his weight on her chair, and watched as she logged in.

An immediate message spread across the screen before Irene could even check her email.

> All non-essential power usage has been cut back in order to
> conserve energy for essential needs. All Librarians who require
> immediate transport for book retrieval have been allotted the
> use of transfer cabinets, command word "Emergency." Abuse of
> this privilege will be noted.

But she'd only been gone a few hours. Had the situation become that much worse in her absence?

"I thought they trusted you to be adults," Kai commented.

Irene bit her lip and focused on the current situation, choking down her rampant and probably entirely justified paranoia. She could think of plenty of reasons why the elder Librarians might monitor Librarian movement. Such as watching for suspicious travel, or attempts to escape, or even outright treason . . . "Maybe it's like being a parent," she said, bringing up a Library map. "You never really see your children as adults."

"You're exaggerating," Kai said, with the easy confidence of someone who hadn't tested the issue yet.

Just you wait till you try to convince your *father that you're grown up and know what you're doing.* But Irene was distracted from her planned retort by the Library map unfurling across the screen. "Aha," she said. "The nearest cabinet is"—she checked the map—"about half a mile from here. Could be worse."

"Do we actually have any plans yet?" Kai asked.

"Oh, the usual." Irene typed as she spoke, writing Coppelia a quick email covering Alberich's messages and Zayanna's rumours, as clinically and unemotionally as she could. "We get there, we review the situation, then we decide how to get in and we snatch the book. We may be lucky: if there are enough books stored in the Hermitage, or at least in some bits of it, then I might be able to force a gate to the Library from there. That would speed up our getaway."

"I'm hearing a lot of *may*s and *might*s in that," Kai said.

"That's because I'm desperately trying to find any good points at all in the current situation," Irene admitted. "As opposed to thinking of it as . . . well, an unplanned theft from a royal palace at very short notice. You know I don't like short notice." She hit the send button. "Still, at least we won't have long-term identities to protect."

"What do we pose as when we get there?" Kai asked.

"I'm thinking religious pilgrims, at least until we can get a feel for the place and find something better. Our background information's years out of date." She began typing again, a quick appeal to Bradamant to visit Vale and pick up any information that he'd collected. Despite their enmity, Bradamant's curiosity should spur her into action. "The Library portal to that world opens into the Jagiellonian Library in Krakow, in Poland. At least we'll be on the same continent, when it comes to travelling to St. Petersburg. It could be worse. We could be having to get there from Africa or Australia, or similar."

"And no Librarian-in-Residence?" Kai asked.

"There was one, but she died twenty years before that report was written." Irene hit send again. "Natural causes—it's at the back of the report; she was in a traffic accident. Hit by a crashing flying sleigh. The sleigh was flying, that is, and then it crashed." The thought gave her a little unwanted shudder. Living outside the Library was never safe. Flying sleighs could come out of nowhere and hit you, however careful you were.

Her email pinged. Bradamant had replied.

Can we talk?

Kai was leaning over Irene's shoulder again. "What does she want?" he asked suspiciously.

"Well, I did just ask her a favour," Irene pointed out, trying to repress her own doubts.

Currently in transit on way to mission, she typed in. *Can it be quick?*

It took barely ten seconds for Bradamant to reply—just enough time for Irene to run a status check on her parents and to be reassured that they were still out on assignment. And still hopefully alive.

I only want a few words. Will you be stopping by your quarters?

"You've been the one saying we're in a hurry," Kai said.

"Yes," Irene agreed reluctantly. "But we do need to stop by my rooms, so I can get some emergency cash and whatever."

Yes. Meet you there in fifteen minutes?

Irene was assuming Bradamant had access to a transfer cabinet as well. If not, she decided, then there wasn't time for Irene herself to go out of her way for a conversation.

See you there, the answer came.

Damn. Now she didn't have an excuse to avoid the conversation. "Let's go," she said, turning the computer off. "It'd be embarrassing to be late."

The transfer cabinet was cramped for two people. Irene braced herself against Kai, rather than against the walls, as she pronounced the command word in the Language, then gave her quarters as the destination. The cabinet slid sideways and then down, like a barrel going over a waterfall, jolting the two of them, and Irene muttered an apology as she felt her foot bang into Kai's ankle. He steadied her, the two of them together in the darkness, his arms around her, and Irene briefly let herself relax.

So Alberich's trying to kill me. So Lady Guantes is trying to kill me. So maybe other people are trying to kill me, too. At least there's one person upon whom I can rely. Whom I can trust.

A moment later they stopped, and the doors swung open. They were in the residential area that included Irene's quarters, in a central passageway that opened onto a dozen small suites of rooms. Like the rest of the Library so far, it was barely illuminated now, with only a strip of lighting glowing dimly along the floor. Irene was grateful that the shadows hid her flushed cheeks.

"Which one's yours?" Kai asked.

"Third along on the left," Irene said. "I haven't been here for a while: sorry about the mess." She tapped the code number into the combination lock on the door, trying to remember if she'd left anything particularly embarrassing lying around.

As it turned out, the most embarrassing thing was the dust.

"It's been months since I was here," Irene muttered. Kai was staring down the corridor, making a deliberate show of not looking into her rooms, but clearly very curious. "Oh, come in—I've got nothing to hide, and it'll take me a few moments to find the gold." She led the way into her room, flicking on the light-switch. Fortunately, it worked.

As usual with Irene's rooms—and with most Librarians'—there were stacks of books piled against the already-stuffed bookcases, forming a danger to navigation. The only actual decorations were framed photographs of her parents and of some of her friends from school. The desk was still piled with translation notes from the last time she'd been here, when she'd had a couple of weeks without assignments. She'd been trying to improve her written Korean from appalling to merely bad. The side door to her bedroom was shut, sparing her any comments from Kai on her wardrobe. She began going through the desk drawers, trying to remember where she'd left her emergency stash of gold sovereigns. Even if it was foreign currency, basic gold was usually good anywhere.

"Thanks for waiting," Bradamant said.

Irene looked up quickly and saw Bradamant standing in the doorway, elegant as always in a fitted grey jacket and shin-length skirt. A cameo brooch at her collar caught the light and glittered. It was the sort of outfit that a female millionaire entrepreneur would have worn in the 1940s, in a world that had female millionaire entrepreneurs. Every inch of her screamed personal tailoring and extreme expense.

"Not a problem," Irene answered. She had to remind herself that she'd decided on a new policy of mutual coexistence, rather than automatically taking offence at everything Bradamant said. "I hope you didn't have to come out of your way to get down here?"

"Well, the whole point was to speak with you." Bradamant stepped into the room and the door swung shut behind her. "As you said some time back, we shouldn't be wasting our time sniping at each other. Especially in an emergency."

Kai had shuffled to one side and was taking a polite interest in the nearest bookcase, ostensibly not part of the conversation, even though Irene knew he'd be listening.

"Fair enough," Irene agreed. "So why did you want to speak with me?"

"Well." Bradamant hesitated, picking her words. "We *are* among the very few Librarians who've actually met Alberich."

"We are among those fortunate few survivors, yes," Irene said.

"Has he tried to communicate with you?"

The words hung in the air. *I've already told Coppelia—it's not as if there's anything treasonous about it,* Irene thought. *There's no reason to be ashamed of it or afraid to admit it.* But actually saying it out loud took an effort. "Yes," she finally managed. "It happened since the meeting this morning, and it was definitely him. You?"

"No," Bradamant said. She sounded more irritated about it than thankful. "Probably because I'm stuck here."

"Not on assignment? I assumed that all the able-bodied—"

"Kostchei's keeping me here." Bradamant folded her arms crisply. "He says he needs someone on hand for emergency pickups."

Saying *Not because of what happened during your last assignment?* would have been unforgivable. But the thought ran through Irene's mind, and she hastily suppressed it before it could show on her face. "I suppose it makes sense," she said neutrally.

"It doesn't make sense to keep me here when we could actually be tracking Alberich down," Bradamant snapped. "We both know he's the sort who holds a grudge. It'd be much more *useful* if we were bait in a trap!"

"I beg leave to argue about it being in any way useful for Irene to get herself killed," Kai commented from where he was leaning against the bookcase.

"Oh, you could be there too—he could come after you as well,"

Bradamant said. "I'm not trying to keep you out of it. I'm sure you'd be very useful." She gave him a polished smile, discreet and a little sly. "And I'm sure your family wouldn't object to having Alberich out of the way."

"Does everyone know about my family?" Kai muttered.

"Not everyone," Bradamant said quickly. "But you actually warded an area against chaos when we last confronted Alberich, so you're from an important family. Not all dragons could do that." She turned back to Irene before Kai could agree or disagree. "So what do you think?"

"Can we take this by stages?" Irene asked. The basic idea of *let's all trap Alberich* sounded good in itself, but the specificity of *let's go and play bait for an insane murderer* left her less enthusiastic. "Have you run this past Kostchei yet?"

"No," Bradamant admitted. "I thought I'd discuss it with you first."

"Do you think he wouldn't approve, then?"

Bradamant shrugged. "It'd depend how feasible we could make it. If we could come up with a plan that might work . . ."

Irene still wasn't convinced this was a good idea. "When Alberich contacted me, he funnelled raw chaotic power into my location, once he'd established where I was." She ran through the details of the morning's encounter in response to Bradamant's raised eyebrow. Though she did leave out the bits where she'd been drugged and kidnapped by werewolves and lost her Library documents. *No point in confusing the issue.* "I concede that this means we could get a two-way link," she finished. "I'm just not sure that it would be to our advantage, rather than to his."

"That's a bit defeatist, isn't it?" Kai said quietly.

"You didn't get nearly fried by raw chaos this morning—" Irene started.

"No," Kai said. "Because I *wasn't there*, because you went off to the Library on your own. You would have thought that by now we'd know better."

Irene took a deep breath. "All right. Point taken, Kai. Bradamant, can you give me a moment to think about this? I need to change my dress anyhow." She looked down at her wrecked clothing. Days like this were hell on her clothing budget. "Give me five minutes and I'll be with you."

Both Kai and Bradamant nodded, and Irene slipped quickly into her bedroom. She ran through her options as she dropped her ruined dress and coat on the floor and speedily changed into something long-skirted, modest, bland, and unobtrusive. She had a lot of those in her wardrobe.

Two main questions were nagging at her. Was it just her distrust of Bradamant that was making her discount her colleague's idea? And, ultimately, could it actually work?

As Irene walked back into her study, Bradamant was just saying, "Nobody's disputing her *talent* . . ." She glanced at Irene. "We're talking about you, of course."

"Well, of course," Irene agreed. "I'm not in the room, you talk about me—some things are a fact of life. I'm sure Kai and I will be talking about you as soon as you've left."

Bradamant smiled icily. "So? Your thoughts?"

Irene tucked the pouch of gold sovereigns into an inner pocket. "It's a plausible idea," she admitted. "If Kostchei and Coppelia, or whoever, agree to it, then I'll help with it. But I'm not going to go running off solo with you now. Or even if we take Kai with us."

Kai opened his mouth, then shut it again, apparently mollified by the idea that he'd be invited along too.

But Bradamant frowned. "If you think this is a good idea, then I can't see why you're not more enthusiastic."

"I don't see that it's being *un*enthusiastic to wait for our superiors' opinion first," Irene said. "Actually, I don't see why you want me to be *enthusiastic* anyhow. Even if this is a good idea, it's not going to be remotely safe or easy."

"Always such a cynic," Bradamant said. Her smile was a little brittle. "Irene, tell me . . ."

"Yes?"

"Do you think our superiors actually have the right idea here?"

"Right idea in what sense?" Irene asked cautiously.

"In the sense that they're fighting a strictly defensive strategy," Bradamant said. She was picking her words just as carefully as Irene. *Neither of us wants to be the first one to say something that could be reported and held against us.* "I'm . . . concerned."

"We don't necessarily know everything they're planning," Irene said, but the words rang hollow in her own ears, and she remembered her earlier complaint to Coppelia.

"And you know what the corollary to *that* is."

"That what they're planning is too horrendously dangerous to tell us?" Irene suggested.

"No," Bradamant said. She lowered her voice. "That there are spies among us."

"That doesn't work," Kai said firmly, cutting through the sudden silence. "Seriously, it doesn't work. If there were Librarians who were working for Alberich and who could access the Library, then couldn't they just open a door for him and invite him in? Even if he can't enter because he's chaos-contaminated, they could be actively sabotaging the Library, passing him information—whatever. There wouldn't be any need for all these threats and ultimatums."

If Irene had been the praying type, she would have said a prayer of thanks for that simple common-sense point. It short-circuited her paranoia. "Right," she agreed.

"I'm sure there are other things that spies could be doing for him," Bradamant suggested. But that line of argument was clearly weak, even to her own ears, and she gave up with a shrug, looking disappointed.

"And what do you actually want us to *do*, anyhow? You and me, that is. Are we supposed to stand around and yell, 'Alberich, we're here, come and get us' until something happens?"

"There's no need to be like that about it," Bradamant snapped. "I was only putting forward a suggestion. And there's something you aren't taking into consideration."

"What?"

"I saw you talking with Penemue."

"Then you probably saw her cutting me dead once she realized I wasn't going to be immediately useful to her," Irene answered. "Has she been talking to you, too?"

"She's tried." Bradamant looked smug. "Give me some credit here, Irene. I probably know more about what's going on in the political landscape here than you do. I knew more about it even before I got stuck here for the last few months. And to give Penemue credit, she isn't just doing this because she sees herself as the new representative of the working classes. She honestly thinks some reform is needed."

"Fair's fair," Irene said. "I accept that she's not wholly selfish. But I have the impression that you've got reservations about her too."

"Her current timing isn't impressing me." Bradamant folded her arms. "I'm not going to argue the Library's power structure with you, because we'd probably end up debating aristocracy versus oligarchy versus democracy. And, frankly, we both have more urgent things to do. But I think we can both agree that long-term change is at least worth discussing?"

"Possibly," Irene agreed cautiously. "But the Penemue thing—I get that she's looking to rock the boat, and going on the attack makes sense from her point of view, as a counter to official policy. Are you suggesting that if we don't consider this option of us playing bait, then she'll bring it up herself?"

"It could happen," Bradamant said. "So I'm wondering if the two of us should be proactive about it and take that political option out of her hands."

Irene considered, then shook her head. "No. Our superiors know about our previous encounter with Alberich. If we've had the idea of playing bait, they've certainly had the idea of using us as bait." It wasn't a comforting thought, but it had the feeling of truth to it. "Us trying to run off and do this on our own isn't going to help anyone's political position. It might even make it worse for the authorities, if Penemue tries to push the idea that they're losing control of their own juniors."

Bradamant nodded slowly. "You might have a point there. All right, I'll leave it for the moment."

Little tendrils of paranoia wove themselves together at the back of Irene's mind. Bradamant was perfectly capable of using Irene as bait, with or without Irene's permission, if she could get support for it. Or, on a darker note, who was to say that the mysterious woman behind Irene's kidnapping had been Lady Guantes? What if it had been someone much closer to the Library . . .

"I'll check with your friend Vale in a day or two," Bradamant said. Her expression was perfectly pleasant, as graceful and enigmatic as an Erté statuette. "And if he finds anything urgent, I'll pass it to Coppelia or you. Will that do?"

"It will," Irene said. She forced away her fears. She might not *like* Bradamant very much, but she could trust her not to betray the Library—couldn't she? She smiled in return. "Thank you. I appreciate that. And if you have any useful thoughts about how to lure

Alberich out, then please tell me. But you're right, we both need to be getting down to work."

Bradamant hesitated, glancing between Irene and Kai, then inclined her head in a nod and stepped outside. The door closed behind her with a very soft click.

"Was she seriously suggesting mutiny?" Kai demanded.

"Of course not," Irene said quickly. "She was trying to put a stop to it. You heard her."

"On the surface, yes. But she was also sounding you out, to see how far you'd go along with it."

"That's a hypothesis."

"I may be a novice in the Library, Irene, but I was raised in my father's court." Kai didn't even sound angry. He just sounded depressed. "As Bradamant said, she knows the political landscape. But I know how these things work too. In times of war, anyone might rise to power."

"We should be going," Irene said, trying to steer the conversation back to safer grounds. "Priorities, remember? Collecting a book? Before we were sidetracked by . . ."

"By Bradamant, who wanted to suggest that your superiors were incompetent and you should take independent action," Kai said, showing no sign of being steered.

"You're not helping."

"I'm not *trying* to help. You're bending over backwards to be fair to someone whom you have no reason to trust." Kai set his jaw stubbornly.

"She's another Librarian, and I trust her." Irene rethought that statement. "That is, I trust her not to be working with Alberich. Look, Kai, do you want me to run to Coppelia and tell her Bradamant was questioning her authority? Especially when Bradamant can perfectly well deny that she said it, or claim that I misinterpreted her?"

Kai tapped his chest. "You have an independent witness."

"Bradamant would say that you'd lie to support me." She saw Kai's face darken at the insult. "Don't lose your temper at *me*—it's what she'd say, and it's what enough people would believe."

"Then what can we actually do?" Kai demanded.

"Keep our eyes open and pay attention. And, in the meantime, go and get our book." She opened the door. "Coming?"

Kai muttered to himself but let the subject drop. As they were crowding into the transfer cabinet, he asked, "Are you going to check the status of any other Librarians? If people have been killed . . ."

"I checked on my parents," Irene said. "They haven't reported any problems." And she could hardly go running off to check on them in person. At least Alberich would have no idea who they were or how to find them.

"And your other friends?"

There was a pause as Kai worked out that Irene wasn't going to give him a list of other friends. "Surely you know other Librarians," he said, sounding disappointed.

"Of course I do," Irene replied. "That doesn't mean I'm going to throw a panic fit and run round looking for a list of casualties. What are you getting at here, Kai?"

He shrugged. "Your sisters and brothers in arms are in danger. Irene, you went into danger to save me. Wouldn't you do that for them too?"

This was getting more emotionally fraught than Irene enjoyed. The cramped quarters didn't help, as they were now standing extremely close. "Well, yes, of course I would, but what exactly do you expect me to *do* here and now? Should I be panicking because there's a chance that someone I know is . . ." *Dead.* She knew a lot of other Librarians as casual acquaintances, even if she didn't know them well. Coppelia and Kostchei had said that people had died. She didn't want to speculate. It would be too hard to stop. "... in danger," she substituted. "I—we—have a *job* to do. **Gate of B-1165.**"

The transfer cabinet jolted into motion, sliding sideways through darkness and cutting off any rejoinder Kai might have made. As it dropped like a lift, Irene was forced to recognize the thing that annoyed her most about Bradamant's proposal. It was that Irene desperately wanted to do it. She *wanted* to strike back against Alberich, to save the Library. Putting herself in danger to get the job done was hardly new. But her common sense revolted against the idea of putting herself in danger if it wasn't actually going to accomplish anything. Bradamant didn't have a plan beyond using themselves as bait. She just had wishful thinking.

If only they had some way of locating Alberich ...

The cabinet slammed to a stop, and Irene and Kai staggered out into a windowless room, with barely enough light to avoid tripping over piles of books. There were no warning signs here about current dangers, no threatening posters, and no special seals on the door out of the Library.

"Ready?" she said.

"Ready," Kai agreed, adjusting his cuffs.

Irene took hold of the heavy brass handle and shoved the door open, then stepped through into another world. She had to push aside a plush red rope cordoning off their door. There was an OUT OF ORDER sign in Polish dangling from its handle. Beyond, the room was full of display-cases and tapestries. Another place that had once been a true library and now was nothing but a museum.

Kai grabbed her wrist, his grip hard enough to hurt. "Irene," he said, his voice shocked. "Some of my kindred are in this world."

CHAPTER 13

I rene stared at Kai in surprise, and was about to ask for more details when the door at the other end of the room boomed open, thudding against the wall. She and Kai both turned to see who it was.

The man standing in the doorway was presumably a museum guard, though the cudgel hanging from his belt looked too well-used for Irene's peace of mind. His clothing was stark black with red accents, with a high-necked jacket over breeches and boots. A brutal scar marred one side of his face. Two other guards filled the space behind him: the bulk of their shoulders made Irene seriously wonder about their normal duties. Museum guards weren't *usually* this well-organized, beefy, or clearly ready for violence.

"Who are you and what are you doing here?" the lead guard demanded.

It was a reasonable question, and it was one that Irene had been asked quite a number of times in her career. Unfortunately, *I'm Irene and I'm here to steal books* was rarely the answer that interrogators wanted to hear. More immediately, she couldn't think of any good answer that would adequately explain her presence in an apparently heavily guarded area. She might as well go directly to the next usual step.

"You perceive that I and this man are people who have a right to be here and who should be allowed to leave," she said firmly in the Language. The effort took her by surprise. It felt as if she were having to push the words uphill. The universe didn't seem to want to accept the Language's effect. Was this how it felt to work in such high-order worlds? She'd generally been employed in more middle-of-the-road ones before, or even chaotic ones.

Nevertheless, the Language worked. The guards all looked a bit confused, but the arrogant intimidation drained from their posture. "Apologies," the first one said, saluting. "We hadn't realized, ma'am."

"Carry on," Irene said with a casual nod, sauntering towards the door. She swayed a little, still light-headed from the effort, but Kai steadied her. The guards melted out of her way like butter before a hot knife, their eyes lowered in respect.

She and Kai were halfway down the corridor when there came a furious yell of "Stop them!"

"Faster than usual," Irene muttered as the two of them sprinted round the corner. The guards had the advantage of knowing the terrain, but fortunately the place was a tangle of rooms. Very elegant, beautiful rooms, as far as Irene could tell while running through them, and full of interesting-looking books. More to the point, these were rooms where one could lose pursuers.

She took stock of the situation while hiding behind a display-stand with Kai. The guards thundered past, yelling something that Irene's Polish wasn't good enough to translate.

She waited till they were out of earshot, then said, "We may need to rethink our usual strategy."

"Why?" Kai asked.

"Because normally that effect lasts for longer."

"I assumed it was just bad luck."

"No. I think it was the high-order nature of this world. It was harder to get it to work, too."

"Oh." Kai frowned. "Normally I'd have loved to take you to a high-order world, but this might make things inconvenient. I never expected to be actually stealing a book with you on one of them. And why did those guards come in just then? They seemed very prepared for action. I thought that sort of thing only happened on high-chaos worlds."

"Life has a tendency to be awkward," Irene said with deep bitterness. "All right. Let's try to find the exit before they come back."

Some very cautious exploration brought them to the more public areas of the building, and they were able to slip into the general comings and goings without attracting attention. Most of the visitors seemed to be students or scholars, and very few of them looked well off. Battered overcoats and an air of genteel poverty were the norm.

The guard at the door demanded to see Irene's pass but was willing to take a gold coin and her apology for having "forgotten" it instead. Probably there would be trouble once he and the guards who'd been chasing them compared notes, but Irene planned to be well out of the city by that time.

She and Kai found a café several streets away, collecting newspapers as they went, and settled down in a corner with a pot of tea and a plate of fried cakes stuffed with plum jam. For half an hour or so they were silent, except for occasional requests to pass a newspaper. Irene took the Polish papers, as she had at least a basic grasp of the language, while Kai read the international ones, since his Polish was non-existent.

Finally Irene put down the last paper and signalled for a new pot of tea. "This is going to be inconvenient," she said. "I don't like trying to steal books in the middle of secessions and revolutions."

"Maybe not as inconvenient as it might have been." Kai tapped the French newspaper *Le Monde*. "According to this one, the troubles are in the outlying countries, not Russia itself. Once we're in St. Petersburg we'll be safe." He thought about that. "Well, safer than we are here, at least."

"Maybe, maybe not." Irene stacked the papers thoughtfully. "They're using terms like 'terrorism' and 'foreign agents' and 'fifth column.' I've found that when that starts happening, homeland citizens get suspicious of any oddly behaving foreigners. The sooner we're out of here, the better."

"Do you think it'll have made the security around the Hermitage any heavier?" Kai asked. "Given how out of date the rest of our information is . . ."

"No way of knowing, unfortunately. That's the problem with not having a Librarian-in-Residence." She remembered his earlier comment. "By the way, what did you mean when you said there were dragons here?"

"Not here in Poland," Kai said, a little too quickly.

"No, in this world," Irene said.

"I can tell they're in this world. I don't know where, without trying to find them. I'm just not sure that trying to find them would be a good idea."

"Why not?" Irene asked, genuinely surprised. She'd thought Kai would be only too pleased to spend time with other dragons.

"Well. You know." It was never a good sign when Kai went mono-syllabic. He fiddled with the cakes. "Questions."

"Kai, we've talked about keeping dangerous secrets before," Irene said patiently. To be more precise, she'd talked and he'd listened. "Is this something I should know about?"

"I'm worried about my father." Kai's voice was quiet and uncertain. "I've already caused him inconvenience by being kidnapped and needing rescue. I don't want him to be embarrassed by any further shameful behaviour on my part. What I do in private is one thing, but . . . Well, I know you understand what court intrigues can be like, Irene. Nobody's going to actually *challenge* my father, but there are other things they can do."

"Delayed taxes and tributes?" Irene guessed. "Orders getting accidentally lost en route? Polite semi-public insubordination? Negotiating with other monarchs?" She'd learnt earlier that there were four dragon kings, and Kai's father was one of them. However, Kai himself was one son among many, by far the youngest and lowest down the scale of inheritance. "Long-term consequences on the grounds that misconduct in the son can imply weakness in the father?"

"You do understand," Kai said with relief. "My uncle's loyal to him, of course, and Li Ming's loyal to my uncle, so it doesn't matter if they know about my affiliation with the Library. But I don't know which other dragons are actually here. It might even be representatives from one of the queens' courts. I don't want to be accused of intruding on someone else's territory."

Irene knew she should be getting on with the job, but Kai so rarely discussed dragon politics that she couldn't resist the urge to ask a few more questions. "Are the queens enemies of the kings?"

"Oh no," Kai said, sounding a little shocked that he might have given that impression. "But they're established in the more secure worlds, the ones that you call high-order. The kings go there to visit them on state occasions, or for mating contracts."

"Were you brought up in your mother's court or your father's?" Irene asked.

"My father's. Male children are given to the father, and female ones to the mother. At least, with royal matings. Dragons of lower rank may have different arrangements." He caught the look in her eye. "Oh, you shouldn't think that I grew up without any female dragons around. My royal father has many female courtiers and servants, and female lords under his command. It's just that the royal households themselves are of the same gender."

"Why?"

Kai shrugged. "That's how it is."

Irene would have liked more detail, but the current urgent situation was more important. "All right," she said. "To get back to matters at hand, are any dragons who are here likely to interfere with us stealing a book?"

"Not *interfere* as such," Kai said carefully. "But they would certainly be curious."

"In that case, we'll be discreet and hope they don't notice." She saw the relief in his eyes. "Next step: we need to get to St. Petersburg, possibly with a stop to obtain clothing first."

She nodded at the people passing by outside. While many of them wore some sort of dark coat over their clothing, as Kai and Irene did, these were distinctively heavy wool or felt coats, often with fur cuffs and collars. The clothing beneath the coats comprised long skirts for women, but with a bodice and blouse rather than a dress. These were banded with bright colours. The men wore heavy boots and thick trousers, with shirts and waistcoats. Both genders wore hats: Irene and Kai were unusual in being bare-headed.

"Not too cheap, I hope," Kai said. Even though he could make a scruffy shirt and trousers look like the latest catwalk fashion, that didn't mean he wanted to. He shopped with all the exquisite taste of a prince who'd been raised in personally tailored silks and furs.

Irene was something of a disappointment to him there, and she knew it. "Sorry," she said. "I don't want us spending too much of our spare cash before we get there. Fashions may be different in St. Petersburg—"

"I told you we should have bought *Vogue*," Kai put in.

"That's high fashion, not regular fashion," Irene said firmly. "It wouldn't have been any use. Come on. We should get started." She commandeered the last cake, then signalled the waiter over, combining a tip with a request for directions to a local clothing shop.

She was grateful that Kai didn't make any comments about urgency, or this errand taking up too much time. Running into a heavily guarded royal property without the right disguise would get them *killed*. And working out the details kept her stable. Whereas if she let herself start thinking *the entire Library may be destroyed*, her mind went into a terrified hamster-wheel spin. It was too large a concept to imagine.

In some versions of Krakow there would have been a huge central railway station, but here there was a grand travel-hub building with sleighs being constantly flown in and out. They were drawn by reindeer and horses that galloped through the air. It was a more obtrusive use of magic than Irene had seen elsewhere in the city—which, come to think of it, seemed generally worn-down. The place desperately needed some renovation, which suggested a financial depression.

The whole situation was probably linked to the general uncertainty in this world's Russian Empire and to the rigid state control of magic. Irene noted it as background detail, considering how it would impact their mission, in the same way that she would have studied the grammar and vocabulary of a new language.

Fortunately the guards at the gates didn't ask for passports, but the tickets were expensive enough that Irene winced for her dwindling finances. A pageboy who cast sideways glances at their cheap clothing led her and Kai to a sleek black-and-silver sleigh with six large reindeer fastened to it. He opened the small side door and bowed them inside. It was crowded: there was barely room for them to squeeze into a corner, and everyone else was better-dressed than they were. She spotted bright clusters of ribbons on sleeves and at throats, or smooth sable gloves and high-heeled red leather boots.

"Good evening," the woman sitting next to her said brightly in Polish. She was the rich elderly type, with furs that showed their age but had once been very expensive. Her rouged cheeks matched a red nose. "How nice to have young company on this overnight flight! What brings you on this trip?"

Kai smiled in polite incomprehension. Irene was left to carry the conversation and the cover story, which at least took her mind off the sleigh rising into the air and the heights it reached. And the speed. Zeppelins or high-technology shuttles were *so* much better than this sort of transport. One could shut the windows and didn't have to see the landscape below spooling past at an impossibly fast rate, from far too high up. She concentrated on making her narrative sound convincing.

"... and so my cousin here came to get me after my mother's heart attack," she concluded. It was a tragic tale of family illness and breakdown, complete with a father's alcoholism and accident. Irene had apparently had to spend all her savings on the fast sleigh home, to be with her dying mother. She'd borrowed from some of the worst tear-jerker family epics she knew, and she was quite proud of the result. "Of course, my cousin's never been outside Russia in his life, but he knew where I was living . . ."

Several of her listeners sighed in sympathy. In-flight entertainment consisted of looking over the edge or passing round bottles of vodka and slivovitz, and Irene's story had drawn more attention than she'd really wanted. She pressed her knuckles against her lips. "Please forgive me—I'm just so worried about poor Mamma."

Kai might not have been able to understand the Polish, but he could take a cue. He slipped an arm round her shoulders and held her close. "Please forgive my cousin," he said in Russian. "I think she needs to rest."

To general nods, Irene let herself relax. It was true that she was exhausted. It had been a long day, and far too full of excitement. Forgotten bruises were making themselves felt, now that there was nothing to do but sit and wait for the flight to end.

"Get some sleep," Kai murmured in her ear. "I'll wake you if . . . well, if anyone attacks."

Irene quirked a smile. "Thank you," she whispered and let her head rest on his shoulder, closing her eyes. She tried to clear her mind for sleep, difficult as it was. But Kai was warm against her, even through the thick layers of their clothing, and despite her dislike of heights, next to him she felt safe. *He's a dragon. He'll catch me if I fall . . .*

When she opened her eyes again, the sky was bright and pale and cloudless, and the air was bitterly cold. They joined a queue of incoming aerial traffic diving in towards a huge hexagonal building sheathed in panes of glass and mother-of-pearl. A huge clock on the side, gleaming with brass and surrounded by astronomical symbols, showed that it was six o'clock in the morning.

Irene rubbed her eyes and looked up at Kai. "Didn't you get any sleep?"

"Enough." He didn't look rumpled or half-asleep, though; he looked keen and sharp, as though the wintry night air had put a new edge on his energy. "Look at the city below. You can see all the landmarks."

Irene gritted her teeth and peered over the edge of the sleigh at St. Petersburg below them. "It's . . . big," she said, not very helpfully. Her understanding of the city's geography would have been better if she hadn't been trying not to think about falling out of the sleigh and landing on said geography.

"I think that's the Winter Palace down there." Kai pointed at a building on the waterfront, which sparkled gold and blue in the morning light. "Lovely architecture."

It was very efficient of Kai to be scouting out the terrain and spotting buildings that were part of the Hermitage complex. Irene should be complimenting him on his good work, rather than fighting motion sickness and vertigo. "How nice," she muttered.

Kai gave up on her and continued leaning over the edge to watch as the sleigh came in to land. The reindeer cantered through one of the archways in the building's walls and downwards, until they were drawing the sleigh over the ground rather than through the air, landing with barely a bump. They touched down inside a huge open hall: it was crowded with other sleighs, shuffling passengers, guards, and heavily loaded porters. The sound of hundreds of people shouting at each other was almost physically painful.

Irene was halfway through saying polite goodbyes to the other passengers when she noticed the bears. They were crouched in pairs by the exit gates, each with a handler next to it: iron collars circled their necks, and chains ran from their hind legs to pegs set into the ground. "Kai," she murmured, nodding to them.

Kai's eyes narrowed as he considered them. "I'm not sure if they're crowd control, guards, or what," he said, strolling towards the exit with her. Unlike most of the other passengers, they had only a minimum of luggage. "How shall we play it?"

"Act normal," Irene said. "At least nobody else seems to like them, either." People going through the exit gates were flinching away from the bears, or treating them with lofty disdain and then twitching at their slightest growl. Nobody was actually being stopped, though. Perhaps they were just a threat? Or some sort of ceremonial guard? But who posted ceremonial guards at an airport-equivalent?

They joined a queue shuffling towards the nearest exit. Irene ran through a mental list of possible contraband. She wasn't carrying a gun, or any drugs or explosives, something that she slightly regretted—after all, they might be useful on this mission. But for the moment she couldn't think of anything illegal concealed on her or Kai. Of course, it might depend on what this regime considered illegal . . .

Then the nearest bear growled. It wasn't the casual little noise that it and the other bears had been giving earlier when they shifted position or licked their muzzles, but an on-point, attention-all-guards noise. It rose from its crouch, the chains on its hind legs creaking, and leaned towards one of the people in the queue.

Its handler stepped forward. "Good morning, friend citizen," he said briskly. "Are you carrying any illegal magical components, as defined under section four of the law against importation of hazardous or treasonous materials?"

"Of course not," the accused man said flatly. His face was still rosy from the windburn that all the sleigh passengers had suffered from, but Irene thought that he'd lost a little colour. Other people were backing away from him—or, rather, from him and the bear. "There must be some mistake."

The handler raised a silver whistle to his mouth and blew a shrill blast. The sound carried through the noise of the crowd, and Irene could see several men in long dark coats hurrying towards them. "I'm sure you won't mind going with these guards to have your luggage checked, then," the handler said. "Please be aware that this is your duty under the law, and any resistance will be considered an illegal act."

Everyone else was looking at each other and muttering nervously. That made it safe for Irene to lean over to Kai and whisper, "They've got bears sniffing for sources of magic?"

"It looks that way." They shuffled a step closer to the exit. The bear had gone back down on its haunches again, looking as tame and unthreatening as one might reasonably expect from a large grizzly bear. In other words, not very.

"Interesting." They were second from the front of the line now. The man ahead was being waved through.

"Business or pleasure?" the handler said, with the bare minimum of interest.

"Family," Irene said. She decided to go for the earnest-but-confused approach. "I'm visiting my mother. I mean, that's not really pleasure, but I suppose it's not business either—"

"Yes, very good," the handler said wearily. "Please go through the exit ahead of you."

With an inner sigh of relief, Irene walked past him, with Kai in her wake.

And then the bear leaned forward and sniffed at Kai.

CHAPTER 14

There were gasps as the crowd pulled back from Irene and Kai. And from the bear, of course. It was difficult to ignore the bear. For a moment Irene considered feigning innocence and signalling to Kai to make a run for it, then meeting up with him later. Common sense told her that she'd probably be arrested as an accomplice. Besides, she was reluctant to leave him on his own in a strange place. He might get into trouble. Into even *more* trouble.

The handler frowned. "Are you carrying any illegal magical components, as defined under section four of the law against importation of hazardous or treasonous materials?"

"Absolutely not," Kai said. He eyed the bear sidelong. "There must be some mistake."

The bear gave vent to a long, rolling eructation. It lowered its head and tried to nuzzle against Kai, straining at its chains. There was nothing aggressive about it now.

Kai looked at Irene for a moment, then sighed and reached over to scratch its head, his fingers sinking into its fur. "Good girl," he said gently. "Good girl."

The security men in the long black coats had reached the scene. "Will you step away from the bear, friend citizen," one of them demanded. "Please place your hands above your head, and don't make any threatening moves."

This was not the surreptitious entry to St. Petersburg that Irene had been planning. She edged over to the handler. "What if it hurts him?" she demanded, letting an edge of panicked concern sharpen her voice. "It's a bear! What if it bites his head off, if he stops stroking it?"

"Our bears are all very highly trained, friend citizen," the handler reassured her, watching the bear nervously. "There's absolutely no way it would harm anyone. If your friend just steps away from it, I'm sure it won't do anything to him."

But the idea had been planted and had taken root. The security men looked at each other. "Perhaps you'd better not try to move till we can get one of the controllers over here, friend citizen," one of them said. "See if you can keep it calm."

"What's going on here?" The woman striding into the growing circle of empty space had a long black coat like the men, but there were green stripes on her shoulders and cuffs. Her long hair was braided back cruelly tight, and instead of the skirts the other women wore, she was in trousers and heavy boots, like the men. She glared around suspiciously. "Is there a problem?"

"That's the problem, Mistress Controller," the lead security guard said, pointing at the bear that was cuddling up against Kai.

The woman peered short-sightedly. Then she walked up to the bear and laid a hand on its head, murmuring so softly that Irene couldn't hear what she was saying. Kai took a step back, but the tilt of his head suggested that he was listening.

"Galina says that he smells of the sap in the tree as it goes thundering towards heaven," the woman announced, frowning. "She says that she salutes the lord of the powers of the earth and the sky, ruler of seas and shaker of mountains. I want her on immediate medical leave. And I want him questioned." She pointed at Kai.

"On what charges, Mistress Controller?" the guard asked.

"I don't know. Public nuisance, maybe," the woman said. "I'm sure he's done something. Take him into custody, and anyone with him." She rubbed the bear's shoulder affectionately.

The security guard did his best to look confident. "If you'll just come along with me, friend citizen," he said to Kai. "And the lady who's with you. I'm sure we'll have this all sorted out in a few minutes."

Damn, they remembered I exist. Irene stepped forward to Kai's side, giving him a little nod. "Please let's do as they say, cousin," she murmured.

Kai reluctantly let the bear be—it was fawning on the woman now, anyhow—and he and Irene followed the security guards to a side door. Irene was assessing the guards' visible weaponry as they led the way. Heavy truncheons, like the guards in the museum. Coils of thin rope on their belts at the opposite side—some sort of magical restraint? They wore silver whistles like the handler's at their necks, so that was probably a quick way to give the alarm. All most inconvenient. And just because Irene didn't see any missile weapons, that didn't mean the guards didn't have them.

They were ushered into a back corridor that was very different from the opulent sleigh-port exterior or the grand central hall. It was utilitarian, efficient, and lacking any external windows that one could escape through. The doors spaced along it were open frameworks of heavy steel bars. "Just along here," the guard said, the reassurance in his words diluted by the nervousness of his voice. "If you friend citizens will wait in this room, someone will be along to see you in a moment."

He gestured Irene and Kai into a sparsely furnished room—bare and cell-like, with white-tiled walls and floor, and only a single chair—and then tapped his hand against the side of the doorway and mumbled a few words. A shimmering glow of light sprang up across the open doorway, hissing like magnesium in water.

"What's going on?" Irene demanded.

"Just to keep you here till the investigators arrive," the second guard said. "We'll be back in a moment, friend citizens." He slammed the metal bars into place and locked the gate in position. The guards strode off quickly, with the air of men who were about to pass a dangerous problem on to someone else.

Irene looked around the cell. No obvious peepholes or ways of listening, but she couldn't be sure. "So much for a quiet arrival," she muttered.

Kai spread his hands. "I really am sorry. I had no idea the bear would do something like that. But what do we do now?"

"Wait for the investigators and explain everything to them," Irene said mildly. She tugged at her earlobe significantly. *We may be listened to.* "I'm sure that once they find out what's going on, they'll let us go. Didn't that lady say the bear needed a medical check-up?"

Kai wandered across and poked the screen across the doorway with a careful finger. It spat thick sparks in all directions, and he drew back. "That's a surprisingly powerful magical field," he said, picking his words. "I suspect that even if someone simply *tried* to jump through it, it might knock them out—and give them bad electrical burns."

"The government seems to have a firm hold on the use of magic round here," Irene said. She was trying to orient herself geographically. Even though she hadn't enjoyed the view when they came in, she'd seen that the sleigh-port was surrounded by the city, rather than being out in the countryside. If they could escape into St. Petersburg, they could hopefully lose any pursuit. They just had to get out of here. Preferably before more guards came back.

There was no point wasting any more time. "Can you guide me to the nearest outside wall? Bearing in mind where we are, in reference to the river?"

Kai nodded. He knew what she was about to do.

The Language wasn't magic. It was something else again, an entirely different sort of power. Irene couldn't use it to work with magic, and she couldn't use magic herself: it varied from world to world, and she'd never been trained in it. Her parents had always told her that a flexible mind and good use of the Language were more valuable than studying the minutiae of a given world's magic, and she'd generally agreed. It was only at times like this, when locked up behind a magical force-field, that she felt their argument might have been a bit one-sided.

However, what the Language *could* do was stop magic working. It was wholesale and unconditional, which sometimes made it a poor tool for delicate thefts. But for break-outs like this, it was perfect.

"**Magical barrier, deactivate,**" she said. Her words ground in the air like millstones, heavy with a current of power, and the shield fizzled and vanished. She was sweating as though she'd been running uphill. "**Steel-bar door, unlock and open.**"

The lock clicked and the door swung open, hitting the wall with a thump that rattled the tiles. Kai was already moving, dragging Irene along with him as she panted for breath. This place made using the Language *hard*. Everything was too settled, too real, too orderly. If she'd had the breath, she would have complained to anyone who'd listen.

They ran down the corridor, away from the central hall and in the direction of the outer walls. A guard turned the corner ahead of them and stood there, shocked, raising a hand for them to stop. Kai let go of Irene, caught the man's extended wrist and spun, slamming him into the wall, before catching Irene's shoulder again and pulling her on. He barely missed a step.

"Halt!" several voices were yelling from behind them. *Well, if they had any doubts about us, we've now convinced them.*

They turned a corner. It was a dead end. Offices lined the walls on either side, but the end of the corridor was solid stonework, without even the luxury of a window.

"You're sure it's outside, on the other side of this?" Irene demanded ungrammatically. Well, she was in a rush.

"Absolutely," Kai said. He glanced over his shoulder towards the noise of approaching booted feet. "Though I don't know how thick the wall is."

"Let's just hope the support structure holds," Irene said. She stepped forward and set her hands against the cold stone surface. **"Stone wall directly in front of me, measured by my height and my hands,"** she said, trying to define it as specifically as possible, **"crumble to dust all the way through to the outside."**

For a moment Irene thought it wouldn't work. Doors were made to open and did it all the time, but stone was not friable by nature. It seemed to shiver under her hands, as though it was trying to throw off her command as easily as a human could refuse an order.

No. She was not going to let it disobey. She bent her will on it, focusing, summoning her determination, gritting her teeth as she stared at it. And slowly—far too slowly—the surface grew rough and pitted as she watched, and dust began to cascade down over her hands.

"Irene!" Kai shouted, sweeping her off her feet. The two of them tumbled to the ground together, as a spray of cross-bow bolts sliced through the air above them at waist height.

Irene felt as if her bones were having a temporary holiday and had been replaced by jelly, but the situation couldn't be postponed until she felt better. **"Cross-bow strings, break!"** she shouted.

Dust came cascading down over her and Kai. He rolled to his feet, balanced and ready, as the guards approached. Irene coughed and pulled herself upright less elegantly, turning to check on the wall. There was a roughly person-sized gap in it by now, and she could see clear sky on the other side. "Time to go!"

"You first!"

There wasn't time to argue. Irene ducked her head and shuffled through the hole—it was about five feet long, suggesting very thick outer walls. On the far side, it came out on the first-floor level of the building, meaning that there was a drop of ten feet to the ground below. People were already gathering and pointing.

Irene bent down, grabbed the lower edge of the hole, and let herself drop, landing safely on the pavement. Those tumbling lessons had definitely been worth it. "Kai! Now!"

He followed her down in a swirl of dust, another spray of cross-bow bolts rattling above his head and into the building opposite. They must have restrung in double-quick time. "Which way?"

"Just a moment. **Dust, gather in a cloud in that hole in the building!**" The eroded rock dust drew together like time-lapsed fog, blowing backwards into the building. "All right. Now—"

Irene looked around, gathering her wits. The street was full of people: pedestrians on the pavement, small carriages and riders in the road, and all of them looking at her and Kai. This seemed like yet another situation that could be resolved by running away.

It was.

Two streets later, having outpaced any witnesses, she and Kai slowed their run to a casual stroll—pausing to look in the occasional shop window. The back of Irene's neck was prickling with paranoia. Even if they'd been miraculously lucky in their escape—mostly because the guards hadn't expected them to break out, and *nobody* had foreseen them blowing a hole in the sleigh-port wall—the local police equivalent had to be on their tail by now. Or, worse, the Oprichniki. She expressed this in a murmur to Kai as they stared at a wedding-dress display.

"The Oprichniki?" Kai frowned. "Oh yes, their strangely obvious local secret service."

"Why strangely obvious?"

"They *all* wear long black coats," Kai said.

"Those are probably just the ones that get mentioned in the newspapers." Irene pursed her lips at the dress, as if she were considering herself in white silk. "We need to break our trail, we need cover, we need a plan. You know, I should be asking you for more ideas. I am supposed to be mentoring you."

"But your ideas are usually better than mine." Kai shrugged. "Why waste time asking me, when we can simply go straight to whatever you have in mind?"

Irene knew she should probably argue, but it was hardly the moment for a performance-development review. She added *Convince Kai to provide more input into planning* to her growing list of Things to Do Once We've Averted the Apocalypse. "All right. Then give me your thoughts on the magic here. You may have noticed things that I haven't."

"We know there's a government monopoly on its use," Kai said. "The magically powered flight we came in on was state-owned. The municipal building works that originally drained the land that this city's built on were magically assisted. And the current walls holding the water back are magically reinforced and state-funded—that was in your notes. It was one of the main stories in the newspapers we read, too, about Slavic countries wanting secession from Russian authority. They were calling for their own magical traditions and industries to be back under their own control. And we haven't seen any private magical workers in these shops so far."

Irene nodded. "Yes, I agree with all of that, but do you have any conclusions?"

"We're going to be in trouble from the government, but not from casual practitioners," Kai said. "If we want to avoid pursuit, perhaps we should split up . . ."

He didn't sound enthusiastic about it, and Irene could guess why. Getting captured by werewolves earlier wasn't her finest hour. And it would only have strengthened Kai's conviction that she'd get into trouble the moment she was out of sight. "Perhaps not," she said. "We don't know the local geography and I don't have any convenient way of finding you. Could you find me? The way you could navigate to Vale's home world?"

He shook his head. "It doesn't work inside a world, no. My father or my uncles could do better, but dragons like myself or my brothers are lesser creatures."

"The word you want is *younger*, not *lesser*," Irene said firmly. "Anyhow, point settled: no splitting up. Next step, when and how to get into the Hermitage. In particular, the Winter Palace."

Kai brushed his fingers against his stomach. The packet of documents was lodged inside his shirt, held in place by a couple of bandages. It was safer than carrying them around in an attaché case. "You could do what you did to the sleigh-port wall?"

"Probably not. Now we've done it once, they'll know to watch out for anyone trying it. Besides, there are going to be external ground-level patrols. That's not something you can hide. It said in the papers there was going to be a grand state reception tonight. That means increased security." However, a big reception would provide useful cover, if only she and Kai could get *in* there . . .

"Speaking of ground-level patrols, I think some police just came round the end of the road," Kai said urgently.

"Let me do the talking," Irene said, leading the way into the bridal shop.

She had a plan. And it was beginning to come together.

"Excuse me," she said to the assistant who'd come bustling up to greet her. "My fiancé and I have been invited unexpectedly to a party tonight, but I haven't a *thing* to wear. My friend Ludmilla said her friend Greta always recommended your shop. And I know you don't do evening wear yourself, but could you direct me to somewhere that does?"

Five minutes later they left, with directions to a tailor a few streets away who could provide suitable clothing at short notice—and, more importantly, the police had gone past without spotting them.

"Are we going to talk our way into the reception disguised as guests?" Kai asked.

"Not exactly," Irene said. "I can't forge an invitation without seeing one, and we won't *get* to see any. Plus, if I try to alter their perceptions, the guards on the door will realize what's going on before we get inside, given how badly that tactic's working here."

"Then what?"

"I've seen your uncle call a storm simply by losing his temper," Irene said thoughtfully. "Can you do that?"

Kai tilted his head, considering. "Yes," he said. "Well, a small one, at least. Why?"

This was shaping up nicely. It was a drastic plan, yes, and not the sort of operation that could be repeated, but it was manageable. "Good," Irene replied, and smiled. "We're going to come at this from a different direction."

INTERLUDE
Vale and Silver

"You may tell him that Peregrine Vale is here to see him."

The Liechtenstein Embassy was always difficult to penetrate. Of course Vale had entered it before on multiple occasions, but he had generally been in disguise. This time he was present as himself and had barely managed to penetrate the front lounge. The place scarcely did its duty as an embassy for its country. Would-be visitors to Liechtenstein could barely make it through the front door.

One might even think, he reflected sourly, *that they had something to hide.*

"And I must inform you that Lord Silver is not available." The words came out like honed icicles. Johnson was Lord Silver's manservant, factotum, and general dogsbody. He'd lasted for five years now, longer than any previous holders of that position. But, like all of them, he'd developed a fanatical devotion to Silver within a week of signing on.

Vale inspected the fellow carefully as he spoke. While Johnson's clothes were cut like an upper-class servant's, the fabric was unusually high-quality and the shoes shone with a blackness that suggested champagne had been used in the polish. His voice had been neutered of anything resembling an accent—Fae-induced, to make him the "perfect servant," or a deliberate choice on his part? Johnson didn't have a criminal record, but more suspiciously there wasn't *any* record of his past before taking this post. He quite obviously (well, obviously to Vale) wore a concealed pistol beneath his coat.

Vale raised an eyebrow. "Really. Unavailable. I take it that he is unaware of ongoing events, then?"

That made Johnson pause. He stared back at Vale as if he could somehow force information out of him just by glaring hard enough. Vale could track the calculations behind the man's eyes: if Vale was bluffing and managed to trick his way into a meeting with Silver, Silver would make Johnson regret it. However, if something important really was going on and Silver missed out on a chance to meddle, he would *really* make Johnson regret it.

"You'll have to wait," Johnson said abruptly. "His lordship hasn't yet risen."

"I suppose it *is* barely four o'clock in the afternoon," Vale agreed drily. "No doubt he needs his sleep."

Johnson's lips pursed to a thin line of suppressed rage. He neatly inclined his head, refusing Vale the courtesy of a bow, and stalked out of the lounge.

Vale took the opportunity to inspect the room. The carpet and wallpaper were cheap and plain, hardly worthy of an embassy: it was a room to repel callers and persuade them to leave as quickly as possible. The only decoration was the oil painting of the Queen over the fireplace, which was poorly executed and badly dusted. Two chairs, no desk or table. One of the chairs was a comfortable armchair. A thread of silver hair, caught in the antimacassar, betrayed its usual occupant. The other chair was a more rigid specimen, designed to make the sitter uncomfortable. The fireplace hadn't been cleaned out since last night, and had apparently been used to incinerate a number of handwritten documents. Vale itched to take a closer look.

The door behind him creaked open, and he turned to see that Silver had indeed arrived—being upright, if not particularly aware. The Fae sagged against the door-frame, hands fumbling as he tried to tie the sash of his black silk dressing-gown, still in his nightshirt and slippers underneath. His silver hair was tousled from sleep. And though he attempted to narrow his eyes menacingly at Vale, they were blurred and out of focus.

"My dear Vale," Silver yawned. "I was told you were here. I didn't think you'd come to rifle through my fireplace."

"I was curious about what you've been burning," Vale answered. "Far too many mysteries in London have their roots under your roof."

"Johnson, fetch me some coffee, for the love of God. It seems Mr. Vale is going to be witty, rather than actually getting to the point." Silver swayed across the room to his chair and collapsed into it with a sigh of relief. "You mentioned something about current events, I believe?"

"I suggest you drink your coffee first," Vale said. The traces of last night's dissipation were plain on Silver's face—and the marks on his neck suggested one or more partners. Although Vale might extract more truth from the Fae while he was still half-asleep, that approach risked missing some vital bit of information.

"You're unduly concerned for my welfare. I should probably be worried." Silver yawned again. "I hope you won't make me regret getting up at this ungodly hour. Amuse me, detective. Tell me something interesting while I'm waiting for my coffee."

"Very well." Vale nodded to the maid standing by the door. "The woman over there is one of your private assassins."

"I have private assassins?" Silver said, frowning. "I'm sure I'd remember if I had such a thing. Though they would be useful."

Vale walked over to the maid, who had frozen in position. "This woman is apparently low-ranking in the embassy staff, as demonstrated by her ill-fitting cuffs." He tapped her wrist. "And the concealed darns at her elbows. Higher-ranking servants would have better-fitting clothing and would receive it first-hand, rather than having it passed down. And yet you've brought her to a meeting with a guest, rather than keeping her in the kitchen or upstairs. Her tendency to peer and the hunch of her shoulders suggest far-sightedness." The words came tumbling out, each link in the chain of evidence clear and certain. For a moment Vale's malaise lifted and he was able to focus on his deductions. He leaned in more closely to examine her face. "The bridge of her nose shows that she *does* normally wear glasses or pince-nez. When she entered this room, her gait betrayed that she is carrying a gun secured to her left leg, under her skirts. What sort of agent carries a long-barrelled gun, has darns at her elbows from positioning herself to aim her weapon, and would have long-sightedness as an asset? A sniper."

"So why did she take the glasses off?" Silver asked. "Vanity?"

"I confess I am not yet certain." He stepped back from the woman. "But the fact that this young woman has simply stood here, without moving or objecting to my examination of her, or protesting at my conclusions, is in itself quite suggestive."

"I have my staff well-trained . . . Ah, thank you, Johnson." Silver took the proffered cup of coffee and drained it with a shuddering gasp. His eyes were more focused when he opened them again. "Can I offer you refreshments, detective?"

"Certainly not," Vale said. He wasn't eating or drinking anything from a Fae's hands. They were prone to claiming it as a personal debt and trying to exercise their glamours over the recipient. "As to your maid, the matter's easily settled. Have her expose her ankles in front of a policeman. While the law permits some concealed weapons, it tends to draw the line at unlicensed guns."

Silver ran his fingers through his hair. "Johnson, I'm going to need a pick-me-up. And take Mary with you, before our great detective can jump to any more conclusions."

Vale snorted and turned away, strolling across to the window. As in the rest of the room, smears of dust marred the window-sill and the corners of the panes. "I do not jump to conclusions. I deduce, based on evidence."

"Yes, yes, I know," Silver said soothingly, "and very elegant it all is. But you said something about current events. You make a very unlikely angel to wake me from my flowery bed, Vale. Do explain."

"Very well. Have you heard any recent news about Alberich?"

The name hung in the air between them. Silver slowly steepled his fingers, watching Vale over them. His expression was hard to define, but it certainly wasn't surprised. "I wonder why Miss Winters isn't the one here asking that question."

"Winters is a busy woman," Vale said. "I thought I'd save her the time and drop by myself."

"Where is she at the moment?" Silver's tone was casual, but his eyes were narrowed in thought.

"Oh, elsewhere." Vale waved a hand vaguely. "Out and about. She's remarkably bad at leaving a forwarding address, I find. Is there something you feel you should tell her?"

"Well, I might speculate," Silver said. "I don't have a horse in this race myself, but it does seem to be a free-for-all to all comers. From what I've heard, at least."

Vale dropped into the chair opposite Silver, ignoring its uncompromising design, and focused on the Fae. "I've yet to come across a situation where you *didn't* take one side or the other. It'd be unusual for you to be genuinely neutral."

"You know me so well." A smile of wry amusement flickered across Silver's face. "I should be flattered you spend so much time scrutinizing my habits."

"Don't be," Vale said, his tone as caustic as he could make it. "I hardly enjoy the experience. You are one of the most notorious roués in London."

"One tries," Silver agreed. He reached out to take a glass of hangover remedy, which had been swiftly fetched by the attentive Johnson, and downed the contents with a wince. "One tries very, very hard indeed."

"So how do you see the current situation?"

"Well, what *I* know is that Alberich's been looking for assistance." Silver set the glass down on its tray, abruptly serious. "And before we go any further, detective, I want your word that what I'm about to say will clear any debts—which I may or may not owe you from the Venice business."

"May or may not owe me?" Vale said. "That sounds remarkably uncertain."

"I dislike admitting that I owe anyone a debt. I'm sure you can understand that."

"And so you're weaselling around your obligations."

"If owing a favour ever becomes a matter of life or death for you, too, then perhaps you'll understand," Silver snapped. "For the moment, you will just have to accept that such things can cause a great deal of trouble. So if I tell you what I know about current goings-on, will you consider our debt cleared?"

Vale knew that the Fae were bound to keep their given word. It was one of the more useful pieces of information about them, together with the fact that cold iron weakened their powers. He wasn't going to object to these little advantages: the Fae were irksome, and their glamours were inconvenient, as well as borderline illegal. "You have my word that I will consider the debt cleared, in return for you telling me what you know about 'current events.' I can't speak for Winters."

"Yes, such a pity she's not here," Silver said. "I'd be enjoying this discussion a great deal more if I were having it with her." While he did not quite lick his lips at the thought, his expression suggested a barely restrained carnality.

Vale could only be grateful that Winters *was* elsewhere. Even if she was quite capable of handling Silver, she would certainly not enjoy being exposed to his insinuations. Her behaviour two nights ago, towards Vale himself, was something quite different from this... impropriety. "You overrate yourself," he said briefly.

"And I thought we were going to be civil."

"You are the instigator of a dozen conspiracies here in London. You're running at least one spy ring that I know of out of your embassy. And in the Venice affair you knowingly sent Winters into a situation that might have killed her, or worse, purely to save your own miserable hide. I would say that I'm being remarkably civil." Vale leaned back in his chair, as much as it allowed. "Would you like me to go on?"

Silver looked up at the ceiling as though demanding patience from some unseen deity. "Oh, by all means go on. I'm hardly unaware of your opinion of me. I rather appreciate it. But if you actually want information, then perhaps you should let *me* speak."

Vale was forced to concede Silver's point. "Continue," he said tersely, mentally saving a few choice insults for a later opportunity.

"Alberich has a number of allies among the Fae," Silver began. "To put it bluntly, he's done favours and he's owed favours. A couple of months back, shortly after the Venice business, I heard rumours that he'd been looking for . . . collaborators, shall we say. A step up from agents, but far from being equal partners. The sort of Fae who are weaker than I am, but still strong enough to walk between the worlds on their own."

"Indeed," Vale said neutrally. His mind flashed back to the woman Zayanna and her plausible but unsupported tale. "Do go on."

Silver spread his hands. "That's pretty much all I've heard."

"Was Lady Guantes one of these Fae?"

"I wouldn't know," Silver said. "The lady has vanished from sight—and good riddance. I'm sure we'll have trouble with her again, but it'll take her a while to build up her power base." He was remarkably casual about the subject, Vale felt. "But the epilogue to the Alberich business is that some of those who were taking an interest in his offers have since dropped out of circulation. Or so I'm told. Which leads me to wonder why you're here and asking after him."

"But what was he wanting collaborators *for*?" Vale asked. "Surely there must have been some talk about his ultimate plans? Offers of potential rewards? Even speculation would be useful."

"Yes. Yes, you have a very good point there." Silver frowned thoughtfully. "There has been significantly little detail available. My best guess would be that his offers were vague enough that only the desperate were attracted. Sadly, there are enough of those—people who've lost their patrons, who've come out as losers in intrigues, and so on. Poor fools."

"You're surprisingly sympathetic."

"Not sympathy so much as pity," Silver said. "Sympathy would imply I might even try to help them. Pity is much safer. It can be delivered from on high without getting involved. I pity them. I sympathize with you, detective."

"Me?" Vale said, surprised.

"I warned you not to go to Venice." Silver's gaze was very direct now, and there was an odd intimacy to his tone, a suggestion that the two of them shared some kind of connection. "I know what sort of effect a high-chaos world has on an unprepared human. I didn't want to lose you, detective. And I'm still not sure whether I will or not."

Vale drew back, affronted by Silver's manner. But if he was to be honest with himself, what truly repelled him was that he somehow *understood* what Silver meant. It was as if Silver were talking to another of his own kind—another Fae—and the thought of that revolted every atom of his being. The brief enjoyment he'd taken from sparring with Silver faded, and his earlier ennui threatened to sweep over him again. He'd been able to hold it off, convincing himself that his actions would somehow be worthwhile and make a difference. But now it all seemed so shallow once more, and ultimately irrelevant. He hungered for the sheer fire of their earlier conversation, the keen delight of matching wits with Silver. And at the same time he found that desire disturbing.

"So all you know is that Alberich had a plan in mind," he finally said, trying to get back to the subject at hand. Winters needed his help. That much *was* important. "And while some of your kind may be involved, they are currently incommunicado."

"Succinct and accurate," Silver said, and yawned again. "If anything else has happened within the last few days, then I haven't yet heard. But you must agree that you now know more than you did. My debt is paid."

Vale was forced to nod in agreement. "I accept this. I could only wish, for once, that you knew a little more than you do."

"But my dear Vale, we're hardly finished." Silver leaned forward, his face avid and hungry for information. "You haven't yet told me what *you* know, or why you came here to ask all these questions. Obviously Alberich's making his move. Is there nothing I can say or do that would persuade you to share information?"

It was an interesting quandary. Silver would pay dearly for news on Alberich's attack on the Library, but telling him might put Winters and Strongrock in danger. "I'm not sure what you have that I might want . . . ," Vale said.

"My turn to play detective!" Silver said gleefully. His lips curved in a smile, much as they usually did when appraising a woman. "The fact that you *won't* tell me is information in itself. I deduce that Alberich has caused, or is causing, some danger to the Library, which explains Miss Winters's absence. Naturally you don't want to tell me *that*. You'd be far too afraid of what I might do with the information."

"You'd be taking quite a gamble if you tried to sell that to other Fae as reliable intelligence," Vale said blandly. But he felt his stomach sink. Silver's speculation was far too accurate, and there was no convenient way to turn aside his guesses without an outright lie.

"You aren't denying it," Silver pointed out.

"Our deal doesn't involve *me* giving *you* any further details," Vale said. "By agreement *or* by denial."

Yet . . . was news of the attack really that significant? It seemed to be generally known that Alberich took an interest in the Library. And there was one thing Vale very much wanted to know, and Silver might just be able to tell him. "On the other hand . . ." he said thoughtfully.

Silver's eyes glittered. *"Yes?"*

"Have any Fae of moderate power entered London recently? The sort of person whom Alberich was recruiting? Or Lady Guantes herself?"

"Really, my dear Vale, how do you expect me to know something like that?" But the smirk on Silver's lips suggested that he had the answer.

"You are the spider in the local web," Vale said. "Any flies entering it would catch your attention. My question stands."

"Reasonable. And in return, *my* question would be: what precisely is going on?" Silver inspected his fingernails. "Do take your time. I'm sure we're not in a hurry."

"Alberich has begun an attack on the Library," Vale said. The tension in the room hummed like a violin string as Silver locked eyes with him. He shrugged. "As you guessed."

"That's all?" Silver demanded.

"It seems quite enough to me." And Vale knew that he had far less grasp of the wider implications than Winters or Strongrock. One more demonstration of his insignificance. One more indication of how little power any mere human had, in the greater chess game between warring powers. "Now I believe you were going to answer *my* question."

Silver scowled petulantly. "Very well. No. Nobody with that level of power, or stronger, has come to London within the last month. Or to be fair, if they have, then they've been lying remarkably low. And certainly Lady Guantes isn't here."

"I see," Vale said. Zayanna claimed to be a refugee from her previous patron and to have just arrived in London. But why should she have avoided Silver, to the extent that he didn't even know she was present? It was definitely suspicious. He was tempted to ask for Silver's assistance in locating her, but that would have placed too much information in Silver's hands.

Vale rose to his feet. "Thank you for your assistance. Incidentally, I'd recommend getting more discreet guards. If I could notice that sniper, then so could others."

Silver didn't bother standing up. "Most kind of you to suggest it," he said bitterly. "Unfortunately, due to *certain people* stealing my transport a few months back, when I was in Venice, I was forced to leave most of my entourage there."

The full implications of that statement trickled into Vale's mind, forming a horrific picture. "Your servants, your maids and body-guards—you *left* them there? In another world, with no way of returning here?"

"I could hardly bring them back myself," Silver complained. "I had enough trouble bringing Johnson and my luggage along. Don't look at me like that, Vale. I'm sure they're quite capable of making new lives for themselves. They're young, strong, healthy . . ."

"I'll see myself out," Vale said, and slammed the door behind him.

CHAPTER 15

It was ten o'clock, and the reception should be in full swing. Irene clung to Kai's scaled back, her oilcloth cloak floating out behind her in the rising wind, as he hovered high above the Winter Palace. The city beneath them was a grid of lit points against the darkness: they were too high for Irene to see any of the buildings clearly at this time of night, but she could make out the street lamps and the glaring illuminations around the larger buildings. The lights on sleighs in flight flickered in regular paths around the sleigh-port. There weren't any clouds to block her view. Yet.

Kai was concentrating as he glided through the air, which barred conversation on his part and allowed Irene to run through her mental check-list for the operation.

Evening clothes for both of them: obtained. Even if they were ready-made, rather than personally tailored. (Kai had been rather upset that he couldn't get a military uniform, since that was apparently the thing for young men to wear to balls. But Irene had pointed out everything that might go wrong, such as Kai not knowing the details of his supposed regiment, and he had reluctantly given in.) Map of Winter Palace and theorized location of book: memorized. And all papers had been destroyed. It was now more dangerous than useful to be carrying the Library documents around. Transformation of Kai into dragon, to rouse storm and land on roof: successfully achieved.

The next step was the storm itself. There would of course be sentries on the roof, but very few would be looking *up* while being hammered by wind and rain. This explained Irene's heavy hooded oilcloth cape, which would hopefully keep her mostly dry. Enough to pass as a guest when inside, anyway. If she and Kai were subjected to serious scrutiny, then they were already deep in trouble.

"I hold the winds and am ready to release them," Kai said. His words echoed in the thin air, and Irene tightened her grip on his scales. "Are you prepared?"

"Do it," Irene said.

The storm gathered as she watched, clouds spinning together into a great dark whorl that hid the city below. Gusts of wind tugged at her, and she plastered herself even closer to the dragon's back, drawing her hood around her face. He swung through the air in a tightening spiral, his wings glittering against the darkness on either side of her. Deep in the clouds lightning flashed, and thunder followed without a moment's pause.

Kai had said this wouldn't tire him, but she'd insisted that he get a few hours' sleep earlier. He'd watched through the night while she slept on the sleigh, and she didn't know how much sleep dragons needed, but she knew they needed *some*. They'd taken a room in a cheap hotel, where the woman at the desk had leered at them, jumping to obvious conclusions. The break had kept them off the street, too, enabling them to avoid the increasing numbers of police. Kai had slept like the dead, his chest barely moving. Irene sat in the rickety chair and memorized their maps and plans, and wondered from time to time: *What would I do without you? It's been less than a year, and already I rely on you to be there when I need you, I fall asleep on your shoulder . . .*

Imminent disaster first, she reminded herself. Personal issues later.

"The storm's as heavy as I can make it without risking a gale," Kai rumbled. "I'm taking us down."

He dropped like a hawk through the clouds, accelerating as if the laws of gravity and air resistance were optional rather than obligatory. Maybe they were, to him. The bitter chill cut into Irene's hands, her elegant lace gloves offering no protection, and the wind moulded her cape against her body. Suddenly there was rain all around them, lashing against them, streaming across Kai's body in thick rivulets and outlining his scales. He kept on descending through it, as gracefully and uncaringly as if navigating a summer breeze. Irene lowered her head and clung on for dear life.

They broke through the cloud and continued falling, like a lift in a high-speed crash. Irene wished she could think of less dramatic similes, but then it became difficult to think at all. The rain slammed down on her and Kai like a waterfall, oozing under her cape and slashing at her face, making it impossible to see clearly.

Kai's wings spread with a thud of air like a miniature thunder-clap, and their descent abruptly slowed. It was probably a contradiction of the natural laws of inertia and force equals mass times acceleration, or whatever the relevant equations were. But if the universe wasn't paying attention, Irene wasn't going to raise the issue. He settled gently on a level stretch of roof, his claws grating on the slate surface. If there were guards up here, then they were all sensibly out of the rain and not watching the roof. Good. First objective achieved.

Irene slid from Kai's back and peered through the pouring rain, getting her bearings. Over to her right she could see the onion-dome of the palace church. That must mean that the nearer cross-piece building, between the Winter Palace and the Hermitage proper, was St. George's Hall. The imperial throne was there—though hopefully they wouldn't be running into Her Imperial Majesty tonight. Further round to her left was the Great Hall, scene of the night's reception, its windows blazing with light despite the enshrouding rain. So she and Kai should be directly above some of the unoccupied royal apartments. Well, technically they were directly above the servants' attics, which were directly above said royal apartments, but servants' attics never made it onto the official maps.

Next to her, Kai shuddered, and the air rippled around him. And then he was standing next to her, also shrouded in an oilcloth cape. "There's a door and stairs over there," he said, pointing to a shadow on one of the roof's exterior crenellations. "Let's get out of the rain."

It was close enough, and Irene nodded. She had to hold his arm to make her way across the wet slate, even barefoot as she was. The door was locked, but it opened to the Language, and they both breathed a sigh of relief when they were inside and out of the storm.

As expected, these were the servants' attics, and therefore utilitarian rather than Models of Great Architecture. Irene pulled her bag from under her coat and carried out emergency repairs to her hair. She dried her feet with the towel she'd been carrying, before pulling on stockings and dancing slippers. Then they bundled capes and towel into a convenient cupboard and headed down the nearest flight of stairs, hopefully looking like lost reception guests. They didn't pass any servants on the way, though Irene heard the odd soft-shoed scuffle in the background.

When they reached the second floor, the décor abruptly changed to luxurious, but not overdone. The floors and walls of the rooms were inlaid marble, the corridors were also of marble, and the furniture featured gilt, carving, and velvet cushions. The paintings on the walls had probably been commissioned or collected from famous artists. (Visual arts had never been Irene's best subject. She could barely tell a Rembrandt from a Raphael without a guide-book.)

Kai looked around with clear approval. "Not bad," he said. "Quite tolerable. Which part are we heading for now?" He paused to straighten his cravat in one of the mirrors.

Irene shoved a comb back into a wind-tossed section of her hair and looked glumly at her elegant though slightly damp reflection. It was a *nice* dress, a pretty light green silk-and-tulle affair with puffed sleeves and full skirts (damp around the edges), which left her shoulders and neck bare. She'd accessorized it with arm-length lace gloves and silk slippers and had put up her hair with combs and pins, but despite all that, next to Kai she looked like . . . well, like someone who'd dressed up for the occasion. Kai, in his frock-coat, cravat, waistcoat, and well-cut trousers, looked like someone who *should* be at an imperial reception. Even hosting the reception. On him, the clothing looked natural.

She decided it wasn't worth unpicking that little knot of resentment, and she thrust it aside. "Along here and down the staircase at the far end," she instructed. "Then down two floors. And if we can avoid anyone noticing, so much the better." The storm was still crashing down outside, and when she passed the windows she could hear the wind like ripping fabric and the rain rattling against the glass.

They made it to the ground floor without being stopped. As they descended, the architecture became more and more lush, heading towards sheer extravagance, but retaining just enough control to avoid gaudiness. Rich marble sheathed everything, as pale and smooth as cream. Gilt ornamentation gleamed as if it had only been polished within the last hour. The sounds of music drifted very faintly through the corridors.

A servant approached, sleek in his black uniform. "I beg your pardon, sir, madam," he said, effortlessly identifying the more aristocratic of the two of them and addressing him first. "The reception is taking place in the Great Hall. If you require directions . . ."

Kai looked down his nose at the man. "You may go about your business," he said. "The lady and I know our way."

With a bow, the servant retreated. But Irene knew he'd only be the first in a line of helpful minions trying to herd them towards the other guests. She took Kai's arm and led him round a corner, into a slightly less impressive side corridor and through an only moderately impressive doorway, into an unimpressive plain stone staircase leading down.

Kai sniffed. "I can smell food," he murmured.

"The kitchens are down here, in the basements," Irene replied. It was a narrow staircase, and she had to pull in her skirts so that they wouldn't brush the walls. "They should be over, um"—she consulted her mental map—"west and north-west-ish. Thataway. We need to go north-east from here, heading under the church."

As they hurried down the dark corridor, Irene pondered the likelihood of their getting stopped by guards. She was astonished they'd come as far as they had. True, the Winter Palace must be afflicted by the usual security blind spot, as in *the outer walls are well-guarded, so anyone inside must belong there.* But even so, given the rumours of rebellion and secession, and the government crack-downs, shouldn't there be a *bit* more security inside the palace? The farther they went, the more nervous she became. She started to worry that they were actually being lured into some vast trap, and were being drawn well inside so that they'd have no chance of escape . . .

"Stop right there!" came an order.

It was almost a relief. Irene obediently stayed where she was, one hand on Kai's sleeve. Only three guards defended the archive's doorway, their ultimate goal—good heavens, what on earth were they thinking? Though to be fair, the door behind them did look heavily locked and barred.

"Approach and identify yourself!" came the next order.

Perfect. Irene walked forward. Even better, she could see which of the guards was clearly in command. She slipped a hand into her bodice, then withdrew it and showed it to the lead guard, as though she'd just pulled something out that only he should see. **"You perceive that this is full identification, and that we are authorized to view the contents of this archive,"** she said.

The guard snapped into a terrified salute, his back straight with the rigidity of panic. The other two guards followed suit a moment later. "Yes, ma'am," he said quickly. "Absolutely, ma'am!"

"You may open the door and assist me," Irene said briskly, wondering exactly who he thought she was. *Probably Oprichniki. Only secret police get that sort of reaction.* "Your men will remain outside. There's no need for them to hear this."

He nodded and pulled a key from his belt, which he quickly turned in the lock. There was a small noise, almost a sigh, from the door as he pulled it open. Irene suspected there had been some sort of magic alarm on it. Now, just so long as the guard stayed confused until they were inside . . .

They were into the next room, and Kai had closed the door behind them, before the guard shook his head and frowned. But Kai had been expecting that and had him in a choke hold before he could raise the alarm. Irene left him to throttle the fellow into unconsciousness—there was no need to kill him, after all—and looked around. They were in a small anteroom, with another heavily barred door on the far side. All right, so the security wasn't that laughable. There were rows of ledgers in bookshelves to one side, presumably with lists of items held in the repository beyond. And there was a little desk, with a woman in heavy robes trying to hide under it.

Irene walked over and leaned on the desk. "That's not actually working, you know," she said gently.

The woman pulled herself upright, flinching back against the wall. "I won't help you. I will defend this place with my *life!*"

Irene nodded. "That's quite understandable," she agreed. **"But you now perceive that I am someone who has a right to be here, and a right to be given the location of a particular item."** Her head was starting to ache.

"Oh." The woman stayed pressed against the wall. But she looked a little calmer now, as if Irene was a known and understandable threat, rather than something completely unpredictable. "Ah, what item would Your Excellency wish to see?"

"A book," Irene said, daring to hope. "It's called *The Manuscript Found in Saragossa*, and it's by Jan Potocki. Where is it?"

The woman edged from behind her desk, staying on the opposite side from Irene, and hurried over to the ledgers. She pulled one out and leafed through it, muttering to herself. Her heavy embroidered sleeves swung as she turned the pages. She finally came to a stop and rested her finger on an entry. "Here it is— Wait, who did you say you were again?"

Kai rapped her on the back of her neck and caught her before she could hit the ground, while Irene bent to look at the ledger. It was indeed an entry for the book they wanted, but as Irene read it she blinked in shock. "I don't *believe* it," she said out loud. "It was released to the empress herself two days ago, for *personal bedtime reading!*"

Kai propped the woman up against her desk. "Please tell me you're joking," he said.

"I wish I were." Irene weighed *steal book from palace's underground sanctuary* against *steal book from imperial bedroom*. An imperial bedroom was probably even *more* heavily guarded than an underground sanctuary. Marvellous. "Well, we can't just stand around here," she said with a sigh. "Let's go and try again."

"How do you know it was for bedtime reading?" Kai asked.

"The lady in question signed it out herself. Apparently she has a sense of humour." Not that that was likely to save Kai's or Irene's neck if they were caught mid-theft. "I almost regret accepting the mission now."

"Why?"

"Because I'm quite happy to steal a book from storage, where nobody's ever going to read it," Irene explained. "But I do feel a bit guilty about snatching it mid-read from someone's bedside table."

The guards on the door were only too happy to wave them past, after being told that their commanding officer was checking the security inside. Irene led the way back in the direction from which they'd come. "Back up the stairs," she murmured, "up to the first floor; then we take a run at the bedroom."

"That's not a very detailed plan." But Kai wasn't complaining, simply resigned.

"There have been times when I had detailed plans," Irene said wistfully. "I look back at them and wonder why I never realized how lucky I was."

They'd reached the ground floor and were heading for the stairway they'd descended earlier, when the same servant as before caught them. This time he had several other guests in his wake and was clearly chivvying them along. "Sir!" he expostulated in Kai's direction. "Her

Imperial Majesty is about to give her address. You should be in the Great Hall."

Kai glanced at Irene, and she read the same thought in his eyes. Better to go along and blend in with the crowd than make a scene. They could edge out later and get back to the search. And it really would be suspicious to be caught elsewhere in the Winter Palace while the empress was giving a speech. "Thank you," he said to the man. "I was just heading in that direction. I take it this is the quickest way?"

The servant refrained from rolling his eyes at the boundless idiocy of the aristocracy and quickly led Irene, Kai, and the rest of his flock down a succession of corridors, each more luxurious than the last. They accumulated more bystanders on the way, and Irene was grateful that she and Kai could hide in the middle of the growing crowd.

The Great Hall itself was vast: the floor consisted of inlaid marble mosaics, but the walls and ceiling were white and gold, as perfect as snow and sunlight. Huge blazing chandeliers hung from above, the candlelight glaring off the gilt so brightly that they were a challenge to behold. At the far end of the chamber, more than fifty yards away, a throne on a raised dais was canopied and draped in scarlet. The silver dress of its occupant seemed to gleam with its own light.

Between them and her, the crowd shifted and jostled for position. Young maidens in their first season at court were in plain white, with ostrich feathers and flowers pinned into their hair, and huge masses of silk skirts. Older women like Irene, or married ones, wore pastels or deeper shades—and jewellery rather than flowers. Most of the men present were in military uniform, often with a dress-sword hanging at one hip and a short staff at the other. A few were either in well-cut civilian clothing, like Kai, or in robes that were somewhere between academic and ecclesiastical. Some older women wore those robes too, and Irene noticed that they generally stood apart from others of their gender. Around the edges scurried servants in the palace livery, but nobody was looking at them: all attention was on Her Imperial Majesty.

As the last group was shooed into the Great Hall, the empress rose to her feet. Everyone went down on one knee, from the advisers surrounding her dais to the guards by the entrance. And it wasn't just overdone obeisance or the effect of magic. The Undying Empress, to give her the full title, had genuine presence and charisma. The loyalty that the crowd offered her wasn't feigned. Irene had been in the presence of dragon kings and Fae lords, and while she wouldn't rank this Catherine the Great's authority on quite that level, she was still extremely impressive.

Fortunately the empress wasn't in the mood for a long speech. After a few firmly delivered statements about the unity of her empire, the loyalty of her subjects, and her maternal love for said subjects, she resumed her seat. Everyone promptly rose to their feet, conversation broke out like wildfire, and the small orchestra in a corner of the room started playing.

"Irene . . . ," Kai said hopefully.

The only way out of the hall was the way they'd come in. Well, there was another exit behind the empress, but that wasn't an option. And it would be too obvious if they tried to get away immediately. "We just circulate," Irene said firmly. "I'm not dancing unless we have to."

Kai sighed and offered her his arm as they began to drift round the edge of the hall, catching snippets of conversation. While this included topics normal for any state occasion—upcoming wars, family history, possible betrothals, big-game hunting in Mongolia—there was a nervous edge to the talk. People weren't precisely paranoid, but every so often spontaneous praise for the Undying Empress and her glorious empire would get thrown into the talk, as though it would grease the rest of the conversation and slip it past any listeners.

There was a noticeable gap in the crowd ahead of them. At the centre of it stood a man in formal clothing like Kai's, having a casual conversation with some of the robed men and women. At least, it looked casual on his part. From *their* attitudes and posture, one might think it was a matter of life and death.

"What do you think?" Kai murmured. "High authority, definitely, but which area?"

"Secret police," Irene answered. "Think nice innocent thoughts—"

She broke off as the man turned to sweep his gaze across the ballroom. He was nobody she'd ever met before. His flaxen-pale hair was cropped short and he was clean-shaven. And though he was middle-aged, he showed no signs of belly or jowls. His eyes were a clear grey, as cold as marble, and they looked out over the crowd with a glitter of absolute hunger: for power, for answers, for domination. But there was something about those eyes that she recognized, and she added it to the man's posture, the way he tilted his head, the way he looked at her . . .

"Alberich," she breathed, her throat dry with terror.

CHAPTER 16

He had stolen a new body, looked quite at home here, and knew exactly who they were. Surely this was positive, Irene tried to convince herself as she tried not to panic. It was an unparalleled opportunity to get information—maybe even to end the whole threat, here and now. She should think optimistically.

But cold dread ran the opposite way in her veins and spread ice round her heart. This was also an unparalleled opportunity to get killed, or worse. Alberich was as much above her as she was above the thugs they'd dodged in Poland, when they'd first entered this world. He was hundreds of years old. He'd betrayed the Library and learnt the Fae's darkest secrets. He skinned Librarians for fun and profit and then wore their skins as disguises. He wasn't careless. And if Irene had recognized him, then the odds were ten to one that he was prepared for that.

"Irene," Kai murmured, reminding her of his presence. His

muscles were tense under her arm. "Shall I take him down? If I reached him before he could react . . ."

"Too obvious," Irene said regretfully. "He knows you're a dragon, Kai. He's not stupid."

"Oh yes, you did say he sold information about me to the Fae—and caused my kidnapping." Kai's eyes were like dark ice. "But he might be overconfident. Shall I test that?"

Irene weighed the possibilities. An open assault on Alberich, against all his defences and in the middle of a hall full of soldiers and wizards, might well be suicidal. And she didn't *want* to get herself killed. On the other hand, if it disposed of him and ended his threat to the Library, then it might be worth it. She'd refused Bradamant's suggestion that they act as bait, because they didn't have a good way to reach Alberich. Well, here he was, right in front of her. What was she going to do now?

She reached out and caught the arm of an older woman, a gaudy battleship in violet satin and diamonds. "Excuse me, madam," she said hastily, before the other woman could shake her off, and nodded towards Alberich. "Who is that gentleman over there?"

The woman went so pale that the rouge stood out on her cheeks in two scarlet spots. "You must mean Count Nicolai Ilyich," she said, trying and failing to sound casual. "I thought *everyone* knew who he was."

"We've just arrived from Paris. I don't know anyone. Except the empress, of course." Irene forced a laugh. "Is he someone important?"

"He's the head of the Oprichniki, and if you have any sense you'll stay well out of his way." The woman shook Irene's hand off her arm and sailed away, as fast as was commensurate with dignity.

Alberich was still watching, though he didn't try to approach. A growing space was forming around Irene and Kai as well, probably because people could follow Alberich's gaze and didn't care to be associated with its target.

Irene took a deep breath. "Kai, I'm about to do something reckless," she said, "and I need you to be standing by as backup."

"No," Kai said flatly. "That is not going to happen. I will not let you do this."

"I'm not particularly wild about it either." That was the understatement of the decade. She'd rather walk up a volcano that was emitting little pre-eruption burps. "But he can use the Language as well as I can, if not better. And you know what *I* can do . . ."

Kai scowled, not even trying to hide his anger. "So you want me to stay out of range of his voice."

"I may need you to rescue me." She squeezed his arm. "I don't trust just *anyone* to rescue me, you know."

"Besides, he can't do anything dramatic to you without exposing himself, in a public place such as this," Kai said, coming to the same conclusion as Irene.

"Yes, that's rather what I'm hoping," she agreed. "And if you hear him yelling something like *Guard, arrest these rebel spies!*—then that's the cue to run."

Before Kai could delay her any further, she turned and walked towards Alberich.

Her curtsey was the polite dip and ruffle of skirts appropriate for a young woman when approaching a man of superior rank. There was certainly no genuine respect behind it. Alberich knew that, and Irene knew that he knew it. But she couldn't risk being noticed as unusual. Yet.

"As polite as ever," Alberich said. His voice had a different timbre from their last encounter, but of course he'd been wearing someone else's skin that time. Some other victim who'd died so that he could disguise himself and use their identity. "I was afraid that you'd try and lose yourself in the crowd, Ray."

Irene smiled sweetly, not wanting him to see how much his use of her birth-name annoyed her. "But then I might have lost sight of you, Alberich. You're far too dangerous for that."

"And you didn't even bring me a glass of champagne."

"Oh, come now. You know I'd poison it."

"You must have so many questions." His thin-lipped smile cut across his face like a scar. "Why don't you ask some of them?"

"Let's be frank, shall we?" There was no way of knowing whether or not he'd tell the truth. He might even be playing for time, simply keeping her busy until a trap closed on her. But possibly—just possibly—he was vain enough to boast, or careless enough to give something away. "Why are you here?"

"To speak to you, of course." He spread his hands in mock confession. "All this way, just to talk to one little Librarian. I hope you aren't going to waste my time."

Irene ignored the threat. She was ignoring so many other possible dangers, so it was comparatively easy to add one more to the pile of Deliberately Burying Head in Sand and Hoping They'll Go Away. "What I don't understand, to be entirely honest—"

"Oh, please be honest," Alberich cut in.

Irene smiled again, because it was that or glare back at him. Her fear hadn't disappeared; it was a constant whisper at the back of her mind. But her anger let her keep her composure and snipe back at him, looking for an opening. It was the best argument she'd come across yet for the deliberate cultivation of certain deadly sins. "I'm not sure how you knew to be here," she finished.

Alberich looked pleased. "Now, that *is* an intelligent question.

You're trying to find out how much I know, before deciding on a course of action."

"Well, wouldn't anyone?"

He shook his head sadly. "You'd be painfully surprised. But in return for my answer"—he glanced towards the couples currently occupying the central area, moving in pairs through the steps of a polonaise—"I believe I'd like a dance."

Irene was momentarily taken aback. "Why?" she demanded.

"Mostly because it'll put you off-balance and annoy your associate," Alberich replied. "You're only irritated because you didn't think of suggesting it first."

Irene considered her position. Being out on the dance floor didn't seem much more dangerous than standing here talking. She was already well into the danger-zone. She might as well play along and see where it went. "Very well," she agreed. "So, how did you know to be here?"

"Once I found out which world you were coming to—dear me, you weren't expecting that bit, were you? I assure you it's quite true." Alberich's eyes were penetrating again, cataloguing her reactions. "In any case, once I knew you were heading here, I came here myself and took a position of authority. The head of the Oprichniki hears all the news, after all. When I received reports of the disturbance at the sleigh-port, I knew you were in St. Petersburg. And when that storm blew up so suddenly over the Winter Palace tonight, well . . ."

Irene seethed. In retrospect, she'd left an obvious trail for anyone who knew the signs to follow. Her only excuse was that she hadn't expected anyone here to be looking for her. But like all excuses, when actually tested, it sounded rather hollow. Her professional pride was stung. "I'm extremely embarrassed," she said through gritted teeth. "I had no idea—"

"Well, of course not," Alberich said. "Now, as we agreed, a dance. They're playing a waltz. You can waltz, I hope?" He offered her his hand.

"Of course," Irene said, taking his hand. Her skin crawled as he touched her, even through the lace of her glove. Farther out in the crowd she could see Kai and the leashed tension in his body. She caught his eye and shook her head slightly. *Don't do anything. Yet.* "But how did you find out I was coming *here*?"

"My dear Ray, you're far too trusting." He led her out onto the floor, and she could feel the stares of the assembled dignitaries.

"Will I regret agreeing to this dance?" Fear was spreading again, like ice in her heart and throat, but she met his gaze as she turned to face him.

Alberich paused just long enough for the fear to blossom into terror; then he smiled at her again. "Did you think I meant you're too trusting of *me*? Well, yes, but not right here and now. I need answers, and it's difficult to get those when the other person can't trust you enough to make a deal. Torture really isn't as effective as they say."

"I'm sure you'd know," Irene said, keeping her tone as light as she could. All around the floor, partners were smiling at each other as the musicians picked up the pace of the waltz. She set her lips in a deliberately upward curl, gazing into Alberich's eyes as he settled his other hand on her waist. "But then *who* shouldn't I trust—what did you mean?"

"I mean that I was told you were being sent to World B-1165." He was ready for the stutter in her gait and smoothly guided her into the first steps of the dance. "Surely you're not so naive as to think that all Librarians are as faithful to their cause as you are?"

Irene kept the smile pinned on her face, but her thoughts went round in little circles. *He's suggesting someone in the Library betrayed me. But is he telling the truth or dissembling to stop me from suspecting someone else? Or is it a double-bluff because he* knows *I'll assume he's lying* . . . "Nobody's perfect," she said eventually. "Not even me."

"So you've been thinking about what I said." They turned together in the smooth pivots of the waltz.

"Well, I'm not *stupid.*" Unless one counted getting into this entire situation as total stupidity, in which case Irene had already lost that argument—and probably her life, too. "But I want to know more about your threat to the Library before I make any irreparable decisions."

"That's easy enough." They moved in a bubble of space amid the other dancers. Nobody wanted to get too close to the head of the Oprichniki. "Unless it submits to me, the Library will be destroyed. And unless you give me the information I want . . ."

"I will be destroyed too?" Irene suggested.

"You're taking this very well."

"I've had practice," Irene said regretfully. "Death threats seem to crop up twice a week these days. I'm working on getting past the sheer terror and on to the bargaining stage."

"I knew there was a reason I liked you," Alberich said approvingly. They negotiated a corner turn stylishly, and Irene took the opportunity to glance across the crowd and spot Kai. He was still there. In retrospect, perhaps she should have told him to steal the book while Alberich was occupied. But she wasn't sure he'd have agreed to leave her there with Alberich.

"When we spoke before—well, when you sent me those threatening messages—you said you wanted to know what 'the book' said. You meant the volume of Grimm tales, I assume?" He'd tried to kill her over it, after all. If there was yet another book involved, that introduced a whole new level of complexity.

"Correct. There was an anomalous story in that edition." Alberich must have caught the flicker in her eyes as she considered claiming ignorance. "Come now, Ray, we both know you read it. Anyone would have done so under the circumstances. Someone like yourself certainly would."

"Someone like myself?" Irene asked, playing for time.

"Someone who's good at being a Librarian. Notice that I don't say 'a good Librarian.'" They moved together in the waltz, their steps balanced and precise. "Someone who does the job well—not just someone who's devoted to the Library's philosophy. That's why I want to recruit you."

Irene's first impulse was a rather stupid pride. After all, how many people were complimented by the Library's arch-traitor, who admired them enough to want to recruit them in person? The second impulse was sheer revulsion. *If he thinks I'd work for him, after everything he's done, then what* does *he think of me?* But the third impulse, the one that kept her feet moving and her face smiling, was simple, cold calculation. *How can I use this?*

"I can't trust you," she said. He'd expect her to be suspicious. "Perhaps I should just run for it."

"The Palace is guarded." He swept her round another turn, his hand warm on the small of her back, gloved in a dead man's skin. "I don't mean just by casual guards, either. I mean by alert guards, who have been warned about possible revolutionaries—guards ready to shoot to kill and have the necromancers ask questions later. There are even guards on the roof now. The Language can't outrun a speeding bullet."

Was he telling the truth? She wasn't sure. But was it possible? Yes, very possible. "And if I answer your questions and tell you what you want to know?"

"Then you'll be kept under arrest here till the Library has fallen. But you'll live."

"And Kai?"

"He can have the cell next to you," Alberich said generously.

"You're very certain that the Library will fall."

"If I had the least doubt, I wouldn't be stopping to have this conversation with you here and now."

Irene would have liked to think Alberich was lying about that, too. But nothing in his voice suggested falsehood or even uncertainty. He meant every word of it. "How are you doing it?" she asked.

Alberich shook his head. "You find out if you join me."

Well, she hadn't really expected that one to work. And now she really was beginning to panic, in a carefully controlled way. He wasn't even going to gloat and conveniently provide information. Her whole attempted interrogation was a total failure. She hadn't learnt anything, except how he'd managed to trace her here.

Perhaps it was time to go for the nuclear option.

"Don't," Alberich said. His smile had gone, and now his expression was all cold business.

"Don't what?" Irene said innocently. Damn, if he'd guessed what she was thinking . . .

"You're considering using the Language to strip my skin from me and expose me in public." His hand tightened on hers. "You already did that to me once before, Ray. I don't make the same mistake twice. I've taken precautions."

He might be telling the truth. Or he might be bluffing. This situation was impossible. But if he was bluffing and he was vulnerable in that way, then surely he wouldn't have brought it up in the first place. Irene cursed silently. That would have worked so well. Alberich distracted, everyone turning on him, she and Kai escaping in the confusion. "I want a guarantee of safety for my parents," she said.

"Why should I care about your parents?" Alberich sounded like one of her mentors from the Library now. "Ray, you're good at think-ing outside the lines, but your problem is that you think too *small*. Your parents haven't inconvenienced me. I don't hold a grudge against them. I'm not the sort of sadist who'd hunt down your fam-ily to spite you. When you're in my service, you can keep them as safe as you like."

He doesn't know. The thought detonated at the back of her head in a sunburst of illumination. *He doesn't know my parents are Librar-ians, or he wouldn't be so quick to agree. He thinks they're just ordinary humans. And everyone in the Library who knows me, knows that my parents are Librarians. Which almost certainly means that whoever told him to find me here* isn't *a Librarian.*

Her sudden surge of relief must have shown in her face, for Alberich nodded paternally. "There, you see? You need to learn to trust me, Ray. I'm not your enemy here."

The circle of waltzers turned on its invisible hub, spinning Alberich and Irene towards the end of the room where the empress sat among her advisers, watching the reception with a gracious smile.

"You're very good at making me forget what you are," Irene said. That was true. She could dance with him like this, trading insults and questions, and it was almost . . . entertaining. Challenging. Excit-ing. Perhaps it was the feeling of security at being in such a public place, with so many other people present. But it was a false security, as threadbare as her fake identity here, and she was still entirely vul-nerable.

"Redefining oneself is something we all have to do." Alberich's tone was oddly serious, as if this were more important than the secu-rity of the Library itself, or her own life. "You have to ask: Am I just a Librarian? Is this all I am, all that I ever will be? Or can I actually transform myself into something *more*?"

"This sounds like an argument for transhumanism," Irene said. "Evolution to the next stage."

"Is that what they're calling it now? It's hardly a new idea. The only problem is that it's difficult to imagine something entirely new. We use the words and definitions of the past to shape our ideas. Something that is genuinely the next evolutionary step is unlikely to resemble anything we *can* imagine. Even the best books on the subject are limited."

She'd never thought of Alberich as a science fiction reader before. "Maybe you're right about the limitations of imagination—and not just for humans. I spoke with an elder Fae a few months back. She was encouraging the younger ones to leave humanity behind, to become defined by stories instead. She'd never consider anything outside that sphere."

"That's where both the Fae and the dragons fail." Alberich's eyes had that hungry look again, though it wasn't directed at Irene. It was directed at the whole *world*. "They are defined either by narrative or by reality. They don't go beyond that. The only person who can ever set bounds on you should be yourself."

It all sounded perfectly reasonable, but from Irene's perspective, the fact that Alberich was a murderer and a traitor suggested there were flaws in his philosophy. "But you're allied with the Fae . . . ," she said.

"I *use* the Fae. Both sides in this struggle are ultimately doomed to failure. The dragons, the Fae—both of them incapable of coming to any agreement, blinkered by their own limitations. They're sterile, Ray. Moribund. What's the point of preserving a system where nobody wins? The most you can achieve is that everyone continues this stalemate for eternity."

"And neither side actually cares about the humans in the middle . . ."

Irene could see where this argument was going. She'd had it demonstrated to her only a few months ago, when Kai was kidnapped. Both sides had been on the verge of a war, and neither had seemed particularly interested in the worlds in the middle. The closest they'd come had been a suggestion that the humans would ultimately be better off under their control.

Alberich nodded. "You see my point. Humanity is the future. And the Library should be leaders in that future, rather than just collecting books. We should be uniting worlds, not keeping secrets from them. Building alliances. Recruiting the best and the brightest. Using the Language to change things for the better. How are you actually *helping* anyone by supporting the current status quo?"

She could have said *I'm stopping things from getting worse*, but she was sure he'd have a counter for that as well. This was like being in an argument with an older Librarian, where she knew she was going to lose and the only question was how . . .

Common sense kicked in. Why, precisely, was she trying to argue a point of logic with the person who was trying to destroy the Library? Did she actually think she was going to convince Alberich to change his mind? This wasn't about winning an argument. It was about getting information out of him. Pride was not the issue. Stopping him was.

Of course, simply getting away from him right now would be game, set, and match to her. "I do see," she answered, her voice barely audible above the murmuring of the reception crowd and the music. Let him think that she was considering. Let him think anything, as long as she had a moment to act. Because she'd thought of something to slow him down, just a little.

She broke away from him mid-twirl, wrenching herself out of his hands—and was that a faint stickiness that she felt against her skin, where he'd touched her? No, she wasn't going to even consider that. She'd picked her location: they were barely ten yards from the empress.

Her Imperial, Undying Majesty looked down at Irene from her chair on the dais, raising an eyebrow at this public display of bad manners. The advisers around her, in their sumptuous robes and their heavily medal-bedecked military uniforms, were looking at her too. Even the two white tigers that lay at the chair's feet raised their heads to regard Irene with great yellow eyes.

"Your Imperial Majesty," Irene cried out, "that man is an impostor!" She dodged a grab from Alberich to stumble a few paces towards the dais. The music had come to a jangling halt, and the room was full of shocked whispers. Hands fell to the hilts of dress-swords.

This had better work.

Irene focused on the Language. **"Your Imperial Majesty must perceive that I speak the truth!"**

The exquisite marble floor came up and hit her in the face.

CHAPTER 17

The floor was such a pretty colour. The bit directly in front of Irene's face was golden marble, though it was spattered with the blood that seemed to be dripping from her nose. She tried to work out exactly how that had happened, but her brain wasn't cooperating, and all the screaming and shouting made it hard to think.

Fire blazed somewhere above her, reflected in the polished floor before her in a burst of rainbows. A woman shouted something, her voice a whip of command, and a choir of voices answered. And the fire lashed out again.

Then another voice spoke from behind her, in a tone that roused her to full consciousness like a cold shower in the morning. It wasn't the voice of the man she'd been speaking with, the voice of the man whose skin he'd stolen. It was the voice of the *real* Alberich, the Librarian who had willingly contaminated himself with chaos and become something other than human. It sounded like buzzing wasps, like water on molten metal.

The air boomed, and a gust of freezing wind washed over her and outwards. Then it switched to a hissing suction in the opposite direction that dragged at her clothing. Chaotic power throbbed against her bare skin, aggressive and growing.

Irene was almost certain she wouldn't like the answer, but she had to know what was going on behind her. She rolled onto her side, her head still swimming, and turned to look.

There was a hole in the air where Alberich had been standing. It hung in empty space like an obsidian mirror twice a man's height, blackness seething around its edges and struggling to expand. In its depths, Irene thought she could see a man's figure, half-defined and obscured by the shadows. It was diminishing every second, as though it was somehow retreating from her without actually moving. It raised an arm in a beckoning gesture, and for one stupid moment she thought, *Of course, this is how I catch Alberich—all I have to do is get up and walk forward . . .*

Darkness boiled out of the hole in the air, reaching out in tentacles that curled towards the bystanders. And towards Irene. One shadowy tentacle coiled round her ankle, cool through the silk of her stocking, but with sparks of chaos fizzing through it like bubbles in champagne. She shrieked, momentarily unable to phrase anything in the Language through sheer terror and disgust. She struggled to pull herself away, flailing her feet wildly.

The woman's voice spoke again, but this time it was like the first line of a psalm: other voices from around the floor chanted a response in thunderous unison, and the floating void in the air shrank as lightning crackled around it in a halo.

Irene's conscious, professional mind was trying to take notes, even under the current circumstances. *So this is what happens during a chaos incursion in a high-order world. It has significant difficulty in*

sustaining itself, and even local humans are able to force it shut—
assuming they're powerful enough. Of course it would be easier to be
analytical if that damned tentacle weren't still trying to drag her
towards the hole. And the beautiful marble floor was so smooth that
there was nothing to halt her inevitable slide towards it. Even her
fingernails could gain no purchase.

"Chaos power, release me!" she gasped, trying to project her
words loudly enough to be heard. But this time the Language failed
her. She knew she was forming the words properly—she could hear
them—but there was no power behind them. She was a reservoir
that had run dry. Her head ached as if someone were drilling screws
into her temples, and she lost what little grip she had on the floor,
slipping inexorably towards the hole in space.

Kai stepped between her and the void and went down on one knee,
seizing the tentacle in both hands. Irene could see the scale patterns
showing on his skin in the flaring light of the shuddering chandeliers
as his nails lengthened into claws. The great choir of massed voices
spoke again, and their force beat against the air like hammers in a
foundry. Kai's features were frozen in concentration, and his hands
tensed with the effort as he wrenched them ferociously apart.

The tentacle spasmed between his hands, then snapped in a burst
of shadow.

Kai dropped it, ignoring it, and swept Irene up in his arms. He
swung her away from the rapidly closing abyss, carrying her effortlessly back towards the surrounding line of robed sorcerers. Irene
didn't have the strength to do more than hang on to him as her mind
raced. She was aware that they needed to get out of here before attention shifted to them, but what about the book in the empress's quarters? And was there something useful in her conversation with
Alberich that she'd missed?

The hole closed with a snap, and the howling of air, which had become a background noise, abruptly ceased. Irene took a shuddering breath of relief. The air suddenly seemed to taste so much cleaner. The room was still full of the gabble of voices and the shrieks of panicked civilians—but it was a human noise, and less apocalyptic. Kai backed a few paces towards the door, Irene still in his arms, then came to a stop as several military types shouldered into his path.

"I believe Her Imperial Majesty would like a word," the oldest of them said. His hair and beard might be snow-white with age, but he had the build and muscle of a serving officer. And there was nothing elderly about his attitude. "This way, young man, if you please."

Irene tugged at Kai's arm. "Put me down, please." Her voice was cracked and dry. She coughed, and her next words were more audible. "Please. I can walk."

And she would rather face the Undying Empress on her own two feet.

The gentlemen escorting them up to the steps of the dais were polite, but she and Kai were still prisoners, under guard. The crowd was beginning to settle down now, and more and more interest was focusing on them.

The empress herself barely had a hair out of place. A maid had appeared from somewhere and was restoring the varnish on the nails of her left hand, while to her right an anonymous-looking man in plain black, possibly Oprichniki himself, was delivering answers to her rapid-fire questions. As Kai, Irene, and their escort arrived and respectively bowed or curtseyed, the empress turned to them, waving her servants away. The light seemed to cling to her, flowing over her silver dress and crown. Physical details, such as her white hair and heavy build, seemed unimportant in comparison with the power at her command.

The crowd fell silent, not wanting to miss any of this.

Irene attempted to think of a good excuse for what had just happened. She'd been trying for the last few minutes, but her best idea so far—*we're loyal subjects who wanted to expose an evil impostor*—wouldn't stand up to much investigation. *This* was why she liked to get away before anyone could start asking questions.

"If she speaks," the empress said, pointing at Irene, "knock her unconscious."

Irene mentally cursed while plastering on her best politely confused but helpful expression. And *that* was the problem with hanging around after using the Language to affect people's perceptions. They remembered what you'd done to them.

"Your Imperial Majesty—" Kai began.

"Him, too, for safety's sake," the empress said.

Kai shut his mouth.

The empress looked at them both critically. "Young woman, young man, you may both have done me a service, but I cannot be sure until I have fully investigated the matter. It is clear that some foul entity possessed my loyal servant Nicolai. You will be interrogated later and will give me your full story then. In the meantime"—she turned to the elderly man in charge of the escort—"maximum security, the cell with the highest wardings, and shackles."

Kai's arm stiffened under Irene's hand, and she knew without looking that his face would be showing every one of his feelings, and none of them good. She squeezed his arm reassuringly. As long as it wasn't Alberich organizing their accommodation, they should be able simply to walk out of any cell once she had her voice back.

The empress turned back to a man delivering his report, and Irene and Kai were marched out of the Great Hall in dead silence. The subbasements they were led to weren't on Irene's maps of the Winter

Palace. And the heavy shackles on their wrists were applied with the utmost politeness. The guards were clearly aware that Irene and Kai were accused but not convicted, and might still come out of the affair smelling of roses. The prison cell even had beds. And candles. And a heavily locked door, of course.

And now that they were theoretically restrained from working magic, and theoretically alone—except for the person probably listening on the other side of the wall, of course—they could talk.

Kai sat down heavily on the bed, his shackled hands between his knees. "What language?" he asked. He'd deduced the probability of a listener, too.

"English," Irene said. After all, in this alternate world the British Isles were a small country that had never risen to empire. If there *was* someone eavesdropping, it'd take a little while to find a translator.

"Well, you spoke to Alberich, and I hope you're satisfied." He stared at his chains. "I suppose my relatives will get us out of here. They're certain to investigate a chaos incursion like that one. But they'll ask questions . . ."

Irene sat down next to him and patted his hand. Her chains clanked unmusically. Both sets of shackles were overwritten with complicated runes and embossed with gold and lead. No doubt they'd completely annul the magic of this world. But they couldn't bind the Language. "Kai, I intend for us to be well out of here by the time anyone comes to investigate."

"You're in a damned good mood," Kai muttered.

"And you're in an unusually bad one."

"Given the last half-hour, I have reason." Even though their bodies weren't touching, she could feel the tension in him like a vibrating wire. "How am I supposed to keep you safe when you keep on—"

"No," Irene said, cutting in. "This is *not* the time." She was distracted.

An idea was bubbling through her mind, trying to take shape and concrete form. In comparison, Kai's little fit of temper was unimportant. "I'm trying to work something out."

"It never is the time," Kai muttered. Then, curious, he asked, "What?"

"Let me ask you some questions." It would clarify her own thinking, and there were a few points she wanted to be certain about. "This is a high-order world, so the power of chaos is hindered. Alberich in particular couldn't use much of his strength here, since he's made himself a creature of chaos."

Kai nodded. "That's correct. I think he must have been shielded by his stolen skin. When the empress and her servants attacked him, it shredded away and he had to escape into the void."

"Were they the ones who closed the hole into chaos, then?"

"No, that was the world's natural stability. Humans couldn't affect something like *that*." The thought seemed to cheer him for some reason. "What they did was basically to keep him in the void with their spells until it closed. It wasn't very efficient, of course, but they threw enough raw power at him to hold him back, and the hole closed on its own. Though they probably don't realize that."

Irene nodded. "So, since Alberich was severely weakened by being in this world, we can assume that if he had had a less dangerous method of achieving his goals, he would have taken it."

Kai frowned, then relaxed. "Ah, you mean that he can't have any allies among the dragons! Yes, that's a relief."

"Not *exactly*," Irene said. "Or at least, that's not the point I'm making here."

"Then what is your point?" The candle cast huge shadows on the wall as he leaned forward.

"Alberich told me he traced us here because of the disturbances we caused. The mess at the sleigh-port, the storm you raised. He was waiting in the Great Hall and watching for us to show up." Irene saw Kai frowning in thought and decided to jump straight to the conclusion. "If he had known which book we were after, then he'd have gone straight there and laid a trap for us. He wouldn't have needed to chase us down."

"That's logical," Kai agreed. "So?"

"So he *didn't* know which book we're after." Irene held up a finger. "But he *did* know which world I was coming to. He even quoted the Library designation, he was so busy trying to impress me."

Kai shrugged. "So he knew some things, but not others. That in itself isn't—" He broke off, making the connection. "Wait. Someone from the Library would have had access to the records to report our destination *and* would have known the book you'd been assigned to collect."

Irene nodded. "Which suggests that whoever passed Alberich the information *wasn't* a Librarian. But he discovered the world's designation from *someone*."

"The werewolves who stole your folder?" Kai suggested. "If they saw your mission papers?"

"Possible, but unlikely. The documents in the folder were in the Language, remember. Anyone who read them would have read them in their native tongue. If one of them passed on the information, why just the world's designation? Why not the name of the book as well, and the place where it was located?"

"I'll allow that. But that means—"

"Yes," Irene interrupted. "Exactly! The only people who'd know the world's designation, but not the book, are the ones who saw the *outside* of the folder, but not the *inside*. Which means the people who were waiting in Vale's rooms when I arrived." As she said it, the theory became near-certainty. However, her pleasure at the logical construction drained away as she accepted the conclusion. "Which means one of them is working for Alberich."

"Not Li Ming," Kai said at once.

"Hopefully not." Irene didn't necessarily share Kai's faith in the other dragon, but she'd really prefer it if Alberich didn't have dragon allies as well as Fae ones. "And surely not Vale, either."

"Of course not," Kai said. "And there's no reason for it to be Singh. Which leaves Zayanna." *Obviously,* his tone added.

Irene nodded reluctantly. "I didn't want . . . ," she started, then fell silent, trying to think what she had wanted. There had never been a reason to trust Zayanna.

"She's Fae," Kai said dismissively. "It's all a game to them. Probably her patron did throw her out, like she said, and Alberich offered her a better deal."

"If her patron did throw her out, it was because she helped rescue you," Irene said quietly.

"For her own reasons." Kai jingled his chains. "And speaking of rescues, how about our own?"

Irene pulled herself together. "Yes. We need to get out of here and get back to Vale's world. If Zayanna's been communicating with Alberich, then she can tell us how to find him." And then they could work out what to do next.

Irene had never had a reason to trust Zayanna. But she'd wanted to. She'd felt sorry for her. She'd chosen to trust someone whom she'd been warned against by Kai, by the Library's own guidelines, by simple common sense . . .

And now everyone she'd left behind might be in mortal danger.

A sullen swell of anger built inside her. This was a *personal* betrayal. She'd never really appreciated how much worse this felt than professional treachery. Perhaps because she'd never faced quite so personal a betrayal before, and certainly never with such high stakes.

"All right," she said, bringing her hands firmly together. She could feel a solid strength growing in the back of her mind, which had been lacking earlier: the power to use the Language and the force of will to command it. She'd exhausted herself against the empress, but now her strength had returned, like rainwater collecting after a drought. "Kai, once we're out of this cell, I'll need you to find the shortest path towards the waterfront."

"Certainly," Kai said. "Is that how we're leaving?"

"Eventually. I'm assuming that you can command the waters, or the water-spirits, in the way you've done before. This world being a high-order world won't stop you?"

"It'll make it easier, if anything. I won't need to summon the local spirits." He sounded quite definite about that, and Irene wondered if they'd report on him to the local dragons. "But what about the book? It'll be difficult getting up to the empress's bedroom, as security is bound to be on high alert . . ."

"We're leaving it behind."

Kai stared at her, shocked. "But it was your mission. We have to get it—"

"It's even more important to find the link to Alberich," Irene said. She hated abandoning a mission, and hated abandoning a book even more, but the *real* threat was Alberich. If they went to grab the book and lost the chance of finding Alberich himself, then they'd have treated the symptom but died of the underlying disease. "Our priority is getting out of here and finding Alberich's accomplice—whether it's Zayanna or anyone else—and using them to stop Alberich."

"Using them how, precisely? Alberich doesn't seem the type to stop attacking the Library just to keep someone else safe. Shouldn't we actually do our assigned job first?"

"I could be wrong," Irene said. Her anger was still burning, making her want to spit out every word, to shout at someone who deserved it, to hammer against the cell door. She controlled it. Kai's objections were reasonable and deserved an answer, even if the answer was going to be a flat no. "In which case I will have weakened the Library by not obtaining a vitally important book. And in which case I will take full responsibility, and I will feel every damn bit of guilt that I deserve to feel. But I don't think I am wrong. I think Zayanna is part of Alberich's plan. I strongly believe that at this precise moment getting our hands on her, or whoever's helping him, is the most important thing we can do."

"But what do we do when—" Kai started.

"We'll work out the details when we've caught the accomplice," Irene said firmly. "Let's do this in manageable stages. Are you ready?"

"The sooner, the better," Kai said. He was still as tense as a stretched wire, his shoulders hunched and his expression guarded. Irene silently scolded herself as she became aware of at least part of the problem. He'd been imprisoned only a few months back, depending on others to rescue him. It was hardly surprising if being chained in a cell again left him on edge.

"Right." She stood up, and he followed. **"Shackles, unlock and fall off."**

The shackles were human magic, not Fae or dragon work, and they yielded to the Language like any other piece of mortal metalwork—falling to the ground with a clang.

Irene stepped to one side of the door, leaving the path clear for Kai. **"Door, unlock. Wards on door and entrance, fall. Door, open."**

Her head throbbed with the newly returned headache, which had apparently only left for a brief holiday. It had now come back with its friends to stay. But at least there was a convenient stone wall to lean on. She did that for a moment while Kai exploded through the just-opened door and "reasoned" with the guards on the other side. They didn't even have time to level their cross-bows.

When she followed him out into the guard-room, everyone was unconscious. This included a robed man, who was presumably the mage unfortunate enough to have been posted on guard-duty. "A bit wholesale," she said mildly.

Kai shrugged. "None of them are dead. Besides, we don't want them raising the alarm earlier than necessary."

"True," Irene admitted. She tugged at the mage's heavy over-robes. "Give me a hand with these, please."

Kai frowned for a moment, then looked at her bedraggled, blood-stained ballgown and nodded. When Irene had donned them she still looked badly dressed, but at least she might be a little less conspicuous.

"The Neva River is that way," Kai said, pointing helpfully down the corridor.

Irene led the way, stalking along in a businesslike manner and hoping that anyone they ran into would look at the robes and not at her face. Her personal worries drew her face into a scowl, and she saw no reason to attempt a smile. There was the threat to the Library. There was Alberich, who was an ongoing terror just as much as a current danger. There were all her friends and family who were in danger. And there was Zayanna, who, barring a miracle and a very implausible explanation, had lied to her.

She'd *liked* Zayanna.

From the distance came the sound of running feet and a clanging bell. They were several corridors away from the cells by now, in a direction that Irene would have described as *hopelessly lost*, but which Kai claimed led straight towards the river. These passages, deep beneath the Winter Palace, were far from the glorious corridors of the upper levels—or even the prosaic but businesslike archives beneath the cathedral. They were floored with flagstones and walled with granite, clean but old. These passageways were cold with the deep bone-chill of freezing water seeping through earth and stone. Even the air felt damp.

"The hunt's up," Kai said concisely and obviously.

"We knew it would be," Irene agreed. "Is it much farther?"

"A bit. I'm assuming that you want to get as close as possible?"

"Right. The less wall and foundation I have to remove, the easier it'll be."

"How are we leaving this world, after that?"

"Through the closest library to the Library itself." She caught Kai's frown. "I know it might be faster in some ways for you to carry us out as a dragon, but I need to leave word at the Library as soon as possible. If something does go wrong when we try to catch Zayanna, I don't want to be the idiot who didn't tell anyone where we were going or what we were up to—"

She came to a dead stop as a roar echoed through the passages. Panicked back-brain instinct urged her to cower and hide or to look for a nice high tree to climb. "What the hell is that?" she hissed.

"The empress's tigers. But I don't think they're nearby." Kai kept on walking, far more casual about the noise than she was, and Irene had to hurry to catch up.

"You mean those big white Siberian—"

"They'd have to be Bengal tigers," Kai said seriously. "You only get white tigers from Bengal. My uncle gets quite annoyed about it. His subject kingdoms often send him furs as tribute, but Siberian tigers are always orange, never white. He once said—"

"The operative word is *big*," Irene cut in. "How good are tigers at tracking by scent?"

"Well, hounds are better for coursing game," Kai began. Then he caught Irene's glare. "Quite good," he said meekly. "I've never tried training them."

"I don't suppose they'll go to their knees and worship you, the way that bear did?"

"Probably not," Kai said regretfully. Another roar split the air, closer now. "They're cats, after all."

Irene wished that the Undying Empress had preferred bears as pets.

"This is about as close as we're going to get." Kai stopped at a bend in the passage and laid his hand against the wall. "I can feel the flowing water some yards beyond this. They laid the foundations well."

"I would apologize to the empress, but maybe she'll be glad of the opportunity to redecorate." Irene approached the wall and laid her hands next to Kai's, bracing herself. **"Stone wall and foundation and earth that lies between me and the river beyond, crumble and give way, and make a passage to the river large enough for us to pass through."**

It was bad, but not as bad as trying to influence the empress. *What fun,* Irene thought grimly through the band of pain pressing on her temples. *I now have a whole new standard for how bad things can get. Travel is so educational.* She dimly felt Kai's arm round her waist, supporting her as she leaned against him. *I almost think I prefer travelling in worlds on the chaos spectrum; at least I don't get a headache every five minutes . . .*

"Irene!" Kai was yelling. "Tigers!"

Oh, right, tigers. Tigers were relevant in some way. And tigers were beautiful when there were heavy iron bars between her and them . . .

There were two big tigers pacing down the corridor towards her and Kai. Panic gave Irene a shot of icy-cold adrenaline and yanked her back to awareness, then retired to gibber in the back of her brain and let her take care of things.

Kai snapped his fingers and pointed at the ground. "Lie down," he said firmly.

One tiger yawned, baring huge white teeth and revealing an implausibly pink tongue. The other simply snarled.

"Cats," Kai muttered. "Irene, can you just put them to sleep or something? I don't want to kill them."

"Any particular reason?" The tigers were getting closer now. They were walking rather than running. Presumably they were meant to guard Irene and Kai till the human guards arrived.

"They're such beautiful specimens," Kai said. "I wish we could take them back for my uncle."

Irene winced at the thought of trying to drag a couple of unwilling tigers through the Library. "Absolutely not," she said firmly. "You can come back and negotiate with the local dragons on your own time."

Behind her, the stonework groaned and began to shudder. Irene turned and saw it parting like a pair of lips, as though it were opening its mouth to speak.

But instead of words, water rushed out in a mighty gush that would have plastered Irene against the opposite wall if Kai hadn't dragged her out of the way. The tigers fled, turning tail and racing down the corridor as water came flooding in and gushed knee-high along the passage.

"I've got this," Kai said calmly. "Hold your breath." He advanced into the flow of water. It softened as he touched it, curling around him and Irene, the current weakening to the strength of a gentle stream as he walked forward through it. The narrow hole in the wall was just large enough to admit the two of them. Irene followed him into the darkness, feeling the water brush her face and trail her dress and robes out behind her. And Kai's power somehow channelled air around them, allowing them to breathe. Icy tendrils stroked her forehead and soothed her headache.

And then they were out into the full force of the river. It swept them up and along till they surfaced in a bursting wave. Irene was gasping for air now, her arms round Kai's neck as she let him support her. Her shoes were lost somewhere at the bottom of the Neva, and her clothing was a sodden, unwieldy mass that would probably have drowned her if she weren't hanging on to a dragon. The water was bitterly cold. She thought about that, then rephrased to *merely* bitterly cold, because without Kai's influence it would be freezing and she'd be passing out from the chill. Thin raindrops scythed down from the overcast sky and stung her face. Street lamps along the embankment cast orange shimmers onto the water, glaring in the darkness.

But they were outside and free to act.

"Right," she said, once she had her breath back. "Now for the Library."

CHAPTER 18

The Library was still dark when they reached it—if anything, it was darker, with lonely oil lamps flickering in the silence. It was pouring down outside there, too, and the windows of the nearest corridor were smeared with long streaks of raindrops. Irene half-imagined she could hear the ticking of a distant clock, but when she tried to listen there was only silence. The air seemed hot, and she wondered how much of that was real and how much was her own fear.

She sat in front of the first computer they found, turning it on and then tapping her fingers on the table as it took its time booting up. She begrudged every passing second. Time was not her friend tonight—there were too many emergencies seething in her mind: Alberich, the Library, her parents, Zayanna, *Vale*...

The email screen came up. Irene leaned forward to start typing, but an incoming email immediately filled the screen.

Need talk urgentest, where to meet? Bradamant

"Typed in a hurry," Kai deduced, leaning over Irene's shoulder.

"Check this room's designation, please," Irene replied, ignoring him. She was typing up her own email to Coppelia, in prose not much better than Bradamant's own.

"A-21, Italian Giallo Novels, Late Twentieth Century," Kai reported.

A-21 Italian giallo novels late twentieth century, or entrance to Vale's world, which is easier? Irene sent to Bradamant.

Entrance Vale's world, see you there ASAP, the message came back.

"We should hurry," Kai said, pacing up and down and ignoring the spare chair. "If she has something urgent to tell us . . ."

"Give me a moment," Irene said. She was checking current announcements on the network. Unfortunately there weren't any along the lines of *Alberich is dead, everything's been sorted out, you can all relax and go back to normal.* But there were lists of worlds whose gates had been destroyed—a longer list than she'd hoped to see— and there was a list of dead Librarians. She scanned down it, her heart cramping in her chest at the thought that she might recognize a name.

And she did recognize a couple.

Kai had stopped pacing and was staring over her shoulder again. "I knew Hypatia," he said.

It was one of the names on the list. "I don't think I ever met her," Irene said.

"She was a bit older than you. She used to say, 'It isn't your job to die for the Library, it's your job to make other people die for your Library—'" He cut himself off, straightening, and his next words were cold and polished. "She gave her life honourably in service to the Library. I shouldn't demean her sacrifice."

Irene closed the window, logging out of the computer. "I don't think there's anything shameful in repeating a joke she liked. At least you're remembering her. Isn't that better than not remembering her at all?"

The Library's shadows hung around her, a silent promise of the future. After all, when Irene herself died, what would be left of her? A handful of unread books in an unused bedroom. A footnote in the memories of a few other Librarians.

And vital books on the shelves of the Library, which wouldn't have been there without her.

"Come on," she said. "The transfer cabinet's this way."

"Irene, your parents—" Kai broke off, his tone uncertain.

"Not on that list," Irene said. "Still safe. As much as anywhere's safe at the moment."

Bradamant was waiting for them outside the room containing the portal to Vale's world. She was leaning against the wall under one of the lamps and was scribbling in a notebook. The dim light threw her into shadow, making her look like a slender pen-and-ink sketch in a dark pencil-skirt and jacket. Her eyes widened as she caught sight of them. "What *happened*?"

Irene looked down at herself. She was mostly dry, but her dip in the river had left her gown and stolen robe hopelessly crumpled. And the marks from her nosebleed all down her bodice proved that cold water didn't always get rid of bloodstains. "The mission went wrong and we ran into Alberich," she reported succinctly. "We got away."

"Well, of course you got away, or you wouldn't be here now," Bradamant said impatiently. "What about Alberich?"

"He escaped too." Irene reminded herself that she was actively trying to be on better terms with Bradamant these days; plus Bradamant had a right to know, plus professional courtesy, et cetera. So she described recent events.

Bradamant nodded calmly as she listened, but her knuckles were white on the edge of her notebook. But when Irene described her recognition of Alberich, Bradamant nearly bent the book in half. "Why didn't you just kill him?" she demanded.

"I did think about it," Irene admitted. "I just didn't have the opportunity."

"Surely you could have tried a bit harder." Even in the dim light, Bradamant was white with fury. "Grabbed a cross-bow off a guard, used a gun or dropped the ceiling on him."

"You tried shooting him in the head before. Remember?" Irene recalled it perfectly well, and from the expression on Bradamant's face, so did she. "Three shots. In the forehead. And all it did was stagger him for a moment. As it was, I provoked the most powerful mages in the empire to do their best, and all that did was make him retreat. I'm not sure what *would* kill him."

"Dragons?" Bradamant suggested. This time she was looking at Kai.

"There wasn't time to call for assistance," Kai objected.

"Let's leave the blame till later," Irene said wearily. Was Kai now regretting that he'd wanted to avoid the local dragons? She might ask him later, but not in front of Bradamant. "This next bit's more urgent." She ran through their conversation and her deductions.

Bradamant was nodding by the end of it. "It makes sense. It has to be one of the people in that room. Someone in the Library could have found out where you were going . . ." She had the grace to blush a little, perhaps remembering her past actions. "But in that case, they'd have known what book you were after. And as you've pointed out, that brings us down to the people in Vale's rooms who saw the folder."

"And it's the Fae, obviously," Kai said. "I don't understand why the two of you are even considering anyone else."

"Simple logic makes Zayanna the most likely," Irene said, "but there's the possibility that someone else was being manipulated. Or that we were being observed."

"Vale's room being spied upon?" Kai snorted. "You just don't want to admit that the Fae—"

"Excuse me," Bradamant cut in. She stared at Kai until he fell silent. "Thank you. Look, Irene, you need to do something about your friend Vale. When you have a spare minute, which admittedly isn't now. I went to see him."

"Had he discovered anything?" Irene demanded.

"Yes, and that's what I wanted to tell you. I've passed it on to our elders, too, of course."

"Of course," Irene agreed, irritated that Bradamant felt the need to point that out. Irene wasn't her junior any longer and didn't need that sort of reminder. "So?"

"Vale says that Silver says that apparently Alberich's been hiring. That is, word's out amongst the Fae that Alberich has been looking for junior Fae to do . . . jobs. Exactly what the jobs are, Silver didn't know, but . . ." Bradamant shrugged. "I can think of half a dozen things, from distracting and assassinating Librarians all the way to his big anti-Library plot. Silver also said that some who'd expressed an interest had then dropped out of circulation. Apparently once you're in on Alberich's plan, you don't talk to anyone else about it."

"That's interesting. I wonder what he's offering them."

"Power," Bradamant said. "And the chance to be part of a good narrative."

"Yes, that would work," Irene agreed. One way for Fae to gain more power was to obey all the stereotypes of a fictional character. Conforming to patterns in this way strengthened the chaos within them, acting against the universe's natural inclination towards randomness. Destroying the Library would make a *marvellous* story, she thought sourly. Her mind flickered back to Bradamant's earlier words. "And yes, I know Vale's not in good shape. He contracted chaos contamination during our Venice mission. And I really need to get him to a high-order world when we have time."

Bradamant looked aside, avoiding Irene's eyes. "There is another option, you know."

"What?" Irene demanded. If there was a way to help Vale, something that she could do without betraying her other obligations . . .

"Force him through the full process," Bradamant said coldly. "Increase the level of contamination till he's full Fae."

Irene stared at her. "Are you *insane*?"

"He'd never agree to it," Kai said, as sharply as Irene had.

"Where do you think Fae come from?" Bradamant retorted. "And do you want to keep him alive and sane? At least this way he'll be stable. It wouldn't be difficult. Get him to interact with other Fae, or become more of a stereotype. He's a detective. Make him detect." She must have seen the disgust in Irene's face, for she took a step back. Her expression settled into a bland smile, one familiar to Irene from all the years they'd known and disliked each other. "I'm trying to help you. Don't blame me if there aren't any good options."

"You clearly know more about this sort of thing than I do," Irene said before she could stop herself.

"I have my own contacts," Bradamant said.

"Oh?"

"None of your business." The statement was delivered flatly, leaving no openings for argument.

Irene took a deep breath and forced herself back from the edge of anger. She was going to be an adult, even if everyone around her felt the need to be children. She'd save her fury for the person who actually *deserved* it. "All right. Thank you for your input, but I don't think Vale himself would tolerate it." She glanced to Kai, who nodded in agreement. "And thank you for passing on this information. I've put the basic facts in an email to Coppelia—"

"She won't be reading it till she gets back," Bradamant said. "She's out of the Library at the moment. So's Kostchei. So are many other elders."

"Seriously?" Irene was genuinely astonished. By the time anyone was promoted to Senior Librarian, they were generally old enough and injured enough to merit honourable retirement. Elder Librarians didn't leave the Library, didn't return to alternate worlds where time resumed its normal flow and where they might be in danger. It just wasn't done. She'd only seen Coppelia do it once before, and that time it had been a matter of stopping a war. If *many* of the elders were now taking this step . . .

Bradamant nodded, her expression sour. "They're collecting information. From *their* contacts. It's all very well to know Alberich's working with the Fae, but if we can't find him, it's useless."

"I hope Penemue's out on assignment, too."

"That's rather harsh," Bradamant said. "Yes, she is. Just because she plays politics doesn't mean she doesn't do her job."

"Has she been talking to you?" Irene accused.

"I talk to a lot of people." The shadows were very deep around

Bradamant. "Things aren't necessarily as black and white as you'd like to think. And not everyone gets good assignments."

"I wouldn't call our last few months' jobs good assignments," Irene said bitterly.

"Technically you're being punished, remember?" Bradamant sighed. "Some people pull worse jobs for less reason. Just because you haven't noticed that doesn't mean there isn't resentment. And no, this isn't the time to quarrel about it. But there's a reason why other Librarians are talking to Penemue."

"What's she saying at the moment?"

Bradamant hesitated, then lowered her voice. "The Library is reducing its energy levels to free up more power for transporting things. Penemue is saying that's an excuse. That the lights are down and the air's getting stale because the Library's been weakened. She's saying it's not simply a case of burning gates, but that the whole Library is slipping into entropy. And a lot of people have noticed that they can hear a clock ticking."

She fell silent for a moment, and all three of them listened. Irene could hear her own pulse, her own breathing. She strained to hear anything else behind the noise of her own life, but she couldn't be certain. Imagination supplied a whispered ticking in the background, counting down seconds, but . . .

"I know," Bradamant said. "Once you start listening, you can't be sure if you're imagining it or not. And some are starting to murmur that we should consider talking to Alberich. Just possibly. Just maybe. Just as an alternative to be considered."

"Just never," Irene said harshly.

"You're snapping at the wrong person," Bradamant said. "And a few Librarians suspect history of being inherently revisionist and written by the winners. They ask me if perhaps I provoked him during our last confrontation. They suggest that he might have had a perfectly good reason to be doing whatever he was doing, and that it was our fault if we were almost killed in the process. Who'd have thought that a few days of panic would make so many colleagues and friends . . ." She gestured, unable or unwilling to finish the sentence, her mouth twisting sourly.

"Come with us," Irene said on sudden impulse. "We could use your help." It was perfectly true. Bradamant was good at her job, and Irene was past the need for pride and trying to manage things all by herself.

Bradamant avoided Irene's eyes again, her mouth twisting wryly. "I can't. I'm supposed to stay here and act as a coordinator. Stupid, isn't it?"

Irene was opening her mouth to express disbelief when an unpleasant supposition hit her. The last time they'd worked together, Bradamant had been working under secret orders. She'd pulled a nasty trick on Irene, which had put the whole mission in danger. While Irene hadn't actively blamed Bradamant for that in the debriefing, the truth had been there for their superiors to see. If Bradamant's supporting role was her punishment, Irene would only be rubbing salt into the wounds by asking for details. So instead she said, "I'm sorry to hear it. I think you'd be more use in the field."

"Yes, so do I." Bradamant's tone was as dry as dust, and even less sympathetic. "Very well. I'll make sure your information is passed on if Coppelia or anyone else returns before you do. Good luck."

"And you." Irene turned away before she could say something tactless and ruin the moment. Then she led Kai into the next room, which held the door to Vale's world.

There was even less light in this room. With only a dim fluorescent bulb glimmering on the ceiling, they had to pick their way carefully across the floor, avoiding barely visible piles of books. They were halfway to the portal when Irene stopped dead.

"What is it?" Kai demanded, startled out of his brooding.

"I'm thinking." And for once, she was doing it *before* walking into a trap. "What happened the last time I came through this door? I was jumped by those werewolves. Whoever's operating in Vale's world— whether it's Zayanna or not—knows this is our way in. And if it were me, I'd use that knowledge."

"Point taken," Kai said. He eyed the door thoughtfully. "It's past midnight now. Anything could be waiting for us. We could travel via another world instead, and I could carry you to Vale's world?"

Irene considered it. "We'd lose time," she decided. "The longer we delay, the more chance there is that Alberich's agent will escape— then we lose our lead."

"So what do we do?"

Apparently Kai didn't have any brilliant ideas. This was a pity, because Irene didn't have any either. "We're careful," she said firmly. "And we stand on either side of the door when we open it." She was trying to think of all the possible things that could be on the other side. Thugs. Explosives. Poisonous gas. Gun-fire. "And we look before we go in," she added. It wasn't much, but it was something.

She and Kai took up positions on either side of the door, and Irene turned the handle carefully before shoving it open into Vale's world beyond.

The shotgun blast roared between them, at chest height, and spat-tered lead pellets into the shelves and books on the far side of the room. Irene wasn't sure if it would have killed a dragon, but it would certainly have killed a human. The sudden blast of sound left her shaking her head, and a hum still seemed to hang in the air.

She peered round the door-frame. Even though the room's ether lamps had been turned down for the night, there was enough light to see the main attraction. The shotgun was obvious enough. It was tied to a chair, with a wire leading from it to the handle of the door she'd just opened. It was textbook stuff, drawn from classic murder mysteries. And like all such murder methods, it wasn't half as entertaining when encountered for real.

"That could have killed you," Kai snarled.

"It could have killed you, too," Irene pointed out. "Especially if whoever it was thought you would insist on going first." Which he might very well have done. She thought of him taking that shotgun blast to the chest and mentally shuddered.

There was a rising whine in the air. She didn't know what it was, but there was no time to lose. If they waited any longer, the room might become totally impassable, and then they'd have to take Kai's alternate route and lose hours in the process. "Come on," Irene directed, leading the way into the room at a run.

Kai kicked the door to the Library shut behind him as he followed her in. The room looked empty enough, apart from the chair with the gun. There were just a few disused display-cases and folding-tables stacked against the walls. There were no other immediately obvious threats—no lurking black mambas, no sticks of dynamite with lit fuses, no skulking thugs with knives.

But the buzz was growing louder, and it was coming from *above* them.

Irene looked up.

Three pale things resembling paper bags sagged from the ceiling, each of them held in place by a couple of leather straps. They were swaying in position, each of them vomiting a growing swirl of buzzing darkness. Having a shotgun go off in their vicinity would have woken even the most sweet-tempered nest of wasps. And Irene was willing to bet these weren't the more friendly variety, which could be persuaded away with a fly-swatter. Assuming they were wasps at all. What was worse than wasps? She didn't want to find out. Abandoning subtlety, she ran for the door, shouting, **"Corridor door, unlock and open!"**

The lock clicked audibly and the door swung open, slamming into the wall behind it, but the way was still blocked. The doorway was filled from floor to lintel with crates. Someone had clearly piled them up outside—after setting the shotgun and nests and closing and locking the door. Marvellous.

The dark swirl arrowed towards her and Kai. Irene flung her arms up to protect her face, a purely instinctive move, and felt burning needles jab into her hands. Crawling buzzing things, which she couldn't even *see* clearly in the near darkness, landed on her wrists and tried to crawl down the sleeves of her clothes. Flickers of motion touched her face as vibrating wings brushed against her and tiny insect feet settled onto her skin.

"Wind, blow these insects off me!" she screamed.

She found herself at the centre of a mini-hurricane, which thrust away from her as if she were the centre of a sonic boom. It left her gasping before she could breathe properly, but it flung the creatures back for a moment. Her hands burned with their stings, and next to her she heard Kai cursing. This was worse than seeing a pair of hunting tigers approach. Here in the darkness, unable to see what was attacking, locked in a room with these things . . .

It was a trap that had been set for a Librarian. Very well, she'd meet it like a Librarian.

"Kai, down!" she ordered, throwing herself to the ground as the things came buzzing back for her. **"Glass, shatter! Glass fragments, impale the insects!"**

She heard Kai hitting the floor as well. Then the display-cases and lamps flew to pieces in a scream of breaking glass that almost drowned out the furious buzzing. Shards flew in all directions above her head, scything through the air. She kept her head down and covered, hoping against hope that this would actually work.

The noises were promising. Repeated thwips, like arrows, only on a smaller scale. Three heavy scrunching sounds, as if someone had dropped large bags of cereal. Then only a faint buzzing, still furious, but not so immediate. Then silence.

"I think they've stopped," Kai said. His voice was muffled, suggesting that he hadn't yet uncovered his head to look.

"Right," Irene said. She forced herself to move her arms and look up. The floor was littered with the glitter of broken glass, intermingled with small things that still twitched and scrabbled, their little wings moving them across the floor in futile, painful millimetres. Some of the insects still zoomed around the room, flecks of darkness in the shadows, but they'd retreated to the ceiling. The three nests were shattered masses where they'd fallen to the ground, jarred loose and weighed down by the amount of glass they'd taken on board. "Kai? How badly did they get you?"

"Enough to hurt quite a bit," Kai said, coming to his feet and shaking his hands as though he could physically expel the venom. Which gave Irene an idea—but one better tried out of insect range. He was deliberately keeping his tone even, but Irene could tell that he was annoyed. "Of all the petty, humiliating ways to try to murder you!"

"I'm not totally sure it was meant as murder," Irene said thoughtfully. She turned to the crates blocking the doorway and pitched her voice to carry. After all, someone might have double stacked them to add to their trap. **"Crates, move aside from the doorway."**

Her head ached a little as they slid sideways, but the Language worked much more easily here than it had in the world they'd just left. *I never thought I'd be preferring a high-chaos world to a high-order one.*

With her and Kai outside and the door safely shut behind them, she took advantage of the corridor's lighting to get a good look at her hands. They looked . . . uncomfortable, to put it mildly. They felt hideously painful, but there was something about actually seeing the multiple sting wounds on both hands that left her feeling queasy. Or perhaps that was the venom. But she'd never get used to seeing her own injuries. "Kai, hold your hands out while I try something. **Insect venom, exit my body and the dragon's body through the wounds by which you entered.**"

Clear liquid bubbled from the puncture holes in her skin, and she watched queasily as it dripped to the floor. Her hands still stung and ached, but it wasn't quite as bad, and at least it wasn't getting worse.

Kai frowned at his hands as the venom left them. "Irene, what did you mean when you said you weren't sure it was murder?"

"It could have been meant to drive us back into the Library," Irene pointed out. "Or repel any other Librarian who tried to get through. I don't know. Add it to the list of questions we have to ask." Her hands seemed to have finished dripping venom for the moment. She shook them dry and regretted not having any bandages. She also regretted shaking them. "Anyhow, priorities. We need to find Zayanna. And Vale. And Singh. And Li Ming, while we're at it. And the fastest way to all of those is through Vale."

And please let the Library hold on a little longer, she thought. *And let Vale be all right.*

CHAPTER 19

"Thank God you're here, Miss Winters," Singh said. He actually looked pleased to see her and Kai, which in itself worried Irene. As a general rule, the inspector tolerated the two of them, or at best considered them useful resources. If he was glad to see them, then Vale must be worse than she'd feared.

"How is Vale?" she asked, getting straight to the point. It was three o'clock in the morning and the street lamps outside were barely visible through drifts of smog. Here in Vale's rooms the lights were all turned up high, viciously bright to her tired eyes, and showing no pity to the room's clutter. The place was even more disarrayed than usual, with papers lying in drifts as though thrown there.

Singh frowned. He was in ordinary civilian clothing rather than his usual police uniform, and his tie-pin, Irene noticed with the precision of fatigue, was a little sword. "He's not good, not good at all. May I speak frankly, Miss Winters?"

"Of course," Irene said, mentally resigning herself. Anything that started off with *May I speak frankly* never ended well.

"I've seen Mr. Vale under stress before. I've seen him caught up in a case before." Singh folded his arms. "I have even, I must admit, seen him dosing himself with substances that I would prefer not to notice legally. But I have never seen him in quite this driven a state. And given that you know all about it, Miss Winters—you and your friend Strongrock here—I would be grateful if you could tell me exactly what's going on."

"Where is Vale at the moment?" Irene glanced at the closed bedroom door. "Is he . . ." She trailed off, not wanting to actually say *hitting the morphine again* out loud.

Singh shifted his weight from foot to foot. "I confess that I put a little something in his tea to help him sleep. When I arrived earlier this evening he was pacing the room, throwing out theories with one hand and digging himself deeper into depression with the other. Mr. Vale's a man of moods, and they've been getting worse over this last month. But in all the time I've known him, I've never seen him this bad."

Singh's words *in all the time I've known him* hung in the air like an accusation. He was a long-time friend of Vale. They'd worked together for years before Irene and Kai had shown up. From Singh's point of view, Irene was the interloper who'd swept in bringing trouble, and who'd then brought this down on Vale.

And it was all entirely true. Her guilt was a sour taste in her mouth.

"It's my fault," Kai said. Irene began to protest, but he brought up his hand to cut her off. "Let's be honest about this, Irene. I was the one who was kidnapped, and when Vale tried to help, he was exposed to a toxic environment. That's why he's in trouble now. There isn't anything I can say except that I'm sorry, Inspector Singh, and I will do my best to make amends."

"You can claim responsibility all you like, Mr. Strongrock," Singh said. "And I'm not denying that you may well *be* responsible. But even though I'm only a police inspector, and not up to Mr. Vale's standards of detecting, it's still very obvious that Miss Winters is in charge. She brought you here. *And* her friend was visiting earlier today. I think I'd like my answers from Miss Winters."

Irene didn't bother asking how Singh knew that Bradamant had visited. Vale might have told him, or the housekeeper, or anyone. It didn't matter. What *did* matter was that, several months ago, Bradamant had sold Singh a whole pack of lies while they'd been hunting for the Grimm book. Singh wasn't inclined to trust any Librarian after that.

"May we sit down?" she said. "This may take a little while."

At least there was brandy. All three of them knew where Vale kept it.

Irene knew that Singh was aware of the Library and the concept of multiple alternate worlds, though he wasn't as well-informed as Vale. They'd had to tell him the basics when Alberich had previously interfered in this world. And even though Irene herself hadn't gone into further detail, she was sure Vale had passed on a lot more information. Probably including Irene's own rap sheet. So she luckily didn't have to start right from the very beginning. She ran through Alberich's new threat to the Library, Vale's contamination by chaos, and their current need for Vale's services. "We stopped off at the hotel address Zayanna gave us on our way here," she finished. "The hotel clerk said that Zayanna had taken a room, but she hadn't been staying there, just using it as an address to collect mail. I know it wasn't likely, but we had to check."

"I'm more interested in what you've said about helping Mr. Vale." Singh hadn't taken any of the brandy for himself and had made do with a glass of water—more to keep Irene and Kai company than out of any actual need for a drink, Irene suspected. "If Mr. Strongrock takes him to *another world*"—he pronounced those words with scepticism but managed to get them out—"then that will help him get back to his normal self?"

Irene looked down at her hands, which were throbbing painfully. She wouldn't be getting to sleep anytime soon. No problem; she didn't have time to sleep anyhow.

She had to find Zayanna, and the fastest method was to get Vale to do it. No question about it: he could find anyone hiding out in London. But if she did ask Vale, he would be in danger of going over the edge. And if she tried to save Vale instead, by getting Kai to take him to a high-order world, her chances of locating Zayanna dropped significantly.

Bradamant wouldn't have hesitated. Bradamant would have known that the Library was her highest priority, just as it should be Irene's. Saving the Library justified putting one human in danger. And Irene herself put people in danger all the time when she was stealing books. So why was she hesitating, simply because this one person was a friend and she'd got him into this in the first place?

Next to her, Kai was looking deeply concerned, but he didn't seem as stressed as Irene herself felt. With a nasty shock, she realized that he was gazing at her as though she could wave her hand and sort everything out. As if she knew how to fix things. She'd done a dreadful job of mentoring him, she reflected bleakly: he shouldn't be relying on her like this.

"Yes," she finally said. "Yes, I think taking him to another world could do the trick."

Kai nodded. "In that case, I'll—"

He was cut off by a hammering on the front door. It was shockingly loud in the quiet house. Singh put down his glass and crossed to the window, standing to one side as he twitched back the curtain to peer out. "It's Lord Silver," he reported in a voice so very neutral that he must have been battling to control his feelings. "If we let him stand out there, he's going to wake the whole neighbourhood."

"Can't you arrest him?" Kai said hopefully.

"For that I'd need a charge or two, Mr. Strongrock. I don't suppose either of you knows of anything illegal that the gentleman's done lately?"

"Well, not *personally*," Kai said. "But doesn't this come under making a public disturbance?"

"That's one of those difficult lines to draw," Singh said. "Crash-landing a stolen zeppelin on the roof—now, that might be creating a public disturbance, and a few other things beside."

Irene knew he was referring to her own past escapades, where only Vale's involvement had allowed them to escape charges. It was a nicely subtle way to make a point. She'd have applauded, if the point hadn't been aimed at her. "It might be simplest if I just went down and asked him to go away," she said wearily. "I don't think he'll stop until he's got someone's attention."

"Leave that to me, Miss Winters," Singh said. He was out of the room and heading downstairs before she could agree.

"He was pleased you didn't want to bring Silver in," Kai said. He leaned back in his chair. "So am I. But I don't like leaving you alone in this world while you're looking for Zayanna."

"I'm not that thrilled by it, either, but I don't see any other option if we're to help Vale." Irene realized that she'd come to a decision. "I can ask Singh to help me find Zayanna; I won't be alone. And you can't simply take everyone with you. From what you were saying earlier, you'd have problems carrying two people."

"Problems," Kai said. "Well, yes, problems, but it might still be possible. And then we'd all be in one place when it came to finding Zayanna afterwards."

He was treating this as if it were something that could be handled on a schedule. Irene took a deep breath, controlling her temper. "Kai, which bit of *emergency* do you not understand? If Zayanna's our target, she's already shown that she's a good enough operative to try to kill us several times—and get away with it. We can't afford to give her any time to hide. We don't have any time to waste . . ." She realized she was talking herself back into her earlier moral dilemma, and hesitated.

There were voices on the stairs. Kai frowned. "That doesn't sound like anyone's told anyone to go away. Surely Silver couldn't have—"

"Couldn't have what?" Silver enquired, entering the room. He was in full evening dress, a gardenia in his button-hole, and looked as if he'd just come from some disreputable party. (Well, perhaps the disreputability wasn't immediately obvious, but it was Silver. Irene assumed immorality on principle.) Singh was a couple of steps behind him, looking disgruntled.

Kai didn't bother to get up. "I was going to say that I couldn't think of any reason for Inspector Singh to admit you."

"I couldn't think of any reason myself," Irene admitted. "Unless it's about our current investigation?"

"Tangentially." Silver tossed his hat and gloves onto the crowded table, where they landed next to a bloodstained pile of legal documents with a knife through them. He looked around the room as if it were a wild animal's habitat at the zoo. "Fascinating. I've always had trouble penetrating Mr. Vale's privacy."

"I've allowed you in solely because you said you had important information for us, Lord Silver," Singh said. His voice was still impeccably polite and his manners could be held up in a court of law, but there was a growl behind it. "I must ask you to tell us what brought you here in such a hurry."

"I came to stop you making a terrible mistake," Silver said. He strolled farther into the room and leaned on the back of Kai's chair. Kai stiffened and shifted forward, twisting to look up at the Fae, distrust written all over his face.

On the one hand, Irene mused, this was no doubt filtered through Silver's self-interest. On the other hand, he might have something genuinely important to say. And time was ticking away: she had to know now, she couldn't afford to wait. "Please go on," she said cautiously.

"You're considering taking away the very thing that makes Mr. Vale great." Silver held up a hand, even though nobody had tried to stop him. "Oh, don't interrupt. You're talking about taking him to a high-order sphere, the sort of place that's most uncongenial to someone like me, to drain away his nature. I'm right, aren't I?"

"You're absolutely right," Irene agreed. "It would be most uncongenial to someone like you."

Silver sighed. "Consider this, all three of you. Has it ever occurred to you that your friend Mr. Vale has more than a streak of Fae in him already? The fact that he continually meets the people whom he *should* meet? His abilities? His behaviour? The way he makes deductions that seem beyond the scope of human ability? I've always thought I should investigate his family more closely."

"This is ridiculous, sir," Singh said. He'd taken a position by the door to Vale's bedroom, possibly to stop anyone else getting in, and stood there in cold disapproval. "Mr. Vale dislikes the Fae more than most people I've ever met."

"Of course it's ridiculous!" Kai agreed forcefully. He glared up at Silver as though he intended to challenge the Fae to a duel on the spot. The only thing keeping him in his chair must be the suspicion that Silver would sprawl in it if it were empty.

"I notice that Miss Winters isn't disagreeing as strongly as you gentlemen," Silver said. His voice slipped under convictions like a knife prising up the seal on an envelope, leaving naked facts behind it.

And the reason Irene wasn't denying it was because the suggestion was uncomfortably plausible. The first time she and Kai had met Vale, he'd commented that he had a gift for meeting people at convenient times and knowing if they'd be important to him. Taken down to its essentials, that was far too close to the Fae sense of narrative and the way they fitted themselves into a story. Vale was an archetype of the Great Detective, and this world itself was on the high-chaos spectrum. Not as much as the Venice they'd all visited, but still more than a step away from balance. She'd never thought about this before—but had she subconsciously refused to consider it because she liked Vale?

"I don't believe that Vale is Fae," she said.

"Not in the present tense, maybe," Silver agreed. "But the future holds potential."

Irene thought of Alberich and his words about limitations and what we make of ourselves. She could feel Kai's stare of disappointment because she hadn't leapt to deny the whole possibility. "If this was true," she said, "why did you try to stop him going to Venice? I'd have thought you'd be in favour of it. And don't try to tell me it was reverse psychology."

Silver paused. "Well, my little mouse, I was indeed going to tell you that, but it seems I must confess that I was actually wrong about something." He smiled in a charming display of vulnerability. Irene had to mentally pinch herself to push back the compulsion to believe him, the tug of his glamour. The fact that he was insulting her helped. "I didn't think Vale would make it. I'm only too glad to find out that he has. I want to bring him properly into our kind. It'd be the easiest thing in the world. Or in any suitable world, really. But if you drag him off to a high-order sphere and force him to be merely human, you won't just cleanse him; you'll *destroy* him. You'll wipe out everything that makes him what he is."

"I can't believe you're seriously considering this," Kai broke in. "This is all lies—"

"No, it isn't," Silver said. He leaned forward, his eyes on Irene like a caress. "And you know it isn't."

"Will you swear it's true?" Irene asked.

Silver nodded, his hair drifting round his face as if touched by an invisible breeze. "I will, and do."

"And even if it isn't lies, he's only saying it because it's to his benefit!" Kai said furiously. "He's just as bad as Zayanna! The two of them are only involving themselves because of their perverse obsessions."

Irene put her glass down carefully before she threw it at someone. "Kai," she said, and something in her tone made him cut short whatever he'd been going to say. "Please be quiet for just a moment. Lord Silver, thank you for your input into the situation. Inspector Singh . . ."

"Yes?" Singh had retreated into himself while Silver and Kai were talking, watching the rest of the room like a cat at a mousehole. Now he gave Irene his undivided attention.

Irene knew this wasn't going to go down well, and she steeled herself in anticipation. "I think we're going to need to ask Vale for a decision."

Silver brought his hands together in applause. "Oh, *very* nice, Miss Winters. An excellent way to ease your conscience. You're more of a hypocrite than I'd given you credit for. Do you honestly think he'll make any choice other than the one you want?"

"Which is *exactly* why he shouldn't make that choice." Kai turned to Singh, looking for an ally. "Inspector, you must see that we need to get Vale out of here now, before he deteriorates any further . . . Do you want him to become like that?" He jerked a thumb over his shoulder at Silver. "We can't risk that happening to him."

"I take offence at being called a 'that,'" Silver remarked. "Don't push me, dragon. Just because I have a fondness for Mr. Vale doesn't mean I like *you*."

"I have to question your motives, Miss Winters," Singh said. He showed no sign of moving from in front of the bedroom door. "Lord Silver's quite likely right in his guess. I'm sure Mr. Vale would want to help you, no matter what the risk to himself was. Lord Silver may or may not be correct in there being a risk to Mr. Vale if he leaves this world. But it seems there's a lot more risk if he stays put."

"That may be so," Irene said. She found that she had risen to her feet without realizing it. "All right, that probably *is* so. And I don't want that risk any more than you do. But can't you see that if we make this decision for him, he's never going to forgive us? Lord Silver's been talking about *what* Vale is." She tried to find the words to convince Singh. "That's how he sees him. But you talk about *who* Vale is. I don't know him as well as you do, I haven't been his friend as long as you have, and I'm sorry for the trouble I've got him into. And under some circumstances, maybe I *would* drug him and drag him out of trouble without him having a choice in the matter. But he has a right to *choose* whether or not he takes this risk. And none of us, whether we're his friends or his enemies, have the right to make that choice for him. He won't thank us for taking the decision out of his hands."

Singh hesitated, then shook his head. "I'm not concerned with Mr. Vale's thanks, Miss Winters. I'll do what I must to save him, even if it means losing his friendship—"

"Then it's a good thing you won't need to." The door behind Singh swung open and Vale stood there, clearly fully awake. He was in his shirtsleeves, his hair dishevelled, and his eyes glittered with a focus that was almost frightening. "Singh, old fellow, I appreciate what you've said. But there are some situations where a man has to make his own choices." He glanced at Silver. "A man. Not necessarily a Fae."

"There's far less difference than you might think," Silver drawled casually. But he was watching Vale with the same sharp focus, ignoring the others.

Vale ran a hand through his hair. "Lord Silver, when I had far too close an encounter with some of your kind in that other Venice, I found they were quite incapable of making real choices. They'd already made the only real one that they were capable of, in choosing to be what they made themselves."

"So be yourself!" Silver said. "You've bored me on the topic often enough. The law needs you, justice needs you—"

"Yes, this is true . . ." Vale hesitated, and for a moment the air in the room seemed as thick as honey, full of potential, full of choice. "But what is also true is that a particular person needs my help."

He took a deep breath. His eyes and voice were steadier now. "I would be a shallow stereotype of myself if I took cases *purely* for the sake of intellectual curiosity. I am quite capable of providing assistance to a friend who has asked me for it. Winters, as one human being to another, is there anything you want to ask me?"

"Yes," Irene said firmly. Kai looked as if the ground had been cut from under his feet, or as if a book for the Library had decided to complain about being stolen mid-theft. Singh was watching Vale cautiously, but at least he wasn't interfering so far. Silver had shut his mouth, which was an unquestionable improvement. "I need you to help me find someone."

"Then please sit down," Vale said. "And, Lord Silver, thank you for your time and attention, but I have an urgent investigation in progress. Don't let us detain you."

Silver slammed the door behind him.

CHAPTER 20

I have my notes over here," Vale said, striding across to a pile of documents on the table. It was surrounded by a morass of maps, clothing bills, death threats, and newspapers. Vale swept them all away with a casual gesture, and Irene had to catch them to stop them from sliding off the table. "Combine the purchases made from certain exotic animal suppliers to provide the spiders that infested Winters's home, the deposits and withdrawals of money at various banks, Zayanna's desire to avoid Lord Silver, and the current movements of various gangs for hire . . . While not conclusive, it leads to a clear angle of investigation."

"Which exotic animal suppliers?" Irene asked. A nasty thought came to her. "And has Zayanna been buying anything *else* besides spiders and wasps?"

"Which wasps?" Vale asked.

"These ones." Kai reached into his pocket and pulled out a rather mangled example of the ones that had attacked them. It still had a sliver of glass through it. The stinger looked even larger than Irene had thought, and her stung hands throbbed with new pain at the reminder.

"Ah!" Vale picked the thing up by one wing and inspected it. "Not a wasp, but a giant Asian hornet! The size is quite distinctive."

"Personally I'm *glad* there aren't many hornets out there that are two inches long," Irene said with a shudder. "Is that any help in locating her?"

"It confirms my suspicions." Vale leaned over to tap a spot on a map of London. "A great many things can be bought at Harrods, but this isn't one of them. She must have been shopping at the Belgravia Underground Market."

Singh was nodding, but Irene and Kai exchanged glances of mutual incomprehension. "The Belgravia Underground Market?" Irene asked.

"An establishment in Belgravia," Vale said. "It facilitates the sale of rare animals, and frequently highly dangerous ones. A number of the vendors there skirt the edge of the law, but given the price of the wares and the social rank of the buyers, it's difficult for the police to interfere."

Singh nodded grimly. "The lady's broken some laws. But I can't bring in a few constables to turn the Belgravia Underground Market upside down and shake it to see what falls out. I'd never get a warrant for it. I'm afraid we're going to have to be *subtle* about this, Miss Winters."

"But you think we can find a lead on Zayanna there?" Irene said, going for the main point.

Vale nodded. "Let me get my coat. I'll only be a moment."

As Singh headed downstairs to call a cab, Kai drew Irene into a corner. "I'm concerned," he said flatly.

"So am I," Irene agreed, "about a lot of things." Such as whether she'd just destroyed Vale by forcing him into this investigation. She'd known he wouldn't say no when she'd insisted on offering him a choice. And both Kai and Singh had insisted on trying to help Vale instead. If she'd ruined him by making him stay here to help her . . . she felt ill at the thought. She didn't need Kai questioning her right now. She was far too busy questioning herself. "Which one are we considering at the moment?"

"I'm concerned about your motivations." Kai folded his arms defensively. "You've already shown that you're irrational about Zayanna."

It was far easier for Irene to contemplate Zayanna's betrayal than to consider how she herself might have betrayed Vale. Her voice dropped to barely a whisper, but she could hear her own anger in its absolute chill. "Since when have you been *my* superior? Since when have you been in a position to judge *me*? Do you think I'm going to let Zayanna go with a slapped hand, just because I thought she was a friend?"

Kai looked as if he'd like to back away, if he could only find a way to do so without looking as if he was doing so. "You listened to her before," he tried.

"She had a plausible story before. It made sense. She had helped me. I felt sorry for her."

"You felt sorry for a *Fae*."

"I'm only human." Irene's fury—at Zayanna, at herself—was a ball of acid in her stomach. "And because of that, as you are no doubt going to point out, I made a mistake. I trusted someone who was better at acting harmless than I've ever been, I got us both into danger, and I risked the Library." *And I just endangered Vale.* "You don't *need* to tell me, Kai. I am perfectly capable of seeing this all by myself."

"It's more than just that. In order to get hold of her, you were willing to risk—" Kai cut himself off, but the glance he shot in the direction of Vale's bedroom door finished his sentence for him.

"I was trying to get all the facts before I made a decision," Irene replied. "Just because Bradamant had said . . ."

A memory unexpectedly jarred into place. The conversation with Bradamant and Kai in the Library, when Bradamant had mentioned how Vale could become fully Fae. Kai had said without hesitation that Vale would never agree to it. But Kai hadn't asked any questions or suggested it would be impossible for Vale to become Fae. He hadn't even needed to pause to consider. Which meant that he'd already known about the possibility.

"You knew that was an option," she said flatly. "Vale becoming a full Fae. You knew and you didn't tell me."

The betraying flicker of guilt in Kai's eyes gave him away before he could try to deny it, and he knew it. "It would have been worse than death for him," he protested. "It still may." He'd dropped his voice now as well.

I always thought Kai was the sort of person who'd lie to protect the people he loved. Why should I be so bitter when it turns out that he'd lie to me? "It wasn't your decision to make."

"It was." He assumed that air of hauteur again. "Would you trust a drunken man to make the right decision when it came to saving himself? If I was incapable of making decisions, wouldn't you make the choice that was right for me?"

"That's not the point," Irene said. Her anger was still there, heightened by that irrational sense of betrayal. "Vale *was* capable of making decisions."

"Nobody who's that contaminated by chaos can be trusted." Kai looked down at her, and for a moment she had the same sense of absolute distance, of inhuman pride, that his uncle had carried with him when they'd met before.

She could argue about it with Kai for a hundred years, and all she'd get out of it would be wasted breath. And she wasn't going to make tearful eyes at him and say *If you were really my friend, then you'd agree with me.* She'd never wanted her friendships to be on those terms.

Irene took a deep breath, tasting the air and the familiar smell of Vale's rooms. Paper, ink, chemicals, coffee, the old leather of the armchairs, the constant overriding fug of pipe smoke. "Let me be honest," she said. "This is not a situation I've been in before. I may have been let down in a professional way, but I've never actually been betrayed by someone whom I considered a friend." *And I've never sacrificed a friend, either. Not like this.*

Kai had enough sense not to say anything along the lines of *Well, obviously Zayanna wasn't a friend and never could have been, and this proves it.* He simply nodded.

"And you're right. I am feeling more than a little irrational about this." Her anger was a saw-blade, honed and ready to rip. She was tired of splitting hairs with him, tired of arguing comparative morality, tired of wasting time when the Library was in danger. The clock was ticking. "But don't worry. I'm not going to let that stop me from getting the information we need. There's no more time for this. I need to capture Zayanna, and I need to know that I can rely on you. Do you trust my judgement?"

"I trust it enough to tell you all this to your face." He touched her shoulder and did his best to smile. "But do be careful. I'd rather not have to train a new superior."

Irene was trying to find a good reply to that when Vale emerged from his rooms, properly dressed and swinging a coat over his shoulders. He hustled them down the stairs to where Singh had managed, somehow at this time of night, to find a cab.

The Belgravia Underground Market didn't make any particular attempt to hide itself. Their cab-driver recognized the address. When they arrived, the houses were dark at street level, lightless behind drawn curtains. But the windows of basement flats all down the road gleamed with the dazzle of strong ether lamps. Passers-by strolled in pairs or groups, very few of them alone: even in this expensive part of London, the night was dangerous.

"It was started over a century ago," Vale explained. He gestured down the row of elegant pale houses, their black iron balconies gleaming with reflected light from the street lamps. "Lyall Mews. The properties were all owned by the same noble family. Unfortunately, their heir wasn't as good with cards and dice as he'd thought, and the family ended up mortgaged to their eyebrows. They eventually signed a contract with a syndicate, permanently renting the entire set of cellars to them for a nominal fee, though they kept the houses above."

"And that same syndicate still owns the contract," Singh agreed. He'd turned up his collar against the night air, and his moustache bristled above it. "Even if all the houses are owned by different families these days. How do you want to handle this, Mr. Vale? There are two main exits, one at each end of the market. We don't want to risk our quarry bolting out of one the moment we walk in the other."

"You think Zayanna will actually be here?" Kai asked.

"It's possible," Vale said. "Not very likely, but certainly not impossible. Or we can question stallholders who might have seen her. She is Fae, after all. And even if she doesn't actually need any more pets, she may not be able to resist the urge to come shopping."

He pointed down the street again towards a square of light on the pavement, indicating an open door. "That is one of the two entrances to the market. The other is beside us. There are approximately three vendors who might have supplied king baboon spiders, giant Asian hornets, and snakes—you did mention that she was fond of snakes? If two of us use this entrance and the other two enter by the other door, we can work towards the middle. If we check with vendors on the way, then we can intercept the lady if she is present; and we may hope to find her delivery address, if not."

Irene was not wildly enthusiastic to find herself heading down to the far entrance in Singh's company. Singh was too professional to show it, but she didn't think he was happy, either. But Vale had proposed the division of labour, and Kai had agreed to it.

Are Singh and I supposed to realize each other's good points while working together and bond over the job? She was perfectly well aware of Singh's good points. He was intelligent, professional, ethical, and probably a better influence on Vale than she was. It was more a question of Singh disliking *her*—on the grounds that she was a book thief from another world who'd broken the law more than once, and who had put Vale in danger. And she couldn't really argue with that.

The open door at the far end of the street also leaked light out into the foggy night, together with a mixture of aromas—an overriding smell of cheap incense, and beneath it undertones of hay, mould, and dung. The room behind the door was small and bare, lit by a single ether lamp, and might once have been a storage cupboard. Two large men were sitting behind a table, anonymous in overcoats and mufflers. A cash-box sat on the table in obvious invitation.

"How much is it?" Singh asked. He'd pulled his hat low over his eyes and, like the men, he'd now covered his mouth and chin with a scarf. Irene had collected a spare overcoat and veil from Vale's rooms and was similarly well covered. The whole thing was verging on the ridiculous. If this was the general standard of dress for the Belgravia Underground Market, no wonder people with more money than sense spent their time and cash here. Still, it did increase the chances of their finding Zayanna here. She'd love it.

"Five guineas each," the man on the right said. It wasn't an attempt at bargaining. It was a simple statement of fact. Irene revised her opinion of this place's customers, placing them even higher up the idle-rich scale of finance.

Singh and Irene dropped money into the cash-box, and the man on the left nodded them towards the inner door.

Noise washed over them as they stepped inside, and the smell made Irene draw her veil closer across her face. The long stretch of cellars wasn't well lit: the occasional lamps were turned down or muted with coloured shades, and the far end of the market was hidden in shadows. The cellars were wider than she'd expected, and she realized they must run under the front street on one side and also out under the back gardens of the houses on the other side. Vendors had laid out their stalls in little islands in the centre of each cellar, or jostled each other along the walls. Some displayed tanks and aquariums with snakes, lizards, and fish. Others showed off gauze-covered boxes and hives, or cages, or even animals on small leads. A pair of white owls in the corner overlooked the room with furious yellow eyes, glaring down like offended deities, their legs tethered to their owner's table by paired chains. The clothing of the shoppers ranged from the expensive to the ridiculous, but given the time of night and the fog outside, most people were muffled in heavy coats.

"Miss Chayat's stall first," Singh said, nodding over to the right-hand wall. "She's one of the main insect suppliers, I believe."

The stall in question was obvious, standing between purveyors of armoured lizards on the right and of Siamese fighting fish on the left. Its shelves were filled with tiny cages, each containing a single insect or a pair of them, walled with gauze and sealed with wax. The air around it hummed with the sound of struggling insects. The stall-holder herself was as untidy as her wares were neat, with long greying hair that tangled around her face and blended indistinctly into her tattered shawl and beige dress. She peered at them suspiciously as they approached.

"King baboon spiders," Irene said, getting to the point. "And giant Asian hornets."

The woman pursed her wrinkled lips. "It'll take a week to order the hornets in. I can do you the spiders, though—there's currently a glut on the market."

Irene had almost forgotten their earlier sale to the pet shop. It was interesting to see the free-market economy in action. "That's annoying," she said, affecting her best upper-class accent. "I'd been told I could find giant Asian hornets here. If it's because someone else has placed a prior order on your stock, I'm sure I could pay more . . ."

The stallholder shook her head, cutting Irene off. "Whoever told you that told you wrong. Those hornets need to be ordered from abroad. You just can't keep them in this climate, and nobody here would keep them in stock on the chance of a sale, least of all me. There's no call for them. The only one in this market who *might* be able to get them for you in less than a week is Snaith. You'll find him two cellars along, in the middle, if that's what you're after."

Irene glanced at Singh and he nodded. This didn't sound like a vendor who'd sold any within the last month. Snaith—who was also one of the other sellers Vale had named—was a more likely bet. "Thank you," Irene said and moved on.

It was difficult to make one's way through the market in a straight line. The stalls were laid out haphazardly, in some defined pattern that had evolved from rationality into chaos. And the buyers clustered around them, examining their wares, rather than clearing the way for others to get through. Singh and Irene had to take a wide detour round one stall, where the vendor was shouting down a group of buyers who wanted armadillos—claiming that the recent leprosy scare was making imports impossible. A pair of men in overcoats, similar to the men at the entrance, were already shoving through the crowd towards the disturbance. The market's internal security, no doubt.

They had to pause again in the second cellar. A woman with huge glasses like an insect's faceted eyes was complaining vociferously. Apparently her new cheetah cub, Percival, was too fond of eating her food and chewing her fingers—and she'd specifically asked for one with better training. The cub in question was trailing behind her on a silver chain, chewing it and staring at the tanks of piranhas on the next stall along. Between the woman and her secretary, and the stall-holder, and all the interested onlookers, there was no way past. Singh and Irene had to circle round laboriously towards the third cellar.

It was then that Irene recognized a face.

It wasn't a particularly distinguished face, and it had a brand-new black eye since last she'd seen it. But it was the face of Davey, one of the werewolves who'd kidnapped her earlier. He was speaking to one of the stallholders Vale had pinpointed. And even more importantly, due to their sidelong approach, he didn't seem to have noticed her.

She drew Singh to one side, ostensibly to examine some duck-billed platypuses, and murmured an explanation to him as she watched Davey surreptitiously. She was grateful for the animal smells all around them—it should cut down on the chance of his recognizing her.

Davey was complaining about the failure of an order to arrive. The order—a mated pair of spitting cobras—had apparently been delayed in transit from Mandalay, due to prevailing winds. Davey was whining about the inconvenience of it all: the stallholder polished his monocle, unimpressed.

"It might be a trap," Singh muttered. Irene nodded. She'd had the same thought. Zayanna could quite easily trail a known agent in front of Irene and Kai in order to lure them into a prepared ambush. Then again, they had come to the market because Vale had deduced that Zayanna was shopping here. It was plausible that she'd send an agent rather than come herself. This might be for real.

"I'll follow him," Irene said, keeping her voice low. "You can find out from the stallholder where the order's supposed to be sent. Then find Vale and Kai and send them after me. I'll try to leave a trail to show where I've gone."

Singh's brows drew together. "I don't think so," he said. Irene turned to glare at him, but he shook his head very slightly. "Miss Winters, I know this is serious, but what if this Davey fellow takes a cab the moment he steps outside? Or what if you're several streets away before I manage to find Mr. Vale and Mr. Strongrock? Having you off on your own somewhere won't help the situation. We'll do better to find out where he wants the stuff delivered and then go there together."

Irene gritted her teeth. "We may be almost out of time. I don't think we can afford to wait. If he gets away from us, or if the address is a fake one—"

"Miss Winters." Singh's hand tightened on her arm, and when she looked at him, she saw genuine concern in his eyes. "Think it through, madam. It's because the matter's so urgent that we can't take any risks. You're the one person here who can reach your Library. We can't risk losing you."

"You know damn well that Vale would be going after him alone," Irene muttered.

Singh sighed. "Indeed I do, Miss Winters. Indeed I do. And I'd say exactly the same thing to him, madam. You are not making my life any easier by suggesting precisely the same thing that he'd have in mind. A little bit of self-preservation would make life a great deal easier for all your friends. This is no night to be splitting up and losing you in the fog. Nor is it a good thing for them to be getting into trouble because they lose track of you."

He had a point. Irene locked down the rising panic that was her constant companion, the sense that every second she wasted was a second the Library couldn't afford to lose. "Very well," she agreed, and tried not to sound too grudging about it.

A few minutes later, with the stallholder's voice greased by the application of a lot of money, they had an address.

CHAPTER 21

The delivery address was a warehouse in the East End of London. The cab had dropped them off a few streets away.

"Zayanna is going to have a back exit," Irene said, repeating a point she'd already made several times in conversation in the cab. "And we know she has henchmen. Maybe even better-quality ones than Davey. We can't risk letting her escape out the back while we come in the front. Or vice versa."

"What's the roof like?" Kai asked.

"I wouldn't trust any roofs in this area," Vale said. Now that they were about to swing into action, he seemed entirely his normal self, and Irene could almost persuade herself that the febrile edge in his eyes was her imagination. "Not without a chance to check them first. I don't like Winters's idea of us splitting up any better than you do, Strongrock, but it seems our best option."

"Then *I'll* distract Zayanna," Kai suggested. He drew himself up, every inch the young prince and commander. "Irene would be much more effective getting in round the back and using the Language to open the locks."

Irene had been wanting him to demonstrate his independence and decision-making ability. Just not right now. She didn't need an argument at this moment. She had too many other balls in the air. "Kai, in case you didn't notice, Zayanna doesn't *like* you."

"So? She's Fae. She'll welcome a confrontation—"

"I'm not talking about pandering to her love of drama," Irene said, thinking of the Fae fondness for declaring eternal enmity against a rival, then spending their lives plotting obsessively against such a target. "I'm trying to establish that she actually, genuinely doesn't like you. I think she might even seriously try to kill you if she sees you in the firing line. With me, she'll want to talk first."

"And you want to talk to her, of course," Kai said coldly.

"If you know any other method to get information out of her, then kindly tell me now and don't waste my time being facetious," Irene snapped. "And a lock pick will work just as well as the Language. You don't need me to open locks." She considered saying, *It's three to one*, since Vale and Singh had already agreed, but she didn't want Kai being half-hearted about his side of the job. Also, it wasn't a democracy. "Please be careful, gentlemen. If Zayanna's expecting us, she may think we'll use the back way as a matter of course and may have set up all her traps there accordingly."

Vale nodded. Singh looked as if he was questioning exactly why he was there—and about to run into danger on her account—but he nodded, too. Kai finally made a reluctant noise of agreement.

"Right." Irene checked her watch. "Ten minutes for you to get into position; then I go and knock on the door."

A distant church clock was chiming five when she finally rapped on the warehouse side door. The skies above had begun to pale a little, but the fog still clung at street level.

There was no answer from inside the warehouse.

Irene stepped to one side and inspected the area in the way that Vale would have done. An arc of dirt on the pavement showed that the door had been opened recently, and the mark of twin wheel-tracks demonstrated that something heavy had been pushed or dragged in or out. It also suggested that Zayanna did indeed have minions in there, if this was her base. Zayanna was not the sort of person to push heavy trolleys herself.

She tested the handle, still standing to one side of the door. Locked. All right. This was manageable. **"Warehouse door lock, open."**

It was quiet enough on the street at this hour of night that she could hear the tumblers in the lock click into place. She gave it a moment to see if anyone inside reacted, but there was no answering noise. Mentally crossing her fingers, she tugged the door open and peered into the room.

To her relief, there weren't any shotguns or harpoons or axes, or whatever, wired up to the door. The room inside was an ordinary small office, an ether lamp still burning on the wall in spite of the late hour, complete with chairs and desk. Another door in the far wall led farther into the warehouse.

The thought of incriminating documents and invoices led Irene across to the desk, but she hesitated as she reached for the top drawer. For one thing, it was far too convenient a location for traps. And another thought had struck her. Why should the ether lamp be on at this time of night? Either because someone had just been in here, or because someone—like Irene—was expected . . .

"All right," she said, looking around. Her voice seemed too loud in the silent room. "Zayanna? I came to see you."

For a long moment there was no answer, and Irene was able to consider all the ways in which she'd bollixed up the plan. Then Zayanna's voice called from beyond the inner door, "In here, darling!"

Irene advanced cautiously, looking through into the room beyond. It was the heat that hit her first. The large space beyond the door, nearly one-third of the warehouse interior, was as warm as a greenhouse. Thick black cloth had been nailed up against the walls and across the ceiling, covering the windows and blocking draughts. Cages and terrariums stood at careful intervals, interspersed with large electrical-coil radiators and blazing ether lamps. It all looked vastly unsafe. At the centre of the room were a couple of divans with a small table between them.

Zayanna had made herself comfortable on the farther divan, leaning her chin on one hand as she contemplated Irene. She was in clinging black satin that trailed over the edge of the divan, giving her a serpentine air. "Do come in," she murmured, her eyes mocking. "My pets are all perfectly safe."

"I remember you used to look after snakes for your patron." Irene wasn't quite certain that she wanted to walk between those cages to reach Zayanna. The scorpions in the closest terrarium looked too active for Irene to be comfortable anywhere near them. And far too big.

"I do prefer snakes," Zayanna admitted. "But I like other pets, too."

"This many of them?" Irene indicated the cages and terrariums with a gesture.

"Oh well, I might have got a tiny bit carried away there. I just went to do a teeny bit of shopping, to get a few little ones to start with, and you know how it is." Zayanna shrugged. "Wasn't it Oscar Wilde who said that nothing succeeds like excess? I thought I'd try it with giant hornets and see if it was true."

"Sadly—well, I suppose it's sadly for you, not me—it didn't quite work," Irene said. She ignored the impulse to ask exactly where Zayanna had read Oscar Wilde. "I'm here, after all."

"I did hope you'd make it, darling." Zayanna reached across to pick up one of the bottles that stood on the table. "Can I offer you something to drink? Strictly no obligations, my word on it."

"And no poison?"

"My word on that, too," Zayanna promised. "Darling, I do realize you might be a tiny little bit suspicious of me at the moment, but we're not going to have a proper conversation if we have to keep on shouting at each other across the room like this. Won't you come and sit down? I'm not going to try to kill you while you're walking over here—it'd spoil everything."

It was the same logic that Irene herself had used, after all—*she won't kill me because she'll want to gloat at me*—but it was a little less comforting when she was face-to-face with it. "All right," she agreed, knowing that her caution was audible in her voice. "But you must understand that I'm rather annoyed with myself at the moment."

"Why?" Zayanna asked. "And what would you like to drink?"

Irene began to walk carefully between the cages and heaters, holding her full skirts close to her legs. Her multiple layers of clothing—overcoat and ballgown—were swelteringly hot. "Well, I am supposed to be good at my job, rather than falling for the first sob story that comes along."

"But I was *convincing*," Zayanna said smugly. "And let's be fair, darling, we had history and I was well prepared."

"Oh?" Irene tried to make the question sound only mildly curious. "And do you have any brandy there?"

Zayanna shook her head vigorously, her dark curls tousled over her shoulders. "Brandy's so dull. I've got tequila, absinthe, jenever, *baijiu*, vodka—"

"Brandy is *not* dull," Irene protested. The feeling of time running through her hands like sand gave her a nagging ache of urgency. But the more Zayanna relaxed and focused on Irene, the easier it would be for the men to break in unobserved. Thinking of it as a military operation helped Irene suppress her own anger. "And aren't you hitting the spirits a little bit heavily?"

"Who needs a liver?" Zayanna picked up a bottle whose label proclaimed it BEST-QUALITY AMSTERDAM JENEVER and splashed clear liquid into two glasses. "Now then, darling. Sit down and we can talk. I'm sure you have lots of questions for me."

Irene seated herself on the divan opposite Zayanna's, with the table between the two of them. "I should probably get to the point. Zayanna, you *are* the person who's been trying to kill me, am I right?"

"I'm definitely one of them," Zayanna said. She pushed one of the glasses across the table to Irene. "There may be other people, too. I wouldn't necessarily know."

"Why?" Irene tried to keep her tone level, to treat the subject as casually and lightly as Zayanna did, but the word twisted in her mouth and turned sharp. "Perhaps it was stupid of me, but I hadn't realized we were on those terms."

"Which terms?"

"The terms that involved trying to kill each other."

Zayanna tilted her head, looking puzzled. "Well, on a practical level, we are, but that doesn't mean we have to be unpleasant to each other. It's been such a challenge!"

"A challenge," Irene said flatly. The stings on her hand throbbed as she reached across to pick up the glass.

Zayanna nodded. "You were an *inspiration* to me, Irene darling. When we met in Venice, you were so calm, so controlled, such a perfect agent! I did tell you at least a bit of the truth. My patron threw me out. He showed me the door. He turned the metaphorical dogs loose on me. And the real dogs, too! He said I should have been more proactive, more aware. So when Alberich offered me a job, I thought, I can do *better*. I can be just as good as you were!"

Irene stared into the jenever. She couldn't quite bring herself to take a sip, even though alcoholic oblivion was oh-so-very-tempting at that precise moment. "You know, Zayanna, usually I'd be pleased and proud to think that I was an inspiring teacher, but right now I'm feeling a bit conflicted on the subject."

Zayanna took a swig of the jenever and licked her lips. "I can understand that you're feeling a bit depressed about losing. But do cheer up! Maybe next time you'll win."

"There won't *be* a next time if I'm dead," Irene felt the need to point out. "And I'm not dead yet, so saying I've lost seems somewhat premature."

"It's like having the king in check in chess," Zayanna said. "When the next move is going to be checkmate, you can say you've won, even if the other person hasn't agreed to it yet. The front door locked itself behind you. I've got men next door, and they'll come running if I shout. There's a button under my foot, darling. It's wired to all the cage doors. If I press it, then everything gets opened—and I promise you some of my pets have very fast-acting poison. And I've taken the antidotes. So you see, I *have* won."

It was an interesting theoretical situation. Irene would prefer to avoid the practical experiment. "All right," she agreed. "Technically, I suppose that does count as check, and I can't immediately move my king out of the position. It's a pity. I'd hoped I could get the answers to some questions before, well . . ." She wiggled her fingers in a manner suggestive of poisonous snakes.

"Hmm, we might be able to come to an arrangement," Zayanna said. There was a sly, bargaining note to her voice. "Technically my contract said 'kill or otherwise take out of circulation,' so as long as I keep you out of the way, darling, I think that fulfils it."

"Your contract with Alberich." Irene nodded knowingly.

Zayanna smiled. "I couldn't possibly tell you, darling. That'd be betrayal and . . . let's just say that would be bad for me." She tried to make a joke of it, but there was a flutter of nervousness behind her voice.

"How bad?"

"Permanently bad." Zayanna sighed. "One would almost think he didn't have faith that we'd stay loyal or avoid being captured. Speaking of which, how *did* you find me here? I was expecting you, but I still don't know how you did it."

Irene needed a plausible reason that didn't draw Zayanna to any conclusions about possible allies showing up. "I used the Language," she lied, gambling that Zayanna wouldn't necessarily know everything it could or couldn't do. "I was able to track one of the giant Asian hornets from the British Library to here." And where had the men got to, anyhow? She could use a rescue, or at the very least a diversion.

"Oh," Zayanna said. She looked around at the cages and terrariums. "Drat. I hadn't thought of that. I'm so glad you didn't try it with the spiders. It would have absolutely spoilt things if you'd caught up with me that early."

Irene wanted very badly to grab Zayanna by the shoulders and scream at her that this wasn't some sort of game—that the Library might be destroyed, that Irene could have been killed. That things didn't just happen in a vacuum, but that cause led on to effect. She saw that her hand was shaking, and she put the glass of jenever down before she spilled it. "I can see that would have cut things short," she agreed. *Why aren't the men here yet?*

Zayanna sighed. "Darling, I'm not getting much of a sense of engagement from you here. You're being very analytical about it all. Don't you want to swear vengeance or anything? I did betray you, after all. I knew that you'd be protective if you thought I was in trouble, just like you were with that dragon you saved . . . Where is he, by the way?"

"I sent him home," Irene said. She'd been expecting that question. "It was too risky for him to stay in this world."

"Probably a good thing. I'm certainly not in this to start a war with his family," Zayanna poured herself more jenever. "And he's so incredibly possessive. Such a bore."

"Some people might say that was the pot calling the kettle black," Irene remarked drily.

Zayanna pouted. "Irene, you're being unfair. I don't want to keep you out of danger or stop you doing your Librarian thing. Totally the contrary. That's why I don't want . . . anyone to kill you."

"But if Alberich destroys the Library—" Irene tried.

Zayanna looked blank. "You can find another patron, can't you? You won't stop being what you are."

"And nor will you, it seems." Regret fought with anger, and for a moment Irene wished she could be stupid enough to drink that glass of jenever. It might help her feel a little better about the fact that Zayanna wasn't, and didn't *want* to be, anything other than a manipulative Fae who was far more interested in playing the game than in why it was being played. Irene thought of that list of destroyed gates and dead Librarians. They were real. Compared to that, the fact that she'd once liked Zayanna and thought of her as a friend was as important as . . . well, as a dead giant Asian hornet.

"So what now?" Zayanna leaned forward eagerly. "Do tell me, darling. Are you meditating a simply devastating counter-move? Will you leap across the table and attack me? Or are you going to flee into the London night?"

"Fleeing wouldn't work very well," Irene said. "You'd probably have the werewolves hunt me down."

"Oh, drat—you guessed that one. I could drop you into a pit of snakes, maybe? We always used to do that back home. And then we'd have cocktails."

"You have a pit of snakes?"

"Next door," Zayanna confirmed. "Or I can keep you in chains or something."

"Which you also have next door?" Irene leaned forward, resting her hands on the drinks table, casually sliding her thumbs under its lip. "Don't worry. I do understand that you don't have a choice in the matter. Being what you are."

Zayanna looked hurt. "Irene darling, that didn't sound very kind."

"It wasn't meant to be." Irene gave up trying to categorize her feelings and settled for the fact that she could feel both anger and pity for Zayanna without their being mutually exclusive. "It really wasn't."

"But we're friends." Zayanna gave her the most human smile she'd given yet that evening. "Don't you remember? We went swimming together in Venice, and you told me about your old school?"

"And you got drunk and complained about how you always had to milk the serpents and you never got to seduce any of the heroes," Irene agreed. This conversation had reached the point where awkward choices were going to have to be made, and she couldn't wait for the men any longer. "I'm sorry that you lost your patron."

"Bah," Zayanna said dismissively. "I've had more fun in the last few months than I did for decades before that! This is what I was meant to be, darling."

Irene nodded understandingly. And then she thrust the table upwards, bottles and all, dumping them all over Zayanna.

CHAPTER 22

The table went over in a crash of bottles and glasses. Zayanna cried out in anger, shoving it off her, but she was well doused in a spray of vodka, gin, and other expensive spirits. The floor was littered with broken glass. Irene sprang to her feet and took advantage of the other woman's confusion to grab her by the shoulders and drag her off the divan, dropping her on the floor. "No pressing any buttons," she said. "No releasing any snakes or scorpions, or whatever."

"Guards!" Zayanna shrieked. There was an undertone of panic to her voice. "Guards! Get in here now!"

The far door swung open. Kai was standing there with Vale and Singh. "I'm afraid they're not available," he said. "Will we do?"

Irene was just starting to enjoy the look on Zayanna's face when a single click sounded. She half-glanced sideways, not taking her attention off Zayanna for a second. A cage door had swung open, and a long green serpent was tentatively wriggling out of its enclosure. More clicks sounded, like a house of cards ever so slowly collapsing, as other cage doors opened.

"It was a dead man's switch," Zayanna spat. She touched her throat nervously. "It was supposed to activate if I took my foot off it. Do you think I'm *stupid*? Now let me go!"

"No," Irene said firmly. "Not an option. You're going to tell me the truth."

Zayanna came to her feet in a sudden motion, but instead of charging towards Irene, she bolted away. Irene had been expecting some sort of reaction, but the other woman's sheer speed took her by surprise. So she ended up rugby-tackling Zayanna rather than anything more elegant. The two of them went down together, rolling across the alcohol-splattered floor. Little scratching noises of skittering insect feet sounded uncomfortably close.

Irene managed to hold Zayanna down, getting a knee in the small of her back and twisting an arm behind her. "You're not getting away," she grunted. "Stop wasting time—"

Zayanna started to choke, and she scrabbled at her neck with her free hand as she gasped for breath. A string of words in the Language was appearing around her throat, dark characters rising to the surface of the skin and stamped there like a tattoo. Irene could make out odd words through the coils of Zayanna's hair as she struggled. **Betray. Captive. Die.**

That would be bad for me, Zayanna's voice echoed in Irene's memory. *Permanently bad.*

Irene abandoned her grip on the Fae and rolled her over onto her back, tilting her head back to get a better view of the Language. It was tightening like a noose, and the words were growing from thin sketched outlines to full shaded images, stamped as black as bruises on Zayanna's throat. Zayanna clawed at them, but her fingers found no purchase, and her chest heaved as she struggled for breath.

"What's going on?" Kai demanded from behind Irene's shoulder.

"A trap from Alberich to stop her talking. Keep the snakes off us," Irene said. She sorted through her mind for words in the Language to block this. She could read the full sentence now, clasped in a deadly circle round Zayanna's neck. **Before I should betray you, or be forced to speak, or be made captive, I shall die.**

Irene opened her mouth, but a sudden thought stopped her before she could try using the Language to break Alberich's death sentence. Alberich had sent Zayanna—and other Fae—out to kill Librarians. He'd expect Librarians to be trying to question them. He'd *expect* people to use the Language to save Zayanna.

She ignored the thuds and crashes from behind her and fumbled in her pocket for a spare coin, pulling out a silver shilling. That would do. If she couldn't break the Language with the Language, then she'd have to find another way to damage that sentence. Running more on instinct than with a plan in mind, she folded her coat-cuff around her fingers and grasped the coin.

"Silver shilling in my hand, rise in temperature to red-hot heat," she ordered.

Coils of smoke rose as the hot metal charred the fabric of her coat. Zayanna was barely struggling now, her eyes glazed and her breath coming in tiny whistling gasps. Irene put one knee on Zayanna's left wrist to hold her arm down, grabbed the other woman's hair with her free hand to drag her head back and bare her neck, and pressed the red-hot coin against the word *die* on her neck.

Zayanna screamed. Irene gritted her teeth and held the coin against Zayanna's flesh, watching as the circle of burned flesh blotted out the word below it.

The noose of Language around Zayanna's throat twisted like a living thing, balked of its final verb and forced into incoherence. Then it snapped, and the words dissolved into swirls as they faded. Zayanna could suddenly breathe again, and she gulped down great swallows of air, tears running from the corners of her eyes as her body went limp.

"Irene," Kai said urgently. She turned to see him stamp on a scorpion. He pointed at blue flames rising from where a pool of alcohol had reached one of the flaming heaters. The fire was starting to spread across the floor, and Irene flinched back away from it. "We've got to get out of here."

"I can put that out," Irene said, controlling herself. She dropped the coin. A red brand marred Zayanna's neck where it had burned her. "Give me a moment . . ."

"It might be easier to let the place burn down," Singh suggested. "I'm not generally in favour of arson, but given the number of deadly creatures loose in this place, one might call it public sanitation."

"Singh has the right of it," Vale agreed. He paused to knock aside a cobra with the remains of the table. "I suggest we retreat and call the fire brigade."

"That sounds good to me," Irene said quickly before anyone could change their minds. The sooner she was away from flames, snakes, insects, and whatever—and able to question Zayanna—the better. "And then we can get some answers."

Half an hour later they were in the upper room of a nearby pub. The fire brigade had been called (and had been in time to save the rest of the neighbourhood), Zayanna's minions were in custody at Scotland Yard, and Zayanna herself was sitting up and demanding gin.

Irene had searched the room and dumped any printed paper in the corridor outside. She hoped that would cut down on the risk of Alberich interfering. She hoped even more fervently that he wouldn't be trying to find her and that he'd assume she was still in prison back in St. Petersburg.

Vale had turned up the ether lights and drawn the curtains, cutting out the light from the warehouse fire outside. The sound of fire engines and crowds drifted through the window. Zayanna had draped herself over one of the rickety chairs in the centre of the room and sat there smoothing her skirts, her new brand scarlet on her neck. Irene sat facing her, while Kai stood by the door and Singh and Vale hovered watchfully.

Zayanna had completely recovered her good mood, in spite of having lost her pets and probably her cash reserves. No doubt it was because she was the centre of attention. No Fae could resist that. "I suppose I could tentatively surrender, darling," she suggested. "It'd be difficult for me to manage to kill you now."

"You did try your best," Irene agreed. "I'll give you extra points for effort. And I did just save *your* life."

"It was only in danger because you'd captured me anyhow. So what now?" Zayanna tilted her head enquiringly. "Do I get imprisoned?"

"'Killed' sounds more appropriate," Kai said coldly. Irene had agreed with him that he'd be the bad cop to her good cop. But from the tone of his voice she was worried that he'd be an extremely homicidal cop.

Zayanna batted her eyelashes. "Are you threatening to kill me in cold blood? In front of an officer of the law? Isn't that *illegal*?"

"You're right, madam," Singh said. "I'm absolutely shocked to hear those sorts of threats. Mr. Strongrock, if you'll excuse me for a moment, I should go and check on the firemen. Let me know when I should come back in."

"Don't bother," Zayanna said sourly. "You've made your point. So, Irene. You said you wanted me to surrender. I'm surrendering. What happens now?"

"Tell me about Alberich," Irene said. The name was bitter in her mouth. "What's he doing?"

"Trying to destroy the Library, darling," Zayanna said. Then, after a pause, "Oh, you want *details*?"

"Yes." Irene kept her voice patient. "And, Zayanna, let me be clear about this. I'm saving your life. In return I want the full truth, and I want you to be helpful about giving it to me."

"Saving my life?" Zayanna pouted. "I know that you did destroy Alberich's curse, and that I did cause you a few problems and everything, but would you really *kill* me?"

"Yes," Irene said. The word came out with difficulty. She looked Zayanna squarely in the eyes. "Listen to me, because I am being absolutely truthful. The Library is more important to me than you are. If I have to, I will give you to the dragons, or I will sell you to Lord Silver, or I will shoot you in person. That's three things that could kill you. I'm the only person in this room who's actually interested in keeping you alive." She saw doubt in Zayanna's eyes and shifted to the Language, making the words a promise and a truth. **"If you don't tell me what I want to know about Alberich, then I am going to kill you."**

Zayanna flinched back against her chair, as if Irene were the poisonous snake and she were the threatened victim. Perhaps it was the Language. Or perhaps it was something in Irene's face. "Don't!" she cried out. *"Please!"*

"Vale." Irene extended her hand. "Your gun, please."

Vale slapped his pistol into her hand without a word.

He doesn't think I'd really do it. He thinks I'm bluffing to convince her.

Irene thought of the darkened corridors and rooms in the Library, of the gate going up in flames and of the list of dead Librarians. She raised the gun to point it directly at Zayanna.

Zayanna stared at the gun. She wasn't doing her usual trick of playing with her ringlets. Her hands tightened on the sides of the chair, and her breath was fast and panicked. "I—" She swallowed. "All *right!*" She flung herself from her chair, going on her knees in front of Irene. "I'll tell you what I know, and I swear I'll tell you the truth. I surrender. I really *do* surrender."

Irene handed the gun back to Vale, trying to calm her racing heartbeat. That had been too close. She had never thought of herself as the sort of person who was genuinely ready to kill for information. She'd manage a few convincing threats, maybe, but those would just be bluffs. It was an unpleasant surprise to find out that she was ready for lethal action, and that she'd go through with it so easily, so unhesitatingly. "Get up," she said wearily. "Back in your chair, please. I accept your surrender, but you have to tell me the whole truth."

Zayanna picked herself up off the floor and slid back into her chair, her stockings miraculously unladdered. "What he's doing is—"

There was a banging at the door. "Gentleman for Mr. Strongrock!" the barmaid from downstairs shouted.

Irene turned—well, everyone turned—to stare at Kai. Even Zayanna looked interested, though possibly because the interruption took the pressure off *her*.

Kai himself looked dumbfounded. "I didn't tell anyone to meet me here," he protested. "How could I have? I didn't know we were going to be here."

This could be a cunning ploy to get into the room and kill them all. Or it could be a genuine message for Kai, in which case it was almost certainly from his family or Li Ming. And in *that* case, Irene needed to hear it. "Let's see who it is," she suggested.

It was Li Ming, led by a curious barmaid, dapper in his usual grey and with an attaché case in one hand. While he didn't actually look around the room and sniff in disgust, clearly it was only because he was far too polite to do so. "Your Highness," he addressed Kai. "I hope that I have not come at an inconvenient time."

"Your presence is always welcome," Kai said, court-trained manners coming to his rescue as he closed the door and shut out the barmaid. "We were just interrogating this Fae."

"May I be of assistance?" Li Ming enquired.

Irene watched Zayanna out of the corner of her eye. She could see the Fae reassessing the situation and slumping even further in her chair. "Actually, Lord Li Ming, Zayanna here was about to tell us more about Alberich's plan." Would it be a good thing for the dragons to know what was going on? Irene couldn't see any way in which it was a particularly *bad* thing. They'd never cooperate with Alberich, which made them allies in the current situation. "If your message for Kai could wait a few moments, would you permit her to speak first?"

"I would be glad to," Li Ming said. "Might this have something to do with a world that Your Highness was investigating recently—I heard there were some disturbances?"

"Ah yes, I was going to speak with you about that," Kai said, a little too quickly. "Perhaps after we have dealt with the current problem?"

Li Ming nodded. He stood beside Kai, an inch taller than him and currently much better-dressed. They might have been part of a matched set of statues, frozen in marble but ready to break free at any moment, their power chained and controlled but always present.

Irene turned her attention back to Zayanna. If Kai was in trouble because of their Russian mission, she'd handle that later. "What's Alberich doing?" she asked bluntly.

"It's sort of a cosmological thing, darling. Please hear me out—I'm not sure how to explain this properly. I know your Library's connected to spheres all over, isn't it?"

Irene knew that *spheres* was the Fae term for alternate worlds. "It is," she agreed. "So?"

"Well, the spheres that are more comfortable for my people—the ones that Aunt Isra would have said were ones of high virtue . . . Do you remember her?" Zayanna waited for Irene's nod. "There's a point at which they become really unstable. They're dangerous even for us. I admit I don't know for sure, but I suppose it's the same thing at the other end of the scale, too?" She looked at Kai and Li Ming. "Are there places that are so rigidly ordered that even you can't exist there, without losing your personality?"

Kai and Li Ming exchanged glances. Finally Li Ming spoke, and he was clearly choosing his words with care. "It's true that human life requires at least a very small amount of chaos, to be recognizable as human. But there are worlds that are entirely static. They are necessary to the functioning of reality, but they are not places where humans or dragons can live. They are indeed too rigid." He fell silent again—though it wasn't clear if it was because of some obscure embarrassment at the idea one could have too much order, or because he didn't want to reveal anything more.

"I can accept that both ends of reality are dangerous," Irene said. "So how are these unstable spheres relevant to Alberich?"

Zayanna ran her fingers through her hair. "I really wish you'd captured someone who understood this properly. What I took from Alberich's explanation, darling, is that he's somehow linking one of the really unstable spheres to other spheres, more stable ones. And he's doing it by using unique books from those stable spheres, which he stole before your Library could get them."

She waved her hands in the air, trying to find the right words. "Imagine your Library's a sphere at the centre of a web of chains. All the worlds it influences are linked to it by these chains. And the chains are created through the power of special books, unique books. And I know how much you love your books, darling. So if a book is taken from a world, then kept in the Library, this forges a connection and brings the chain into being. You know these chains as gates to your Library. 'Traverses'—isn't that what you call them?"

Zayanna waited for Irene to nod, then went on. "So the more books the Library holds from a particular world, the stronger the connection will be. But then Alberich brings along his own sphere, the unstable one. He steals a book from one of the Library's existing 'satellite worlds,' if you like, but instead of it going to the Library, he links it with his chaotic world. And he does this time and time again—no, I don't know how often, but I did get the impression it was one of those gloriously long-term plans."

Zayanna took a breath. "But the universe won't allow a world to be linked to two centres of influence; it just doesn't work that way. So the problem for your Library is that these new linkages are pulling the unstable sphere into the same place as your Library. Now Alberich's unstable domain is actually replacing your Library in a metaphysical sort of way. And the more other worlds start synchronizing with the unstable sphere, the stronger this replacement effect becomes. So, in time, it blows up your Library's gates to other worlds entirely—even where Alberich hasn't hijacked any linking books. The sphere he's using is taking over all the links instead."

Irene could feel the blood leaving her cheeks. "Surely that can't be possible."

"Well, you tell me, darling." Zayanna shrugged. "How should I know what's possible and what isn't? It does sound plausible, though. Isn't there some sort of law about how two things can't occupy the same space at the same time? Inspector?"

Singh frowned. "I believe that's more of a scientific principle than a legal one, madam."

"But if this is an ongoing process," Irene said, "then what happens if—"

"*When*, darling," Zayanna corrected her. "The way he talked about it, it's definitely when."

"When it reaches . . . full synchronization," Irene finished. Her mouth was dry.

"Well, he said there were two possibilities." Zayanna frowned with the air of someone trying to remember the exact words. "Either the unstable sphere would shunt the Library out of time and space by usurping all its links to other worlds. Alberich's new domain would knock the Library completely out of touch and make it completely impossible to reach, and so on. Or the process would just blow up both the Library and the unstable sphere. He was really very conflicted about it, because the second idea sounded more effective—in terms of utterly destroying the Library. But it'd mean that he'd lose all his books."

"A few more questions," Irene said, still trying to process the magnitude of this potential destruction. "Did Alberich say how the process could be stopped?"

"Darling, he's not that stupid. Granted, we'd all sworn to obey him and carry out his plan, and he'd threatened us with fates worse than death if we disobeyed. He'd also put that binding on me and all the others, so we'd die if we were captured or betrayed him, and so on—but even so, he wasn't going to tell us *everything*."

Irene nodded regretfully. "And the fact that I broke that binding on you means that now you're free to disobey him?"

"Or you're playing for time," Kai suggested.

"I admit it would solve all my problems if he blew up the Library right here and now. No more conflicts of interest!" Zayanna smiled at Irene cheerfully.

Irene's stomach lurched at the thought. "How much time do we have?" she asked bluntly.

"I don't know," Zayanna said. "I honestly don't know—my word on it. But I don't think you've got long." Her expression was friendly, even sympathetic, but there was no genuine understanding of Irene's emotions behind it.

She grasps that it would hurt me if the Library was destroyed, Irene thought. *She just doesn't really perceive why it would hurt me, or how much.*

The nearby fire had been put out by now, and the sounds of conflagration and fire engines alike had died away. The street hadn't yet begun to stir with morning activity. For the moment everything was quiet as Irene considered how to frame her next question.

"Can you take people to his unstable sphere?" she finally asked.

Zayanna's smile vanished. "Darling, that's a terribly, terribly bad idea."

"But you aren't saying no."

Zayanna chewed on her lower lip. "I'm saying let me think about it. I'm not playing for time. I suppose it might be possible . . ."

Irene nodded. "Good." They could take in a strike team of Librarians, disable whatever Alberich had done, and hopefully dispose of Alberich while they were at it. Problem sorted. Admittedly it was a very sketchy plan, but it was one hundred per cent more of a plan than she'd had half an hour ago. She turned to Li Ming. "I apologize for the delay. You have a message for Kai?"

"For His Highness, and for you by implication. My lord knew that His Highness would pass you the information anyway." Li Ming favoured Irene with a quick, understanding smile. He put his attaché case on the battered table, opening it and exposing the written documents inside. The black ink of the writing seemed to draw the light, as if the fact that they could see it now gave it an unhealthy significance. "We have a proposal—"

Then the air pulsed as though it were the surface of a drum struck by a careless hand, and the buzz of chaos-tainted Library power washed through the room.

CHAPTER 23

Li Ming's attaché case sprang fully open, as though an unseen hand had flipped back the lid. The writing on the papers inside writhed and coalesced, shifting and re-forming in unstable patterns. Li Ming recoiled from it, and behind him Kai was flinching as well, similar expressions of sheer disgust on their faces. The papers rustled against each other, humming like a nest of wasps.

Irene knew the taste of Alberich's power by now, and the power was building to dangerous levels.

"Open a window!" she shouted.

This had happened in the werewolf caves, when three ingredients had been present: some form of writing, a Librarian, and Alberich's will at work. Alberich had again zeroed in on where she was—and this time Li Ming's documents had given his corruption a focus. If this was a message, it was the sort that left people dead.

Vale fumbled with the window latch, but it was rusted in position. "It's stuck," he reported calmly. But then, he couldn't feel the mounting power in the same way Irene did, and he didn't have the same revulsion to it that the dragons had. "Singh, try yours—"

"No time. Stand back, gentlemen. **Windows, open!**"

Both windows in the room flew open, dragging their latches out of the sockets. They were sash-windows, the up-and-down vertical sort, and they rose to their full height, hitting their upper limits with enough of a bang to crack the panes. Glass came tinkling down on the window-sills and fell into the room as the cold morning fog rolled in.

The writing on the papers had dissolved into a constant wash of words in the Language: tangled, nonsensical vocabulary but no actual sentences, not even coherent phrases. The attaché case was shuddering where it lay on the table, jerking in place as though it had been electrified, and the rising buzz of power was clear enough now that even Vale and Singh could hear it.

Irene sheathed her hands in the battered folds of her skirt in an attempt to protect them, and flipped the lid of the attaché case shut. There was a jolt as she touched it, a painful vibration that echoed in her bones and made her grateful that the contact was only momentary. "Kai," she ordered, "help me with the table!"

Fortunately Kai understood her meaning instantly. Gritting his teeth, he grabbed one side of the table as she caught the other. They ran across to the window together, pitching the case and its papers into the empty street outside.

The explosion shattered the remaining glass in the windows and seared the air with a wave of scorching heat. Everyone in the room ducked, even Li Ming. Then there was silence, except for the clinking of broken glass falling to the ground.

Muffled shouting started outside, with the thumps of people throwing open their own windows and leaning out to see what was going on, to complain, or both.

Irene shook her hand, trying to work the vibration out of it. "I'm very sorry about your papers," she said inadequately to Li Ming. "I hope there was nothing too significant in there?"

Li Ming looked wistfully in the direction of his attaché case, then shrugged. "Nothing too important," he said, and Irene couldn't work out if he was being ironic or not. He continued, "Only some possible drafts for a treaty, in the event that the Library might wish to petition my lord and his brothers for protection. I take it that was Alberich's interference just now?"

"It was, yes," Irene agreed, part of her responding automatically while the rest of her mind registered that they had hit dangerous political waters. Throwing themselves on the mercy of the dragon kings was certainly an option for the Library, in terms of sheer survival. But it would mean they'd lose their all-important neutrality. However nicely the dragon kings might put it, from that point onwards the Library would be their dependant. And however much autonomy might be promised in those treaties, at some point the Library would end up taking orders.

She glanced across and saw Kai frowning, clearly going through the same mental calculations. She couldn't really *blame* the dragon kings for taking advantage of the situation. It was the practical, politically sensible thing to do. That was how rulers reacted when they saw an opportunity. But that also put limits on what she could expect from Li Ming, here and now, in terms of help against Alberich . . .

Also, how much had Alberich seen just now? She didn't know how much the person on the far end of this sort of connection—whether it was the Library or Alberich—could pick up from the other side. Maybe Alberich could merely sense she was present, and his actions were the metaphysical equivalent of tossing a grenade into the room. Or maybe Alberich could actually see who else was present. Such as Zayanna. In which case . . .

Irene swore, ignoring the looks of shock from all the men in the room, who apparently either considered her to be above such things or refused to admit such words existed. Then she grabbed Zayanna's shoulder. "Zayanna. Can you get me to Alberich's sphere? Right this minute?"

Zayanna blinked in confusion. "Well, possibly, yes, darling, but why the hurry?"

"Because I don't know whether or not Alberich could tell you're here. He targeted that effect on me." Irene pointed at the window through which she'd thrown the papers. "If he knows you're here as well, if he realizes you're sharing his plans—"

"But I had to—you threatened to kill me . . . ," Zayanna protested.

"Whatever. You did tell us, and he won't care *why*. Now we know what's going on, and if he finds out, he'll find some way to stop us. And your life will probably be short and interesting, but mostly very, very short." Irene turned to the others. "I'm sorry, but I don't think we have a choice. Zayanna's going to have to take us here and now."

"Irene," Zayanna said quietly. "I think this is an absolutely thrilling idea, darling. And you're absolutely right that Alberich will kill me horribly if he realizes I've talked—or even that I *might* tell you anything at all, once he realizes I'm not already dead. But there is one tiny little problem with your plan."

"Which is?" Irene said through gritted teeth.

"It's the *us* idea. I can get to Alberich's sphere, and I can probably take one person with me, but that's all." She spread her hands in apology. "Darling, I'm not Lord Guantes or Lord Silver, or anything like that powerful." *If I was, I wouldn't be in this situation* went unsaid but understood.

"Then you take me," Kai said, stepping forward.

Li Ming's "No, Your Highness!" clashed with Irene's "Certainly not!" and Zayanna's own "Impossible."

Irene gestured at Kai to stop him from protesting and said to Zayanna, "Why impossible?"

"He's a dragon," Zayanna said. "He's harder to move. I don't even know if I could take him at all. And I don't think he'd like the level of chaos there, anyhow." Her smile wasn't pleasant.

"So I go there myself—" Kai started, then came to a stop. Irene remembered how he'd travelled between worlds. It was entirely different from the way they'd travelled with the Fae before, and he knew it. How would his method of travel mesh with Zayanna's own technique—and how would he know where to go, without her leading the way?

Kai and Vale exchanged glances. Singh saw it and said, "Mr. Vale, surely you can't be considering—"

"He won't," Irene said. "Vale, I value your abilities, but if only one of us can get to Alberich's sphere, then I'll be able to do more there than you will. I'm the one who's going." She offered Zayanna her hand. "And we'd better be going now, rather than standing around talking."

Kai stood there fuming, obviously considering the idea of simply knocking Irene over the head or holding her down, rather than letting her waltz off on such a suicidal proposition. "This is quite possibly a trick so that she can lure you out there and claim credit for your capture," he said, with surprising control.

"Is it?" Irene asked Zayanna.

"I won't deny that I thought about it," Zayanna said. "But would Alberich actually believe it, or would he simply kill us both on general principles? Darling—darlings"—her gesture took in the whole room—"I swear that I'll just take Irene here to Alberich's sphere, and I'm not planning to sell her off to him or anything."

The word *sell* drew a twitch from Kai. No surprise, given how it had nearly once happened to him. "And are you telling the truth about only being able to take one person?" he demanded.

Zayanna put one hand on her heart and took Irene's hand in the other. "I am. I swear it."

While the two of them were glaring at each other, Irene had formulated a plan. It wasn't much of a plan, but it would have to do. "Kai, there is something I specifically need you to do."

"What?" Kai asked suspiciously.

"This isn't just me trying to get you out of the way so I can run off into danger," Irene said. The way he avoided her eyes told her that he'd been imagining exactly that. "I need to get this information to other Librarians. You can do that for me."

"But I can't reach the Library," he pointed out. "You'll need to get me in there."

"Kai, you're being deliberately obtuse." Irene could hear the edge to her voice and made herself calm down. It wasn't easy. Panic at what she was about to do was nibbling at the edges of her control. "You said you could find *me* in different alternate worlds, a few days back. Well, you know Coppelia, and Bradamant told us she was out on assignment. Go find *her*. Go and find all the Librarians possible, whether they're students or full Librarians."

"I know you better than them, so you're easier to find," Kai said flatly. "You *are* deliberately trying to get me out of the way. I won't accept this."

"Do you have a better idea?"

"I'm sure she can work out some way of taking me along." Kai's glance at Zayanna was almost as unfriendly as the look she gave him in return. "Just because she says I'm harder to move doesn't make it impossible. The important thing is to reach Alberich's sphere."

"Which is high-chaos by its *nature*," Irene burst out in exasperation. "Weren't you listening? Kai, you're a dragon—that is the *last* place you can go."

"Miss Winters is quite correct." Li Ming had come up to flank her supportively. "Your Highness, surely you must see how it would look if Miss Winters took you into a high-chaos world. You'd barely be able to maintain your true form there, let alone help her. Worse still, she'd be doing it purely in order to support her own faction. Your uncle would disapprove. Your *father* would condemn it."

Kai opened his mouth, then shut it again. Vale and Singh were talking in the corner, their voices lowered, and even though she couldn't make out what they were saying, it was fairly obvious that Singh was doing his best to talk Vale out of a proposition, and it wasn't hard to guess what.

Sorry, Vale. This is one trip that you can't secretly infiltrate in disguise.

"We have to go," Irene said. She was trying not to think about the main reason she was hurrying: the longer she delayed, the more reasons she'd find why this was a *bad* idea. All the words she'd thrown at Bradamant earlier came back to echo at her now. *Reckless. Foolish. Dangerous.* Running off solo with a Fae whom she *knew* was untrustworthy, all the way into the private turf of the Library's worst enemy, who already had a grudge against her . . . Possibly two grudges, depending on how Alberich felt about that business at the Winter Palace. It could hardly be worse.

No, that needed rephrasing. It *could* be worse. This was a chance, an opportunity, but only if Irene took it now. She reached out to take Kai's hand and squeeze it. "I trust you. Warn Coppelia, warn the others. When I get to Alberich's sphere I'll either force a passage to the Library so that we can bring in reinforcements, or I'll find some other way to mark it and bring people back." She was aware that it might be impossible to reach the Library from high-chaos worlds, but that was just one more of the things she was trying not to think about. Another was whether she'd be able to function there herself. She'd soon find out.

He returned the clasp. "Irene, do one thing for me."

"What?"

"Tell me in the Language that you'll come back."

Oh, unkind. She glared at him, but he wouldn't release her hand. "Is this really necessary?"

"It'd make me feel better."

"When did you get so manipulative?"

"No doubt from watching his teacher," Vale commented. "Winters, this is a foolhardy enterprise, but I appreciate that you don't have a choice. Telling us that you intend to return seems to be the least you can do to reassure us."

"**I fully intend to come back to you.** There, are you satisfied?" Her words in the Language were a promise to herself as much as to them. She would have liked to complain that she didn't know why they were so annoyed, for *she* was the one who was going into danger. But honesty compelled her to recognize that if they'd been the ones going, then she would have done her utmost to follow them. Honesty was most unhelpful: it got in the way of a satisfying whine of complaint at their overprotectiveness and made *her* feel like the one at fault.

"Not remotely satisfied." Kai pulled her into a hug, his grasp almost tight enough to hurt. "I know I can't talk you out of this," he murmured in her ear. "But when you get back, we are going to discuss the future."

Irene sighed, returning the embrace, trying to convince herself that she was only doing it from habit and not because she actually needed the comfort. "Just make sure there's brandy," she murmured back.

Kai released her. But Li Ming was stepping forward, his face set in unusually stern lines. Ordinarily he was content—or at least seemed content—to be a figure in the background, merely offering Kai his advice. Maybe he had some vital suggestion to offer?

"This is quite unthinkable, Miss Winters," he said. The room was abruptly colder, and the ether lamps whined in their sockets like dying flies as they flared bright and translucent. "You cannot possibly go."

That was not a helpful suggestion. "It seems the best option," Irene began.

Li Ming made a brief cutting gesture with one hand. It would have suited a judge's pronouncement of a guilty verdict. "The Fae's untrustworthy. Even if she swears she's telling the truth, she's not reliable. You're risking yourself and all those who depend on you. My lord would not approve of your taking this step. I don't approve of it."

"I'm sorry," Irene said. "I appreciate your opinion, but—"

"This is no longer a time for courtesy." The familiar scale-patterns flowed across Li Ming's skin like ice on the surface of a river. The windows rattled as the wind rose outside. He was beautiful, remote, untouchable, and utterly certain of what he was doing. "I will not permit this folly to take place."

"That's *not* your decision to make," Irene snapped.

"Any rational being has a right and a duty to stop you committing suicide." The cold wind had a biting edge now, harsh with the taste of oncoming winter and frozen streams. Irene had never really wondered how powerful Li Ming might be. He'd always been acting the servant or the counsellor, staying in the shadows. That might have been a serious mistake on her part. "You are a junior servant of the Library. This duty should be left to others. My lord would forbid you to take this action. Your Highness, help me restrain her."

Zayanna was shivering, folding her arms around herself. Rage warmed Irene: she looked sideways to Kai, letting him respond.

But Kai hesitated.

Irene realized how clear it must seem in his eyes. The logic would be beautifully tempting. Irene was endangering herself: her judgement was faulty, her assessment of the situation incorrect. He should stop her for her own good. He would be serving the Library by keeping her safe. It all made sense, and it was still the most profound sort of betrayal that he should even be *thinking* it, that he could look at her and entertain those thoughts and not be ashamed.

Irene turned to Li Ming. "You may try to restrain me," she said, her voice as cold as the rising wind. "You will not succeed. I must be on my way. *Zayanna.*" She grabbed the Fae's wrist.

Li Ming nodded, as if he wasn't surprised, and extended a hand to grasp Irene's shoulder.

Kai caught his wrist a moment before Li Ming touched her. The chill that sheathed Li Ming's hand brushed Irene's skin like fresh snow, and she pulled away, dragging Zayanna with her.

"Wait," Kai said, and all the subtones of hierarchy and command were suddenly in his voice. But he was saying it to Li Ming, not to her. "She has my permission to do this."

"Your Highness, this is folly . . . ," Li Ming protested. Irene glanced over her shoulder as she and Zayanna hurried to the door and saw that even though neither dragon moved, they were locked in position as they struggled against each other. This wasn't mere courtesy. It was two forces of nature, both looking less human by the second, as scales marked their skin and their eyes gleamed draconic red. The wind outside howled, denied its target.

Irene didn't waste any more time. With a nod of farewell to Vale and Singh, she was out of the room and rattling down the stairs, Zayanna right behind her.

The street outside was full of wind: it rolled through like a physical thing, rattling windows and slamming shutters, ripping the fog away to show the lightening sky. Irene hadn't let go of Zayanna, for fear that she might vanish around a corner and never come back. "So how do we get there?" she asked.

Zayanna sighed. "You take my hand and we walk, darling. Or perhaps we just keep on running. I can't manage a horse, much less a carriage. I'm afraid it's going to be tedious."

"You can tell me about Alberich's sphere as we go," Irene suggested. They turned left down a dark side alley. It was the sort of place that Irene would normally avoid, but Zayanna sprinted down it without a moment's hesitation.

"It looks mostly like a library," Zayanna gasped. "I'm not sure whether it originally looked that way, if he made it look that way, or if it's getting to look that way because it's moving into the place of your Library. I told you that metaphysics really isn't my thing. So confusing." She turned left into another side street. This had slick grey concrete walls that reached farther above their heads than should have been possible in that area of London. The wind had gone, and the air was still and hot, stinking of oil.

"Well, does Alberich have guards?" Irene asked.

"I didn't see any." Zayanna frowned a little, a thin line between her elegant brows. She'd slowed her pace from a run to a fast walk. "I mean, there were a few people there, but they were just people. *You* know—or have you never been that far into chaos before? When you go too far in, normal humans don't have very much real personality. They're awfully responsive when they're needed for background parts, but they don't have much staying power, if you take my meaning. They're not as meaningful to work with as other Fae, or even dragons or Librarians like you."

Irene mentally shuddered at the thought. People with no genuine personality of their own, simply walk-on scenery or character parts for Fae psychodramas. "You should be careful," she said sardonically. "At this rate you'll be convincing yourself that if the Fae did win, and chaos took over all the worlds, you'd still ultimately have lost—by missing out on all those interesting interactions with other people. It sounds rather self-defeating."

"Maybe, darling, but we're hardly the only contradictory ones." Zayanna turned left again, her frown deeper. They were walking between grey stone walls, the cobbles beneath their feet damp with the morning dew. Lilac overhung the walls, its scent sweet in the morning air. "What was Li Ming saying about places that are so orderly and mechanical that even dragons or humans can't exist? People do keep on talking about wanting a war so that their side will win. But ultimately all they *really* want is for their side to be a bit better off. Nobody wishes for their side to triumph completely." She paused, considering that statement, and clarified it. "Nobody *sane*, that is."

"Ay, there's the rub," Irene muttered. She tried to remember where in Shakespeare that was from. Hopefully not one of the tragedies. "I wish I was simply back amongst the books again."

"We could go hunting books after this," Zayanna suggested. "We'll steal them from that silver dragon's private library—"

"Oh no we won't," Irene said hastily, before Zayanna could make that bad idea any worse. "Besides, you can't be a Librarian."

"I think that's very prejudiced of you all." The passage was now so narrow they were forced to walk in single file, though Irene kept her grip on Zayanna's hand. "Why can't I steal books too?"

Irene considered and rejected all the arguments that started *There's more to it than just stealing books.* "Because you'd have to swear yourself to the Library," she said. "Permanently, full-time, life and death. Would you actually do that, Zayanna?"

Zayanna laughed, but there was something a little forced about the sound, and Irene couldn't see her face. "How true, darling! I'm just a frivolous, self-obsessed little mayfly. How well you know me."

Part of Irene wanted to kick herself for saying the wrong thing while depending on Zayanna to lead her to Alberich's sphere. Another part felt unreasonably guilty. *She's admitted to working for Alberich and against us, to trying to kill me and Kai, and I'm embarrassed because I hurt her feelings. This is neither logical nor intelligent.* "I'm sorry," she said. Whether or not Zayanna deserved an apology, it felt like a good idea to give one. She couldn't afford to have the other woman turn against her now. "I know you were just doing your job. And I'm sorry for branding you. It was the only way I could think of to save your life."

Zayanna rubbed at the angry burn on her neck. "Try to be more artistic about it next time, darling. That's all I ask."

For a while they walked in silence. Irene wanted to go faster, but Zayanna was the one setting the pace. The Fae's steps had grown slower, and she forced herself forward as though she were struggling against a high wind. The air was thick and close, like the end of summer, full of dust and smelling of dry grass and overripe fruits. Zayanna's face was marked with sweat, and she pushed her hair back from her face with her free hand, muttering a curse.

"Can I help?" Irene asked, breaking the silence.

"No." Zayanna sounded as if she were in the middle of running a marathon. "Told you it was going to be difficult to bring someone else along. Just keep on walking. Keep on going."

The walls on either side were red brick now, and the two women had to turn sideways to squeeze between them. Beyond the walls Irene thought she could hear the sounds of machinery, great pumping presses and turning gears.

Zayanna stopped, and Irene went up on her toes, peering over her shoulder to see what lay ahead. She saw a small door set into the wall, unobtrusive and constructed of plain metal, looking positively unimportant. An incongruous letter-flap was set into it.

"Ah," Zayanna said. "Here we are." She opened the door before Irene could stop her.

CHAPTER 24

I t was something of an anticlimax to find the space beyond the door full of bricks. They were cemented in place, and even dusted with cobwebs in places. For all that Irene could tell, the doorway might have been bricked up for decades.

"It wasn't like that before," Zayanna said. She tilted her head to look at it from another angle, but that didn't make the bricks miraculously disappear.

"Is this where anyone trying to get to this sphere would arrive?" Irene asked. "Or is it just that you used this door last time, and so you came here again?"

"Not exactly, darling." Zayanna rubbed her nose thoughtfully. "It's more as if this sphere is like a carriage in motion, and we're running alongside and trying to jump on, and this is the point where you can scramble into the carriage from the road. I know that's a really bad simile—or is it a metaphor?"

"It's a simile," Irene said, glad of a question she could actually answer. "You said 'like.'"

"Simile, right," Zayanna said. "But that's basically how it is. This is how anyone would get in if they tried to reach it the way I just did. It does look rather as if Alberich doesn't want visitors." Implicit in her tone was a suggestion that perhaps now that she and Irene had made the effort, they could turn around and leave, with honour satisfied.

"And the letterbox? Was that there before?"

Zayanna nodded. "It was there so we could pass urgent information to him."

"Like about what I was doing—yes, quite. And it's a reasonable supposition that he wouldn't want Librarians getting in here, either," Irene said, thinking out loud. "So if I were him, I'd booby-trap it against someone using the Language, in case one of us told the bricks to get out of the way."

"He's not really giving us much of a chance," Zayanna said unhelpfully. "How are we supposed to get in there?"

"But he doesn't *want* us getting in there . . . ," Irene started, then paused. Alberich had hijacked a high-chaos world. In high-chaos worlds, stories came true. No narrative would ever finish with *And so the protagonist shut himself up in a convenient castle until his plan came to fruition—tale over.* He could brick up doors and lay traps, but in any classic story the intruder would eventually enter the castle. "Are we in a high-chaos area at the moment ourselves?"

Zayanna wobbled her hand. "Fairly. Quite a bit. Not as much as Venice was, but more than that world you were living in. There's a strong gradient between this sphere we're in at the moment and the one through that door."

"Do you think we could get through the wall at any point other than that door?" Irene asked.

"No." Zayanna was quite definite. "At least, not by any way I know."

Irene nodded. "All right. We need to stand well back."

Zayanna looked alarmed but interested. "What are you going to do, darling?"

"Substitute brute force for caution." Irene had a nasty feeling that trying to use the Language *directly* on the barrier might set off some sort of trap. It was the logical thing to set up, if one was expecting Librarian intrusions. And there would no doubt be alarms. But if she could hit fast enough and hard enough, then perhaps that would work. She stepped back and focused. **"Bricks from the walls on either side of me, smash open the brick wall blocking that doorway!"**

Using the Language in a higher-chaos world had benefits and drawbacks. On the positive side, the Language worked more easily and more powerfully. But on the negative side, Irene had to sacrifice a corresponding amount of energy. It was like shoving a weighted trolley downhill: once it started to roll, it really *went*. But it was that much harder to steer or stop, and the first shove came at a cost.

The walls on either side groaned. Moss and dust fell from them as they shuddered in place, pattering down on the narrow passage where Irene and Zayanna stood. Then, with a rolling thunder of crashes, bricks flew through the air like bullets, slamming into the wall that filled the doorway. The first few shattered on it, but the successive pounding impacts of brick after brick drove cracks into the wall. Powdered cement drifted down and mingled with red brick-dust in a choking cloud that made both Irene and Zayanna cover their faces.

It took half a minute of constant pounding for the wall filling the door to crumble. Finally, a brick went through it like a bullet through a pane of glass, leaving cracks in all directions; then more followed, widening the gap and landing on the other side of the doorway with booming thuds that echoed over the crashing of brickwork. More and more bricks zoomed through, till the doorway was denuded of its barrier, with only fragments of cement and broken brick lining it like the edge of a jig-saw. Finally they stopped.

"Now!" Irene coughed, her voice betraying her in the dusty air. She caught Zayanna's arm and dragged her forward, stumbling over fragments of brick to the doorway. Fear caught at her, trying to slow her pace. What if she'd made a mistake? What if passing through would mean instant and horrific death? What if Alberich was waiting on the other side?

Well, if he was, he'd just received a faceful of bricks. She gritted her teeth and pulled Zayanna along with her, stepping through the doorway.

Nothing went boom or splat. Irene was still alive and moving freely. She decided to call her mission a total success so far.

The room on the other side was unexpectedly large. Globes of crystal on the distant walls cast a pale light, which filtered down through the clouds of brick-dust to illuminate shelves of books. The floor under Irene's feet was dark wood, aged and polished. The place could easily have been a room from the Library itself. She guessed that was the point. In the distance, a clock was ticking, a low steady pulse of noise in the heavy silence.

There were three passageways leading out of the room. "Which one do we want?" Irene asked Zayanna.

"No idea, darling," Zayanna said. "Pick one at random?"

Irene tossed a mental coin and chose the right-hand passage. It opened almost immediately into a smaller room: this one had floor-level exits, but also a curving oak staircase that went up through the ceiling and down through the floor. Again, the walls were covered with bookshelves.

She managed to resist the temptation to examine them, reminding herself that the priority was getting away from the entrance before any security came. But several rooms later (two to the left, up one, three to the right, forward two) she finally gave way and paused for just a moment to look at the titles. She frowned at what she saw. "These don't make any sense. They're not in any language I know. They're in the English alphabet, but I don't recognize it. Zayanna, do you know what language this is?"

Irene pulled out one of the thick volumes for Zayanna to inspect. It was bound in dark blue leather and was heavy in her hands, and while the pages seemed clean and stable enough, there was an after-smell that made Irene wrinkle her nose. It wasn't quite a proper stink that could be pointed to and complained about. It was the sort of faint odour that might come from a piece of decaying food somewhere in one's home, which couldn't be precisely tracked down, but which would slowly infiltrate the entire place. It suggested unwholesomeness.

Zayanna gave the book a cursory glance. "Nothing I know, darling. Perhaps it's code?"

Irene scanned a few more books, but they all contained the same jumbles of letters. They weren't in the Language. They weren't in any language Irene knew, either. She wasn't even sure they were in a proper language at all. "Is this a real library," she said, her voice quiet in the echoing room, "or is this just the stage-set of a library?"

"Does it make a difference?"

"I don't know." But one worrying thought in particular nagged at Irene. If this wasn't a *real* library—if all the books it contained were simply garbage—then would she actually be able to create a passage from it to the Library itself, to fetch help? That would be singularly unhelpful.

"This place is like a beehive," she said. "It's three-dimensional."

"Buildings usually are," Zayanna pointed out.

"I mean, in the sense that all the rooms we've been through so far have exits up and down, as well as on the same level," Irene explained. "And all the rooms we've been through so far seem to be more or less the same. Was it that way when you were here?"

"The important stuff was farther in," Zayanna said. "I didn't see much of it, but there was a big open area, absolutely huge, and a pattern in the centre with a clock—and lots of stairs. One of the others did ask about it, but he never got an answer. But this bit here, where we are at the moment, was different then. It wasn't so . . ." She waved a hand. "So *definite*."

Irene tried to work out what that meant. "Has this place become less chaotic since you were last here?"

"Yes, that's it exactly!" Zayanna said. "It's being much more stable now. I wonder why."

Irene was also wondering why, among quite a number of other things: the most important and puzzling of which being why they were still safe. There was no sign of anyone chasing them so far, and the lack of alarms or pursuit was getting on her nerves. It made no sense for them to have been able to penetrate this place so easily. Paranoia suggested that Alberich was watching the entire place, could see every movement they made, and was merely waiting for the right moment to strike.

The problem with paranoia was that if you let it rule all your decisions, then you would miss some perfectly good opportunities. Irene

GENEVIEVE COGMAN

reviewed her priorities. She'd identified Alberich's hide-out, and she knew his plan. The next step was to open a passage to reach the Library and bring back the metaphorical heavy artillery.

"This will do as well as anywhere else," she said, more to herself than to Zayanna. She walked along to the closest door and reached out to touch the handle, focusing her will. This was where things either went perfectly right or horribly wrong. "**Open to the Library.**"

The words in the Language shook the air, and the door trembled on its hinges. The wood of the frame creaked, bending and straining against itself, and Irene felt the connection forming. It sucked at her strength like an open wound, but it was *there*, practically within her grasp. Just a little farther, just a little nearer . . .

All the doors in the room slammed open. The handle Irene was holding jerked loose from her hand. Zayanna pulled Irene back just before the door could hit her. The forming link was broken now, snapped like a piece of overstretched string. All the lights in the room flared up and then guttered to a dim glow. Irene had the impression of a dozen eyes turning themselves in her direction.

Nobody else had entered the room. Nobody at all. But a shadow drew itself across the wall in a dark stretch of overly long limbs and a crooked neck, a shadow cast by a person who wasn't there, and the sound of feet echoed from a long way away. Where the shadow touched them, the books turned white and green with decay, rotting where they stood on the shelves.

"Ahhhhhhh . . . ," a voice whispered, thick and dank. "Now, tell me, Ray, why is it that a thing's always in the last place you look?"

"The malice of inanimate objects," Irene answered. Her mouth was dry and the words stuck in her throat. From best-possible outcome to worst-case scenario, all in the space of a few seconds. She wanted to scream like a child that it wasn't *fair*. "Is that Alberich?"

"Who else would it be?" The shadow reached out towards her, two-dimensional across the floor, its fingers lengthening into claws. Irene and Zayanna stepped hastily away from it. When the shadow drew back again, the wood of the floor was thick with mould.

"You could be one of his servants." Irene's mouth was running on automatic while she tried to think of a productive next step. There was always the tried-and-tested option of *run away in any convenient direction*, but common sense indicated that would be a short-term solution. She needed something better. "But if you are Alberich, then where are you? Where's your body?"

"Always so many questions, Ray." Alberich's laughter dripped through the room as if it were a physical entity, mingling with the ticking of the distant clock. "It's one of the things I like about you."

"And yet you hardly ever answer them."

"I can put myself into all sorts of containers. Skins, bodies, libraries . . ." The shadow leaned away from the wall, spreading its arms across the floor towards Irene and Zayanna. The dark limbs curved around them on the floor to join at the far side, making a circle a few yards across, with Zayanna and Irene in the middle.

"You took your time answering when I came knocking on your door." Irene mentally reviewed all the words in the Language that she knew for *shadow*. Though would Alberich have taken this form if she could affect it? He knew the capabilities of the Language as well as she did. Probably even better.

"It can take me a little while to focus. We're almost at midnight; there's hardly any time left for games. You two are like tiny moths, fluttering through my library, and just as hard to catch." The shadows on the floor deepened, swirling closer to their feet. "But that ends here—"

Irene had been waiting for this. **"Light, strong and clear!"** she shouted, shielding her eyes with her hand against the sudden dazzle, as all the lamps on the wall instantly blazed as bright as high noon.

But the shadow didn't vanish. It was a black stain on the wall and floor, as flat and two-dimensional as dried ink, but it was still there, even in the multidirectional glare of the lamps. And it was still seeping towards them, only a foot away now. Alberich's glutinous laughter dribbled from the walls again. "Silly child. Did you really suppose I wouldn't think of that?"

Panic jump-started Irene's imagination. So what if she was about to demand something impossible? That shadow was already impossible in the first place. She really hoped the universe agreed with her. **"Floor, hold that bodiless shadow!"**

The entire room shook, and the distant clock's ticking jarred for a moment like a stuck record. Books went tumbling from the shelves in a cascade of crashes. A spike of pain twisted in Irene's head, the premonition of what was clearly going to be an appalling headache, assuming she survived the next few minutes. A trickle of blood ran from her nose—but the shadow had stopped in its tracks. Pulling herself together, she threw herself into a jump across the ring of darkness. Her heel came down on its far edge, and wood crumbled into mouldy dust under her foot.

Irene slipped and fell to her hands and knees, but scrabbled to her feet again as she felt the floor tremble under her fingers. She might have held the shadow back for a moment, but there was no way that could last. Zayanna had made the leap more elegantly than Irene and was already through the nearest door. Irene ran after her.

"Which way?" Zayanna demanded, her eyes wide with panic. The room was like the one they'd just left, except that the books were bound in purple leather. There was a door at each compass-point, and a curving stairway running up and down. "This is all your fault!"

Irene couldn't really argue with that statement. She'd been wondering how long it would be before Zayanna brought it up. She decided to focus on the first question, even if she didn't really have an answer. "Try going up," she suggested, taking the lead and heading up the staircase. Her feet hammered loudly on the wooden stairs: neither of them was willing to sacrifice speed for stealth.

On the floor above, the room followed exactly the same pattern, but green-bound books filled the shelves. The covers seemed to mock the two of them with their unhealthy shade, the glistening emerald of a fly's body. Zayanna looked around and cursed. "You should just have put the lights out," she accused Irene. "He couldn't *have* a shadow in darkness—"

"And then we'd be trying to find our way round here in pitch black," Irene snapped back. "It's bad enough trying to find our way in here with the lights *on*."

"Darling, he's going to kill me." Zayanna was apparently calm now, but Irene had the impression of a lid hastily nailed down over a seething cauldron of panic. "And you too, but frankly I'm more worried about me. *Do* something!"

It didn't take a great detective to see that Zayanna was having multiple second thoughts about the whole expedition. "We keep moving," Irene said, sounding calmer than she felt. "If he's got to find us first, then let's make him work to keep up." She pointed farther up the staircase.

"And then?"

That was the question. How could she fight Alberich in a library where he controlled the environment? This whole place was a perversion of the true Library, with books that contained only nonsense, rooms that were indistinguishable from each other, without even an index . . .

Alberich's voice rose from the depths towards them as they ran up the stairs. "I'm impressed," he murmured.

"Is he really?" Zayanna asked.

"No," Irene said.

"Why shouldn't I be impressed? You found your way here. You persuaded your companion to help you. I'd thought you were competent, but I didn't know you were *that* competent."

Irene was only half-listening to the words. Either they were merely one more attempt by Alberich to persuade her to join him, or he was simply playing with the two of them and something horrible would happen the moment they let their guard down. Neither option was useful. Then, as she and Zayanna stumbled out into the next room, she caught sight of Zayanna's face. An unpleasant thought brought Irene up straight, as though someone had yanked her hair. *Which of the two of us is he trying to convince? And what if Zayanna listens to him?*

She needed to find the centre of this place fast. She needed a map. But all she had was books of nonsense . . . which, come to think of it, were an essential part of this place. She could *use* that.

Zayanna screamed and pointed. The shadow was levering itself up the staircase. Long twig-like fingers splayed across the floor, reaching for them. They ran.

Irene grabbed a book off the shelf in the next room as they stumbled inside. It seemed to throb in her hands, its dull orange leather binding the shade of rotten autumn leaves. She flipped it open, but the contents were just as much nonsense as the ones she'd looked at earlier.

"Is this the time for reading?" Zayanna snapped.

"Depends on the book." Irene took a firm grip on it. **"Book that I am holding, lead me towards the centre of this library!"**

The book in her hands shivered as if it was trying to squirm free, then tugged unmistakably towards the doorway on their left. But at the same moment the shadow was in the room with them, stretching from floor to halfway across the ceiling. It reached for Irene.

"Lights off!" Irene screamed at the top of her voice. Every light in the room, and in all the adjacent ones where her voice could reach, shut down. Total darkness enshrouded her. She reached out for Zayanna's hand and felt it warm and trembling in hers.

And then something touched her shoulder. "Really, Ray," Alberich's voice breathed just behind her. "Did you think that would stop me?"

Irene bolted in the direction of the doorway, led by the book she was clutching. Her voice had carried well: she and Zayanna stumbled blindly through two darkened rooms before they came to one with lights on. The book tugged her towards the stairway and down. Behind her, she heard Zayanna gasp in shock, and she turned to see what had happened.

"Get it off, darling!" Zayanna pointed at Irene's coat. "*Quick. There's something on the back . . .*"

Where Alberich touched me . . . With the speed of sheer panic, Irene shrugged her coat off and dropped it on the floor. There was a patch of mould on the shoulder, shaped something like a handprint and visibly spreading. She shuddered in disgust, then tried to squint over her shoulder to see her back. "Is it still there—did it seep through?"

"I think a bit got through onto that robe thing," Zayanna said, inspecting it. She pursed her lips as Irene discarded that as well. "All right, darling, I think you're clean. It's a good thing you're wearing so many layers."

The mould was growing faster now, colonizing the overcoat in vile streaks of grey and white, the same shade as the bone-coloured books on this room's shelves. "We have to keep moving," Irene said. "If I don't use the Language and if we don't stay in one place, it'll take him longer to find us. I think. I hope."

"I can't think why it's taking him so long as it is," Zayanna said as they ran down the stairs, following the book's tugging. The clock in the distance seemed to be sounding a counterpoint to their running steps, its steady tick like a constant pursuit. "If he can see everything in here, why can't he just reach out and squish us?"

"I'm not sure, but I'm not going to complain." The book led them to the right, then three rooms along straight, then down again. The tugging was stronger now. "I think we're closer."

"You realize this could all be a trap." Zayanna's tone was more speculative than nervous.

"Some things are worth risking a trap for."

"For you, darling." Zayanna glanced at the violet-bound books they were passing, then shrugged. "I'm a people person, not a book-hunter."

"It'd be nice if I could be just a book-hunter." Irene was on edge, twitching at every creak or groan from an overloaded bookshelf, eyeing the shadows nervously in each new room. The clock seemed louder now, each separate tick a footstep of oncoming doom. "I was happy when it was *just books*!"

"Were you?" Zayanna shrugged. "I'm no judge, darling, but you seemed to me to be having a perfectly splendid time getting along with those friends of yours back there. I wonder if we'll ever see them again." The question was casual rather than serious, toying with the idea, rather than actually worrying about it.

"I have spent most of my life preferring books to people," Irene said sharply. "Just because I like a few specific people doesn't change anything."

"Do you like me?"

Common sense urged Irene to say *of course* and reassure Zayanna. But she was justifiably bitter over those multiple murder attempts and the fact that Zayanna was complicit in Alberich's attempt to destroy the Library. All reason supported a tart response: after all,

Why on earth should I like someone who'd do that? Finally Irene said, "More than I should."

The next room was ominous: it was the first one they'd come to so far where the books were all bound in black. It had no staircase and only two doorways: the one they'd come through and another on the far side of the room.

"This looks terribly exciting," Zayanna said.

"Not my chosen adjective." Irene stepped forward to the far door. "Be prepared for anything."

She prodded it with the orange-bound book that she was still holding.

Rather to her surprise, the door swung open at once. There was a wide-open space beyond, a terrain clustered with free-standing bookshelves that ranged in height from waist high to multiple storey. In the distance, perhaps half a mile away, she could see an openwork tangle of stairs and points of light. The entire space was huge—larger than she had thought could be contained inside the beehive network they'd come through. It extended to either side. And as she looked up, she thought she could see bookshelves hanging from the ceiling incredibly high above. A blood-red light from some unseen source of illumination filled the place, gleaming on the dark wooden floor. The clock's tick rang in the background, imperceptibly faster.

"There is no way there isn't going to be some sort of alarm," Irene said softly. "We'll have to go fast and quiet."

"Where?"

"To the centre, where else?"

"He'll be expecting us to go there."

"That's our hard luck." Irene took a deep breath, tucked the book under her arm, and crossed the threshold.

The sound was like a thousand dentist drills biting into a thousand innocent teeth. It shook the whole area and jarred painfully in the ears. Books clattered down from their shelves: the ones falling from a greater height tumbled like startled birds, in a flurry of bright covers and pale pages that ended in a sudden crash against the floor. Irene reluctantly gave up on any hope of stealth, and simply ran.

"Surprise," Alberich said from behind her.

Irene turned in time to see a set of shelves as high as a Georgian mansion falling towards her. It didn't move with the speed of normal gravity, but like the finger of someone's hand being folded down to touch their palm. Its shadow blocked out the red light, and there was no time left to dodge, no time to use the Language—

Zayanna shoved into her from behind, throwing her forward. Irene lost her balance and went tumbling, rolling forward frantically in an attempt to keep moving and avoid that terrible impact. Then the bookcase hit the floor, and the concussion of the blow knocked her another ten feet. She came to a painful halt against the base of another bookcase. Books tilted out of it and came landing on her in small aftershocks, thudding down on the arm she'd automatically raised to protect her head.

Silence.

She looked up.

Zayanna lay pinned beneath the edge of the bookcase, half her body trapped underneath it, in a spreading pool of blood.

CHAPTER 25

Irene scrambled across to where Zayanna lay. Everything was quiet, apart from the clock's remorseless counting of seconds. No further bookcases fell. The ground didn't open under her feet. Nothing tried to kill her.

Of course it won't, she thought from somewhere in the depths of her rage and grief. *Not yet. Not till after Alberich has seen me watch her die.*

"Zayanna," she whispered, touching the other woman's wrist. There was still a pulse there. But the pool of blood was spreading, black in the red light. "Zayanna, hold on, let me get that off you. I'll pull you out and then . . ." And then what? The Language could temporarily seal a wound or set a bone, but it couldn't heal, and it couldn't bring back the dead.

"Darling?" Zayanna's eyes fluttered open, but her gaze was unfocused. She coughed a little, trying to breathe, and reached for Irene's hand.

"Yes, I'm here." Irene tried to keep her voice reassuring. "I'm sorry I dragged you into this. Just hold on. Let me—"

"Don't waste your energy," Zayanna murmured. "You'll need it." Her hand tightened on Irene's, a silent *we both know I'm dying*. "The funny thing is?"

"Yes?" Irene prompted as Zayanna's voice faded for a moment. Her eyes were dry. Fury was building inside her, hot as lava, and it left no space for anything that would blur her vision or distract her from her aim.

"I didn't have to push you." Zayanna blinked, like a child going to sleep. "I could have been lying to you all along. I could have let him kill you." Her voice was barely audible now, thin and thready. "I don't understand . . ."

Her breathing stopped. The clock ticked on.

"How curious." It was Alberich's voice. Irene looked up to see the shadow splayed across the ruined bookshelves above her. It was thirty feet tall, twisted and hunched so that the head tilted down towards her. "I recruited Fae who had every reason to hate the Library, ones who'd suffered because of things Librarians had done. When Zayanna asked for you in particular, it seemed ideal. Why did she change her mind?"

Irene released Zayanna's hand. "Human error?" she suggested. Her skirts were stained with Zayanna's blood, though in the scarlet light the blood was black rather than red.

"Hers?"

"Yours. She really wasn't the type to hate anyone." Something twisted in Irene's guts at the thought. "She was a much nicer person than I am."

"*Was* being the operative word." She could feel the shadow watching her. No, it wasn't just the shadow, it was this whole place, and

Alberich had somehow embedded himself in it. "I suppose I should give you a chance, Ray. We still have a few minutes before the clock reaches midnight and the Library . . . stops. Have you come to me in order to join me? Is that why you're here?"

"I . . ." Irene let her voice trail off, gulping back an audible sob. This had to sound realistic. She'd only get one chance. "I thought we could stop you. I thought . . . Oh, Zayanna . . ." She bit her tongue hard enough to bring tears to her eyes, and bent down to cradle the dead woman in her arms. Her hand, shielded by Zayanna's body and Irene's own skirts, sidled along the ground until it felt the wetness of the pool of blood. Working by touch and memory, she began to trace her fingers across the floor. It was a trick she'd played before, and she knew it. If Alberich actually paid attention to what she was doing, rather than to her tears, then he might realize, too. But it was the only trick she had left . . .

The clock's tick seemed judgemental, counting down to a verdict. "I am disappointed, Ray," Alberich's voice whispered from all around her. "I thought you had vision. I thought I could make something of you. But you don't learn from your mistakes. You repeat your errors. You are weighed in the balance and found wanting. Any last words?"

It was an obvious opening for Irene to try to say something in the Language. She could feel the floor tremble beneath her, no longer as solid as it seemed, just waiting to gulp her down before she could even finish speaking a word. The bookcases loomed above her, prepared to drop on her and smear her to a pulp. The air hummed with anticipation.

And all Irene could think was, *I may take a while to learn from my mistakes, but I get there eventually. But Alberich hasn't learnt from his at all.* She blindly traced a final long curve across the floor with bloodied fingers, finishing two words in the Language.

Not Alberich.

Power exploded outwards in a soundless concussion that knocked the air out of Irene and threw her right back into the bookcase, near where she'd lain only minutes earlier. She lay there with her head ringing, trying to muster conscious thought and stand up and *move*. That quality of presence, suggesting imminent movement, had been withdrawn from the floor and bookcases around her. She'd guessed correctly—she hoped. Alberich was possessing this entire library, and since it was all a metaphysical whole, if he was locked out of part of it through the Language, then he must be locked out of all of it. At least for a little while. It made sense, or she desperately wanted it to make sense, especially when energized by panic and stunned through a minor concussion.

Something wet was trickling down her face. She raised her right hand to touch it, then remembered she still had Zayanna's blood on her fingers, and used her left hand instead. Not surprisingly, she had a bad nosebleed.

There was a noise in the distance, something less even and precise than the deep pulse of the clock. It was footsteps.

Panic seized her heart and twisted. She struggled again to get to her feet. Her head was still empty and buzzing with the after-effect of overstraining herself. She had to lean on the bookcase to pull herself upright, and even then it was a struggle.

That was either Alberich himself, in the flesh, or some trusted servant. She had to reach the centre of this maze before they caught up with her, or before Alberich could fill the Library with his presence again and crush her.

Irene shuffled between two bookcases, trying to keep her steps as quiet as possible. She didn't look back at Zayanna. There wasn't any time for affecting farewells to the dead or last promises of vengeance.

I'm sorry, Zayanna, she thought. *Would you have wanted this as an end to your story? Or would you rather have stayed alive? That's the problem with getting too much into character . . .*

With a wrench she pulled her mind away from morbid self-indulgence and back to the present situation. Her concentration and her sense of balance were coming back now that she was moving. She had got this far. Zayanna had died to get her this far. Irene was not going to let Alberich win now.

While she wasn't tall enough, or situated high enough, to see the overall layout of the library between her and the central point, she could get an impression of it. Main roads of empty space radiated out from the centre like the spokes of a spider's web, and smaller gaps between bookcases ran between them at irregular distances.

The footsteps behind her had stopped now. She thought she heard a voice speaking, very distantly and quietly, but not clearly enough for her to make out the words.

So what would I do if I were Alberich? I'd know that I was making for the centre. So I'd either get ahead of me—damn these pronouns—and wait to ambush me. Or I'd get up high where I could look down and spot me coming . . .

She stopped to look up at the bookcases around her. They were as tall as tower blocks—impossibly high for their size, structurally unsound, constructions that should have toppled over even before they were loaded with books. But nobody was standing on the top and looking down at her that she could see. Yet.

Irene wove a zigzag course towards the centre, taking side turns and avoiding taking a single open roadway between shelves. She tried to combine silence with as much speed as was humanly possible. Alberich might be able to enter the physical environment again shortly. At which point she would be a messy smear on the landscape.

She turned a corner, lurking in the shadow and looking to the left and right. No sign of Alberich. But something was wrong. Her instincts were screaming at her.

Wait. By the angle of the bookshelves, there shouldn't be a shadow there. Which meant that the shadow was being cast by something irregular above her. Which meant . . .

"**Books, form a shield above me!**" she shouted, in the same breath that a voice from above called down, "**Shelves, crush that woman!**"

Books and shelves collided above her head. Irene ran for cover in a shower of wood and pages and dust, mentally cursing her opponent's grasp of tactics. What could she do to stop him? She needed either to be up on the same level as him or to find some way of hiding herself from him.

She looked up at the high bookshelves again. She *did* have an advantage. She was on the ground. *Gravity* was her advantage.

"Ready to surrender yet, Ray?" Alberich called down to her.

Irene pressed her back against her current shelter. The metal corners of an unfamiliar book ground into her shoulders, and she shifted sideways to ease it out from its place on the shelf. That would do. "Are you going to shout 'Come out, come out, wherever you are'?" she answered.

"If you make this a children's story, then I'll make it a cautionary tale," he taunted. There was no sign of any movement in the surrounding shadows. She couldn't get a bearing on where he was. But the shadow she'd seen above her had been cast by a real thing, and the voice talking to her now was a human voice. The earlier *thing* had sounded anything but . . . So Alberich was back in a human form again. Less dangerous in some ways, more in others. "Did you ever read your *Struwwelpeter*?"

The door flew open, in he ran, the great, long, red-legged scissorman!

"My parents never liked me reading horror stories." Irene edged along sideways, squinting up at the tops of the surrounding bookcases. The clock sounded louder now. She prayed that didn't signify anything ominous for her Library. "So of course I read them anyhow."

"You sound like the disobedient type. I should have recruited you earlier." And there he was, just the edge of a curve of a shadow on the bookcase to her left, the equivalent of two storeys up. He'd gone down on all fours, making his shadow smaller, but now that she'd spotted him she could keep track of him. "The offer's still open."

Irene brought the book she was holding to her lips. "I still don't understand what you want from me," she said, trying to make it sound like negotiation. "I'm not the only young Librarian out there. I'm certainly not the only one who's ever been demoted. Convince me that you aren't about to kill me the minute I step out of hiding."

"You're the only one I can find who read that story in the Grimm book."

"It's that important to you?"

"It is. You see, Ray, I need to find my son."

The words *my son* didn't make sense at first. The story in the Grimm book had mentioned his sister's child, not his child, and Irene's first thought was that Alberich must have misread something. But then the concepts fell into place in her mind, and she tasted bile in her mouth. *His son. His sister's son. What he did to his own sister . . .*

Perhaps Alberich expected that reaction from her, for he paused only for a moment before he went on. "The Library kept him from me, Ray. Don't I have a right to my own flesh and blood?"

There were so many things wrong with that statement that Irene found herself incapable of answering. She snapped out of her momentary shock and whispered to the book in her hands, **"Book that I am holding, fly up and knock that man up there from where he stands!"**

The book went up like a comet, scraping her fingers with the force of its ascent. A cry of, **"Shelves, shield me!"** and the meaty thud of an impact came from above her.

But Irene was already running. **"Dust, hide me!"** she shouted, holding a length of tattered tulle across her nose and mouth against the rising clouds of dust.

She trailed her free hand along the bookcases lining the passage so as not to collide with them. Tears ran from her eyes as she blinked frantically, trying to see where she was going. This method of hiding herself did have a few associated problems. But at least it concealed her from Alberich.

Until he loses patience and just levels all the bookshelves in the area, her sense of incoming doom pointed out. *Keep on running.*

The astonishing thing was that he hadn't done what he did once before—sinking her into the floor and calling on all sorts of chaotic forces to destroy her. If it had been Irene trying to destroy *him,* she'd have used whatever she had available.

Unless . . . could she have missed something here? Alberich had created this place, or at least forged it out of a Fae world so far gone into chaos that it had no firm reality left. He'd set it up in a very specific way. Did this mean that he couldn't go round unleashing chaotic power into it randomly, any more than a mad scientist would set off dynamite in the middle of his own laboratory? It would explain a few things.

Though it wouldn't save her if Alberich caught up with her. Even if he left her alive in return for telling him about his . . . son. She couldn't help flicking through a mental list of male Librarians she knew, wondering if they might be the son in question. Admittedly she was better at discussing their literary tastes than their pre-Library histories, but she didn't think any of them could have had *that* sort of history.

The fog of dust blinded Irene nearly as much as it did Alberich, and she was taken by surprise as she stumbled into the central area. She was conscious of a wide-open space in front of her, even if she couldn't see it clearly yet, and some sort of massive tangle of open dark stairs and glowing lights.

"**Bookcases!**" came a furious shriek from above her. "**Block her way!**"

The two high bookcases on either side of her bowed down and collapsed in a great land-slide of shelves and books. Pages filled the air, mingling with the dust and tumbling like huge snowflakes. She had to dodge back frantically to avoid being hit by the falling book-cases, and then her way was well and truly blocked. She'd have to clamber over them, or go round—either of which would lose time and make her far too obvious.

Something that had been nagging at the back of her mind finally broke through. *This is a high-chaos world. Alberich's using the Language far more to frame his intent than in terms of precise description. And I'm doing the same. Just how far can I push this?*

She gritted her teeth and braced herself. "**Floor! Open beneath the barrier and let me pass!**"

The floor groaned, then split with pained creaks and cracking, the two sides pulling apart like the edges of a wound. The resultant gap ran beneath the toppled bookcases, narrow, uneven, dark, and full of splinters . . . but it looked big enough for Irene to get through. With a silent prayer that Alberich couldn't see her and that his next words wouldn't involve such verbs as *close, smash,* or *crush,* Irene squeezed through the crack. She had to lower her head and wriggle sideways, and with every panting breath it seemed that the riven floor was pressing in on her and about to squeeze shut.

She broke through to the other side with a gasp of relief. The dust was not so thick or noxious now—perhaps the barrier of bookshelves had blocked it off, or maybe it was simply settling of its own accord—and she could see the construction at the heart of Alberich's library.

It was an openwork tangle of metal stairs and books, perhaps a hundred yards across at first glance. The stairs writhed around each other, ignoring such petty constraints as railings or supports and rising several storeys high at the corners. The books gleamed amid the dark metal, scattered through the network in some sort of pattern and glowing with their own light. And in the middle of the pattern of books and stairs was the clock, which was still ticking. It was a shadowy clock face hanging in the air, with ivory-pale hands that moved ever closer towards midnight. It didn't give off any sort of gleam or glow. Instead it was a point of immense darkness, the sort of thing that Irene imagined a black hole might look like if given physical form and shrunk to such a tiny scale. And it *wasn't* Irene's imagination that it was ticking faster.

Before the clock reaches midnight, Alberich had said. She was almost out of time.

All sorts of options presented themselves. Stopping the clock or moving the books were the most obvious. Irene ran for the nearest flight of stairs. Her feet rang on the metal steps as she sprinted up them. Fatigue had vanished now that she was so close to success.

She made it to the first landing, where one of the books waited, on display. The part of her mind that became distracted during moments of life-threatening danger couldn't help wondering about it. It must be one of the unique specimens Alberich had stolen. Where was it from, who was the author, what was the title—and if and when this was all over, would she ever get the chance to read it?

And then she saw that there was a fine cage around it. The steel meshwork was wide enough for her to examine the book and allowed its glow to escape, but it certainly wasn't wide enough for her to slide the book out. There wasn't even an obvious lock, let alone a key. Words in the Language were worked into the metal, but she didn't recognize them: they were a vocabulary that she had never learnt.

"Ray!" Alberich called. Irene looked up and saw him walking towards the interlacing open stairs, strolling through the air on a bridge of books that tumbled to the ground as he passed.

It was the first time she'd actually seen him in the flesh throughout the whole wild chase. He was tall, and painfully thin—assuming this was actually a body that looked like his original one, and not just another stolen skin. The hooded black robe that he affected (really, how clichéd) was draped over his gaunt frame, flapping in the wind that blew pages and dust alike across the landscape of bookshelves. His brown hair was streaked with grey and was thinning like a monk's tonsure, but he walked with the firm pace of a young man.

She considered using the Language to drag those books from under him and let him drop, but that seemed too obvious. Besides, he could simply order the books back again. She'd never duelled like this before. One needed to strike in a way that the opponent couldn't simply reverse.

The book lay there in its cage as if it were mocking her. "Yes?" she called back. Could she order all the cages to open so that the books would fly out? But taking the time to give such an order would give Alberich a full sentence in which he could strike back.

He stepped off the bridge of books onto one of the farther staircases, a good twenty yards away from her and five yards higher up. "Have you quite finished with your adolescent rebellion?"

"No," Irene retorted. She reached out to touch the cage, but yanked her fingers back as she felt the prickle of chaotic power in the ironwork. "Come closer and I'll demonstrate." Could she order the metal stairs to bind him? What could she say that Alberich couldn't counter?

"I want to tell you one thing." His sentences were shorter now, more clipped. Was it in case she counter-attacked mid-metaphor? "Your home world? Your parents? I *am* going to find them. You have inconvenienced me. They will pay for it."

It was a petty, spiteful threat. But the sheer malice contained in it, the absolute viciousness of his tone, cut at Irene and made her flinch. "You haven't a chance," she retaliated, edging sideways along a horizontal stretch of walkway. Perhaps she could manage something if she reached the clock.

"Oh? Really? I've had centuries of life. I'm good at what I do." Alberich kept his distance but started to trace a parallel course to hers, clearly planning to keep between her and the clock.

Irene laughed. It wasn't a very good laugh, but it bolstered her spirits. "You don't understand. My parents are *Librarians*. They can run from you forever!"

To her surprise, Alberich actually stopped walking. "They're what?" he said.

"Librarians. Like you or me." She wondered what she'd said that had managed to unsettle him. "So, you see . . ."

Then she saw his face clearly, and her words ran dry in her mouth. He wasn't shocked or unsettled. He was amused. His face *showed* those centuries of age, and they had left lines of cruelty etched around his mouth and eyes that were as clear as the Language itself. His voice was full of a horrible good humour as he spoke. "Ray, my dear, my very dear little girl. That simply isn't possible. I should know. Two Librarians *can't have a child*."

Irene blinked. That statement didn't make any sense. "But you said you have a son . . ."

"That's how I *know*." He began to walk again. "You have no idea what it took. I had to take her deep into chaos to make it possible. All that for a son whom you are keeping from me." His mouth opened impossibly wide, and his tone deepened to a roar. "*So don't insult me with such stories.*"

"Believe what you want," Irene snapped. She was closer to the central clock now. Unfortunately, said closeness involved a vertical drop of about five yards before she could edge any farther on a horizontal level. Manageable with caution and with the Language, but less welcoming with Alberich there to mess things up. "I know—"

"You obviously don't know anything," he cut her off. "And nobody ever told you. No doubt to spare your feelings and keep you loyal. Are you some orphanage brat, Ray? Or were you stolen from a cradle?" He was walking faster now, his steps keeping time with the clock. "If it wasn't for the inconvenience you've caused me, I might even feel sorry for you. I know all about how it feels to find out your whole life was based on a lie."

"Really? So what was yours?" It was a poor comeback, but it was the best Irene could do. The rest of her mind was flooded with the concept that she wasn't what she thought she was. For every sensible objection of *he's lying* and *why should I believe him?* and *he's trying to confuse you*, there was a counter-argument—in the way that he'd seemed genuinely surprised when she'd said she was the child of two Librarians. She would swear it hadn't been faked.

Did it make any difference if she wasn't the child of the people she'd called parents? If the fact of her birth was a lie, then was it such an important lie?

"The Library claims to preserve the balance between chaos and order. But that's a lie. That's what children get told to keep them quiet and obedient." They were on a level with each other now, and he stopped to look across at her. "If you join me, I'll tell you the truth."

Irene remembered a line from that Grimm fairy story she'd read months ago, about Alberich and his sister. "Is it something to do with the 'Library's secret'?" she asked. "One that we all 'wear branded upon our backs . . .' But even if there is a secret, why would that make the Library a lie?"

"Blind faith is just another word for slavery," Alberich said. "You *say* you're preserving some sort of balance, but you're really perpetuating stagnation. Wake up, Ray! Open your *eyes*. And if you're too blind to see anything on a larger scale, don't you feel *anything* for the books that you give the Library? It swallows them up and keeps them and will never let them go. Look at that book next to you." He pointed at the closest metal cage, which held a scroll bound in ribbons of gold and purple. His voice was full of pride and greed, a collector's lust manifest in his every word. But he spoke as if he expected her to understand his desire, his joyful ownership of those priceless books. And perhaps she did. "The complete *Mabinogion*," he continued, "with the full tale of Culhwch and Olwen. *All* of the quests! And that one." He pointed to his left. "Hugo's *La Quiquengrogne*, his sequel to *Notre-Dame de Paris* . . . Other books here, hundreds of them, all *unique*. Books you will never see anywhere else. Books that would be the pride of any collection."

"Which you stole."

"Only because the Library didn't steal them first. **Metal, hold her feet!**"

His use of the Language had come without a change in tone or expression, and Irene was caught by surprise as the stair that she was standing on flowed up and round her shoes, writhing to her ankles. Chagrin bit at her as she realized she'd been distracted by the conversation. *By the promise of books and secrets. What better bait?* No doubt she could unloose the bindings as easily as Alberich had invoked them, but that would give him enough time to do something worse.

The clock hammered away and the air seemed to shiver with a growing power and tension. More torn pages drifted through the air, floating by like huge moths.

"It won't hurt," Alberich said in a tone that pretended reassurance, but his eyes were full of that cruel amusement she'd seen earlier.

"What won't?" There had to be an answer. She had to save the Library. Save the books. Save herself.

"Chaos. There's a point when the body either accepts it or destroys itself. Mine accepted it. And look what I can do!" He stretched his arms out in a gesture that embraced the clock, the twisted staircases, the mad library. "You will join me or you will die. Tell me, Ray, isn't it a relief to come to the end of choices? To know the game's over? You can relax now. Stop being your parents' tool."

He spoke fluidly, with the grand indulgence of a man enjoying his words, but his eyes were on her throughout. He was waiting for her to use the Language to try to either free herself or kill him.

Irene took a deep breath. *Why not just say yes for the moment?* common sense suggested. *Buy time. Tell Alberich some of what he wants to know. Get his trust. Be practical. You said to Bradamant earlier that there was no point in just getting yourself killed.*

And the books here were unique, the fruit of all Alberich's years of theft. Surely anything was worth it to save them? Even if it meant selling herself into slavery and betraying the Library . . .

No. This was a question of priorities, she realized. These books here were a priority. Her own life was a priority. But the Library, all the other Librarians, and all the books *there* were the biggest priority of all.

"You're right," she said. "It is a relief. **Paper! BURN!**"

CHAPTER 26

Irene's shout echoed through the maze of stairways. The books went up like tiny novas, blazing like the hearts of stars. There was no hesitation, no slow kindling at the edges or catching by degrees. They burned as if they were glad to burn. The drifting pages caught fire as well, wafting through the air with a sudden new energy, and the surrounding bookshelves shook with the force of the concussion as their contents flamed up where they stood.

The clock gave one last jarring tick, and stopped.

"No!" Alberich shrieked. He was looking at her as if *she* was the criminal, the aberrant, the lunatic. **"Fires, go out!"**

For a moment Irene feared that he might succeed in extinguishing the flames. But they seemed to rise up with a new fury as he named them in the Language. She remembered her own attempts to put out the fire when she and Kai had been trapped by the broken gate. Perhaps it was due to the mixture of chaos and the Language. Perhaps it was the power of Alberich's own working, turned against him.

Perhaps she should get out of range before he turned his attention back to *her*.

"Metal, release my shoes!" she hissed, and stepped free as the stair retracted its clasp on her feet.

The scroll next to her was withering to ashes inside its cage. It had been a unique document, the lone copy of a story that only existed in one world. And now she'd destroyed it, and hundreds of others too. She'd felt embarrassment before in her life over quite a number of things—petty things, social errors, lack of politeness, moments of stupidity—but she'd rarely known true shame until now.

She tried to push that to the back of her mind, and mostly succeeded, looking around for somewhere to run towards. The prospects were minimal, and getting worse. Fire was spreading out in a great circle, leaping from bookcase to bookcase. Burning pages carried the flames with them like a contagion. High shelves were beginning to lean and topple as their underpinnings scorched and charred away.

For the moment she settled on getting away from Alberich. He was still shouting at the flames and at the clock, as if sheer volume could somehow compel them to obedience. She scurried along the walkway, the remains of her skirts fluttering in the rising heat. Choosing stairs at random, she ran around the outside of the network of steps, looking for a way out.

The clock was silent now, and so was Alberich. The only noise was the growing roar of the flames and the ringing of steps on the metal stairs. Smoke sifted through the air in white coils—thin for the moment, but growing.

"Book-burner!" The sheer fury and betrayal in Alberich's voice made Irene cringe in renewed shame. It wasn't the fact that *he* was saying it, but rather that it echoed her own thoughts. A part of her—a very stupid, senseless part—even felt that death would be an appropriate punishment for what she'd just done. "Ray, you are going to *suffer* for this!"

As threats went, it wasn't the most specific or blood-curdling that had ever been thrown at Irene, but the fury and malice behind it gave her even more incentive to run. Unfortunately she'd come to a corner of the structure, and the only options now were up or down. Down put her on ground level and maybe gave her a chance to escape, if she could somehow find a way out through the burning, collapsing bookshelves. It would also give Alberich a clear advantage of height, to call down obstructions and maledictions on her with the Language. Up . . . well, there wasn't anywhere in particular to go, once she'd headed up. She'd be trapped. Unless maybe she could form a bridge of books in the way that Alberich had earlier?

And falling from a height is one of the quickest and easiest available ways to die, a cold little thread of despair pointed out. *Just for the record.*

She was not going to lose hope. She was not going to give up.

"**Smoke, choke that woman!**" Alberich's voice rang out.

The pale wisps of smoke solidified, massing together as they flooded towards Irene's face.

"**Air, blow that smoke away from me!**" she gabbled.

The first tendril of smoke touched her face and flickered across her lips, and more gathered behind it, flowing around her and up to her mouth. A quick gust of wind scattered the smoke and let her breathe, but there was no real definition or permanence to the moving air. The tendrils of smog began to gather again, and she fled up the stairway, holding a tattered shred of skirt fabric across her nose and mouth.

She passed another of the caged books. It was charred to ashes now, and a thick column of dark, greasy smoke rose from its corpse. It was getting harder to breathe—not just because of the smoke that

Alberich had commanded against her, but because of all the *other* smoke in the air. It wound through the metal stairs like ribbons and rose in billowing clouds towards the distant ceiling high above. It was impossible to see Alberich now.

Surely this was any Librarian's hell, full of burning books and smoke and fire. She would have run onwards, but there was nowhere to run *to* now.

Irene coughed, her lungs burning and her mouth full of the taste of ashes. She had to take the offensive. **"Stairs, open beneath that man's feet,"** she shouted.

The clanging of collapsing metalwork answered her, but there were no human-sounding crashes or screams. Damn. She ran along a long open stretch of walkway, passing more book cages, then stopped as Alberich's form loomed through the smoke ahead of her.

He was opening his mouth to speak, when a huge creaking roar came from the outer bookshelves and a shadow fell across the two of them. Both he and Irene turned to look. One of the tallest book-cases had begun to topple and was leaning towards the central arrangement of stairs, almost in slow motion. Books slid from it, sifting out to scatter in all directions as it teetered down towards them.

There was no time for further reciprocal attacks, and even the Language couldn't have stopped that colossus mid-fall. Both of them turned and ran in opposite directions.

Then it hit.

The concussion shuddered through the tangled structure of stairs, as the timbers of the bookcase sheared through metal and collapsed the walkways under their weight. Irene was thrown off her feet, and she held on to the walkway with the strength of desperation as it shivered and tilted sideways. She crawled along it, coughing in the smoke, until it was more level and she could get back to her feet, then looked behind her.

Even through the haze, she could see that the fallen bookcase had broken the central construct in half. Tangled remains of stairs and walkways still stood—well, leaned—on either side, but the centre, where the clock had been, was a mass of timbers and papers. The ruined shelves were a roaring bonfire that was swelling and burning higher with every passing moment.

"Ray!" Alberich's voice carried over the crackling of the flames. "You haven't won!"

"It looks to me as if I *have*," she shouted back. It was stupid and pointless to be exchanging taunts at this stage of events, when they were probably both about to die horribly, but it did feel good to get in the last word.

"If I must wait a thousand years, I'll find my son." For a moment she could see him silhouetted against the flames, his robe billowing in the hot wind. "He will avenge me. And you will perish with me."

"You can't have all three," Irene said, more to herself than to Alberich. She was swaying from the heat and the smoke, and she had to lean on the railing to hold herself up. Perhaps it would be easiest just to let herself go and fall. She wasn't going to get out of here. She might as well accept it and finish things quickly. "I don't think that works . . ."

A shadow fell across her, and she looked up to see if another building was about to collapse on her.

But it wasn't a building. It was a dragon. It was Kai. The crimson light tinged his blue wings with amethyst. A shadow, indistinct in the smoke and dazzle, clung to his back—Vale? She couldn't be sure.

The shock of seeing Kai was like a wave of cold water in her face, driving away all Irene's despair. First things first. She had to distract

Alberich. **"Metal, seize Alberich!"** she shrieked, putting all her will into it. **"Rails, pierce Alberich, smoke, blind Alberich . . ."**

As she shouted, she was already running for the nearest high point. She couldn't get to the ground, and there was no free space for Kai to land anyhow, so she'd have to get up as high as she could, and pray. Behind her she could hear Alberich shouting angry negations and shielding himself. The smoke swirled around where he'd been standing, briefly as dense as a London pea-souper.

There was a convenient high point just to her left, once a semi-tower of stairs and now a semi-collapsed mass of stairs that leaned at a dangerous angle. Irene inched up it, clinging with one hand and waving frantically with the other. She wished she had a flag to signal with, but there wasn't really enough of her dress left to be worth ripping off and waving.

High above, the dragon dipped and swung round in a turn, heading directly for the half-tower where Irene was perched. He seemed to be moving slowly, almost lazily, his wings extended to glide, but he was halfway to Irene before she could blink.

"Stair unbind from stair." Alberich's voice rang across the fire, and the steps under Irene shuddered. Screws jerked loose and joints came undone. She felt the metal quivering under her, only kept in position by the fact that it was mostly shattered and leaning together in any case. Something came loose with a crash of dreadful finality, and the half-tower slipped sideways.

She began to fall.

Kai spun sideways, one wing to the ground and the other to the heavens, and as he cut through the air and past the half-tower, Vale caught Irene's wrist.

She slammed against Kai's back, his scales grazing her cheek, and her arm and shoulder screaming from the strain. Vale was shouting for her to hold on, but there was nothing for her to hold on *to*. She dug her fingers in as the wind streamed past. Kai tilted again, returning to a horizontal keel, and she slid more towards the centre of his back. Vale was perched just behind his neck, where she'd been sitting before, and was clinging on with one hand while grasping her wrist with the other.

"Railings, gut that dragon!" Alberich screeched, his voice carrying dimly through the rush of wind.

Irene tried to shout something in the Language in defence, but she had no breath to spare and no time to speak. Pieces of metal wrenched themselves free from the broken stairs and flung themselves upwards at Kai. He contorted his body, sliding through the air in a fluid twist that escaped several of them, but one of them sliced across his underside, and another went through his left wing. He cried out in pain, the sound shaking the air like thunder.

"Get us out of here, Strongrock," Vale called. *"I've got her."*

Kai struggled to gain height, streaking away from the central blaze where Alberich stood, but his motions were slow and laboured. "There's too much chaos in this place," he groaned. "I need more time . . ."

Another set of improvised javelins arced towards them. Kai dropped beneath them as they rushed past above, diving between a couple of tenement-high bookcases that were still standing. The tips of his wings brushed them on either side, shaking down a rain of books. Blood pattered from his wounded wing, and Irene could see that he was having to keep it extended and glide on it, rather than use it with the fluidity of his other wing.

He wasn't regaining height. He was barely managing to maintain his current altitude. She could feel his muscles working underneath her body, and the long, shuddering struggle of his breathing. Would he be able to fly them out of there?

But if he'd managed to get here, and if he was managing to stay conscious and functioning, it meant this place wasn't as far out in the depths of chaos as she'd thought. Irene could try to reach the Library again. Without Alberich possessing this place and interfering, she might just be able to get through. And Vale . . . well, they hadn't actually *tried* to get him into the Library before. They would simply have to succeed now. She would drag him in there if she had to tear a way between the worlds with her own bare hands.

"Kai!" she shouted. "Over to the left, there! By the far wall. Do you see that door? Can you get us there?"

"Yes," he rumbled. He winged towards the point she'd indicated, outracing the growing fire. As Irene looked down, she saw the flames overtake the collapsed shelves where Zayanna lay buried.

"Did you succeed, Winters?" Vale demanded.

"I sincerely hope so—" Irene had to break off as Kai landed, his wings curving out and back as he settled to the ground. The left wing didn't move as easily as it should have done, and he groaned in pain again, thumping down hard enough to rattle Irene's teeth. She hastily slid from his back to the ground, then clung to the nearest bookcase as the floor shook underneath her.

Vale swept a quick glance across her. "No serious injuries?" he asked. Behind him, the light flexed and ebbed around Kai as he changed form.

Irene shook her head. "No, nothing serious. Let me—"

The ground shook again, this time in a more directed and precise way, as if some great worm were moving through it. And Irene realized, with the sort of cold terror that swept from feet to brain and through every point between, that if the area where Zayanna lay was burning, then the sigil that Irene had marked on the ground there might be burned away as well. Which might mean that Alberich could inhabit the ground and furnishings of his library once more.

Without even waiting to check Kai's wounds, she turned to the door. **"Open to the Library,"** she demanded in frantic haste, throwing all her strength into the words as she grabbed the handle.

The cold metal fizzed under her hand, buzzing with an energy like static electricity, only more powerful and far more dangerous. The door didn't *want* to open to the Library, or perhaps the Library didn't want to let the door open onto it. Or perhaps Irene was being unreasonable in imagining personalities here, and it was simply the difficulty of reaching from a high-chaos world all the way to the Library.

The door tried to cling to the jamb, holding shut as she strained at it. She could feel the connection, she knew she'd reached the Library again, but the door held closed. Bookcases toppled and books fell as the floor rippled towards them, rising slowly like a tidal wave.

She'd failed in her earlier attempt to open to the Library. But she was not going to lose now, not at the cost of the two friends who'd risked their lives to come and save her.

"Open!" she commanded.

The door wrenched itself open, pulling against its hinges with a creaking scream of wood that was audible above the roaring flames and the falling shelves. Beyond was a dark corridor lined with books, achingly familiar.

Vale thrust the staggering Kai through the doorway, then halted on the step. His expression was one of sheer incomprehension as he pushed at the empty air, his hands pressing at the gap of the doorway as though there were an invisible sheet of glass between him and the safety on the other side.

He's still chaos-contaminated, Irene realized, as though she were reading it off the title card in a silent film. *The Library won't let him in.* She'd thought, she'd hoped, but none of it had been enough. She would just have to do something about it instead.

Once before, she'd expelled chaos by naming herself and forcing out everything that *wasn't* Irene. **I am Irene. I am a servant of the Library,** she had said in the Language, and it had acted to remove anything that refuted those words. She'd hesitated to try it on Vale because she'd been too worried about hurting or even destroying him if she couldn't describe him accurately. He wasn't a Librarian, after all.

But there was no time left. And in this place, the Language had answered her intent rather than her exact words. She could only try, and pray. All her life she had been taught that the Language allowed its users to shape reality. But if reality said that Vale couldn't enter the Library, then she was going to *change* that reality.

She grabbed Vale by the hand. **"Your name is Peregrine Vale,"** she said, her voice audible through the crash of falling books and the rumble of the shuddering floor. **"You are a human being. And you are the greatest detective in London!"**

The shock was like a deep organ-note, humming in her bones and making her stumble. Vale rocked back as if he had been hit by a blast of wind. Chaotic power vented out around him, crumbling the floor underneath him to fragments and transforming the blowing fragments of paper into ash. He fell to one knee, his face white under the smears of dust that marked them both, and his breath came in great heaving gasps.

She grabbed Vale's hand, pulling him forward as she threw herself through the doorway. And he followed her.

The world was blurry in front of her eyes, and she barely stayed on her feet. Both Vale and Kai were shouting at her, holding her up as she swayed, the world swinging round her in huge stomach-churning arcs. She blinked to see the open doorway in front of her, looking out on a landscape that was all inferno, where flames devoured books and shelves and ground and sky, and the wind screamed for vengeance.

There was something she had to do. Yes. That was it.

"Door, close . . ."

The door slammed shut with a thud that echoed down the book-lined corridor, cutting off the flames and fury and leaving the three of them in silence and darkness.

Then slowly, one by one, the lights started to come back on.

CHAPTER 27

"Put your hands there, Winters." Vale positioned her hands to hold the pad in place while he bandaged the gash across Kai's midriff.

Irene tried to focus, but it was too much effort. She simply knelt there and let herself be used as a convenient surgical clamp, while Vale applied strips of torn-up shirt and Kai bled. The gashes weren't life-threatening, but they were nasty and they might leave scars.

"I hope your uncle isn't too annoyed that you came here," she said, vaguely following the thought through to a logical destination.

"And thank you for favouring us with your attention, Winters," Vale said, sitting back on his knees and wiping his hands on the remaining rags. He seemed to have pulled himself together with barely a moment's pause, all self-possession and control once more. "I take it that inferno was a success?"

"It looked quite successful to me," Kai said. He tried moving his bandaged arm, and winced. "Irene, I'm sorry. I should have had more faith in you."

"It was hardly how I'd have planned it," Irene admitted. She was feeling more coherent now, though horribly exhausted. The knowledge of what she'd done to the books lay like a lead weight at the bottom of her mind, dragging all her other achievements down with it. She'd burned them. Unique books—stories that would never be found again—and she'd burned them all. There should have been some other way. There must have been some other way. If she'd tried harder, if she'd been more intelligent, then perhaps she would have found a way to save the books as well as stopping Alberich.

She realized that Kai deserved a better response for his apology, and forced a smile. "I nearly got killed. Several times," she said. "Li Ming was quite right. It was reckless. I wasn't expecting you two. I really wasn't. Thank you." Her voice shook, and she had to bite her lip not to cry.

To Irene's surprise, the arm that went round her shoulders and gave her a comforting squeeze was Vale's. She let herself relax, assuring herself that it would be only for a moment. *I'm not being weak. I'm simply leaning on him for a moment, just till I get my strength back.*

"We should have been there sooner," Kai said firmly.

"What happened to the Fae woman?" Vale asked in tones of academic interest.

A lump rose in Irene's throat. "She's dead," she said, not looking at either of them. "She pushed me out of the way of a falling bookcase. I'd have died if she hadn't. She got me there safely, but . . ."

"Save your sympathy for someone who didn't try to kill you multiple times over, Winters," Vale advised sharply. "She knew perfectly well what she was doing. If she didn't make it out alive, then she has nobody to thank but herself for getting into that situation in the first place."

Irene scrubbed her arm across her stinging eyes. Her face was smeared with ashes. "Believe it or not, that doesn't help much, either." She knew she should try to be more gracious, but her stock of patience had run dry. "I would have liked her to get out of this alive. Even if you don't think she 'deserved' it."

"And your Alberich. Dead, I hope?" Vale asked.

"I hope so. I hope he *burned*." Irene's own vengefulness surprised her.

"Along with his books. It's a shame they couldn't be saved," Kai said.

She was going to have to confess it sooner or later. She might as well get some practice in now. "That was my fault," Irene said. "I started the fire. I ordered them to burn." She could smell the ashes all over her, and she wondered morbidly if any of them came from the unique books in the cages. The ash felt ingrained into her skin, a mark of irredeemable sin more permanent than any scarlet letter.

Vale shrugged. "A shame, but it clearly worked."

"Yes, but . . . they were *unique*," Irene protested. She wasn't getting the sort of disapproval she'd expected. "And I *burned them*."

Vale and Kai exchanged glances. Kai shrugged. "I can sympathize," he said. "Even if I wasn't training as a Librarian, I'd sympathize. They were books. They were unique. But I know you, Irene. You wouldn't have done that if you could have found any other way to stop him. It's *not your fault*. If you're blaming anyone other than Alberich, then you're wrong."

Irene struggled with the urge to tell him that he'd got it all wrong and that she *should* be blamed, but the thorough lack of condemnation from either man made it difficult. "How did you get here?" she asked, changing the subject.

Kai lay back and looked at the ceiling. "I found Madame Coppelia and passed on your message," he said. "Then Vale and I decided to come after you."

"That's suspiciously vague," Irene said. "And rather lacking in details."

"But substantially correct. Besides, this way you can't claim it was all your fault and that you should be punished for getting me into trouble." Kai sounded positively smug.

"True," Vale agreed. "Strongrock can apologize for all of it, together with whatever reparations he needs to make to his uncle's servant."

"Oh dear." Irene wasn't sure she really wanted to know what had happened to Li Ming. She was finally starting to relax. It helped if she didn't think about some of the things that Alberich had said. "I'm having trouble believing it's all over. Part of me is afraid that the lights are going to start going out again, or that I'll open the door and . . ." She let the sentence trail off.

Is Alberich really dead? Irene's paranoia whispered. *I've seen his skin ripped from his body, I've seen him thrown into chaos, and now I've seen him caught in an inferno in a world that's falling apart. It should be enough to kill anyone—human, Fae, dragon, or Librarian. But how can I be sure?*

For a moment there was silence. Then she shook herself and clambered to her feet. "All right," she said firmly. "Time to move." It felt as if time had started again. This little moment of stillness couldn't last. Her personal clock was ticking. There were things to do, people to see, questions to ask. Books to read.

"Couldn't we wait a little longer?" Kai asked pathetically. But he let her and Vale help him up.

"Nonsense, there's far too much to do." Irene finally put a name to the sensation she could feel rising in her, like a kite catching the wind. *Possibility.* Anything seemed possible now.

She looked between the two men. Her two *friends*, here in her *home*, in the Library. This was what defined her, far more than any birth or bloodline. Maybe Alberich was right, or maybe he was lying, or maybe he was simply mistaken. She could ask her parents later. No, she *would* ask them later. That was a promise. But she would be the worst sort of idiot if she let Alberich's malice poison what she had, here and now.

"I should probably be getting back to London," Vale said, a little reluctantly. "There's a lot to be done. I can't leave the place without a wave of crime breaking out, and this time I've gone further than usual." He looked around. "So, this is your Library. I can't say this corridor's very impressive."

Kai chuckled, and Irene found herself smiling. "It's larger than you think," she said blandly. "I can't promise that we have any criminal records, but I'm sure we can find something to interest you. I need to report to Coppelia and to find out if there was any damage to the Library from what Alberich did. So that's our first priority, but after that . . ." She shrugged.

"And I'm free of that taint now?" Vale inspected his fingers as though he would be able to see some sort of visible contamination, or the lack of it.

"I believe so, or you couldn't have entered the Library."

"Then you are absolutely correct, Winters. We've work to do." Vale started striding down the corridor, and Irene and Kai had to hurry to catch up with him. "Which way do we go from here?"

"We look for a room with a computer in it, and Irene can check the map when she contacts Coppelia," Kai said. "You'll *like* computers, Vale."

Vale frowned. "Are you telling me this place isn't properly organized?"

"It's extremely organized," Irene said defensively. "It's just not very *helpfully* organized, from our point of view. Don't worry. Nobody's ever been lost. Well, not permanently."

"You reassure me greatly," Vale said drily. "You'd better take the lead, Winters. We'll follow."

Irene led the way down the corridor under the clear overhead lights, leaving behind the smell of ashes and corruption. New horizons seemed to stretch in front of her. It didn't matter if the Library still wanted to insist she was "on probation." She knew what she had done, and so did the people whose opinions she cared about. Even if there were new mountains ahead of her, she had the energy to face them and to wear them down.

And she had friends to help her.

This sense of possibility might not last, of course. Nothing ever did. But she wasn't going to spoil it by looking too far ahead. They were safe in the Library, and the Library would endure.

ABOUT THE AUTHOR

Genevieve Cogman is a freelance author who has written for several role-playing game companies. She currently works for the National Health Service in England as a clinical classifications specialist. She is the author of the Invisible Library Novels, including *The Burning Page*, *The Masked City*, and *The Invisible Library*.

CONNECT ONLINE

grcogman.com
twitter.com/genevievecogman